Lasting Treasures

LASTING TREASURES

Julie Ellis

G. P. PUTNAM'S SONS   NEW YORK

G. P. Putnam's Sons
Publishers Since 1838
200 Madison Avenue
New York, NY 10016

Library of Congress Cataloging-in-Publication Data

Ellis, Julie, date.
Lasting Treasures / Julie Ellis.
p. cm.
I. Title.
ISBN 0-399-13808-0
PS3555.L597025   1993   92-27612 CIP
813'.54—dc20

Printed in the United States of America
1 2 3 4 5 6 7 8 9 10

This book is printed on acid-free paper.

*For Vanessa Holt—with gratitude
and much affection.*

Chapter One

IN EARLY March 1917 the world was embroiled in a war of terrifying dimensions. In the midst of this war, the Russian people—with their casualties already close to 4,000,000—teetered on the edge of internal revolution. Thousands of soldiers were deserting.

At home the masses struggled to deal with alarming food shortages. Mobs prowled the streets of the cities, looting shops. In Petrograd— the grand old capital—chaos had erupted.

Dr. Maxim Gunsburg, his fragile wife Natasha, and his lovely fifteen-year-old daughter Viktoria were gathered in the luxurious drawing room of the spacious Gunsburg apartment—in a wing of the Veronsky Palace at the edge of Petrograd.

"You must do exactly as I say, my darling," the gentle Dr. Gunsburg told Viktoria. "For weeks I've feared this time would come. I've made the necessary preparations. Your visa and Simone's are in order." Simone had been Viktoria's personal maid since she was nine, when the temperamental Countess Veronsky dismissed the maid she had brought to Petrograd from Paris. "You must travel lightly, appearing to be of the common people. You must—"

"Papa, I don't understand." *Leave Mama and Papa?* Her violet eyes dilated in disbelief.

"Listen to your father," her mother said exhaustedly. "These are terrible times. You must do what he tells you."

"You understand how it is for the Jews in Russia," Dr. Gunsburg reminded Viktoria. His immediate family, as well as Mama's, had been wiped out in a pogrom many years ago. He and his wife had been mercifully taken in by Russian families. "We have lived under special circumstances." Papa, who was not out of medical school at the time, had saved Count Veronsky's life when he had been thrown from his horse. "Jews never know when the czarist government will issue some terrible new ruling to make their lot worse. And the ignorant peasants with their claims of Jewish ritual murders are no better," Dr. Gunsburg pursued. "It's a matter of time before the royal family will be removed—and the masses will take over. Jews will fare no better at the hands of the peasants than under the czars. Always remember, Viktoria, we have been spared the fate of our people."

"Maxim!" Natasha Gunsburg shot a frightened glance toward the door, as though fearful of eavesdroppers. "How can you suggest that the royal family will be overthrown?"

"Even here in the palace this is being discussed. The count himself has said that before the month is over he expects the czar to abdicate. And in his heart, Count Veronsky knows that will not satisfy the people. Viktoria, you must leave the palace tonight. You will make your way to Paris, where my cousin Alexandra lives. She will look after you."

"Papa, the German army is in France!"

"Northern France," her father said, "behind the Hindenburg line. Paris will be safe. The French will not allow Paris to fall."

"Why can't you and Mama come with me?"

"Mama is not well enough to travel," he said. "The rigors that you'll face trying to reach Paris in these times would be too much for her. But one day, my love, we'll be together again," he promised. "But *you* must leave at nightfall."

"Tonight? I must leave tonight?" Viktoria gazed from her father to her mother. *Would she ever see them again?*

"It's best this way," her father insisted. "You'll leave the palace as Simone's niece. You must wear the clothes she lays out for you. You must pretend to be a maid in the palace. I've told her how you are to travel and provided her with ample funds. You can trust Simone to take you to Alexandra in Paris."

"I don't want to go!" Viktoria said, rebelling for the first time in her life. "If you and Mama are staying, why can't I?"

"Because Mama and I love you very much—and we fear for your

life. You and Simone will travel with money and jewels. That will buy your way to a safe haven.''

"What will happen to me in Paris?'' *How would she survive without Papa and Mama?*

"Alexandra will take care of you until we can be together again.'' Dr. Gunsburg strived for an air of optimism. "The world war must end soon. When Mama's health has improved, we'll come to you in Paris.''

"How fortunate that you've studied French and English along with the count's children.'' Natasha Gunsburg tried to emulate her husband's show of optimism. "You've loved Paris each time we've been there.''

"But how are we to arrive in Paris in the middle of a war?'' Viktoria asked.

"Much can be accomplished with money.'' Dr. Gunsburg's smile betrayed a bitterness usually hidden from his family. "And it's understandable that with all the troubles here in Russia, Simone would be anxious to return to her own country. If anyone asks, you're her niece who came to work in the palace—and you, too, are homesick and anxious to be with your own people. You say nothing of your Jewish heritage,'' he stressed. "That is between you and God. In the world as it is today it isn't safe to be a Jew.''

"I can't believe this is happening.'' Viktoria's voice broke. "Mama—'' She crossed to her mother and clung to her. "Mama, tell me it isn't true.''

As though trapped in some awful nightmare, Viktoria embraced her mother and her father while Simone stood by with a shaky calm.

"I hope you're warm enough, my darling,'' her mother said, inspecting Viktoria's shabby peasant attire. Her lush dark hair was hidden beneath a kerchief. "Such bitter weather has come down from the north.''

"She'll be fine, Madame Natasha,'' Simone said. "Soon we'll be on the ship.''

"I don't dare try to drive you to the docks,'' her father said. There Viktoria and Simone were to board a small merchant ship whose captain had promised—for an exorbitant fee—to take them to Helsinki. "We could be attacked by a mob. Remember to talk in French—the crowds will think you are both French and anxious to get to your homeland in this terrible time.''

Carrying small knapsacks and hunching their shoulders against the cold, Viktoria and Simone made their way to the docks, where they found the merchant ship that would take them to Helsinki. Once aboard they remained in the primitive, minuscule cabin assigned to them.

Instinct warning her that she might never see her homeland again, Viktoria tried to etch on her brain her memories of the great city that was Petrograd—the wide streets and canals that made their way through the city, the huge, impressive government buildings, the endless rows of palaces, which Papa warned might soon be taken over by rebellious peasants. She remembered delightful hours of strolling along the Nevsky—one of the great promenades of the world. *Would she ever walk there again?*

At last Viktoria and Simone arrived in Helsinki. Viktoria was startled to discover that the Finns—their country seized by Russia back in 1809—hated the Russians, and talked of the day their country would become a republic. They particularly hated Czar Nicholas II, who had taken away much of their home rule.

Viktoria and Simone traveled by train over the monotonous flat country of Finland. Always, it seemed to Viktoria, she was cold. She felt little appetite for the dark bread and tea that was their usual fare.

From Finland they moved into Sweden—where for a while she was terrified that they would be sent back when their visas underwent minute scrutiny. Now their train sped through the awesome forests of northern Sweden. Their destination, Simone told Viktoria, was Stockholm, a neutral in the war.

Simone sat in the drafty train and knitted. Viktoria's thoughts focused on what her father and mother had told her about the hardship of Jews through the centuries. She sat with her eyes closed and heard her father's voice, almost as if he were beside her.

"You must remember, Viktoria, that for over five thousand years the Jews have fought against repressions of many kinds. We have been blamed for endless calamities that befell this world. We've been forced to live in ghettos, denied the right to own land, to join trade guilds, to practice many vocations. Only because I was taken in as a child by a fine Russian family was I able to go to the university and become

a physician. You must never forget that in times of trouble the Jews are always the scapegoats."

"Simone, will we be able to find my cousin Alexandra in Paris?" Viktoria voiced the fear that had haunted her since she and Simone had fled Petrograd.

"Your papa says she lives at the Ritz. She has been there for many years."

Alexandra, Viktoria remembered, was the cousin Papa had found in Petrograd when she herself was a little girl. He'd thought Alexandra, too, was dead, but Alexandra, a beautiful young girl, captured the heart of a Cossack. Hiding her faith, she married him. At his death, suspecting her Jewishness was about to be exposed, Alexandra had fled to Paris with the expensive jewels he'd given her through the years.

"When will we arrive in Paris?" Viktoria asked, ever conscious of the distance being put between herself and her parents, and of their safety in a country in revolt. "When, Simone?"

"Soon," Simone promised, but Viktoria sensed her growing anxiety. From Stockholm—only a few kilometers to the south—they must travel, somehow, to the east coast of England. From there they had to find someone to ferry them across the dangerous Channel to France. "But we must change our plans," Simone said. "Your papa knows that Denmark is neutral, but he didn't know that the Germans have mined the waters around Denmark—"

"How did you learn this?" Viktoria interrupted, surprised by Simone's shrewdness.

"People on the trains talk. We'll go across Sweden into Norway. Norwegian ships are traveling to England."

"Is it safe?" Surely Norwegian ships were attacked by the Germans! Viktoria's heart began to pound.

"We'll pray," Simone said quietly. "It's a risk we must take."

The next two weeks were fraught with terror. Just when Simone was about to give up on finding a ship that would take them to the east coast of England, she made a deal with a money-hungry sea captain.

"You'll leave us stranded without a krone between us," Simone wailed as she handed over the money she had acquired in Norway by selling a piece of jewelry given her by Dr. Gunsburg. "A woman and a young girl with nothing but the clothes on their backs!"

"You'll be in England," he shrugged. "That's what you want."

Again—proving Dr. Gunsburg's conviction that money could buy almost anything—Simone finally convinced a greedy boat owner to attempt the hazardous journey across the English Channel to France.

Viktoria watched with disbelief when she saw the money that passed from Simone's hands to those of the elderly seaman.

"You're taking the bread out of our mouths," Simone moaned, intent on transmitting the message that they had no further funds.

"I'm putting my life in terrible danger," the old man groaned. "Who knows when a German submarine may approach us? We'll take the shortest route," he said. "We'll set off a little above Dover and land a bit above Calais."

Finally, Viktoria and Simone set foot on soil still in the hands of the French. Three weeks and five days after they had fled Petrograd, Viktoria and Simone emerged from a grimy, third-class train in the huge Gare du Nord in Paris. For an anguished moment Viktoria remembered other arrivals, aboard luxurious trains with handsome drawing rooms and elegant dining cars.

"At last in Paris," Simone said with a reverent whisper.

Hand in hand they left the station. Their destination was the Hotel Ritz, where Viktoria's cousin, Mme. Alexandra Kolikoff, had maintained an apartment for many years. Simone's eyes grew pained as she gazed about her beloved city. Though the first of the spring flowers lent color to gray walls, this was clearly not the Paris Simone remembered.

"So many shops have closed," she mourned, reading fading signs that said *Pour Cause de Mobilisation*. "Nothing is repaired because of the war. So much dust," she said in distaste as a group of Red Cross trucks lumbered past them. Viktoria realized they were carrying wounded from the front.

Still, Viktoria thought the city seemed almost normal. People gathered in the shops and restaurants that were still open. They continued to hail the red taxis and go down into the Métro. But most of all, Viktoria was conscious of the clusters of soldiers in the uniforms of many nations. Soldiers on leave from the front. She gasped at the sight of those maimed by battle. In her sheltered life in Petrograd she had been spared these sights—though Papa spoke painfully about the terrible loss of life among the Russian soldiers fighting the Germans.

Only now—when they paused at a stall to buy still-hot croissants—did Viktoria and Simone learn that the United States had at last declared war on Germany. While they sat on a bench, they listened to a pair of American young men in Red Cross uniforms somberly discussing plans to join the American forces now that their country was involved.

"How far away is the Ritz?" Viktoria asked, already feeling a sense of loss at the imminent parting from Simone, her last tie to home.

"We'll take a bus," Simone told her. "We'll be there soon." Simone was unfamiliarly brusque.

"We'll see each other here in Paris, won't we? And Mama and Papa will be here soon?"

"Viktoria, you ask so many questions," Simone scolded. Almost with anger. "I'll take you to your cousin Alexandra. You will be safe with her. Come, we must find the bus to carry us to the Ritz. I have been away too long to remember these things—" All at once Simone seemed withdrawn.

Hurt by Simone's sudden coldness, Viktoria was silent on the bus ride to the Place Vendôme. They left the bus to walk to the gates of the Ritz, which stood elegant and beautiful on the magnificent square—designed by the French architect Mansard—that is, in truth, octagonal. Eager to greet her cousin, yet reluctant to relinquish Simone's comforting presence, Viktoria walked with Simone through one of the four arches leading into the classical structure that resembled a fine Parisian townhouse.

Simone walked resolutely through the narrow entrance, her head high. She ignored the reproachful stares that their presence elicited. Their appearance indicated the service entrance would have been more appropriate. Viktoria remembered delightful afternoon teas in the small *Salon de thé*, with exquisite silver teapots and almost translucent bone china.

"What is it?" a voice demanded imperiously. Viktoria turned to the owner of the voice with a surge of anger at its lack of respect.

"I have brought Madame Alexandra Kolikoff's cousin to her," Simone said with hauteur. "Her parents wished her to be delivered into their cousin's hands."

"Madame Kolikoff has not been here for over a year." The man gazed suspiciously from Simone to Viktoria.

"It was necessary for Mademoiselle Viktoria to escape from Petrograd dressed as a peasant because of the revolution there," Simone said, assuming the man was trying to dismiss them. "Please inform Madame Kolikoff that her young cousin, Viktoria Gunsburg, is here."

"I have told you," he repeated impatiently. "Madame Kolikoff is not here."

"Then, where is she?" Simone asked, her voice shrill with alarm.

"In the cemetery," he said. "Madame Kolikoff died over a year ago."

Chapter Two

COLD AND TREMBLING, Viktoria turned to Simone. Her eyes were wide with disbelief and terror.

"Simone, must I go back to Petrograd?" Viktoria whispered.

"There is no going back," Simone said tersely, prodding her toward the entrance. "The Russia we knew is gone." Then her face softened. "But you mustn't be afraid. You will stay with me, *chérie*." She reached to take Viktoria's small hand in hers. Simone, too, Viktoria realized now, had dreaded their expected separation. That was why she had appeared so cold. "We'll find a place to live. We'll find jobs. We will survive, Viktoria."

Except for her, Viktoria remembered, Simone was alone in Paris. Her two sisters and their families lived in a village to the south. The sisters had been outraged when she had left their village to move to Paris, and they had refused to reconcile with her before she left for Petrograd. Simone had written them out of her life.

Viktoria and Simone walked out of the Ritz and into the war-drab street. Viktoria was beset by a flood of frightening questions. How would Papa and Mama find her in Paris? From what she'd heard in her travels, she knew the mail system in Russia was in chaos. *She was supposed to be at the Ritz with Cousin Alexandra!* That was all Mama and Papa knew of her whereabouts.

Were she and Simone almost out of money? Simone had said, "We'll find jobs." What kind of work could *she* do? Perhaps be a translator? She spoke three languages. But would anybody wish to hire a fifteen-year-old girl as a translator? The future was a terrifying specter.

"We must find a room for ourselves before nightfall," Simone said, interrupting her anxious introspection. "Not in this fancy part of town," she said with a touch of bitter humor. "A place where people like us can afford to live."

Viktoria walked beside Simone down the stairs of the Métro. Nothing like this existed anywhere in Russia, though she knew from Papa that there were such marvels in London and Budapest as well as Paris. Soon they emerged from the Métro into daylight again. With a growing sense of urgency they began to search for a place to live.

Viktoria fought to conceal her shock at the shabby lodgings that were shown to them. Yet even these were rejected by Simone as too expensive. She and Simone had stayed at hovels on their flight from Petrograd—usually only for a night or two in each town. But here they must live until Mama and Papa came for her.

"The war makes everything cost so much," Simone grumbled. "But we must find something before the lights are blacked out." She smiled at Viktoria's stare of incomprehension. "At night all the lights of the city must be turned off in case German bombers come. I heard people talking on the Métro. At the sound of the *alerte*, everyone must take cover."

It seemed to Viktoria that they had been walking for hours before Simone finally settled down to bargain about a tiny garret apartment, though in truth, it had been barely an hour. In wartime Paris there were numerous apartments available since so many men were in service, and so many people had fled to the south—away from the German army that clearly meant to take Paris.

Now Simone gave money to the woman who had brought them up the five narrow, creaking flights to the garret apartment that consisted of one room—an area half the size of Viktoria's bedroom at the palace. Viktoria gazed about with revulsion at the meager, decrepit furnishings. She and Simone were to *live* in this tiny room until Mama and Papa came for her?

"We must clean," Simone resolved when they were alone. "Whoever lived here before was a pig!" Simone lifted her skirt to rip out the stitches of yet another improvised pocket. "We'll go downstairs to buy food and cleaning supplies. Tomorrow we must look for work.

We have little money left, Viktoria.'' Anxiety crept into Simone's voice, confirming what Viktoria had feared.

"What kind of work?" Viktoria stammered.

"Whatever we can find." Simone paused. "This will not be the life you knew in Petrograd. You must work to support yourself."

"What kind of work?" Viktoria repeated, faintly imperious in her terror.

Simone squinted in thought. "We will be chambermaids at one of the hotels," she decided.

"I am to be a chambermaid?" Viktoria stared at her in shock.

"You must understand," Simone said sternly, "that your life will be different now. You're a very young girl having to earn her own way. I will teach you what you have to know," she said. "You're pretty and have genteel ways. You'll be hired quickly."

Viktoria moved through the next few days in a haze of unreality. What would Mama and Papa think when they found her working as a chambermaid? She felt so clumsy, so inadequate when she tried to follow Simone's instructions on bedmaking, dusting, and cleaning. All her life these things had been done for her.

She sensed Simone's relief when they were both hired as chambermaids at the fashionable Hotel Crillon. She remembered staying with Mama at the Crillon—in a lovely balconied two-bedroom Louis XV suite that overlooked the Place de la Concorde. She remembered the high curving ceiling, and the exquisite crystal chandelier that Mama had so admired.

"You will report tomorrow morning at six o'clock," their interviewer told them crisply. "Remember, to work at the Crillon you must always be courteous and helpful. Every guest is special."

Following Simone's lead, Viktoria made the proper responses. She would be a good chambermaid, she vowed. Hadn't Simone taught her to make up beds, to clean? Still, she fought a feeling of humiliation at performing these menial tasks, so foreign to her.

Her first day on the job—in the required uniform—Viktoria was terrified that she would do something wrong, that the woman who supervised the chambermaids would chastise her. When she walked into the suite she remembered sharing with her mother on their last trip to Paris, she fought an urge to run away from the hotel, away from Paris. But where could she go?

Viktoria forced herself to fit into her new life. She understood that now she and Simone were equals. No longer was Simone her maid, to do her biddings. She loved Simone and was ever grateful for Simone's presence in her life. But she vowed that she would not remain a chambermaid.

Around her throat—hidden by the neckline of her uniform—she wore Mama's ruby-encrusted locket that hung from a gold chain. Simone insisted this last piece of jewelry must not be sold. They would live on their earnings.

In the gray April dawn Lieutenant Gary Barton slid behind the wheel of the staff car and waited for Colonel Ross to join him. They were to drive from the chateau north of Paris—and close to the firing line—into the city. His cap on the seat beside him, Gary ran one hand through his rumpled dark hair in a gesture that betrayed his tension. His blue-green eyes—set in a handsome face—were troubled.

When he'd been transferred to France from London, he'd expected to be on the fighting front. He felt guilty about this privileged appointment—due to his family connections plus his ability to speak fluent French and German. His superior—Colonel Ross—was on a confidential assignment, and he was the colonel's aide and interpreter. Still, he conceded, it was a relief to be away from the nightly bombings that had been their lot in London.

Billeted luxuriously at the Ritz, Gary was pleased to be in Paris—even while he was tormented by guilt at not being on the fighting front. The only thing he'd ever done in his whole life to please Papa, he thought with wry humor, was to enlist. With a wife and a newborn son—himself—his father had been persuaded not to join up with Teddy Roosevelt in the Spanish-American War—which he regretted to this day.

Gary stirred restlessly. What the devil was taking the colonel so long? He hated waiting around this way. His thoughts focused again on his father.

Now, Papa's world revolved about the Barton Tobacco Company. On endless occasions he'd heard the story of how his grandfather had emerged from the War Between the States to become a tobacco farmer and then—when cigarettes appeared in Virginia in 1868—he'd become obsessed by the thought of opening a cigarette factory. It took him eight years to raise the funds to start a tiny factory, but the business prospered under his wily manipulations. As the only son among six children, Daniel had taken over the business twenty-seven years ago and pushed it ahead with astonishing success.

Daniel Barton preferred to forget that his rise in the industry had been accelerated by his marriage to the socially prominent Sara Warren. While Sara's family was in reduced financial circumstances in the years after the War Between the States, the family's integrity was recognized as impeccable. Marriage into the Warren family had assured him the bank credit he needed for expansion.

Gary often wondered what had brought his father and mother together. His mother was a patrician beauty of the Old South, while his father was shrewd, brash, and seemed to enjoy playing the redneck farmer even when he'd become a wealthy tobacco company executive. He knew his father was proud of marrying into the Warren clan—even though he was quick to point out his own humble origins.

Papa enjoyed his frequent trips to New York City—presumably on business, Gary acknowledged, but allowing for social dalliance with willing young ladies. *Didn't Mama ever suspect?*

"Once this bastardly war is over, you're coming into the business, Gary," his father ranted regularly. He'd been out of college a year now. "You gotta stop fooling around, you hear?"

Papa refused to understand that he didn't want to come into the business. He wanted to play the piano—and to write music.

"Sissy stuff!" his father yelled when he talked about becoming a concert pianist, a composer. "Your mother never should have given you music lessons!"

"It's a bloody cold morning for this time of the year," Colonel Ross said, puncturing Gary's thoughts. "Damn it, April in Paris is supposed to be better than this."

On the drive to Paris the colonel studied the reports he'd dragged from his brief case. At intervals he paused for brief conversation with Gary. Like Gary, the colonel was a Southerner—born and bred in a small Virginia town entrenched in the tobacco business. Still, Gary suspected that the colonel was one of those men who enjoyed living close to death.

Gary was sickened by the destruction he'd seen in his brief residence in London. Yet this had not prepared him for what he found in Paris: the parade of ambulances bringing the wounded back from the front, the soldiers missing arms or legs, the men—frequently blind—with faces blown away by shrapnel.

It always amazed him that life seemed to go on so normally in Paris—at least, on the surface. People moved purposefully about the streets. The red taxis were often loaded to their roofs with luggage as they traveled about the city. And there were always men in military uniform on yearned-for leave after painful months on the fighting front.

"We'll hole up at the Crillon this time," the colonel told him. "There's a lady at the Ritz I'd prefer to avoid now." He winked knowingly at Gary, who guessed he was referring to the Parisian mademoiselle who was a model for one of the couture houses. "That's becoming too hot an item to handle." Colonel Ross had a charming wife back home—whom he had neglected to mention. His mademoiselle was thinking ahead already to the end of the war—and becoming the colonel's wife.

Mama loved Paris. She always said if she couldn't live in Bartonville, she'd want to live in Paris. But she was proud that Papa had contrived—a dozen years ago—to have the town's name changed to Bartonville.

He could hear his father's voice proclaiming his pride in this achievement. *"Hell, who built this up from a nothing village to a real town? I made Bartonville. I employ somebody from practically every family in this town. It's my town. I built it—I run it."*

After the war he'd have to have it out with Papa, Gary thought apprehensively. He wanted no part of the business. He didn't even smoke, he thought humorously—and that really teed off the old boy.

After the war he'd move to New York, get himself a little apartment in Greenwich Village, buy a secondhand piano, and concentrate on writing music. Mama would send him small checks now and then to keep him going until he found a job playing the piano somewhere.

Chapter Three

VIKTORIA CONSTANTLY fretted that there was no way to communicate with her parents. She'd tried to send letters, but with the upheaval in Europe this proved impossible. *How would Mama and Papa find her in Paris*? Was Mama well enough to travel yet?

In May a dark period for Paris began to take form. Ominous news of rebellion among the troops surfaced. Many soldiers were refusing to go to the front, and soldiers arriving on leave in the Paris railroad stations were insulting, even attacking, the gendarmes.

What was happening, Parisians wailed. Was this the result of the "Russian movement" spreading into France? Clemenceau declared that the morale of the troops must be boosted and launched a campaign to accomplish this.

That same month Viktoria saw near the Rond Point des Champs Elysées a procession of girls scarcely older than herself. They carried banners that explained they were *les petites mains*—the little hands, as they were called—who worked for the *grande couture*. They were demanding a raise of one sou an hour.

"They dare to do this?" Viktoria whispered in awe to Simone as they paused to watch.

"How else except by striking can they win their demands?" Simone said.

"They're wonderful," Viktoria said in wistful admiration, watching as a group of soldiers on leave joined the strikers in exuberant support.

Simone explained that these girls worked for very low wages at the fine couture houses. Mama and the countess had bought dresses at those same houses—at what she now realized were huge prices. But these very young girls—called *les midinettes* because every working day they poured into the streets for lunch at noon, *midi*—had to fight to have their meager wages raised by one sou an hour.

Suddenly intense summer burst upon Paris. Flowers were lush and fragrant. Day after day the sky was a dazzling blue. The sun hot on the wooden pavements. Vendors sold red roses on the street corners. Strawberries and cherries lured buyers from laden pushcarts.

On the night of July 27th the German "Gothas"—the enormous, new tri-motored bombers—raided Paris, the first such attack. Every Parisian knew their city was the coveted goal of the Germans. To take Paris was to take France. Now efforts were extended to prepare the residents for further such assault.

Every day Viktoria prayed that by some miracle her mother and father—at last in Paris—would turn a corner to find her. The stories that emerged from Russia were frightening. Petrograd, in a state of siege, was encircled by trenches. Mob violence was erupting and food was scarce.

Then on a late August evening, emerging from the Métro station close to the garret apartment she shared with Simone, Viktoria stopped short at the sight of an oddly familiar woman. All at once recognition evoked a surge of excitement.

"Olga!" she called out joyously. "Olga!" One of the seamstresses from the palace. Olga had often sewn for Mama.

The middle-aged rotund woman turned toward Viktoria. Her own face lit up.

"Little Viktoria," she cried out and rushed toward her.

In a surge of Russian—relieved to be able to speak to someone in the only language with which she was comfortable—Olga explained that she and her husband had managed to escape from Russia after he had deserted from the army. They had been in Paris three weeks. Both had jobs.

"What of my mother and father?" Viktoria asked anxiously. "Are they still in Petrograd?"

"Oh, my little one—" Olga's face was distraught. "How do I tell you?"

"Tell me!" All at once Viktoria was trembling. "Tell me, Olga!"

"Your mama died only days after you went away," Olga said. "And your papa—" She hesitated a moment. "He, too, is gone. He was killed in a street demonstration. Almost four hundred were hurt— many died."

Mama and Papa were dead? Viktoria felt faint. *If they were dead, why was she alive*?

"Are you all right?" Olga reached out to her.

"I'm all right," Viktoria whispered, fighting against collapse. This wasn't real. It was a terrible nightmare. "What of the others at the Palace?" she forced herself to inquire.

"Count Veronsky is in prison for sabotage—or so the new government claims. The countess and the girls are still in the Palace—but they fear the Palace will soon be taken over. The countess vows she will not leave Petrograd while the count remains in prison."

"Thank you for bringing me word of my family—" Viktoria heard herself reply. *Mama and Papa were gone forever. Her life was over.*

Gary was ever amazed that despite the rationing and the shortage of food, he and Colonel Ross dined well at the Crillon and Larue's. The Ritz remained out of bounds because of the colonel's avoidance of that certain mademoiselle.

Despite the war, the atmosphere in the elegant Paris hotels was almost gay. Morals and manners were more relaxed than in the earlier years of the war. Chic French women—their hair bobbed short now— considered it fashionable to take a lover—in military uniform, of course. Air force officers were most favored. Thus far, Gary had avoided any feminine alliances—despite disarmingly blatant invitations—probably, he thought humorously, because he knew his father visualized him sleeping with a different French girl every night.

On restless nights he read back issues of *The Tribune*. On Saturdays he went to Brentano's for the New York newspapers. Censorship in Paris papers amused him. Often he'd pick up a copy of *Le Matin*— attracted by a headline—only to discover nothing but white paper in the column below except for the word *Censure* in the center.

On a late September morning he hurried down to breakfast with Colonel Ross, to be told to swallow his breakfast quickly and return to his room to pack.

"We'll head for Boulogne and take the 'leave boat' from there," Colonel Ross said briskly.

"What about the staff car?" Gary asked.

Colonel Ross grinned.

"That car doesn't get out of my sight. A crane will take it aboard ship. It goes with us back to England."

Gary gulped down his breakfast and hurried upstairs to his room. The door was ajar. He realized one of the hotel maids was doing up the room.

"Excuse me," he said in fluent French when the small and very pretty young maid glanced up with a start as she changed a pillow case on his bed. "I have to pack up. I'm leaving unexpectedly. I'll only be a few moments."

"I'll come back later," the chambermaid—her Madonna-like face strangely sad—told him in near-perfect English. She knew from his uniform that he was an American. "Please, there's no need for you to hurry." With a faint smile she darted past him with the grace, he thought, of a young ballerina.

"Thank you," he called after her, wishing there was time for further conversation. He was startled to be so drawn to the French girl who spoke such fluent English.

In the course of her rounds Viktoria could not erase from her memory the face of the handsome young American officer who had unexpectedly returned to his room while she was making up his bed. At unwary intervals their brief exchange of words played across her mind.

Papa always said you could judge a person often by the sound of his voice. The voice of the young American had been so warm and charming! But he'd left the hotel. He'd probably never be back. She felt a surge of guilt at her regret that she wouldn't see him again.

Simone was very strict—as Mama would have been—about her behavior. Simone said it was terrible the way Parisian girls behaved with the soldiers who came into Paris on leave. Paris was the crossroads for soldiers of many nations—from Americans to Senegalese.

"Viktoria, you must always remember you are a lady," Simone said. "You are not one of these Parisian girls who throws herself at any man in uniform."

Wistfully she hoped that the young American officer would be safe.

The war was not going well for the Allies, and fears were beginning to surface that the Russians might make peace with the Germans. That would mean that the German troops, who had been fighting on the Russian front, would focus instead on the French front. *How long before the Germans took Paris?*

And always, in the darkness of the night, Viktoria cried in silence for the mother and father she would never see again.

Chapter Four

PARISIANS LIVED with the painful awareness that the Germans' most urgent objective was to take their city. Their apprehension had been heightened when Russia signed an armistice with Germany in November. Now in late January of 1918 Parisians were weary of the war, the bombs, the shortages, the constant reminders of casualties in the trenches as Red Cross ambulances brought in the injured from the fighting front.

Viktoria loathed the long, monotonous hours she worked as a chambermaid, still haunted by the memories of the time she had been a coddled guest in the elegant Crillon. Her life must change! She could not— *would* not—accept this as her lot. *There had to be more ahead for her.*

Simone had acquired a gentleman friend—a middle-aged Frenchman released from the army after being wounded and left with a slight limp. Simone and Henri dreamt of moving to the country and living and working on the small farm he'd inherited at his father's death just before the war. Now that the farm was in German hands, Henri feared there was nothing left but the earth on which the house and barn had stood.

After a long day at work Viktoria was just emerging from the hotel and into the blacked-out city when the hated *alerte* shrieked its warning of another German attack. She tripped in the darkness and would have fallen except for an unexpected pair of steadying hands.

"Into the hotel," a masculine voice ordered briskly. His French was excellent, but she was sure he was either British or American. "To the shelter."

He was prodding her toward the guests' entrance, she realized in dismay—but in moments such as this the French abandoned protocol. The air raids reduced French society to one level during their duration. Inside the hotel, people were scurrying toward the cellar, some already in nightclothes. A woman struggled to carry a chow in her arms. A waiter called out, "*A la cave! A la cave!*"

All indoor lights were out. Only a flashlight held by a hotel employee guided them to the cellar entrance. Then, as the young soldier—British or American—urged her toward the stairs, Viktoria saw his face for an instant in the meager illumination supplied by the flashlight. Her heart began to pound. *The young American officer who intruded so often on her thoughts.* He was here!

His hand at her elbow, they made their way down to the subterranean refuge. In the dim light provided they saw two men and a woman preparing to play cards. Another pair were already uncorking a bottle of champagne. The woman with the chow sat on an upturned box between rows of dusty wine bottles and ordered her dog to sleep. "*Couche, Maurice. Couche.*"

"We can sit over here," the American officer told Viktoria, and pointed to a pair of chairs at one side of the area.

"Yes," she said shyly. From the glint in his eyes, something fresh in his voice, she knew he remembered her.

"You're the beautiful French girl who speaks English so well," he recalled, abandoning French now.

"I speak French and English, yes," she told him. *He thought she was beautiful.* "I'm Russian. My parents sent me here to Paris when the situation became bad in Petrograd." All at once tears filled her eyes as she visualized those last moments with her mother and father before she and Simone left the Palace forever.

"From word that comes through, we know that Petrograd is in chaos," he said gently. "You're lucky to have gotten out."

"My mother died soon after I left. My father was killed in one of the riots. He was personal physician to Count Veronsky—we lived in the Veronsky Palace." Her voice broke. "Russia will never be the same again—"

"For a few, life in Russia was good," he conceded. "But for many it was a living hell."

"I know," she admitted, fighting for poise. "In our own apartment—away from the count and his family—my father talked about this. It made him very sad. But he was one man," she said defensively. "What could he do? He was good to the peasants under his care. He was the doctor to all the peasants on the count's lands."

"How long have you been in Paris?"

"I arrived here—with my maid who brought me out—almost a year ago," Viktoria told him. "Soon we ran out of money—and Simone said we must find work at one of the hotels if we were to survive." She managed a wisp of a smile. "What about you? When you left the hotel back in September, did you go to the front?" Her eyes were fearful.

"I went with my colonel on special assignment in London," he explained. "I feel guilty that I'm not on the front."

"Be glad!" she said with painful intensity. "We see the soldiers —from so many different countries—who come back after being wounded. I cry for them," she whispered.

"I cry inside for the black Senegalese troops from the French colonies," he said. "Only those close to what's happening realize they're thrown into the front lines to save white troops from slaughter. Perhaps I feel a special hurt because where I live back home there are many colored people—and I've seen how hard their lives can be."

"Where do you live in America?" Up in the night sky the German Gothas were dropping their bombs and the French cannons were responding. Yet to Viktoria it seemed that she and this young American officer were alone on earth.

"In a place called Virginia. It's very beautiful. I miss it so much." His voice was wistful. "I'm Gary Barton," he told her now.

"Viktoria Gunsburg," she said haltingly. Would she ever see him again after tonight?

"Vicky," he decided with a brilliant smile. "I'll always call you Vicky."

He expected to see her again, she thought with a surge of joyous anticipation.

"Tell me about this place. This Virginia," she coaxed, eager to cling to these precious moments.

Gary talked exhaustively about Bartonville—the town which had been named for his family. Viktoria remembered how proud Papa was that there was a town named Gunsburg in Russia.

Gary talked about trips to Paris with his mother before the war, and she guessed that he loved his mother very much. He spoke about his two younger sisters—but, strangely, said little about his father. He acknowledged that though he was not long out of college, he was already fighting with his father about his future.

Now he told her that his father was in the business of making and selling cigarettes. In the United States this was a big business. Americans had begun to smoke before the War Between the States.

"Cigarettes were discovered by British officers in the Crimean War," Gary explained, "but actually the first cigarettes were made by the Aztecs back in 1518. Early in the seventeenth century Spain discovered cigarettes. In Russia, cigarette smoking was discovered in the 1840s—"

"My father said cigarette smoking was an abomination," Viktoria recalled. "There was a cigarette factory in St. Petersburg before he was born. I know the ladies in the Russian court smoked. They considered it exciting."

While the German Gothas spilled death and destruction from the skies, Viktoria and Gary exchanged confidences in the dimly lit cellar as though their lives depended upon absorbing each other's thoughts. Both loved music. Gary was enthralled when she told him that Igor Stravinsky—who had composed the music for *The Firebird* for Diaghilev's great ballet company—was often a guest at the Veronsky Palace.

When at last the Gothas sped away from the city and the French cannons were silent, Viktoria and Gary joined the others in leaving the shelter. The night was cold and clammy and dark. Gary kept a protective hand at Viktoria's elbow.

"The Métro will be running again," she said, reluctant to say good night to Gary. Yet instinctively she knew she would see him again.

"I have the staff car close by," he said. "I'll drive you home. Unless," he teased, "you're afraid to drive with me." Parisians sometimes complained that more casualties resulted from cars driving in blackouts than from the guns.

"That would be very nice," she said softly.

Knowing she was tense from the air raid, he tried to amuse her with stories about his stay in London. In part of her mind she worried

about Simone. Simone always made sure to close the shutters—
against shrapnel—at the first *alerte*. She left the windows open—
against shock, as Parisians advised. But, a direct hit could leave a
gaping hole in the earth where their house had been.

It was necessary to drive very slowly in the darkness. The head-
lights of cars were painted a dark blue to allow only the faintest
illumination to show. Viktoria sighed with relief when they turned a
corner and she saw their street had not been hit. Simone was all right.

"I'll be here in Paris for a while," Gary told her as he pulled up
at the curb before the house she indicated. "Could we have dinner
tomorrow night?"

"I would like that." Simone must understand that Lieutenant Gary
Barton was not just another soldier in Paris. He was not one of those
who arrived at the Gare du Nord on the Saturday "leave train"—
only to disappear quickly with one of the waiting girls into the nearest
hotel, not to emerge until Monday morning. "But I must be home
early," she said. "Simone is very strict."

"I'll pick you up at eight o'clock. Here?" He glanced at the modest
five-story structure.

"All the way up at the top." Suddenly Viktoria felt self-conscious
that she lived in a shabby garret. "Simone will expect you to call for
me at my door."

"Of course," he agreed with a gentle smile. "I'm so glad we met
again, Vicky."

In the weeks ahead Viktoria felt as though she were existing in two
worlds. In one world she was a chambermaid who lived with Simone
in a shabby garret room. Simone was blunt in her suspicions about
the handsome young lieutenant who was in ardent pursuit of Viktoria.

"Viktoria, you know what these soldiers are like in the midst of a
war," she warned. "You must always remember you are a lady. You
are not one of those little *midinettes* or shop girls," she said, "who
allow a man in uniform any liberty he wishes."

"Gary is a perfect gentleman," Viktoria assured her. "He takes no
liberties. He respects me. And once the war is over," she said defensively, her heart beating faster, "he will talk to you, as he would to
Mama if she was here. Simone," she said in a burst of giddy anticipation, "Gary wishes to marry me and take me to America with him."

"When I stand up with you before a judge, I will believe this."

She professed skepticism, but Viktoria knew that Simone feared that she would be hurt.

"After the war," Viktoria repeated. "It will be."

Viktoria's other world consisted of dinners with Gary at such elegant places as the Ritz and Maxim's and Larue's. She'd insisted that they never dine at the Crillon lest she be recognized and risk being discharged from her job. Only because Simone was such an excellent seamstress did she have a proper dress for these occasions. If Gary thought her coat—bought at a secondhand shop at what, to her, was an exorbitant cost—was shabby for such surroundings, he concealed this.

They sat at the secluded little tables they preferred and held hands beneath the fine tablecloths, their eyes telling any onlooker that they were rapturously in love. Gary relished pointing out famous Americans in Paris, and she was always properly impressed. There was the novelist, Edith Wharton, and the entertainer Elsie Janis, and artist Mary Cassatt.

One late March night at Larue's—after the writer Marcel Proust had left with friends—Gary rose from their table in a burst of exuberance and crossed over to the piano.

"Come on over here," he called to Viktoria. "You've never heard me play the piano—"

Viktoria glanced about nervously, then walked to the piano.

"Gary, no one is allowed to play music here while the war is on," she whispered.

"I'll play till they stop me," he chuckled, and began to play—with a skill that awed Viktoria—Chopin's beautiful Minute Waltz.

When he finished, other diners applauded lavishly. Suddenly shy, Gary rose from the piano bench and returned to their table with Viktoria.

"Gary, you didn't tell me how wonderfully you play," she murmured, her eyes adoring him. At the Palace in Petrograd she had heard some of the finest musicians in all Russia. She had learned what was fine and what was ordinary. "I'm so proud of you."

Their dinner was interrupted by yet another warning of a German Gotha raid. They joined the other diners in a rush toward the cellar shelter. Down below they found a private corner, where Viktoria could sit with Gary's arms about her. At covert moments—with the nearest group involved in a heated bridge game—his mouth found hers, and they clung together as though alone in the world. For Viktoria and

Gary, the increasingly frequent air raids provided cherished moments such as these.

"I saw Mlle. Chanel again," Gary said. "I was with the colonel at the Ritz Bar when she met a friend there."

Gary knew that she was fascinated by "Coco" Chanel, the young designer whose shop was becoming so popular.

"Many of the ladies at the Crillon go to Chanel for the new pajamas she's designed." Laughter lit her violet eyes. "They want to look fashionable when they must hurry down into the shelter when the German planes come."

"I'll buy you a pair," he said instantly, "so you'll look fashionable when you're at home in the midst of a raid."

"No," she rejected gently. "That would not be proper."

"When the war is over and I come back to you and we're married, I'll buy you beautiful pajamas and dresses and coats to take back to America. You'll be the most beautiful and best-dressed young wife in Bartonville," he said.

Viktoria was upset when a few days later Gary told her he must go to London with the colonel for an unspecified length of time. She knew that London, too, had been heavily hit by German bombers. She worried for Gary's safety. At least, when Paris was hit, she would see him in a matter of hours and know that he was all right. Now with Gary in London she lay sleepless far into each night.

Late in May he appeared at the apartment door just as Viktoria and Simone were about to sit down to their meager supper. In Paris food was in short supply.

"Oh, Gary, you're all right!" Ignoring Simone's presence she threw herself into his arms. "I was so worried about you!"

"I'm fine, Vicky. I worried about you, too." He turned to Simone with a diffident smile. He was conscious of her skepticism about his relationship with Viktoria. "Madame, may I please take Viktoria off to supper?" he asked ingratiatingly. "I promise to have her home early."

"Would it matter if I said no?" she grumbled. "All right, Viktoria, go out to supper with your young man."

Now word reached Paris that five German divisions had overpowered the Allied forces and were moving toward Paris. The city was in panic. Could Paris defend itself? Must the people be evacuated?

Within the next two weeks a million people fled from Paris. The

Germans were less than forty miles away. Parisians thronged into the Gare de Lyons and the Gare d'Orsay to board trains that would take them to the south of France. The normally crowded boulevards were almost devoid of civilians. Soldiers of half a dozen nations or more lingered in the cafe terraces with female companions, while explosions could be heard above the rumble of Army vehicles.

The long-range "Big Berthas"—named for munitions manufacturer Krupp's wife—fired upon Paris every day from a secret encampment that Allied planes sought frenziedly, but without success, to locate and bomb. Even during daylight hours, shells poured into Paris. The mood in the city was ominous. The populace that had not run to safer areas waited in soaring alarm for the entry of the German Army.

Then Marshal Foch—the new commander of all Allied forces in France—began a determined counteroffensive. Soon, five major battles were being fought simultaneously. Word came back to a joyous Paris that the Germans were fleeing to the north. For now, at least, Paris was saved.

On an intensely hot, late July evening, Gary appeared at Viktoria and Simone's apartment to report that his colonel and their entire staff were heading for the front. Simone pretended to be searching the blacked-out street below for her friend Henri, who had left some minutes earlier while Gary and Viktoria said goodbye.

"Gary, be careful," Viktoria pleaded. "I'll pray for you."

"I'll come back," he promised. "Soon the war will be over, and we can begin to live again."

It seemed to Viktoria that Paris had become one huge evacuation center for wounded soldiers in the French offensive. Ambulances poured into the city day and night. Every hospital bed was occupied. Motorcycle couriers bringing messages from correspondents at the front arrived regularly. The newspapers reported that the American front was fighting furiously. There were few moments of each day when Viktoria was not consumed by anxiety for Gary's safety.

Weeks sped past. The Germans were in retreat, but the fighting was fierce. Casualties were high on both sides. The Germans still remained entrenched in their seemingly impregnable positions in the Argonne Forest, but the Allies were determined to drive them back.

At the end of October the Argonne Forest was cleared by American forces. The Allied armies began their final offensive. Peace at last seemed in sight.

On Sunday, October 27th, Paris was invaded by a host of top Allied officials, generals, and statesmen—including Prime Minister David Lloyd George and Colonel House, who represented President Wilson—and, of course, representatives of the press of many nations. A meeting of the Supreme War Council was scheduled for October 31st—to draw up terms of the armistice. The armistice terms were set at a final meeting on November 4th. The armistice agreement was finally signed early on the morning of November 11th. At eleven AM the war would be over.

Viktoria was dusting a bedroom at the Crillon when the news burst upon Paris. Immediately work was abandoned. All business ceased. Parisians poured into the streets. The boulevards were mobbed with joyful crowds. French girls danced with soldiers of many nations on the Champs Elysées. There was singing, bands playing, and impromptu square dancing.

Viktoria pushed her way through the crowds that clogged every street. She was eager to be home, where Gary would be able to find her. The war was over. *Gary was safe.*

Not until late in the afternoon did Gary arrive at her door.

"Oh, baby, baby," he crooned, holding her close. "The nightmare's over."

"I was scared," she whispered, tears of joy flooding her eyes. "I was afraid I'd never see you again."

"I'll have to go home first to be discharged. Then I'll come back for you. We'll be married here in Paris."

"You'll soon be seeing the last of Paris—" Simone's acerbic voice punctured their magic moment.

Neither Viktoria nor Gary had heard the door open. His hands fell to his sides as they turned to Simone in mutual guilt, neither sure what would have happened if she had not intruded.

"I'll have to return to the States for my army discharge," he said self-consciously, and then reached for Viktoria's hand. "I'll come back then," he added with faint defiance. "Viktoria and I will be married."

"Perhaps you will come back." Simone's face revealed a blend of skepticism and concern for Viktoria. "We will see. Many American soldiers make promises . . ."

Chapter Five

Barton Manor sat beside the James River on the outskirts of Bartonville, nine miles west of Richmond—in the heart of tobacco country. The house itself—surrounded by almost one hundred acres—bore little resemblance to the one to which Daniel Barton had brought his bride, Sara, twenty-four years ago—when he was an ambition-obsessed twenty-six-year-old and she was nineteen. The modest, white clapboard five-room house had expanded through the years into a Southern Greek Revival mansion, with a wide front gallery supported by six Doric columns and a wrought-iron balcony hanging over the large, recessed doorway. The grounds were magnificently landscaped under Sara's supervision.

The tobacco industry had fared well during the war. Daniel Barton had built an addition to the factory early in 1915, and the following year began the construction of a new factory that was double the size of the original. With new jobs opening up, the town, too, was expanding.

"We've got a growing market," Daniel Barton repeated with zest at least once a day to his executive staff and to his wife and daughters. "We're running night and day."

Cigarettes were rushed to the Allies as though, Sara Barton said with distaste, the armed forces could not fight without this stimulant. When the United States became an active participant, American tobacco factories expanded yet again in order to meet demands.

"You know what General Pershing says," Daniel was apt to remind his wife. " 'Tobacco is as indispensable as the daily ration.' "

Though Sara herself loathed smoking, she knew that Richmond women had been smoking since 1902. Their cigarette habit had been discussed in national newspapers and magazines. For a while these pioneer women smokers liked to indulge this habit in the ladies' waiting room of the local depot—until the indignant station master put a stop to it by ordering the maid to cease buying cigarettes for the ladies. They dared to smoke but were timid about buying.

Tonight in the double drawing room—furnished in the elegant English Regency style Sara Barton loved—Gary was spending his first evening home in twenty-two months. Again, he felt guilty that his social connections had brought him back from France a few days before Christmas, when most servicemen would be spending another Christmas far from home. He had crossed the Atlantic with Colonel Ross on one of the first available troopships.

As he'd feared, the announcement he had just made was not being well-received by his father.

"What the hell are you talking about?" Daniel Barton bellowed. He was a tall, overweight, florid-faced man whose once-handsome features showed the rigors of overindulgence. Still, he radiated a sense of power that some women found attractive. Long ago Sara Barton—a blonde, blue-eyed patrician beauty—had learned to close her eyes to her husband's extra-marital affairs. "You see some little French slut," he continued contemptuously, "and you get all hot and bothered. So you had a little fun with her. You don't marry those girls!"

"Don't call Vicky a slut, Papa." Gary struggled to conceal his rage. "And she is not French. She's Russian. Her parents sent her to Paris to get her away from the revolution there. It wasn't safe. Her family was—"

"Now you're gonna tell me she's related to the royal family," Daniel interrupted. "Every little Russian shopgirl in Paris is claiming to be related to the czar."

"Her father was the physician for a titled family and the workers on their estate. She lived with her family in the Palace of a Count Veronsky. She speaks three languages," he said defensively. *How could he have expected Papa to understand?* But nothing was changed. He was going back to Paris to marry Vicky. He would bring her home to Virginia.

"Daniel, why don't you listen to Gary?" his mother said. "He's been through such a terrible time."

"And now he'll come into the business and be trained to take over when I go." As usual, Daniel had little patience for his wife's intervention on Gary's behalf. "Not that I plan for that event to happen any time soon," he added with relish. "I'll still be at the head of Barton Tobacco Company when I'm eighty-five. But Gary's my only son. He'll succeed me."

"Papa, I mean to marry Vicky," Gary reiterated, now pale. He turned to his mother. "You'll love her, Mama."

"Take a few cold baths," Daniel said with a coarse laugh. "Anyhow, it'll be a long time before she can get over here. Every ship has been commandeered to bring home the troops. We sent over a million and a half men. You know how long it'll take to get them home? By that time," he scoffed, "you'll forget what she looks like!"

"I won't forget," Gary shot back grimly.

"You're a boy fresh out of college," Daniel said, changing moods with chameleon-like swiftness. His smile was indulgent. "You did your family proud by going off to fight. So play for two or three months—then come into the business. I'll make a man out of you, Gary."

"The war did that," Gary said quietly. "And if I'm old enough to fight in a war, I'm old enough to get married."

"Gary, you've just been home a few hours," his mother said tenderly. "Why don't we all relax and enjoy your being back? The girls will be so excited when they discover you're here." His younger sisters—Lily and Stephanie—were away at a house party in Norfolk. "I can't tell you how relieved and happy I am to have you home. It's the finest Christmas present you could have given us!"

For the next two weeks, it seemed to Gary that all he did was eat and sleep—and was encouraged in this by his mother. He remembered soldiers—English, French, Australian—coming into Paris on leave after twelve or fourteen months of active duty, yearning for sleep, good food, and a willing girl for the duration of their leave.

He wished that, somehow, he could have arranged to marry Vicky before he was shipped home, that they could have had at least one night together. He was conscious of the passion that stirred low within him as he visualized Vicky's slender but curvaceous frame. But it wasn't just that, he told himself. He couldn't envision a life without Vicky now. They belonged together forever.

He was haunted by memories of the harrowing last weeks of the war, when he had been Colonel Ross's interpreter and driver along the frenzied fighting fronts. They'd made brief forays to the front before, but in those final weeks they'd lived on the front, watching several major battles, seeing the death and destruction from every side. Now, he thought bitterly, those who'd experienced the horrors of war were supposed to come home and resume their normal lives.

Gary knew his mother was upset by his quiet avowals that as soon as it was physically possible he meant to return to Paris for Vicky. But he realized, too, that he was penniless except for the bills his mother tucked into his jacket pocket at regular intervals. The only way he could go to Paris and back was to ask her for the funds.

He'd gone from college graduation into the Army. A major reason for his enlistment had been to stave off a battle with his father about his coming into the business. Up until this point in life he'd felt no need to earn money. He'd had his regular monthly allowance. Even while he was in service, his mother had contrived to send him money.

Now Papa was making it clear that allowances were for students. He could live and eat at home; but as far as his father was concerned, he'd have to work for anything else. Of course, Papa knew that Mama slipped him money regularly. But, Mama could not provide him with funds to support himself and his wife. Nor could he bring himself to accept that.

He slept the mornings away, and roamed about the vast acreage that surrounded Barton Manor. He ate ravenously, spent hours at the piano—though avoiding this when his father was home. He lay sleepless night after night, yearning for Vicky.

Regularly he wrote to Vicky. He explained that it was impossible as yet to arrange for transportation to and from France, but that he was working on the problem. He said nothing of his financial situation. He knew he must come to grips with reality. How was he going to support himself and Vicky?

Each day he felt his dreams of going to New York, finding a job as a pianist in Greenwich Village, composing music, grow more elusive. He'd dreamt of composing concertos and symphonies—but this increasingly seemed a fantasy. *If he was to marry Vicky—and he couldn't accept a life without her—then he must have a job with a regular salary.*

Gary was elated when—after several phone calls to New York City shipping lines—he learned that he could shortly obtain round-trip accommodations between New York and Cherbourg. Now, on a blustery February night, he sat with his mother in the library and geared himself to explain his newly formulated offer to compromise with his father. God, he was glad Papa was up in New York on company business for a few days, he thought, while Effie served coffee to his mother and himself. Lily and Stephanie were off at another of their endless parties.

His mother listened sympathetically while he tried to appear determined yet calm. The birch logs burning in the fireplace grate lent an air of serenity to the spacious room.

"You know how I hate business," Gary said with candor, "but if I have to go in with Papa to support myself and Vicky, then I must." He'd still compose, he vowed to himself. There'd be time for that. Vicky knew how important music was to him. They'd rent a little house for themselves, away from Barton Manor. It would be wonderful, just the two of them alone there.

"You'd like me to talk to your father," his mother said. She'd always been the intermediary in battles between him and Papa. "You'll agree to come into the company if he stops carrying on about your marrying Vicky."

"I can marry her without his approval," Gary pointed out, and smiled wryly at his mother's faint sound of protest. "But I'll need a job." There were few possibilities for a job in Bartonville—except at Barton Tobacco Company—or elsewhere, for that matter, considering his lack of experience or training. "So I might as well work for the company. But Papa must promise he won't be nasty to Vicky when I bring her home." Papa could cut people to shreds with his vitriolic temper. "I won't have her hurt."

"I'll talk to him when he comes back from New York." She tried to appear reassuring, yet he sensed her anxiety. Papa didn't take well to being crossed. "I'm sure your Vicky is a charming young lady to have won you over this way." Her eyes were luminous with affection. "It's sad that her parents are gone, but we'll give you a lovely wed-

ding here at Barton Manor. Lily and Stephanie can be Vicky's bridesmaids and—''

"Mama, no," Gary interrupted, his eyes pleading for compassion.
"Vicky and I will be married in Paris. In a civil ceremony." He tried
for a note of humor. "I doubt that Vicky would travel with me before
we're married. Like Lily and Stephanie she was brought up to observe
all the proprieties." He always pretended not to be aware of his mother's concern about his sisters' frequent departures from the behavior
demanded of them.

But a civil ceremony was important, he reminded himself. He
wished to avoid further hostility with his father by revealing that his
bride-to-be was Jewish. He knew because—ever conscientious—she
had told him. He knew, too, that her father had cautioned her against
revealing this to strangers. He remembered Vicky saying so gravely
that, "to be a Jew in our world is dangerous." She'd spoken with
such anguish about the peasant uprisings against the Jews in Russia
and the devastating pogroms instituted by the Russian government.

It was just as well, he told himself—feeling a twinge of guilt—not
to mention Vicky's background to Papa. His father could be such a
bigot. And in the town of Bartonville the three Jewish families—
though cultured and financially well-fixed—were not received in the
upper social circle.

Now Gary waited impatiently for his father's return. As soon as
things were worked out with Papa, he planned to make reservations
aboard the small French liner. Already rates were rising sharply, but
Mama had made it known she would see him through on this.

Approaching the house shortly before dinner, three evenings after
his talk with his mother, Gary saw the family Cadillac parked in front
of the house. Zachary—who had been with the family since before
Gary was born—was bringing luggage out of the car.

"Your papa's home," Zachary informed him genially. "He musta
had a fine trip. He's sure in a good mood."

"That's nice to hear." Gary smiled, but all at once he was tense.
The confrontation was imminent.

Walking into the house he heard joyous squeals from the girls. Papa
had probably brought them fancy trinkets from New York. Lily was
nineteen already—and Stephanie two years younger—but both sometimes acted as though they were about eight. Mama just wished that

the two of them would stop being so flighty and get themselves engaged to proper young men.

He strolled into the house and down the wide hall to the library,
which was more often the family gathering place than the double-
drawing room because Papa liked its accessibility to his supply of
bourbon and his secret store of Gauloises. He preferred these to the
company brand—though he would have killed anybody who dared to
say this.

"Papa, is that all you've brought us?" Lily scolded as Gary walked
into the room. "Just the necklace and the fur muff?"

"Well, I might just have something stashed away in my luggage,"
he conceded, and Lily flung her arms about him with a fresh outcry
of approval. Gary loathed these noisy displays of affection between
his father and older sister. It was as though Lily was buying Papa's
favors. Stephanie was somewhat less demonstrative.

"Welcome home, Papa." Gary forced himself to exchange an embrace with his father. All his life he'd yearned for Papa's favor—but
Lily always came first, and then Stephanie. Still, Papa was apt to brag
about his "firstborn"—"my son and successor."

They were an insular family, Gary thought. Of Papa's five sisters,
two had died in childbirth and the other three had moved west with
their families. There was bad blood between Papa and his sisters because their father had left the business to his son. Not even an annual
Christmas card passed between them now.

On his mother's side, Gary mused, there were only Grandmother and
Grandfather Warren and bachelor Uncle Rob, who lived in semi-
isolation at the Warren family estate on the other side of Richmond—
still in mourning for the Confederacy. Uncle Rob believed his sister had
married beneath her, but he was not averse to receiving financial aid
from his brother-in-law. Papa found them dull but occasionally amusing. There were "kissing cousins" seen two or three times a year.

In a few minutes dinner was announced. The family moved into
the elegant dining room with its twin Waterford chandeliers, silver by
Tallois of Paris, and delicate ecru curtains flanked by pale olive velvet
drapes that matched the velvet upholstery of the chairs. Mama loved
this room because she had prevailed in her insistence that cigarette
smoke never mar the fragrant Virginia air in here.

After dinner they moved into the double drawing room, for coffee for the gentlemen and hot chocolate for the ladies. Most of the conversation revolved around Daniel's trip to New York City, and Lily's pleas that she and Stephanie be allowed to spend two weeks there the following month. Papa would probably give in, Gary surmised. Lily usually had her way with Papa.

Gary was relieved when his mother finally shipped Lily and Stephanie off to their rooms for the night—despite their protests. Now Mama, with an air of girlish gaiety, contrived to win Papa's favor, would introduce his plans. He tensed, watching his father's face tighten in disapproval as his mother talked.

"Of course, you have to come into the company," Daniel said, turning to Gary with a gesture of impatience. "Who else will follow in my footsteps? But this girl you talk about—it's absurd!" His voice soared in anger.

"Papa, I'll come into the company if my wife is well-received in the family," he said. "If I can fight in a war, I can choose my own wife." His eyes dueled defiantly with his father's. "If Vicky is not welcome here, then we'll live in Paris." Gary knew how much his father wanted him in the company. "We'll manage, somehow."

He saw the flicker of astonishment in his father's eyes. Papa had not expected to be faced with an ultimatum. The atmosphere was suddenly electric. Gary's throat tightened. He didn't *want* to live in Paris—but the threat was a powerful one.

"All right," his father said, his eyes cold and resentful. "Marry the girl. A hundred to one, she'll hate it here. She'll go running back to Paris before your first anniversary. But so be it. You'll start in the company at the machines. Learn the business from the bottom up— as I did. Your starting wage will be eleven dollars a week."

Gary gaped at his father in disbelief. How could he ask Vicky to marry him on weekly wages that would cover no more than a hovel and a near-starvation diet? *Papa was winning again.*

Chapter Six

THE PARIS of March 1919 was a different city from the one of six months earlier. It had become an almost exclusively French city. Most of the foreign soldiers were gone. No tourists were arriving as yet, though the tradespeople were hopeful that travel would soon resume.

Residents complained bitterly about the escalating prices—on everything from fruit and vegetables to clothes and lodgings. Viktoria paid scant attention to these changes. She focused on the conviction that Gary would come for her, that soon she would be leaving Paris. Yet, as she sat down to supper with Simone in their dank, cold garret apartment, she was conscious of the fact that she had not heard from Gary in over three weeks.

"I hate this cold," Simone grumbled, bringing cups of steaming coffee to the table. Only in the mornings—because of the high cost of wood and coal—did they allow themselves a fire in the stove. "When will you agree to move to the country with Henri and me?" she asked. "At least there'll be wood to keep the stove going."

"Simone, I can't leave Paris."

Henri and Simone wanted to get married and move to the tiny farm he had inherited from his father, but Simone kept stalling him because of her.

"Don't worry about me," she continued. "I'll be all right by my-self—" She didn't dare add, "until Gary comes," because she knew Simone was skeptical about this happening.

"You're little more than a child," Simone said in exasperation. "How can I leave you alone?"

"Simone, I stopped being a child when we ran from Petrograd," Viktoria said gently. "I became a woman. I'll be all right alone."

"I'll tell Henri we'll be married next month," Simone decided after a moment. But her eyes were troubled. "I can't wait to get out of Paris. It's not like it used to be. Everything costs so much—and so many things are not to be had at all. Everybody overcharges, and blames it on people above them. Some people are making fortunes," she said bitterly, "while most of us suffer."

"April is a beautiful time to be married." Please, God, Viktoria prayed, let Gary be here by then. She mustn't allow herself to think that he might not come back for her. But even if he hadn't returned to Paris by the time Simone and Henri were married, she couldn't leave. *Gary said he would come back for her.*

"It's been a while since you've had a letter from Gary," Simone reminded. "And he's been gone almost four months."

"He's waiting to acquire passage." How many times had she told Simone that? "Not just to come over, but return passage for the two of us. You know how hard that is right now."

"If I go to the farm with Henri and leave you here, how will you live? You can't pay for this place with your wages. Viktoria, how will you survive?"

"I'm going to look for a job in a shop." Shops were reopening now, hoping for the tourist trade to resume. "I speak three languages," she said. "That should be very useful. I'll earn enough to live." From Simone she had learned to make every sou go far. "I'll miss you. But Gary promises that we can visit France after we're married. It's not as though I'll never see you again—"

"Start looking right away for a job in a shop." Simone's voice was sharp, but Viktoria understood this was caused by anxiety for her welfare. "But say nothing at the hotel. There's always somebody with a friend needing a job as a chambermaid. You could be out on your ear—with nothing."

Gary, unlike some of the other passengers aboard the small French liner, was upset when the ship was detained at Plymouth. The report was that they might be held up another two weeks—in addition to the week they'd already been delayed—because of the cases of influenza aboard. He hadn't bothered to write Viktoria that he was coming because he'd expected to be in Paris before a letter would arrive.

Four days later word came that they could proceed to Cherbourg. With three-fourths of its first-class passengers leaving at Plymouth, the ship sailed late in the afternoon. Early tomorrow morning, Gary thought with relief, they'd dock in Cherbourg. A few hours on the train and he'd be in Paris.

At intervals he worried about how Vicky would receive the news that they would live with his family for a while. Had he been rash in agreeing to Mama's suggestion that they stay at Barton Manor until Papa saw fit to raise his wages to a figure that was practical?

It was the only way, he thought tiredly. They could hardly manage on the eleven dollars a week he'd be earning. The tobacco industry lagged behind others in wages paid, though Papa refused to admit that.

Mama was convinced he'd move up quickly in the company. *"You know Papa. He worked his way up from nothing—and he wants to see you follow in his footsteps. But it won't take years for him to push you forward. He just wants to see you in the company and working seriously."*

Mama had promised that Papa would behave himself with Vicky, Gary remembered. Still, he was apprehensive. And she'd warned Lily and Stephanie that they were not to be snippy, the way they could be sometimes. It was strange how the girls were so much like Papa—in their looks and in their ways, and he was so much like Mama.

As anticipated, by early morning the ship docked at Cherbourg. He dreaded the usual red tape at customs, though the inspection turned out to be casual and lenient. Papa would be amused that their only inquiry had been about tobacco.

A special train supplied by the state railroad was waiting to take them to Paris. Gary boarded the train with a surge of exhilaration. In a few hours he'd be with Viktoria. They'd be married as soon as it was possible. The ocean voyage home would be their honeymoon.

Viktoria fought against tears as she sat with Simone and Henri in a modest restaurant by the Louvre—where luncheon was still available at a moderate price. For two hours now Simone had been a

married woman. Later Viktoria would go with them to the Gare du
Nord and see them off to their new home.

"The food is good here," Henri said, his face radiant. "Of course,
it's crowded, and the service is slow. But still, it is possible to have
lunch without starving for the rest of the week."

"Viktoria, it's not too late to change your mind about coming with
us," Simone tried again. "I know you're pleased about the new
job—"

For a week now Viktoria had been a salesgirl in a small dress shop.
Only occasionally was her knowledge of Russian and English utilized,
but the proprietor talked about how this would all change when the
tourists returned again to Paris: "They will come soon," she prophesied. "The *France* survived the war and soon the new *Paris* will be
sailing. I hear it's magnificent, with lots of iron grillwork and
Lalique."

"Viktoria?" Simone said, interrupting her thoughts. "It's not too
late for you to change your mind. Come with us."

"I can't." Viktoria managed a wisp of a smile. "I must wait for
Gary. Will you come to Paris for our wedding?" Her eyes said she
refused to consider the possibility that this marriage might not take
place.

"I'll come." Simone's eyes said she never expected this day to
arrive.

The three didn't linger over lunch. There was the train to catch at
the Gare du Nord. Though the farm where Simone and Henri would
live was less than two hours from Paris, Viktoria dreaded returning
alone tonight to the apartment she and Simone had shared.

They left the restaurant, and in a grandiose gesture Henri insisted
on their taking a taxi to Simone and Viktoria's apartment to collect
the luggage.

"Henri, when do you ever find a taxi when you want one?" Simone
scoffed. People complained regularly about the independence of the
taxi drivers and their unavailability. "Who needs taxis when we can
take the Métro? The only decent thing the Paris taxi drivers have ever
done was to take six thousand men to the battlefield along the Marne."

"Here's a taxi right now," he said in triumph. "And we're not
going to a battlefield."

"Oh, I don't know about that," Simone chuckled. "My sisters have
always said that marriage is a battlefield."

Viktoria sat back in silence as the taxi headed for their destination. Simone was making a pretense of high spirits, holding hands with Henri, talking ebulliently about their new life on the farm. But Viktoria was conscious of Simone's anxious glances in her direction.

She remembered Simone's frequent exhortation to her: "*Viktoria, you're not the only girl in Paris who thought her American soldier would come back to her. By now most of them have come down to earth again. The war's over—everybody's gone back to their normal lives.*"

The taxi was approaching their street. Viktoria's throat tightened in anguish. It was wrong to be sad because Simone was married and leaving Paris. She should be happy for Simone. But she dreaded walking into their apartment, knowing she'd be there alone tonight. Alone in Paris.

Perhaps Simone was right, she told herself, panic engulfing her at last. Perhaps she *should* go with Simone and Henri to the farm. She could write Gary and tell him where to find her—if he was coming for her. She hadn't received a letter from him in over a month. It wasn't too late to go with Simone and Henri.

The taxi pulled up at the curb. Simone reached to squeeze Viktoria's hand in reassurance while Henri paid the driver.

"This is the last of the cold weather," Simone prophesied as they walked toward the entrance to their building. "In a couple of weeks Paris will be beautiful."

She would go with Simone and Henri, Viktoria told herself while she headed up the narrow stairs toward their room. She couldn't stay here alone. Simone was right. Gary was never coming back for her.

Tears blurred her vision as she climbed up the seemingly endless, murky flights to the garret. She must forget her beautiful dreams. They were not to be. In a few minutes she could pack and be ready to leave with Simone and Henri.

Behind her, Viktoria could hear Henri grumbling about the exhausting stairs. He and Simone were a flight below her. Then—despite the darkness—she became aware of someone sprawled on the landing above. There was something familiar about the shadowed figure. All at once her heart was pounding.

"Gary?" she called out. "Gary, is that you?"

"Vicky—" Gary rose from the landing, his arms outstretched. "Oh, baby, I missed you so much!"

* * *

Three days later—with the help of the American ambassador's office—Viktoria and Gary were married in a French civil ceremony. Delaying their departure for the farm, Simone and Henri were their witnesses. Afterwards, Henri insisted on giving a wedding dinner for the four of them at an inexpensive restaurant where the Chateaubriand was superb and the wine adequate. There was no sugar—an item still scarce in Paris. They were offered saccharin pellets. The bread was excellent, but not yet pre-war white in color—which disturbed none of this party.

"Your mama and papa would have been so happy today," Simone told Viktoria with a sentimental smile. "And just think, you'll spend your wedding night at the Ritz!"

"The American dollar goes far in Paris," Gary said.

Viktoria shuddered for the dozenth time at the thought of how close she and Gary came to missing each other. Another few hours and he would have found an empty apartment—with no inkling of where she was.

Tomorrow they would take the train to Cherbourg and there board the ship that was to carry them to New York. Gary had insisted on buying her a new coat and three beautiful dresses for their trip—their honeymoon, she thought blissfully. She wasn't afraid at all, as Tatiana and Catherine Veronsky had predicted the three of them would be on such an awesome occasion.

After dinner Viktoria and Gary went with Simone and Henri to the Gare du Nord. Gary held Viktoria's hand protectively while they watched the train pull out of the station.

"Now let's go home," he said softly. "To our suite at the Ritz."

Viktoria gazed about the modest, though still quite elegant, Ritz suite.

"Gary, can we afford to stay here?" she asked. He had told her his earnings would be very small, that they must live for a while with his family.

"My mother's treat," he explained. "She's always had a special fondness for the Ritz."

"Gary, I can't believe you're really here," she whispered.

"The waiting was awful," he murmured, reaching for her. "But that's all over—"

Viktoria had lain awake until dawn in the garret apartment and tried to envision her wedding night. Her employer at the shop had insisted on giving her a beautiful, gossamer white nightgown after Viktoria had chosen the coat and three dresses Gary bought for her. But it was clear now that Gary had no wish to delay until she could change into her wedding night gown.

"I missed you every moment we were apart," he told her as his mouth reached for hers. "We have all those months to make up for."

His lips touched hers, and his arms drew her close. She'd thought she might be afraid—just at first. But this was Gary, whom she loved. He released her mouth, touched the high ridge of one cheekbone with infinite tenderness, then lifted her from her feet and carried her into the dark bedroom. She lay motionless while he swept away the clothes that kept her from him. She welcomed the touch of his hands, his mouth that moved from earlobe to throat to a full, high breast.

"You are so beautiful," he murmured. "I knew it would be perfect for us."

Tatiana and Catherine used to whisper and giggle about moments like this, but it was wonderful because she loved Gary, Viktoria told herself exultantly. And Gary loved her. She was eager to learn, to respond, to share this ultimate experience that made them one.

Early the following day, Viktoria and Gary checked out of the Ritz and took a taxi to the train. Viktoria's eyes clung to the passing scenery. When would she see Paris again? She was startled to realize that it had become home in these two past hectic years. St. Petersburg seemed to be a part of another lifetime.

On the train—in a fine first-class carriage—she sat with one hand in Gary's while he talked about the beauty of Virginia.

"Vicky, you'll love it," he promised. "Bartonville is in the midst of tobacco country. All rolling hills and farmland. The house sits on the crest of a knoll that looks down on the James River. But we won't stay there long," he said quickly. "We'll move into a little house of our own as soon as I get a decent raise. And leave it to Mama." He chuckled affectionately. "She'll make sure the old man pushes me up the ladder fast." All at once his face was somber. "I don't care how small a house we have—so long as there's room for us and a piano. It won't be the Veronsky Palace," he teased. "But it'll be our little palace."

"That's all I want, Gary," she said, "a little house for us and your piano. And after dinner every night, you'll play for me."

Early that evening they were settled in their first-class cabin aboard a steamer that—like the ship that had brought Gary to Cherbourg— still lacked the luxuries of the prewar liners.

"I remember coming to England with my mother aboard the *Aquitania*," Gary said. "It was a four-funneled beauty with suites named for famous painters like Rembrandt and Gainsborough and Van Dyck—and decorated with that artist in mind," he recalled, a humorous light in his eyes. "There was a Garden Lounge that was designed to resemble an old English garden. The crew was very British and trained to please. My mother said she suspects the postwar ships will be very different. The *Aquitania*, she says, was the end of an era."

"Gary, what did you tell your family about me?" she asked, all at once fearful. Would they like her?

"That you're a little Russian princess whom I swept off her feet," he joshed. "That you're beautiful, and I love you madly. But I warn you," he said with mock seriousness, "like me, they'll probably call you Vicky."

"I won't mind—" She gazed adoringly at her new husband. "It sounds very American."

Yet already she had to fight off a sense of panic at the prospect of meeting Gary's parents, and his two sisters. Would they be furious that he had married some girl they'd never met? A girl from Russia, who had worked as a chambermaid at the Hotel Crillon?

But she was Gary's wife, she told herself defiantly. They couldn't change that. She clung to this in the days and nights of the rough Atlantic crossing.

Vicky and Gary were happy to be able to keep to themselves— with most first-class passengers spending much time in their cabins. Each night they slept in each other's arms, as though determined to make up for those hauntingly empty months when they'd been apart.

Vicky was delighted that they were to remain in New York overnight. They stayed at the elegant Plaza Hotel, overlooking Central Park, and had dinner in the main dining room at Delmonico's. Gary teased Vicky about not being able to order wine because Prohibition had been instituted in February.

"Not that it bothers my father," Gary chuckled. "He pours his bourbon into root beer bottles and keeps it out in the open. And he smokes Turkish cigarettes transferred into Barton packages because he still prefers the Turkish to his own brand.''

"Your father has his own brand of cigarettes?" Vicky was impressed.

"Honey, I told you he's in the tobacco business." He seemed oddly self-conscious. "The company manufactures cigarettes."

"Yes, you did tell me," she said. "But I thought when you said he was a tobacconist that he ran a shop."

"He's—quite prosperous," Gary said after a moment, seeming to be embarrassed. "You might say wealthy."

"Gary, I'd have married you despite that," she laughed. But, she had not envisioned becoming part of a wealthy family. She knew that the town where they lived was named for the Bartons, but she'd assumed some descendant had been the first to settle there, and that was how the town had acquired its name.

"The house is not the Veronsky Palace," he conceded with a grin, "but it's beautiful."

"To me, wherever you are is beautiful," she declared.

After dinner at Delmonico's, Gary took her to see Broadway. He pointed out the grand new Strand Theater—where movies rather than plays were presented. It was the first real "motion picture palace." But soon they made their way back to the Plaza, eager to be alone again.

The following morning Vicky and Gary traveled by taxi to Pennsylvania Station, to board the train that would take them to Richmond, where they'd be met by the Barton chauffeur. Vicky was impressed by the train station, which was modeled after a Roman temple. But there was nothing of ancient Rome about the people who hurried about its huge public concourses, who populated the arcades of shops, she thought in amusement.

They waited only a few minutes before boarding their train. Now Vicky was tense, trying to prepare herself for meeting Gary's family.

"It's not quite the Orient Express," Gary said while they settled themselves in a car adjoining the dining car, "but the food is great."

"I once went with my mother and father on the Orient Express," Vicky recalled in a surge of pain. But she mustn't mourn today. "We traveled from Paris to Vienna. I remember the dining car. It was paneled in mahogany and teak inlaid with rosewood, and there were paintings by Delacroix and Seymour hanging on the walls. The cutlery was solid silver. The plates were Sèvres porcelain and the glasses Baccarat crystal. Mama adored the dining car—'' Her voice broke despite her efforts to appear in a light mood.

"My mother would be impressed, too," Gary said tenderly. "She loves beautiful things. She'll love you," he promised. Now he hesitated. He seemed troubled. "Vicky, sometimes my father is brusque without meaning to be. It may take him a while to become accustomed to the fact that I have a wife—''

"He's angry that you married me!" All at once her heart was pounding. She'd feared Gary's family might resent his marrying her. Now she knew it was a reality.

"He was—well, surprised," Gary stammered. "And sometimes he can be—blunt. It's just his way. But everything's going to work out fine. You'll see." He reached for her hand and lifted it to his mouth. "I love you. That's all that matters."

Yet instinct warned Vicky that she and Gary must not remain beneath his father's roof a moment longer than was necessary. Her new father-in-law, she suspected, would go to any length to destroy her marriage.

Chapter Seven

TANTALIZING AROMAS drifted through the lower floor of Barton Manor. A turkey roasted in the oven. The scents of cinnamon and curry and peppermint emerged from simmering pots on the kitchen range. Since early morning Lula Mae—the Bartons' cook since Gary was a baby—had been preparing the homecoming dinner for him and his bride.

Sara Barton checked the pendant watch that hung on a gold chain about her slender throat. Zachary was waiting at the depot for Gary and Vicky with the family Cadillac. Theirs was the only automobile in a town of three thousand, though nearby Richmond had over two hundred privately owned autos.

Sara had persuaded herself to remain at the house to welcome them. Of her three children, Gary was the closest to her. It was so much easier to raise a son, she often thought in moments of despair over the flightiness of her daughters, who had been spoiled outrageously by their father.

Walking down the wide, curving staircase to the lower floor, one hand on the magnificent mahogany balustrade, Sara fought for poise. At forty-four, she was an elegant and beautiful woman with a gentility in stark contrast to her husband's coarse ways. She must make Daniel understand he was to behave himself, she told herself for the dozenth time. Gary was bringing his bride home. This was one of the most important occasions in a man's life.

"Sara!" Daniel's voice bellowed from the entrance to the library. He stood there with the customary cigarette in one hand and a glass of bourbon in the other. "When the hell do we eat?"

"When Gary and his wife arrive," she said coolly, walking toward him. "You won't die if dinner is half an hour late."

"Where are the girls?" His eyes swept—in what she recognized as approval—over her classically simple black velvet dress. He would have been surprised to know that she cared. "Damn it, they always dawdle."

"They're gossiping about some young man Lily just met," Sara said. She wished that Lily would marry one of the young men in pursuit. She'd been nervous about Lily's endless flirtations ever since the dean of Ward-Belmont had delicately suggested that her daughter might be happier away from the confines of their campus. She'd never been happy about Lily's vague but indignant report on the escapade that so outraged the dean. "He's a nephew of Tina Duke."

"Buck Duke's family?" Daniel asked with a glint of interest. Buck Duke was one of the few men in the tobacco industry he respected.

"Possibly." Inside the library her eyes settled on the ormolu clock atop the marble mantel. The train had probably arrived by now, she surmised. "But Lily doesn't seem capable of settling on any one prospective suitor."

"So, she's nineteen. Not exactly an old maid. And she's a catch," he pointed out in satisfaction. His face brightened at the sound of his daughters' voices. "Here come the fillies. You better talk to them," he said. "They're spending too damn much on clothes. The bills coming in every month from Thalhimer's and from Miller and Rhoads are outrageous. I don't grow money, you know."

"Papa, haven't they arrived yet?" Lily ran into the library and threw her arms around her father. She was small and very pretty in a voluptuous fashion that sometimes disturbed her mother. "I just can't bear to think of Gary married to some little nobody!"

"Lily, you are not to talk that way," Sara said in distaste. "I won't have it."

When she had married Lily's father, he'd been a nobody, though he'd already acquired a fine fortune. Everybody had thought she'd married Daniel because of the family's situation after the long war years. They were rich in social position and tradition but in dire financial straits. Daniel was poor in social background but rich in cash.

Nobody had realized she'd been obsessed by the dashing figure Daniel Barton had appeared to her all those years ago, before his sensuous good looks became dissipated by too much rich food, liquor, and hard living. She detested the perpetual stench of cigarette smoke that permeated his clothing. It was a source of satisfaction to her that she'd managed to outlaw smoking in both the dining room and her bedroom.

Though she and Daniel had not shared a bedroom for years—and she'd heard endlessly the rumors about the flashy young women in his life—she still never said no on those occasional nights when he decided to avail himself of his marital privileges. She hated herself for not tossing him out of her bedroom—but in those brief swatches of time he made her feel a passionate young girl again.

Gary led Vicky from the handsome Chesapeake & Ohio-Seaboard Air Line depot on Main Street in Richmond to the waiting Cadillac. Zachary welcomed them with endearing cordiality. Gary gave him instructions about the route they were to take to Bartonville.

"This is tobacco country," he reminded Vicky with wry humor. "Tourists always want to see the tobacco plantations. We'll pass two on the way home. Every new tobacco crop has to be planted in soil that hasn't been used for at least a generation. Then it's moved into sandy fields. I know this," he chuckled, "because Papa has drummed tobacco lore into my head since I was three. When I was six, he took me to see how farmers hang the tobacco on cross-sticks over large flues that are connected with hearths fed with huge logs. The tobacco is toasted at temperatures that go up to 240 degrees. Farmers sleep beside the fires to watch over the process."

"All that to make a cigarette?" Vicky marveled.

"Sugar, that isn't the half of it." Gary chuckled but his eyes were somber. "None of which interests me."

Vicky watched the passing scenery with curiosity as they approached Bartonville.

"It's not a pretty town," Gary warned. "I suppose utilitarian would be the word. But Barton Manor is beautiful," he said. "Of course, you'll have to overlook the muddy water of the James River. It's not like the Seine in Paris. Still, it's a lovely sight from the side gallery of the house."

Gary was right, Vicky thought as she gazed at Bartonville. The main street consisted of a few small, unappealing shops—a grocery, a hardware store, a dry-goods store, a tiny bakery. The bank, however, was unexpectedly pleasing to the eye.

Gary pointed out the huge, red-brick factory of the Barton Tobacco Company, then the large addition built during the war years to accommodate the surge of business.

"Workers were brought in by the hundreds from Richmond, but there was no place for them to live. Papa built those dormitories just ahead as living quarters." Gary pointed to a series of low buildings. They were freshly painted but devoid of charm. "The house is two miles on the other side of town."

Beyond the dormitory buildings sat rows of cracker-box houses, with only a few feet of open space between them. Occasionally a tiny front lawn offered a refreshing burst of spring flowers. After a stretch of open fields appeared a cluster of attractive, well-maintained homes. Vicky assumed these were occupied by Barton executives and their families.

Vicky fought against panic when Gary told her they would be at Barton Manor in minutes. She could not erase from her mind the knowledge that Gary's father was displeased that he had married her. Her heart was pounding wildly when Zachary turned off the main road and headed up a winding, tree-lined driveway.

Three hundred yards ahead Zachary pulled to a stop. Viktoria gazed in admiration at the imposing, white templelike structure that stood before Gary and herself.

"We're home, Vicky." Gary squeezed her hand reassuringly as they walked up the stairs to the gallery.

"It's beautiful." Her throat was tight with anxiety. *Would Gary's family learn to like her?*

"Gary, welcome home!" The smaller of the two girls at the massive, handsome front door rushed forward and into his arms. The taller girl—Viktoria instantly knew this was Stephanie—echoed Lily's words and waited to be kissed by her brother in turn.

"Lily, Stephanie, this is Viktoria," Gary said, all at once sounding self-conscious. "My wife."

"Welcome to Barton Manor," Lily said in the musical speech that was so like Gary's. Her smile was girlishly effusive, yet Viktoria sensed a cold resentment at her presence. "But we wished you'd been married here so we could have been your bridesmaids."

"Is that all the luggage you brought with you?" Stephanie stared in disapproval at the two suitcases Zachary was bringing from the car, and Viktoria remembered the masses of luggage when she traveled with Mama.

"We prefer to travel light," Gary laughed and dropped a protective arm about Viktoria. "Our ship wasn't the *Aquitania*."

"This is a lovely house." Viktoria forced herself to make conversation. "Just as Gary told me."

Inside the expansive foyer Gary's face lighted at the sight of his mother.

"Mama!" He rushed forward to embrace her, and then extended a hand to Viktoria. "Mama, this is Viktoria. I warned her that we'll all call her Vicky."

"Welcome to your new home, Vicky." Sara held her arms out to her daughter-in-law.

"Thank you," Viktoria said shyly. Beneath her mother-in-law's gesture of Southern courtesy, she sensed a certain reserve. Mrs. Barton was welcoming her for Gary's sake, she told herself. She must prove that she deserved this welcome.

"You must be starving after that long train trip," Sara said. In truth, Vicky had barely touched her lunch in the dining car. "Let's go into the dining room. I'll have Effie serve dinner immediately."

Viktoria tensed as a florid man with a commanding presence emerged from a side room and stalked toward them. His smile was gracious, even warm—but she saw a calculating glint in his eyes, which belied that smile.

"Gary, you're holding up dinner," he scolded. "And I'm a man who likes to eat on schedule." His gaze settled on Viktoria. "So this is the little lady who captured your heart. I understand you speak English, Vicky."

"Yes, I do," she said softly in the English learned from a British tutor.

"You talk different from us," Lily said. "Doesn't she, Papa?"

"Well, let's get to the table," he ordered, slapping Lily across the rump. "I'm mighty pleased to have you coming into the company, Gary. That's what a man lives for—to see his son training to take over for himself one day."

At Daniel's orders Gary sat on his father's right and Viktoria at his left. Immediately he launched into a monologue about the tobacco business.

"Bartonville—first and last—is a tobacco town," he boasted. "There's tobacco in the air. You smell it the minute you set foot in town. It's in the minds of everybody who lives here. Tobacco is part of American history. It helped the first Virginia colony survive back in the early 1600s. It financed the American Revolution—France loaned us money on the strength of our tobacco crop. And cigarette companies," he continued with relish, "can be proud that they're contributing, too. We perform a public service. We provide the country with a major source of pleasure."

At the other end of the table the two girls carried on a lively conversation about a recent hunt breakfast. Sara Barton seemed strangely removed from the table conversation, Viktoria observed.

"Gary, I tell you we're in the right business these days," Daniel said, smiling smugly. "R. J. Reynolds and Buck Duke had better watch out for Daniel Barton and son. The war did more for cigarette manufacturers than just create more consumers. It pushed us into using more domestic tobacco—instead of the old Turkish leaf. And more and more Americans have taken to smoking. Production has tripled since 1914. Gary old boy, we're going to be so rich by 1930 it'll make your head swim. Not that we're starving right now—" He turned to Viktoria with a grin, but his eyes were cold and appraising. "I expect you know you've married into a family with considerable assets."

"Gary has told me how much he will earn." She was polite, but her violet eyes darkened in defiance. Gary's father thought she was a fortune hunter! "I understand we will have to be very frugal. I learned about that in Paris."

"Gary never mentioned how he met you in Paris," Daniel began.

"In the midst of an air raid," Gary said, jumping into the conversation. "I was coming out of the Crillon. Vicky had just left the shop where she was a salesgirl. We both hurried into the Crillon shelter."

Vicky pretended to be involved in cutting a slice of turkey on her plate. Was Gary afraid to say she had been working as a chambermaid at the hotel? But of course, she understood. She was going to hate living under the same roof with Gary's father. She couldn't wait for the day they could move out of this house.

Viktoria was startled when she realized that Gary was to start on his new job the following morning. So soon she'd be on her own in this intimidating house!

"You'll be in the car with me at seven AM," Daniel told Gary when the family was settled in the library after dinner. "I believe in getting an early start. Be at the breakfast table by six-thirty sharp."

"Yes, sir," Gary said.

Before Gary and Viktoria settled down for the night, he wound up and set the alarm clock and placed it beside their bed.

"You sleep late, you hear?" he ordered tenderly. "Mama wants to take you into Richmond tomorrow to shop for some pretty dresses, but she won't be downstairs before ten o'clock."

"I'll get up with you," Viktoria said firmly. She was ambivalent about the shopping trip, though she understood Gary's mother meant to be kind. She also understood that it was a point of honor for Gary's family that she be properly dressed. Still, she felt uncomfortable—she didn't want to be their charity case. "We'll have breakfast together." She wished that she could prepare breakfast for the two of them in their own little cottage. While she had never entered the kitchen in their apartment in the Veronsky Palace, she had learned to cook under Simone's guidance.

"You'll like Richmond," Gary promised. "It's a beautiful city, built on more hills than Rome. As soon as I can, I'll take you on the grand tour."

"What will I do all day when you're away?" Viktoria asked.

"You'll relax and enjoy life," he said. "Mama will introduce you to people. You and Mama and the girls will do things together. And the evenings will be ours." His eyes were bright with promise.

In the morning—at six-thirty sharp—Gary and Viktoria were at the breakfast table. Viktoria managed a cordial smile as her father-in-law joined them at the table.

"Gary, didn't you tell her?" Daniel asked brusquely and turned to Viktoria. "The women in this household sleep late in the mornings. No need for you to be at the breakfast table."

"If Gary gets up early, then so will I." Viktoria's smile was sweet, but her eyes told him she would make her own decisions.

Daniel grunted, and inspected her with surprise.

"The girl's got spirit," he told Gary grudgingly, and yelled for Effie to serve breakfast.

Viktoria was amazed by the amount of food served so early in the morning. She was content with strong, chicory-laced coffee and golden brown biscuits fresh from the oven. Neither she nor Gary said much over breakfast. Daniel made occasional comments about competitors in the business—which Viktoria understood were meant to evoke Gary's interest in the Barton Tobacco Company. He was smug about the free advertising the government had provided during the war years by sending cigarettes to the fighting forces.

"Old man Reynolds figures he's going to tie up seventy-five percent of the cigarette business with the 'Camels' he brought out back in '13," Daniel grumbled. "Why in hell wasn't he satisfied with plug tobacco?"

"Because he discovered people preferred smoking to chewing tobacco," Gary pointed out. "Which you predicted twenty-five years ago."

"Now Reynolds is trying to change the whole sales approach," Daniel said. "No more pictures of actresses or soap or silk flags being given out as premiums. He puts it right on the damn packages— 'Don't look for premiums or coupons, as the cost of tobaccos blended in Camel Cigarettes prohibits the use of them.' "

"In Russia it was enough to say that the czar preferred one brand of cigarettes to send everyone who smoked to buy them," Viktoria recalled.

"A free testimonial," Daniel nodded in agreement. "Too bad the whole Russian royal family is in prison." He swigged down the remains of his coffee, pushed back his chair. "All right, Gary, let's get to the office."

The house was astonishingly quiet after the two men had left. Uncertain as to how to pass the time until she was to leave for Richmond with Gary's mother, Viktoria went into the library and settled down to read. Reading English required more effort than reading Russian— but now she was an American. She would speak and read only in English, she vowed. Her name now was Vicky—not the Russian Viktoria. She must be a proper American wife to Gary.

In the weeks ahead Vicky strived to fit into Gary's family. She continued to come downstairs to breakfast every working morning at six-thirty, along with Gary. When the two men left for the office, she settled herself in the library to read.

Sara took her to local social activities. It was clear that Sara Barton was the town's *grande dame*. She headed local charity committees, and was president of the Bartonville chapter of the UDC, the United Daughters of the Confederacy. Lily and Stephanie were proud that the town bore their family name—but their contempt for the small town seeped through.

Every Sunday morning Daniel, Sara, and the girls went to church. Vicky gathered that once he had gone off to college, Gary had abandoned this family tradition. Daniel was candid in admitting that his own attendance had nothing to do with his religious convictions.

"Hell, I built that church! I want the congregation to remember that," he said. "And when election time rolls around, I expect them to listen when I talk about the men I want in the Legislature and in Congress."

Vicky—as she insisted on thinking of herself now—was conscious that on the occasions when Sara and her daughters attended afternoon parties in Richmond, she remained in Bartonville. It seemed that Gary's wife didn't measure up to the requirements of Richmond society. Sara Barton had been a Warren—an old and highly respected Richmond family.

On a hot June evening when she and Gary were to dine alone at Barton Manor, Vicky decided on impulse to ask Effie to serve dinner on the side gallery, where they would have a bit of a breeze from the river to alleviate the heat.

"I'd like that," Gary agreed.

"And after dinner, you'll play for me," Vicky said. It upset her that Gary never touched the fine grand piano in the music room unless his father was away from the house. She cherished those rare occasions when she and Sara Barton sat in the music room to hear Gary play. Lily and Stephanie never remained long. Lily sulked because Gary played the classics rather than the popular ragtime she adored.

"Finish washing up—I'll run downstairs and tell Effie."

Hurrying down the stairs, Vicky heard Daniel and Sara arguing behind the closed library door. Not until she was striding down the hall did the voices behind the library door become audible to her.

"Daniel, this is ridiculous," Sara declared. "We have to give a party to introduce Vicky to Richmond society. We can't hide her forever.''

"Give her another few months," Daniel said. "She'll be sick of this house. Sick of this town. She'll pack up and run back to Paris. Stop coddling her. Let her understand she doesn't belong in this family!"

"She's his wife," Sara said. "Accept that."

"I won't accept it!" he bellowed. "Damn it, Sara, you're not helping at all. Don't you understand? I want her out of Gary's life."

Chapter Eight

OVER AND OVER Vicky told herself she didn't have to care how Daniel Barton felt about her. She was Gary's wife, and he loved her. Her father-in-law would not come between them.

Gary was unaware of how isolated Vicky felt in Bartonville. He was putting in long hours six days a week at the company, waiting impatiently to be promoted. He was relieved to relax at home in the evenings and on Sundays.

When Daniel decided that Gary should accompany him to some of the tobacco auctions, he extended an invitation to Vicky to join them on one such jaunt.

"It may not sound like much to you," Daniel said, "but it's an exciting event to folks in the industry. Bring her along to tomorrow's auction, Gary," he ordered.

Vicky sensed that her father-in-law was surprised that she was eager to go with them. At a tobacco auction he felt himself to be the ruling monarch. He wanted her to understand just how important he was.

As they drove to the warehouse where the auction was being held, Daniel explained to Vicky that he had a team of buyers that traveled about the tobacco-growing states.

"When it comes to the local auctions, I like to be there myself. In time, Gary, you'll represent me," he said. "You'll learn to buy heavy when prices are low, so you don't need to bid when prices go up."

Vicky's eyes widened as they walked into the cavernous warehouse where the auction was being held. Immediately she sensed the drama and excitement of the event.

The auctioneer walked down endless aisles of tobacco baskets, with prospective buyers at his heels. Vicky quickly learned that sometimes the buyers bid vocally, and other times just by a simple gesture. Everything happened so fast, she thought, listening to the auctioneer's steady singsong voice, his words intelligible only to those in the know.

Vicky watched—intrigued—as Daniel took a leaf in his hand, gazed with candid wariness. Then all at once he seemed another man. A warm glow came over his face. He liked the leaf he held between his fingers—he seemed to regard it with almost paternal affection. He lifted it to his nose, sniffed, and smiled. She'd never seen such tenderness in her father-in-law.

Gary was bored by the excursion, Vicky realized. She felt guilty that she found it fascinating.

Early in September, Vicky suspected she was pregnant. All at once her world seemed beautiful. There was a new purpose to living. But she mustn't tell Gary, she cautioned herself, until she was certain.

When she told Gary that she was definitely pregnant, he was ecstatic. Daniel was in New York on business with the company's advertising agency when Gary told his mother about the expected baby. Vicky was touched by her mother-in-law's eagerness to welcome her first grandchild. Vicky doubted that her father-in-law would be pleased.

Daniel *was* pleased, Vicky gathered, by the results of his business meetings in New York. He glowed with triumph when he returned. From Gary she learned that he had signed up some important titled personage to endorse Barton cigarettes.

"Papa's so proud of pulling this off that he's invited the man to spend a weekend here at the house at the end of the month. He'll have dinner with the family on Friday evening. On Saturday evening there'll be a formal dinner at the Country Club in Richmond. We'll be there, of course."

Now that she was pregnant, Vicky understood, Daniel Barton was forced to accept her as his daughter-in-law. In a corner of her mind lingered a suspicion that her remark to him some weeks ago—about how most Russian smokers changed to the czar's brand—had triggered his acquiring some important titled European to endorse Barton cigarettes.

She was startled when at dinner, a few nights before their house-guest arrived, Daniel suggested that—considering her condition—she might prefer not to attend either the dinner at Barton Manor or the lavish affair in Richmond.

"Daniel, that's absurd," Sara rejected before Vicky herself could brush this aside. "Only the family knows. She doesn't show yet. Of course, Vicky will attend," she said. "It'll be the perfect opportunity to introduce her to Richmond society."

Almost daily, it seemed to Vicky, Lily and Stephanie were being driven into Richmond to shop for dinner gowns for the festive week-end, plus an assortment of clothes for the other hours they'd be entertaining Daniel's trophy, his titled European who was to endorse Barton cigarettes. Sara went alone with Vicky to choose gowns for the two of them.

"The girls drive me into a frenzy," she admitted. "We'll shop in peace and quiet, then rest ourselves in Miller and Rhoads' tea room." Vicky knew that the tea room—the first in the state—was famous throughout Virginia.

On the humid day of their guest's arrival, Sara decreed that the women of the household would nap all afternoon so as to be fresh when they sat down to dinner in the formal dining salon. Ever sleepy in early pregnancy, Vicky was relieved by this decision.

She was still half-asleep when Gary arrived home—two hours earlier than normal—in order to have time to bathe and dress in leisure. He leaned over to kiss her, and she awoke instantly.

"It's going to be a hot night," he said, "even with every fan in the house turned on."

"There'll be a breeze from the river," Vicky promised. "I put in a special request."

"You're sure you're up to this dinner?" Gary sat at the edge of the bed.

"Of course. I'm up to anything," she whispered, reading the glow in his eyes. She always knew when he wanted to make love.

"In broad daylight?" he teased.

"Close the drapes," she told him. "We'll pretend it's night." She could endure his father's coarse attempts to drive her from the house, she told herself. Nobody would come between Gary and her.

"Papa said he'll talk about a promotion soon," he told Vicky as he rushed to undress by the side of their bed.

"Oh, Gary, how wonderful!" She held out her arms to him as he lowered himself beside her. Maybe then they could afford a little house of their own. "You deserve it."

They abandoned conversation for the moment, caught up in the wonder of their passion, both loathe to relinquish these moments but aware that they must dress and be downstairs to welcome Daniel's guest.

"How the hell do you address titled men?" Gary asked in amusement when he stood before her in his dinner clothes.

"Gary, I've never seen you dressed like that," she murmured in pride. "You'll be the best-looking man at the dinner tomorrow night."

"You didn't tell me," he scolded with mock reproach. "How do you address a Russian count?"

"He's Russian?" All at once a coldness engulfed Vicky, despite the humid heat of the encroaching night. This night would bring back painful memories.

"Papa won't admit it," Gary said humorously, "but he's glad you'll be at dinner tonight. I gather the advertising agency told him the count's English is on the shaky side. You may be called upon to act as interpreter."

"I'd better dress," she decided in sudden guilt. "We should be downstairs early in case I'm needed."

Dressed, Vicky anxiously surveyed her reflection in the bedroom mirror. The daffodil yellow georgette dinner dress—with the Paris-decreed cowl neckline—clung to her slender figure without a hint of her pregnancy. While Lily and Stephanie both sported new bobs, she had not cut her lush, dark hair. Gary liked it long.

As they were about to leave their room, Vicky made a last-moment decision. Tonight she would wear the one piece of her mother's jewelry that Simone had refused to sell—the tiny ruby-encrusted locket on a gold chain.

"Gary, I know I have it—" She searched frenziedly through the drawer where she remembered placing her mother's favorite piece of jewelry, the one that had originally belonged to her great-grandmother. "It couldn't have disappeared!" It was her one link to her family, to life in czarist Russia.

"Sugar, slow down," he said. "You're all excited and not looking carefully—" He reached into the drawer, rummaged about, came up with a small tissue-wrapped parcel. "Is this it?"

"Oh, Gary, yes—" All at once tears filled her eyes. Inside the locket was a photograph of her father and one of herself as a baby.

"Let me put it on for you," Gary said gently.

Now, hand in hand, they left their room and headed downstairs. The sound of convivial voices told them their houseguest had arrived. Lily and Stephanie's excited, girlish giggles punctuated their father's booming voice as he talked about Virginia's proud history.

"No state has given the country more presidents than Virginia," he boasted, as though he were personally responsible for this, Vicky thought in amusement. Dressed in his dinner clothes, Daniel stood in the foyer beneath the glittering Waterford chandelier. His back was to the staircase, with an arm around the shoulders of the man Vicky presumed was his guest. Lily and Stephanie—both garbed in bright green chiffon dinner gowns, with the new draped skirt slit at the side displaying a daring length of leg—gazed up at their father's guest with fatuous smiles. Sara—smartly dressed in gray silk—stood at one side, as though a mildly interested observer.

"Ah, here is my son Gary." Daniel swung about as Gary and Vicky approached, and his guest, too, turned to face the new arrivals. "And Gary's wife," Daniel added belatedly. "I have the pleasure of introducing Count Veronsky," he began with a flourish. "He—"

"That is not Count Veronsky," Vicky broke in indignantly. She stared at the man who faced them now, while Daniel gaped in shock at her audacity. "Mikhail!" she said in sudden recognition. "How dare you call yourself Count Veronsky!"

"There's some mistake—" Daniel turned apologetically to his guest. His face flushed in rage. "Please forgive my—"

"There's no mistake," Vicky insisted. "This is Mikhail, a servant in the Veronsky Palace. I grew up there. I played and studied with the count's daughters!"

"You're the Jew-doctor's daughter," Mikhail shot back in contempt—and froze defensively at having betrayed himself.

"You lied to the advertising agency!" Daniel accused.

"No. I'm Count Veronsky," Mikhail sputtered. "I have papers to prove this."

"Count Veronsky is in a St. Petersburg prison." Vicky struggled to control her anger. "You're Mikhail, who learned to speak a little English when you went with the count on several trips to London."

She launched into a vituperative attack in rapid Russian while Mikhail turned pale in alarm.

"Get out of this house," Daniel ordered. "You have no deal with Barton cigarettes! Zachary!" he yelled. His voice echoed down the long hall to the kitchen, where Zachary was standing by to help with the serving. "Zachary," he said through clenched teeth when the chauffeur-houseman appeared at the far end of the hall. "Drive this imposter to the depot. He's not welcome in my house."

Daniel ordered the family into the library. A grimness about his face told Vicky that Mikhail's epithet—"the Jew-doctor's daughter"—was about to be discussed. In rare silence, the two girls led the way, their mother at their heels. Sara, too, seemed to feel that silence was wise at this moment. Gary prodded Vicky forward, an arm protectively about her waist.

"What is that bilge that bastard threw at me?" Daniel demanded of Vicky when he'd closed the library door behind them. "About your father being 'that Jew-doctor'?"

"My father was the personal physician to Count Veronsky and his family," Vicky explained proudly, struggling to conceal her rage at this interrogation. Daniel had not offered a word of thanks for saving him from making a fool of himself with Mikhail. "And yes, he was Jewish. As was my mother."

"Gary, you never told us that," Daniel said.

"We're hardly a religious family," Gary pointed out. "To me it didn't matter whether Vicky worshipped at a church, synagogue, or mosque."

"You know what it would do to my position in this town if folks here learned your wife is Jewish," Daniel said and turned to Vicky. "You are never to reveal this to anyone. We'll never speak of it again."

"Gary told me that here in America there was freedom," Vicky said, color flooding her high cheekbones. Papa had told her it was wise never to reveal to strangers that she was Jewish—but that was in Europe. *Here in the United States it was supposed to be different.*

"Bullshit," Daniel said. "There're only three Jewish families in Bartonville. There're more in Richmond," he conceded, "and they're accepted in some circles. But here in Bartonville they're not looked upon with favor. I need local support for my candidates for the General Assembly. You'll say nothing about your Jewish parents.''

"Papa," Gary began, but Daniel plunged ahead, ignoring him.

"We've got to figure out how to handle this awkward situation. We have a big dinner party scheduled tomorrow. I'll have to swallow my pride and admit my fancy New York advertising agency—my *former* advertising agency—has led me astray. But the party is not for naught," he plotted. "We're inviting all these lovely people to meet Gary's bride. Gary, you and Vicky will be the guests of honor. You might drop a hint that she's related to the Russian royal family."

"But I'm not," Vicky said.

"Who will know?" Daniel shrugged. "It'll be a dramatic story to spread around—about how you unmasked this charlatan. But you say nothing about being Jewish," he emphasized again. "Not with the way the Ku Klux Klan is growing in the South."

Rebellion simmered in Vicky, but for Gary's sake she was quiet. Gary had told her about the Ku Klux Klan, which had been reborn barely four years ago on a mountaintop near Atlanta, Georgia. It had frightened her to learn that even in the great United States there were those who carried out acts of violence against innocent people. It was akin to the pogroms in Russia.

Vicky was amazed by her father-in-law's commanding presence at the country club dinner. It was clear that respect for him was high— and that he relished this respect. She was startled that he made a point of appearing to be proud of the latest addition to the family—which clearly irritated Lily. Vicky was conscious of her sisters-in-law's hostility beneath a girlish show of affection.

"Vicky just made it out of Russia in time," he told a clique gathered about him while he encircled her waist with one arm. "She fled with her maid through Finland and Sweden, across to England, and then to Paris—where Gary met her."

This was Vicky's first encounter with Virginia society. She marveled at the gaiety, the soft gentility of the women, the gallantry of the men. At Barton Manor she'd grown accustomed to the musical Southern accents around her, but here was a swelling symphony of liquid voices speaking in the caressing manner of those below the Mason-Dixon line.

She was relieved when at last the evening was over. She slept most of the way home, her head resting on Gary's shoulder. Slowly awakening, she heard her father-in-law talking with obvious smugness.

"We handled that just fine," Daniel said. "Gary, you make sure she keeps her mouth shut about her Jewish parents. Right now some of our guests are convinced she's the illegitimate daughter of the czar."

Vicky waited for some word from Daniel about Gary's promised promotion. The baby was due to arrive in April. She longed to be in their own home by the time the baby arrived. Here at Barton Manor she always felt herself an interloper.

At breakfast each morning her father-in-law behaved as though she weren't present. He talked with Gary about the fears of many Americans that the country was about to be taken over by the Communists. Scare headlines appeared regularly in the newspapers. The efforts of some radicals had created near panic the past April when bombs were mailed to thirty-six prominent citizens, including Justice Holmes, John D. Rockefeller, and the attorney general. In June, anarchists set off several direct bombs, one in front of the home of Attorney General Palmer. Now there was talk about passing a sedition bill—though it appeared doubtful that Congress would go along with this. But Attorney General Palmer warned the country about Red plots and vowed to stop them.

Sometimes the two men discussed current business problems, which Vicky struggled to understand. Daniel was angry at the growing need to spend huge amounts on advertising in order to keep up with the four major companies. He was particularly intimidated by the Reynolds Tobacco campaign for their highly successful Camels. Though R. J. had recently died, his brother—W. N., who was now president of the company—carried on in R. J.'s tradition. Daniel resented not being at Reynolds's level, despite the Barton Tobacco Company's impressive volume.

"But by God, I plan to keep my company private," he insisted. "I won't allow us to be intimidated or manipulated by those Wall Street operators. *I* control my company."

When the men left the house each morning, Vicky settled herself in the library. She read voraciously, striving to learn all she could about the history of the Confederacy. She was startled to discover that many of the leather-bound history books had never been opened. She remembered her father's rare caustic remark about the books in the Veronsky library at the Palace: "The count buys culture by the yard."

Often Lily and Stephanie went to Richmond in the afternoons for social occasions. Lily was intermittently outraged by her father's refusal to allow her to drive. "It was all right for women to drive ambulances during the war. But now we're not supposed to drive—it's unwomanly!"

In the early weeks of Vicky's pregnancy Sara made a point of taking Vicky with her to various local meetings involving philanthropic efforts, though now it was assumed that—since she was showing—she would go into semiseclusion.

She struggled to be the proper young Virginia matron-in-waiting. She knitted baby clothes, spent hours with Sara over plans for the nursery—though she secretly told Gary that the baby would sleep in a cradle in their room at night. And always she waited for some sign that they could look for a small house for themselves. Gary's father kept promising a promotion.

She was ever conscious that Gary loathed this first job with the company. He resented his father's insistence that—after four years of college—he begin as a menial laborer. "I spend ten hours a day sitting there like a mindless idiot, just making sure cigarettes are chopped at regular intervals."

She remembered his dreams of settling into a Greenwich Village apartment and devoting himself to his music. He could have done that, perhaps, if he hadn't married her, she tormented herself. But neither of them could imagine life without the other.

It was not until early in the new year that Gary came home to report that what his father called his apprenticeship was finally over.

"Oh, Gary, how wonderful!"

"This is just an interim job," he pointed out, and she realized he was angry about this new assignment. "But it's something I have to do for a while."

"What kind of a job?" she asked fearfully.

"I'll be spending most of my time on the road. Selling." His revulsion—his resentment—lent him an air of exhaustion. *How could Gary's father do this to him*? "I shouldn't be away from home so much at a time like this!"

"We'll manage." She forced a smile, masking her own anxiety. *Would Gary be here when the baby came*? "It's a promotion," she reminded him and fresh hope surged in her. "Does this mean we can have a house of our own soon?"

"Not yet," he said, his eyes betraying his disappointment. "My salary will be only a little higher. But Papa's giving me shares in the company as a bonus." Bitterness crept into his voice. "Each year I'm to receive more shares. He says that by the time he retires, I'll own controlling shares. Damn it, Vicky! I don't want to control the company. *I just want to write music!*"

Chapter Nine

VICKY LAY sleepless, disturbed by Gary's unhappiness over his new assignment. They would get out of the trap, she vowed. By the time the baby was a few months old, they must make a move. They didn't have to live in a big house with servants and a car. After growing up in the Veronsky Palace, she'd survived working as a maid at the Crillon.

Gary was more concerned with writing music than living his father's life. It would be enough for the three of them—Gary, the baby, and herself—to be together. They didn't need to be rich to be happy.

By the time the baby was six months old, she resolved, the three of them would move to New York. Gary would have that Greenwich Village apartment he used to talk about. It was a vague image in her mind, but she understood that apartment represented freedom to Gary. She would work, too. She could do translations or tutor in Russian and French at home. And one day Gary's talents would be recognized—and they'd live well again. But most of all, she thought tenderly, they'd be together and happy.

Two evenings later—before Gary had time to tell Vicky himself—Daniel announced over dinner that Gary was to leave on his first trip as a company agent the following morning. Vicky turned to Gary in dismay. She hadn't expected this to happen so quickly.

"These are modern times," Daniel said. "In the old days—when Washington Duke was starting out—tobacco-selling trips meant peddling in a Nissen wagon. After the War Between the States men were doing that all through the South. Sleeping in those wagons at night because it was cheaper than putting up at a hotel. Duke and his three sons—Brodie, Ben, and Buck—started out that way. And you know how well Buck has done. But Gary here will travel in a fine train, eating the best meals in the dining car, sleeping in good hotels at night. Once you've got the selling routine under your belt,'' he said, turning to Gary, "you'll put in some time in the New York office.''

And that, Vicky told herself in silent triumph, was when they'd look around to set themselves up in New York. Once the baby was born, she'd talk to Gary about what they must do.

"Papa, you didn't peddle," Lily said. "I hope you don't go around telling folks that.''

"I peddled," Daniel shot back. "My old man sent me out with a wagon because that was the cheapest way to get the business moving. When things got better, I traveled by train. We always remembered to cut expenses to the bone. We got rid of the commission merchants. Not until your grandpa died did the company get into advertising. Papa couldn't understand that to sell cigarettes you had to make folks know you were in business. Papa groaned every time I added a new premium—but that was the way to sell." His face was all at once grim. "Then that damned Reynolds came out about six years ago with his bloody Camels. It was bad enough, the way Buck Duke spent money on advertising like he picked twenty dollar bills off tobacco plants every day. Then Reynolds started with his advertising. Premiums went out the window. You can't pick up a bloody magazine or newspaper without seeing some ad for Camels.''

"It must work," Vicky said, involuntarily drawn into the conversation. "You said the other night that Camels are the best-selling cigarettes in the country." Business talk always monopolized mealtime conversations. Though the other three women in the household paid little attention, Vicky listened because this was Gary's world. "You said Camels sell everywhere.''

"I said that in the house," Daniel shot back belligerently. "We don't say that outside.''

"No, sir," Vicky agreed.

"Reynolds just keeps on hammering at Camels," Daniel said. "It's like he's forgotten he makes half a dozen other brands." It was common practice, Vicky had absorbed from table talk, for companies to feature several brands under their banner.

"Isn't that why he sells so many Camels?" Vicky pursued. "Because he focuses on just one brand. I mean—" She was groping for words. "Isn't it natural that people will buy the one they hear talked about most often?"

"You're saying," Daniel said, "that it's smart to put all my eggs in one basket."

"Papa, you're doing fine with the company," Gary said nervously, giving Vicky a warning glance.

"Sure, I've got a solid chunk of the market in the South and in the Northeast. Our profits are fine. But we're doing rotten in the mid-Atlantic states and the West, where we're pushing other brands. Damn it, that little girl just said a mouthful. Without even realizing what she said!" he chortled. "I'm reorganizing. Starting as soon as our inventory allows, Barton Tobacco Company is manufacturing one cigarette—the Barton."

Vicky refrained from uttering the retort that flashed into her mind. She *understood* what she had said—she wasn't some mindless, babbling idiot like Lily. Her parents had taught her to think and to reason.

"Papa, you aren't going to listen to what *she* said?" Lily screeched in outrage. "She's just some silly girl Gary found in Paris."

Gary's sisters couldn't be as stupid as they pretended to be, Vicky thought while Lily and her father exchanged their usual round of noisy debate until Daniel cajoled his favorite child into reluctant calm. Lily and Stephanie seemed to have some strange idea that women were supposed to be pretty and helpless and without a real thought in their heads. Even Gary's mother played this game of always deferring to the men in the family. Not Vicky Barton, she vowed.

Vicky insisted on driving with Gary to the depot in Richmond on the cold, brisk morning of his departure. Being pregnant didn't mean she had to go into solitary confinement, she told herself in defiance.

"I'll only be gone eight days," Gary comforted her as the car approached the depot. Still, Vicky knew he dreaded this separation as much as she did.

"You'll phone me?"

"Every night," he said and chuckled. "I'll call collect. Mama pays the household bills. She won't mind."

"I'll miss you so much," she whispered.

"I'll miss you." He reached to kiss her goodbye in the privacy of the car. "Don't come out in the cold," he ordered.

"I'm getting out with you and waiting until the train pulls out," she said firmly. "I'm not a delicate little flower that'll wither at the first breeze."

"You're bored with being holed up in the house," he said. These days she was never included in outside socializing. "Zachary—" He leaned forward in sudden decision. "I want you to give Miss Vicky a guided tour of Richmond. Drive slowly so she can see everything." He turned to Vicky again. "Stop off at Thalhimer's or Miller & Rhoads and buy yourself something pretty. Just tell them to charge it to Mrs. Daniel Barton. Mama arranged for you to buy on her account, remember?"

"All right," Vicky agreed, happy to escape from the house. Gary's mother had told her that if she wished to charge, the two major department stores in Richmond had been told to accept this. "But I'm going out with you to wait for the train," she added as Zachary opened the rear door.

"Stubborn little one, aren't you?" Gary joshed. "Even Papa recognizes that."

They stood arm in arm by the railroad tracks until the train pulled into the depot. Gary kissed her goodbye again, with an ardor that brought a cluck of disapproval from a woman waiting to board the train.

"You take care of the two of you," Gary murmured and started up the steps to the train.

Vicky watched until the train was a blur in the distance. It was going to be so strange to lie alone in their bed tonight. She returned to the car, where Zachary stood waiting beside the door. The sun was suddenly in retreat. Clouds hovered over the city.

"All right, Zachary," she ordered, fighting against the depression that threatened to overwhelm her. Her smile seemed almost genuine. "Show me Richmond." She would enjoy today, she promised herself. Tonight Gary would phone her—and she'd tell him about her day.

All at once this was an unexpected adventure—to be on her own in Richmond. Vicky had been in Richmond only three times—the evening of the country club dinner and twice when she'd gone shopping with her mother-in-law.

"Zachary," she said on impulse, "first take me to Thalhimer's, please."

"Yes, ma'am," Zachary said. Vicky remembered that Gary said Zachary loved being behind the wheel of the car. No car in Bartonville or Richmond received more loving care.

She'd buy something for the baby, Vicky decided, perhaps a blanket for the cradle. Gary's mother was knitting an afghan, but winters in Virginia were cold. A blanket would come in handy. She had chosen Thalhimer's—opened in 1842 by William Thalhimer, a former history professor at the University of Heidelberg—because it was owned and operated by his highly respected descendants. A *Jewish* family. She'd overheard one of the servants mention this.

She spent a euphoric forty minutes shopping at Thalhimer's. Remembering the status of Jews in czarist Russia. Only because of Count Veronsky's patronage were the Gunsburgs able to live outside the Pale, the huge ghetto where Russian Jews were forced to live. Here in Virginia she shopped in freedom, lived in a mansion.

What was happening to the Jews in Russia now, she wondered. From newspapers and magazines that came into the Barton house she knew that Western Russia had become a bloody battlefield in the course of the civil wars that plagued the country for the past two years. Now Russia was fighting a Polish invasion. *What was happening to Count Veronsky—and to Tatiana and Catherine and their mother?*

Each time she wrote Simone, she asked if there had been any word of the Veronskys. Nothing, Simone said, and coaxed her to concentrate on her new life in America. Vicky's face softened as she remembered Simone's joy that she and Gary were having their first child. Simone, too, was crocheting for the baby.

Vicky left the store and returned to the waiting Cadillac. Zachary rushed to relieve her of her small package and to open the door.

"Now show me the rest of Richmond," she commanded gaily.

Zachary drove along Broad Street, Richmond's shopping area. There were far more cars here than in Bartonville, Vicky noted— though even in Richmond most folks came downtown on the street cars.

"That is T. A. Miller's drugstore," Zachary said, pointing out the car window. "I hear they make fine claret lemonade. And the best banana splits. Miss Lily and Miss Stephanie—they go there all the time."

Further along Broad—at Seventh Street—he pointed out Hellstern's.

"That's where folks go to buy ice cream by the pint or quart or gallon. It's something special."

Zachary drove down the residential avenues of Grace and Franklin en route to Main Street. He pointed out the houses of prominent Richmonders. Main Street, he told her when they arrived there, was the financial district.

He quickly deserted this area to show Vicky the social side of Richmond—the Lyric, which offered vaudeville, the Academy, where Broadway road companies appeared, the Richmond Municipal Auditorium where world-famous artists such as Paderewski, Geraldine Farrar, and Galli-Curci had performed, and the stock companies at the Bijou and the Empire.

Now Zachary weaved in and out of Richmond's streets, pointing out the endless memorials. Gary said that Richmond—the capital of the Confederacy—had more monuments than any city in the South. Zachary slowed down before a modest but lovely building that Vicky instinctively knew was a place of worship.

"That's the Eleventh Street synagogue," Zachary told her. "It's a real nice building."

"Yes, it is." Vicky was startled that he had come almost to a full stop. But, of course, he knew she was Jewish. He'd been in the house the night Mikhail had arrived. He'd heard Mikhail shriek at her, "You're the Jew-doctor's daughter." Gary said the servants in the house knew everything.

Zachary drove on, enjoying his role as tour guide. Soon he slowed down once more.

"That's the Hebrew Cemetery," he told Vicky. "It's got a special place for Confederate veterans."

"Zachary, stop here please," she said. Her mother-in-law talked with such pride about the Confederacy and about the UDC. Jewish soldiers, too, had fought in the War Between the States. "I'd like to see it up close."

"Yes, ma'am," Zachary said and rushed out of the car to open the door for her. She was already on the sidewalk and approaching the cemetery entrance.

Vicky paused at some of the tombstones to read their inscriptions. She was awed by the dates on the older ones. Then she realized she was approaching the plot reserved for Jewish Confederate soldiers. The plot was enclosed by a metal fence, its posts made up of furled flags and stacked muskets with what Vicky supposed were Confederate caps on top. The railings were crossed sabers.

She spied a slender, elderly man rising from his haunches before a tombstone. His beard was neatly trimmed, his carriage erect despite his age. He wore what Vicky recognized, from the family photographs at the Barton house, to be an old Confederate army jacket. As though feeling the weight of her gaze, he looked up with a smile and doffed his hat.

"Good morning, ma'am," he said graciously. "Are you looking for a special grave?"

"No," she said softly. "I just wanted to see the cemetery."

"My brother is buried here." He pointed to the tombstone before him, which indicated that here lay Lieutenant Josiah Ginsberg. "He died from wounds he received in the war. I survived." He seemed apologetic.

"Did many Jews serve in the Confederate army?" All at once she felt compelled to talk with this Jewish war veteran.

"Yes, ma'am," he said proudly. "Over a hundred from Richmond alone. I come here on every holiday—today is Josiah's birthday—in my army jacket because that was one of his last requests. He wanted to know that the Confederacy was remembered."

She gazed again at the tombstone while questions charged across her brain.

"My name before I married was Gunsburg," she said compulsively. "I was born and raised in St. Petersburg, Russia."

"I'm Samuel Ginsberg," he introduced himself. "My parents came here as children from a village near Moscow. Perhaps—many generations ago—we shared relatives."

Vicky remembered how many young Jewish boys—some no more than children—had been pulled from their homes to serve in the czarist army—and were treated with total lack of respect for their feelings and needs because they were Jews.

"Mr. Ginsberg . . ." She faltered, but forced herself to continue. "Were you angry at having to fight in the war?"

"I was proud to serve my country—as my brother was." He bristled for an instant, then she saw a gleam of comprehension in his eyes. "Josiah and I *enlisted*," he explained gently. "We were fighting for our country. And every year I march in the parade that's part of the Confederate reunion.''

"Then it isn't a bad thing in Richmond to be a Jew?'' Vicky asked earnestly. Gary's father had warned her that her Jewishness must be kept a family secret. Papa had told her that it was dangerous in today's world to be a Jew. But what Mr. Ginsberg said denied this. "The Jews in Richmond are not . . . not treated differently from others?''

"During the war years there were problems,'' Mr. Ginsberg acknowledged. "Even here in Richmond. Always in times of trouble the Jew is the scapegoat. Even when we were out there fighting for our country. Right here in Richmond, Jewish stores were looted, and a rock was thrown through the window of a synagogue. Let me tell you, ma'am. Jews have been in Virginia since the 1650s. In 1790— when the population of Richmond was only 3700—there were already one hundred Jews living here. The year before—in 1789—Beth Shalom synagogue was founded and two years later it dedicated the first Jewish cemetery in Virginia. And even in the midst of the War Between the States my mother and my young wife—may they rest in peace—never forgot for one day that they were Jews. With the sound of battle in the distance they attended evening services at Beth Shalom.''

"And today?'' she asked.

He paused and sighed. "There is a social line,'' he conceded. "Forty years ago a Jewish gentleman was president of the Westmoreland Club. Today a Jew could not head a fine Richmond club. Oh, we meet on the street and in the stores, and we're treated with fine Virginia courtesy. But not many of us see the inside of the homes of socially prominent Christians. But that isn't only in Richmond,'' he continued. "This occurs throughout the country. And now we have the cursed Ku Klux Klan,'' he said venomously, "who spread their filth with increasing strength. Not only against us, but against Catholics and coloreds.''

"Thank you for talking with me,'' Vicky said, extending her hand. "It was important for me to understand.''

"My pleasure, ma'am.'' He held her hand in his for a moment. He didn't ask her married name, for which Vicky was grateful. "Welcome to Richmond. It's a fine city. Richmond Jews are joiners,'' he continued with relish. "We have a lively social life.''

"I don't live in Richmond," Vicky said hurriedly, "but thank you."

Back in the car, Vicky instructed Zachary to take her home. The encounter with Mr. Ginsberg had been welcome but disturbing. Gary's father had been correct. Even in the United States, being Jewish caused problems.

Chapter Ten

VICKY DREADED Gary's absences. He was away more than
he was home. Despite her advancing pregnancy, she accompanied him
to the depot on each departure. When he was due to return, she sat
in the large, domed-ceilinged, marble-columned waiting room fully
twenty minutes before his train was due—in the event the train should
arrive early.

She knew Gary was distressed at the possibility of his being away
from Bartonville when she went into labor. She was relieved when he
told her late in March that he'd spoken with his father about his fears
and insisted on remaining in the Bartonville office until after the baby
was born.

On the same night that Gary came home from the office to tell her
this, the family learned that Lily had accepted the proposal of Clark
Thompson, a young Richmond lawyer. Ever seeking to be the center
of attention, Lily chose dinner time to make this announcement.

"What do you mean, you're engaged?" Daniel demanded. "You're
engaged after I've spoken to the young man and approve of him!"
He stared belligerently at his favorite child.

"Papa, he'll come and ask for my hand," Lily promised with mock
demureness. "But I'm marrying him. He comes from an important
Richmond family."

"Meaning landed gentry," Daniel derided. "They own one half a
county but have no money to keep it up."

"Clark will call on you on Sunday afternoon," Lily told her father. "I want to be married in June. Stephanie will be my maid of honor. I'll have six bridesmaids, all Richmond girls. I—"

"Spare me the details," Daniel interrupted. He was annoyed that Lily would be getting married, Vicky guessed. To him she was still his little girl.

"That leaves me less than three months to arrange a wedding," Sara said. "And what about an engagement party and the showers?"

"I leave that all up to you, Mama," Lily said sweetly. "But we must go up to New York for my wedding gown. It has to be prettier than the one Loretta Rankin had made up there. And Clark says we'll live in Richmond."

The house echoed with plans for Lily's engagement party, a series of bridal showers, and the wedding itself. Lily made a point of reminding Vicky that it would be improper for her—in view of her condition—to attend the engagement party.

"My goodness, Vicky, you might have the baby that very evening. I never saw anybody popping out the way you are."

Barton Manor's ballroom was being prepared for the hastily arranged engagement party. The wainscotting, the furniture, and the Waterford chandelier had to be polished for the occasion.

Vicky was engrossed in preparations for the baby's arrival. When she had explained to her mother-in-law that she meant to have the baby sleep in a cradle in its parents' bedroom rather than in the nursery in the next room, Sara had ordered workmen to cut a door through.

"I know how you feel," Sara had confessed. "I felt the same way when Gary was born, though Daniel thought I was mad. You'll feel more comfortable with a connecting door to the nursery."

Vicky understood that her young maid, Mattie Lou, would take on the care of the baby. Still, she meant to be there with him—or her— much of the time. Gary kept saying he didn't care if the baby was a boy or a girl—but Vicky knew his father was counting on a boy. Most men were like that, her mother-in-law said. If it was a girl, Daniel Barton would just have to make do.

At dawn on the day of Lily's engagement party Vicky awoke to the realization that she was in labor. She lay transfixed, her heart pounding. She wouldn't be afraid—this was their baby preparing to make its way into the world. She and Gary would be a family.

No need to wake Gary yet, she told herself. This was a first baby.
It wouldn't be arriving for hours. But Gary wouldn't be going in to
the office today!

As the gray dawn gave way to early morning pinkness, Vicky grap-
pled with the still widely spaced pains, trying not to remember the
stories she'd heard about the agonies of childbirth. *It was their baby
coming into the world. She could cope.* But a particularly sharp contraction evoked an involuntary outcry from her.

"Vicky?" Instantly Gary awoke and sat up in bed. In the morning
light that crept between the drapes, she saw his alarm.

"No need to send for Dr. Roberts yet," she said shakily. "A first
baby is always a long time in coming."

"Is it bad?" he asked anxiously.

"It's going to get worse." She managed a smile. "You'll stay with
me?"

"You bet I will." He reached to take one of her hands in his. "But
shouldn't I call Dr. Roberts?"

"Not for hours," she said, preparing herself for the next contraction.

"I'm going to call Dr. Roberts," he decided.

"Gary, it'll be hours yet," she scolded.

"I want him to know." Gary released her hand and thrust aside the
covers. "I'm going downstairs to phone him. I promise I'll be right
back."

She was relieved that Gary was out of their bedroom when the next
contraction overtook her. She clenched her teeth in pain. Though the
morning was cool, she felt the beads of perspiration rolling down her
forehead.

When Gary returned, she learned that he had told his father he
would not be in the office today.

"I think he's rather proud that he'll be a grandfather by the end of
the day," he reported with an effort at humor.

"Tonight is Lily's engagement party," she remembered all at once.

"I don't give a hang about her party," Gary said, tenderly caressing
her hair. "You're about to make me a father."

Later in the morning—with the pains still eight minutes apart but
growing stronger—Vicky heard Lily's voice rising up the stairs.

"What do you mean, she's in labor?" Lily shrieked. "I won't have
her ruining my engagement party!"

"Gary, I want to move to one of the guest rooms upstairs," Vicky whispered. "I'd be so embarrassed to have the guests at Lily's party hear—"

"I'll have a room prepared," Gary promised. "It won't take long."

With Gary's arm about her—though she protested this was not necessary—Vicky managed the flight of stairs to the third-floor rooms. Only once did she pause to cope with a contraction.

"Gary, this is natural," she told him when the contraction subsided. "But promise you'll stay with me."

"Until the doctor throws me out," Gary vowed. "And maybe even then I'll stay."

Through the long day and early evening Vicky clung to Gary's hand as the contractions grew closer together. Dr. Roberts arrived shortly before the first guests for Lily's engagement party.

"It won't be long now," he promised cheerfully after he had examined her—while Gary hovered in the hall. Mattie Lou, Vicky's young maid, had been sent to the kitchen for hot water. "This baby will come into the world to the sound of music." The orchestra engaged to play for Lily's party was already performing.

"I want Gary here," Vicky said with unexpected firmness between stifled outcries. "It's his baby being born."

"You're sure he can handle it?" Dr. Roberts joked, but he was already heading to the door to summon Gary.

An hour later—while the orchestra played a lively Strauss waltz below—Vicky gave birth to a son.

"He's beautiful," Vicky whispered when the baby at last lay in her arms and Gary hovered adoringly above them. "Michael Daniel Barton." As a conciliatory gesture Vicky had agreed with Gary that their firstborn would carry his father's name. But he would be called Michael, she decreed. Only she and Gary knew that Michael was in memory of her father.

At unwary moments during her pregnancy Vicky had agonized over how to make Gary's parents understand that the baby was not to be baptized, that if a boy he was to be circumcised in accordance with her own faith. Only hours after Michael arrived, Gary promised to see to it that the doctor would circumcise the baby and that his mother would relinquish her plans for Michael's christening. It was unlikely, Sara later told Gary, that Daniel would even be aware of the circumcision.

"Let Michael be well and happy," Sara told Vicky. "We're all children of God."

Vicky and Gary became immersed in the newness of parenthood. She was relieved that Daniel brought Gary in from the road to work under his chief tobacco buyer. Daniel was constantly stressing the importance of understanding the leaf. "It'll take you years to truly appreciate the feel, the smell, the taste of the best leaf," Daniel always told Gary. He was almost gentle, Vicky thought in astonishment when he talked about tobacco. *He loved it.*

Each night when Gary came home from the office, Vicky reported on Michael's activities. When Gary went off on an unscheduled five-day business trip, she waited eagerly for his nightly phone call. They lived in a small, private world in the midst of the frenzied activities revolving around Lily's coming wedding.

Vicky was touched by her mother-in-law's obvious pleasure in her first grandchild. Despite the demands of arranging for Lily's wedding, attending endless showers, Sara made a point of visiting the nursery twice each day.

"He's the image of Gary," Sara said. "And of my father."

If ever she had doubted whether her mother-in-law accepted her as Gary's wife, those doubts were put to rest. Her father-in-law seemed in a perpetually grim mood. Vicky suspected he disapproved of Lily's marriage.

"To Papa no man would be good enough for Lily," Gary told her. "But it'll be quieter around the house with Lily gone."

A week before the wedding Vicky learned that Lily and Clark would not, after all, live in Richmond. Again, Daniel Barton was exercising his will over the family. He was having a house built a quarter of a mile from Barton Manor, which would be his wedding gift to Lily. But Vicky overheard Lily's reaction to this present.

"Why is Papa doing this?" Lily shrieked at her mother. "He knows we wanted to live in Richmond! And Clark's insulted that the house will be in my name! But Clark's a lawyer. He'll know how to change it over into both our names."

"There are special provisions in the deed, as your father told me," Sara explained with the calm she managed to maintain at all times. "The house will belong to you during your lifetime. At your death it'll go to your oldest child. Don't argue with him," Sara pleaded.

"You know he feels he's looking after your interests. It'll be a lovely house, Lily. You and Clark can be proud of it."

Daniel Barton was building a house for his daughter and son-in-law, Vicky thought. But his son and daughter-in-law must live in *his* house. It would mean so much to Gary for them to have a house of their own—where he could always have a piano at his disposal. Why couldn't Gary's father build a house for *them*?

Gary was so happy about the baby—but she knew there were painful hours when he yearned to be away from Barton Manor, away from the business. He hated working for his father. He should be writing music.

When Michael was a few months older, she told herself again, she'd talk to Gary about moving to New York. Gary would find some kind of a job up there that would allow him time to compose. They'd find a little place to live in Greenwich Village—the way Gary used to dream. She'd find work translating or tutoring. After the wedding, she promised herself, they'd make plans.

Chapter Eleven

Vicky was relieved when the wedding was over, and Lily and Clark left for their honeymoon. Lily had prodded her father into providing a wedding trip that included a week in New York City. From New York City the honeymoon couple would sail for France and spend ten days in Paris. It would be a far different Paris from the one she had known, Vicky thought. But Paris would always live in a corner of her heart, for that was where she had met Gary.

Gary was irritated that his father continued to send him out on the road. He loathed these selling trips—not only because of the separation from Michael and her but because he found selling itself distasteful.

"Gary, talk to your father," Vicky said. *Now was the time for them to move on.* "Make him understand you don't want to be in the cigarette business—"

"He's got his mind made up. He's built up this big business, and one day I'm to take over. And when I retire, there'll be Michael," he said bitterly. "He thinks he's building an empire."

"You have a right to live your own life!" Vicky insisted. "You write beautiful music. You have a talent, Gary. It's wrong to throw that away."

"The only talent Papa recognizes is one for making money. It's a religion with him. You know how he carries on—about how he came up from nothing, and now he's one of the richest men in the South.

That's Step One. Next, he means to be one of the richest men in the country.''

"With the way the cigarette business is developing, he probably will be.'' Vicky managed a smile. "He said most of the smaller companies are going out. That means more for the big ones. But we—''

"I feel so sorry for all those small companies that went into business after the Federal government broke up the 'tobacco trust,' '' Gary interrupted. "They thought they had a chance—but there's no place for them in the field. These days a cigarette company needs tremendous capital to stay afloat. But the most hurt of all are the tobacco farmers. The fewer their markets the lower they have to drop their prices.''

"Why must they lower their prices?'' Vicky demanded passionately. "Without their crops there can be no tobacco business.''

"They don't know how to organize among themselves,'' Gary explained. "They leave themselves at the mercy of the manufacturers. The big companies can almost name their own price. The tobacco farmers are hurting badly while the rich cigarette companies are raking in high profits—despite all their cries about the high tax on cigarettes,'' he added with contempt.

"Gary, let's go to New York to live.'' She saw the sudden hunger in his eyes. "We can live cheaply in Greenwich Village, you said. You'll find some kind of job—and I can look for work translating. I can do that at home and still take good care of Michael,'' she said tenderly. "I know we could manage.''

"We can't do that yet,'' he said after a moment. "We'll have to wait until Michael's a few months older—''

"We'll start saving.'' Vicky glowed with anticipation. "We won't spend your salary on anything. Just put it away to see us through those first weeks in New York. Oh, Gary, it'll be wonderful! We'll buy a cheap old piano, and you can compose whenever you're not working. Michael and I will keep out of your way until you're ready to play for us.''

"We won't live in a house like this,'' Gary warned. "It'll be a tiny apartment in some drab building. There'll be little money for anything but rent and food—at least, until I make a connection.''

"Gary, remember the place I shared with Simone? I didn't always live in the Veronsky Palace. We'll manage,'' she insisted. "We don't need a house like Barton Manor. We don't need a Cadillac car. We don't need a car at all.'' She reached to pull Gary close. "We just need ourselves and our dreams. And our love.''

Now Vicky clung to the prospect of their getting away from Bartonville, living their own lives. Just a few months longer, she told herself. Already Gary seemed happier, more able to cope with the job he loathed. *Because they knew they were getting away from Barton Manor.*

A hot spell descended on Bartonville just a few days after Lily and Clark returned from their honeymoon. Mattie Lou and Vicky took turns sitting by the nursery crib or the bedroom cradle and waving a fan over Michael's tiny form. The ceiling fans in every room offered little relief. Not even the breeze from the river alleviated the heat.

In mid-July Sara decided that the women in the family should go to White Sulphur Springs for three weeks. She brought this up at Sunday dinner, with Lily and Clark in attendance.

"This is the worst time of the year in Virginia,'' Sara said with distaste.

"Why can't we go up to Newport?'' Lily said, sulking. "Why do we always settle for White Sulphur Springs? That's for fall or spring.''

"I'm not concerned with following the path of high society,'' Sara said in a rare display of sarcasm.

"Papa, why don't we all go to Newport?'' Lily said. "All the really important businessmen are seen at Newport.''

"Not this important business man,'' Daniel said. "Go with your mother to the Springs.''

"I'll make reservations at the Greenbrier. You'll bring Mattie Lou to help with Michael,'' Sara told Vicky.

"I'd rather stay here,'' Vicky said quickly. "I don't think it's good to take Michael away from his own little corner of the world. And I wouldn't want to leave Gary for three weeks.''

"All kinds of important people come to the Greenbrier,'' Stephanie said, staring at Vicky in disbelief. "Last year the Prince of Wales stayed there when he made his American tour. He danced with Laura Ainsworth from Richmond.''

"Among others,'' Lily chimed in cattily. "I love the Greenbrier's swimming pool and the tennis courts.''

"I'll stay here,'' Vicky reiterated and turned to Sara. "But I do thank you for asking me.''

She was conscious of a covert appraisal by Daniel. He still believed she'd married Gary because he came from a wealthy family. Her refusal of a trip to the fancy Greenbrier surprised him, just as her practice of being at the breakfast table at six-thirty when Gary was home continued to surprise him.

Though the sultry heat continued, enveloping her in unfamiliar lethargy, Vicky enjoyed the quietness of the house with the other women at White Sulphur Springs. Even married, Lily was at Barton Manor every day, and Sara still acted as a constant referee between her and Stephanie.

Two days before the others were to return from White Sulphur Springs, Michael awoke in the morning with a cough that grew worse in the course of the day.

"It's just croup," Mattie Lou comforted. "It gets a lot of babies. My sister's youngest had it last week. She gave him a few drops of paregoric every few hours. Then it just went away."

"I don't want to give Michael paregoric." She touched his forehead. "Mattie Lou, do you think he's running a temperature?"

Mattie Lou brushed her own cheek against Michael's. "No, ma'am, no fever," she said with conviction. "But we better watch. Sometimes the fever don't come on until night time."

By late afternoon Michael's face was flushed. His cough had turned into a bark that ended in a strange whistle. Vicky was alarmed. She hurried to call the baby doctor who cared for Michael. The only baby doctor in Bartonville.

"He's out on a call, Miz Barton," his office nurse reported. "I'll have him phone you as soon as he gets in."

"Thank you," Vicky said, hiding her impatience. "I'll be waiting to hear from him."

Vicky was relieved when Gary and Daniel arrived home earlier than usual.

"No point staying any later in this heat," Daniel grumbled as he walked into the house. "No work's getting done."

"Vicky, what's wrong?" Gary asked, immediately sensing her anxiety.

"I think Michael has the croup," she told him. "And I can't get through to Dr. Herman."

"What do you mean, you can't get through to him?" Daniel demanded.

"I've called three times, and his nurse keeps telling me he's out on calls. Michael's running a fever and his cough is getting worse—" Even as they talked, they heard the harsh little bark that was his cough.

"Get me Herman's office," Daniel ordered. "I want to talk to that nurse."

Moments later Daniel took the phone from Vicky and began to chastise the nurse.

"Look, when my daughter-in-law calls Dr. Herman, she expects to hear from him. Where the hell is he?" He scowled as he listened to her reply. "Why didn't you tell her that, for God's sake?" He slammed down the phone. "He's in the hospital in Richmond—he had an accident with the car. She's stalling everybody until she finds out if he's going to be released right away." He thought for a moment while Vicky exchanged an anxious glance with Gary. "Gary, tell Zach to bring the car out front. I'm going to send him in to Richmond to bring back old Doc Raymond. He may have retired two years ago, but he'll come out here for me. He owes me."

With grim speed Daniel arranged for Dr. Raymond to be picked up with the car and brought to Barton Manor. Gary went upstairs with Vicky to the nursery while Daniel went out to the library. Hurrying up the stairs, they heard Daniel yelling for Effie to bring him a glass of ice for his bourbon.

Walking into the nursery Vicky stopped short.

"Where's Michael?" Her voice was shrill with alarm.

"I'm in the bathroom with him, Miz Vicky," Mattie Lou called out. "The steam from the hot water helps his breathing."

"Zachary's gone to bring Dr. Raymond to the house," Vicky said, fighting for calm. She mustn't fall apart the first time Michael was sick.

"He's going to be all right," Gary said soothingly, but Vicky felt his own anxiety as the two of them approached the bathroom door. It was so *awful*, she thought, to stand by while your baby was sick and not know what to do for him.

"I'll take him, Mattie Lou." Vicky held out her arms. "You run down and ask Lula Mae to fix a pitcher of lemonade for Dr. Raymond. He'll want something cool after the hot drive from Richmond."

The wait for Dr. Raymond's arrival was agonizing. Vicky was grateful for his air of assurance when he arrived and came upstairs to examine Michael.

"Well now, little lady, don't look so upset," he said to Vicky when he placed Michael, who seemed to calm down at the doctor's gentle tones, into Mattie Lou's arms. "A lot of young ones come down with the croup from time to time. Of course, this little fellow is kind of rushing the season." Dr. Raymond wrote out a prescription and handed it to Vicky. "This will help him sleep and give him some relief from the breathing difficulty and the cough. Have Zachary pick me up with the car tomorrow morning around nine. I'll come out to look at him again, but I'm sure he'll be doing fine."

A relieved Gary went downstairs with Dr. Raymond. Then Vicky heard Daniel joining the two men in the foyer, insisting that Dr. Raymond join him for a drink.

"Damn this Prohibition," Daniel boomed. "It's not right to tell a man he's not allowed a shot of bourbon when he comes home from a hard day's work."

Days after Michael was clearly well again, Vicky continued to watch him for signs of a fresh outbreak. At last, she convinced herself that he was all right. This was the time, she decided, to talk to Gary about their moving to New York. Religiously she had deposited most of Gary's weekly salary in the bank so that if they were careful in their spending, they'd be able to survive for several weeks while they searched for jobs.

Tonight Vicky was eager for dinner to be over. She fretted that Daniel lingered over his ice tea. At last, with a glance at his watch, Daniel pushed back his chair and rose to his feet. Her heart pounding in anticipation, Vicky walked with Gary to the side gallery.

They sat on the floral-cushioned glider on the gallery, where the pungent scent of honeysuckle and roses permeated the sultry night air. Occasionally a faint breeze drifted from the river. Good-humoredly argumentative voices filtered from the foyer as Daniel welcomed a few cronies for a poker game.

"Mama and the girls will be home tomorrow night," Gary said. "Mama will talk about how wonderful everything was at the Greenbrier. She always loves going there. Lily and Stephanie will carry on about being snubbed by other guests. Those two are never satisfied."

"Gary, I went to the bank today." Vicky was faintly breathless with excitement. "You know how we've talked about getting away from here, having an apartment in Greenwich Village? We have enough in our savings account to see us through in New York for—"

"Vicky, we can't leave here for the insecurity of New York." The resignation in his eyes startled her.

"Gary, why not? You said we'd wait until Michael was a few months old. We'll manage—"

"You and I would manage," he said gently before she could continue, "but we have to think about Michael. How can we expose him to the uncertainties we might encounter? These last days—when he was so sick—made me understand. For Michael I can live in Bartonville and work for the company. I can keep my music as something private for special moments."

"Gary, this isn't fair to you! You have such talent!"

"And I have a son. Michael must come first." He was resolute. "We brought him into this world. We have obligations. We have to do what's best for our son."

"How do we know it's best?" she challenged him though she understood his feelings.

"It's *security*, Vicky," he said. "But we won't always live here at Barton Manor. You know Papa. He doesn't want to make things too easy for me. In time I'll be earning a fine salary—we'll be able to afford our own house. Michael will never be in want."

"You must have a place with a piano," Vicky said after a moment, her ambitions for Gary refusing to die. "Some little corner where you can write your music in the hours that belong to us. Talk to your mother," she encouraged. "Maybe she'll help."

"Later," he hedged. "This is not the time. Not yet."

Gary's dreams mustn't die, Vicky told herself. Because if they did, then part of them would die as well.

Chapter Twelve

SARA AND THE girls returned from the Greenbrier. Vicky tried to conceal her impatience as Lily and Stephanie daily reproached their mother because they had not remained longer.

"This heat is just awful," Lily stormed while the Barton women gathered on the side veranda of the house for luncheon on a late August day. "Almost everybody we know is up in Newport or Bar Harbor or Southampton. Hardly anybody is in town. They won't be until mid-September."

"Not everybody," Sara contradicted with a wry smile.

"Anybody that counts," Stephanie said with an arrogant toss of her head.

"We'll have Zachary drive us into Richmond and see what's new at Thalhimer's," Sara said tiredly. "And then we'll drop by T. A. Miller's for something cool to drink."

"I don't know why Papa won't put in a swimming pool." Lily exchanged an aggrieved smile with her sister. "You'd think we were ready for the poor house."

"He has an awful fear of somebody being careless at night and falling in and drowning," Sara said. "Vicky, Michael will be napping all afternoon in this weather. Why don't you come along with us?"

"It's so hot I'd rather just stay here and read," Vicky said, her eyes apologetic.

"One of us could just as well fall into the river," Lily continued her complaining. "Papa doesn't worry about that."

"Lily, we're not Rockefellers or Vanderbilts," Sara said. "We spend money like water as it is. Maybe your father thinks that's one expense we can do without."

Vicky was relieved when the others piled into the Cadillac and headed for Richmond. Finally the house was quiet. She lingered at the table and sipped an ice-cold lemonade.

She felt guilty at sitting here with an occasional breeze from the river relieving the day's heat when she knew the discomfort that Gary shared with others at the company. It was bad enough on days like this on the huge office floor—where electric fans did little more than circulate the foul hot air—but for the factory workers it was unbearable. The heat was only exacerbated by the particles of tobacco that filled the air.

In a sudden burst of restlessness Vicky abandoned the frosty glass of lemonade and left the veranda to head for the deserted path beside the river. As she walked along the river's edge, Vicky found herself plagued by the memory of last night—when Gary had sat down at the piano with the belief that his father had gone back to the factory for a long session. However, Mr. Barton returned in less than an hour—grumbling about the heat. Gary had jumped away from the piano the moment he heard his father's voice in the foyer.

This was so wrong, she thought. Gary had such talent—it shouldn't be stifled. Her face softened as she remembered the lovely lullaby he had composed only days after Michael's birth. Tears had filled her eyes when he'd found a few minutes of privacy at the house to play it for her. Now the melody drifted across her mind.

Ignoring Gary's frequent reminder that nobody in the South rushed in weather like this, she hurried from the sun-drenched river bank and made her way through the overgrown bushes and vines that lent a heady fragrance to the summer air. There was no real path here, but she felt a need to escape the oppressive heat of the sun. Here and there was welcome shade, along with the untended growth of honeysuckle, roses, unfamiliar blossoms that offered an exotic blend of perfumes.

Suddenly, she became conscious of an unexpected giddiness. Her eyes searched the area for somewhere to rest for a few moments, perhaps a tree trunk or a cleared area in the shadow of tall trees. Her gaze finally rested on a small cabin in a tiny clearing fifty feet ahead.

She walked toward the cabin. It was no larger than a good-sized room; its windowpanes were broken, the clapboards showed only a hint of paint, and the three steps leading to the tiny veranda were rotted away. But in her mind she saw it restored to its normal state. *It would be a perfect studio for Gary.*

The cabin was at least a ten-minute walk from the house. Here Gary could sit at a piano and play for as long as he wished and know the sounds of his music would not be heard by his father.

Eagerly she made her way up the decaying steps to the veranda and pulled open the door that hung loosely on its hinges. There was a beautiful coolness inside the large, square room, and plenty of room for a grand piano.

She knew what she would do. She would go to Gary's mother and plead with her to allow Gary to have this quiet, secret room for his music studio. The money they had in the bank would pay for a secondhand piano and a bench. If need be, she would clean and paint it herself. She was impatient to approach Sara about this project. Instinct told her it would have to be kept a secret from Gary's father, but his mother would understand.

Back at the house Vicky waited for a few private moments with her mother-in-law. At last Sara and the girls returned from Richmond. Lily and Stephanie went up to Stephanie's bedroom to try on the dresses they'd bought at Thalhimer's. Sara went to sit on the veranda. Vicky rushed to join her, told Sara about her adventure in the woods—in such a rush that her words tumbled over one another. Gary must have a place where he'd feel free to compose.

"I've been saving most of Gary's salary," Vicky concluded, "so we could use that for his piano. Oh, Mrs. Barton, he'd be so happy!"

"Vicky, it's time we stopped this 'Mrs. Barton,' " Sara said gently. "I want you to call me Sara. And yes, I agree. Gary must have his studio."

"That's wonderful!" Vicky's face glowed.

"The piano will be my present," Sara said. "And remember, Daniel is not to know about this. We won't even tell Gary until all the work has been done and the piano is in place. How lovely of you to have thought of this, Vicky," she said tenderly.

*   *   *

This new project was another bond between Vicky and her mother-in-law. Sara brought in workmen to renovate the cabin. She went with Vicky into Richmond to choose a piano. Vicky was simultaneously shocked and elated at the fine grand piano Sara chose. In addition to the piano, Sara decided the cabin must have a beautiful rug and a club chair. Then she instructed the workmen to make sure the fireplace was useable and saw to it that they added a pretty marble mantel. When Vicky remembered there was no electricity in the cabin, she and Sara searched until they found a trio of exquisite hurricane lamps.

At last everything was in place. A pair of happy but wary conspirators, Vicky and Sara returned from the hideaway in the woods to the house. Though both were impatient to show Gary what they had put together, they were nevertheless aware that they must wait for the opportune moment.

At dinner that evening Vicky and Sara exchanged an excited glance. Daniel had just announced that he was leaving in the morning for a four-day business trip. He seemed in high spirits tonight, Vicky thought. Moments later she understood the reason for this.

"This is a fine time for business," he said exuberantly. "Everybody's amazed at the steep drop in leaf tobacco." He grinned at Gary. "You know what that means. Profits are going to soar."

"Why are prices dropping?" Vicky asked.

"They're bringing in bumper crops—at a time when export sales are taking a nosedive because of the exchange rate. If they want to sell, they're going to have to accept lower prices than they counted on."

Now Daniel launched into a monologue about an article in the current *Wall Street Journal*. Vicky knew he enjoyed holding court about the business, though Sara and Stephanie made it plain they were not interested. Gary looked somber, Vicky observed.

"We're looking ahead to a great year coming up," Daniel continued complacently. "Of course, manufacturers can't raise prices any higher than what they are now without losing sales. Twenty cents a pack is the top we can ask—and out of that six cents is tax. But the tobacco farmers know they can't expect high prices at auctions this year, and that guarantees us a substantial margin of profit."

"But what about the farmers?" Gary said, his voice tense. "How are they going to survive? You know a lot of them will go into bank-ruptcy if they have to drop their prices.''

"Gary, be realistic." Daniel waved a hand in dismissal. "This is a world of supply and demand. The farmers have a bumper crop and a diminished market. They have to drop their prices or sit with their crops. Some will go out," he shrugged. "But new ones will come along to take over. Barton Tobacco will have a banner 1921," he predicted, relishing the prospect.

The following day, Vicky and Sara waited impatiently for Gary to return from the office. They were pleased that Stephanie was in Rich-mond, along with Lily, for a baby shower and dinner with a recently married friend and her husband.

Guessing that Gary would take advantage of his father's absence to come home early, Vicky and Sara sat on the veranda and watched for the car to pull up in front of the house.

"I hope the piano has been properly tuned," Sara said. "I want Gary to be pleased."

"He will be," Vicky promised. It had been so hard these last few days not to blurt out the secret to him. "Oh, there's the car!" She leapt to her feet with a dazzling smile as the car came into view.

Gary was bewildered yet amused when his mother and Vicky in-sisted he go for a predinner walk with them into the woods.

"But I haven't seen Michael yet," he protested.

"You'll see him later," Vicky told him. "Anyway, he's asleep now."

The sun was low, lending a rosy glow to the river. The heat of the day had subsided. The air was fragrant. And then Vicky clutched at his arm as the pristine white cabin—its tiny veranda offering a vine-covered railing now, the broken steps and broken windows repaired—came into view.

"Gary, this is your studio," Vicky told him breathlessly. "Your mother's had it all fixed up for you. And there's a grand piano inside! You can come here and play whenever you're free!"

"It was Vicky's idea," Sara said. "She realized—even more than I—how important your music is to you."

His face reflecting a blend of pleasure and gratitude and tenderness, Gary silently walked to the door of his new studio, opened the door, and went inside. The two women trailed behind him, pausing inside the door as Gary walked to the piano, sat down, and with an exuberant smile began to play.

Words were unnecessary, Vicky thought. She and Sara had given Gary what he needed most in this world. He would be happy now despite the job, she promised herself, because he would have a place to play and to compose.

Vicky prodded Sara to the club chair across from the piano and went to stand at Gary's right. Dinner was forgotten as he moved from Mozart to Tchaikovsky to the lullaby he had written for Michael. This was one of those precious times she would remember forever, Vicky thought, tears of joy flooding her eyes.

"Now," Gary said as the last strains of the lullaby faded away, "let's go see Michael." His eyes luminous, he rose from the piano bench and placed his arms around his wife and his mother.

This was the Gary she had known in Paris, Vicky told herself. He would write his music, and the world would love it. And they would move away from Barton Manor to a little house of their very own.

Sara sat in her favorite armchair in a corner of the library and listened to a Caruso phonograph record while Vicky and Gary played chess. She closed her eyes as the magnificence of Caruso's voice singing "Vesti la giubba" filled the room.

Sara knew that the calm of these past four days would soon be disrupted. Daniel was due momentarily. Stephanie was spending the evening at Lily's house and would be driven home soon by her sister.

A faint smile touched Sara's mouth as she considered the tug-of-war currently being waged between Daniel and Stephanie. If it had been Lily, the battle would have been shorter. Still, Sara guessed that Stephanie would soon have her wish. Daniel had never allowed either of the girls to drive, but Clark had bought a new Pierce-Arrow two-passenger Runabout and taught Lily how to drive. Now Stephanie alternately sulked and fought with her father about her learning to drive.

The last of the aria died away, and Sara rose from her chair to remove the record. She relished the sight of Gary and Vicky, both so absorbed in their game of chess. There was none of the fierce competition between them that Daniel displayed when he played with

Gary. Daniel had played chess with Vicky only once. Laughter lit her eyes. He'd been outraged that Vicky won.

She paused, listening to a car door slam. Daniel had arrived. Moments later she heard his voice in the foyer. A dozen years ago she would have rushed to the foyer to welcome him home. Now, she was too proud to concede that, even after all his infidelities, she still loved him.

"Zach, take the smaller valise into the library," she heard Daniel order. He never dared return from a business trip without gifts for the girls.

"Yes, sir!" Zachary said happily and charged ahead of Daniel with the valise in tow.

Sara rose to her feet and crossed to her husband for his perfunctory kiss on the cheek.

"Did. you have a good trip?" she asked as always and frowned at the scent of cheap perfume that clung to him.

"I don't find pleasure in sitting in overheated railroad cars for hours on end," he grumbled, accepting Gary's welcoming handshake. He managed an airy wave of one hand to Vicky. "But I needed to be in Washington right now." He glanced about the room. "Where're the girls?" Even married, Lily was still his "baby girl"—and she made a habit of being at the main house when he was expected home from a trip.

"Stephanie spent the evening over at Lily's," Sara told him. "Lily and Clark had people over for a couple of tables of bridge." Daniel accepted Clark with reluctance, she thought. Maybe the Prince of Wales might have been acceptable as Lily's husband.

"That sounds like them now," Vicky said, as girlish laughter drifted down the hall.

"Papa!" Lily charged into the room and into her father's arms, with Stephanie close behind her.

"You're early, Papa," Stephanie said. "I was sure we'd be home before you arrived."

"Where's Clark?" Daniel demanded.

"Home with our guests," Lily said with a glint of triumph in her eyes. "I drove Stephanie home."

"What did you bring us?" Stephanie asked.

"From Washington, D.C.?" Daniel grumbled. "I wasn't in New York."

"They have department stores in Washington," Lily reminded. "You know Woodies. And Hecht's."

They were still playing this childish game, Sara thought, striving to hide her annoyance while her daughters persuaded their father to open his valise and bring forth gifts. He was making a big production of releasing the locks and reaching inside for two small gift-wrapped boxes. Then, with a furtive glance in her direction, Daniel was hastily trying to conceal a wayward item.

Sara's face tightened as she spied the tulle and ruched pink ribbon brassiere beneath a shirt. Had she expected him to behave any differently on this trip?

"I'll tell Lula Mae to prepare you a tray," she said coldly, her eyes meeting his. He knew that *she* knew he'd had some little whore in his hotel suite in Washington.

Usually when she caught Daniel in one of his escapades, she went to Thalhimer's and Miller & Rhoads and shopped with an abandon she showed at no other time. Daniel never dared utter one word of censure. But this time, she promised herself with a new defiance, she would give herself some fine personal pleasure. Daniel would recognize this as another of her silent retaliations—but he wouldn't fight her.

The following morning Sara phoned a Richmond architect and commissioned him to build a cottage for Gary. This would not be just a cabin, she reported to Vicky later. There would be a large room for his piano, plus another room where he could stretch out and rest, a kitchen, and a small bathroom.

Sara asked herself why her anger toward Daniel for his infidelities seemed more intense than in the past. She forced herself to admit the reason for this. She saw the love shared by Gary and Vicky, and she asked herself where her own marriage had gone astray. In those early years Daniel had seemed to be in love with her, so proud of her. What had she done to lose that?

She tried to focus on the cottage she was building for Gary only a hundred yards away from his present studio. In time, of course, when the bills started coming in, Daniel would find out about it. But she found such satisfaction in Gary's joy in this show of her support for his music. She should have stood behind him before, she chastised herself. Vicky had made her understand how much Gary's music meant to him.

* * *

Daniel waited in astonishment for Lily to be ushered into his office. Lily never came to the office. Was she having trouble with Clark, he asked himself. She was a handful, he thought. Probably too much woman for that young bastard.

"Papa, I think it's just awful!" Lily stormed into the room with the air of a passionate crusader. "Mama lying to all of us this way! But then she's never cared about anybody except Gary."

"Hold on," Daniel ordered. "What's your mother lying about?"

"That cottage she's having built down in the woods. It's closer to the main house than to our little place. But I never would have known about it if one of the carpenters hadn't taken off in the wrong direction and got lost. He came to our little place—" Fourteen rooms wasn't a little place, Daniel thought in irritation. It was just a reminder that she would never forget that Gary would inherit Barton Manor one day. But that was something that had to be. Gary carried on the Barton name.

"He told us how Mama's building that cottage so her darling Gary can have a quiet place to play the piano whenever he likes," he heard Lily say.

"What gave you the idea that your mother was lying about that?" Daniel demanded. Damn Sara for making him look like a fool! "She mentioned it to me. I told her to go ahead. If she wants to have a little project to play with, I don't mind." He managed an amused smile. "Now stop getting yourself upset for no reason. Your mother wants to give Gary a little toy, so be it. After all, you got a fourteen-room house."

"And Gary and that stupid Vicky will get Barton Manor!" she shot back.

"Not for a while," he promised. "I don't plan on kicking the bucket for another thirty or forty years." He reached into his pocket, pulled out his wallet, extracted a few bills. "Now you go down into Richmond and buy yourself something pretty. But first, you come over here and give your old Papa a big hug. I promise you, nobody's ever going to cheat my two little girls."

Later, Daniel stood by a window of his office and watched while Lily climbed behind the wheel of her bright yellow Runabout. He returned to his desk and reached for the phone. Damn Sara! He waited impatiently until she came to the phone.

"Lily was just here telling me about that cottage you got into your head to build. What the hell's the matter with you?" he yelled. "Just when Gary's getting away from his damn music, you're throwing him back into it!"

"Open your eyes, Daniel. Don't you see how unhappy he is?" Sara sounded cool and composed, as always. "Giving him the cottage—a place where he can be alone with his music—is the only way to keep him at the company. Think of something besides your tobacco empire," she said scathingly. "Help me keep Gary here in Bartonville."

"Why didn't you tell me what you were doing?" He was both sullen and defensive.

"Because I knew you'd try to stop me. I've lost my husband. I want to keep my son."

Chapter Thirteen

VICKY LOOKED forward to Sunday mornings at Barton Manor. She and Gary slept late, had coffee in their bedroom, and then spent an hour in the nursery with Michael. Only after Sara, Daniel, and Stephanie had left for church did they come downstairs for breakfast. If the weather permitted, Vicky instructed that their breakfast be served on the veranda. These hours on Sunday were a precious interlude in their lives.

After Sunday breakfasts Gary took off for the studio, with a thermos of coffee and a sandwich to see him through until he returned in mid-afternoon, while Vicky took over Michael. She told herself that Gary relished his hours at the studio, yet she knew he still chafed at the demands of his job with the company. When would he understand that they didn't have to stay here? Together they could provide for Michael.

As on the previous year, Vicky enjoyed the American holiday of Thanksgiving. This would be Michael's first. At Daniel's insistence, Michael was propped up in a highchair and seated at the dinner table with the family, though she suspected that both Lily and Clark were irritated by this. Lily was annoyed, too, by her father's jibes about the lack of a prospective second grandson.

A week after Thanksgiving Sara began what were to be elaborate preparations for Christmas. For the first time Vicky would meet Sara's parents and brother. The previous Christmas Sara had explained that her father was too ill to leave his house. Vicky had often wondered why Sara's parents and brother were never seen at Barton Manor, though Sara went to visit them regularly.

"My folks lead a very reclusive life," Sara explained one afternoon while Zachary drove the two women into Richmond to shop. Her eyes were apologetic and wistful as she talked about her family. "The three of them still live in the shadows of the War Between the States." Vicky understood that what was recorded in the history books as "the Civil War" was never known as that in the South. "My brother Rob was conceived when our father came home wounded in battle, and he was born while Papa was fighting again at Appomattox." Vicky knew that Sara was ten years younger than Rob. She seemed of a later generation. "The family goes back to the early settlers in Richmond," Sara added with pride. "There were Warrens in Richmond since 1741."

They were part of Michael's family, Vicky thought, along with the Gunsburgs of Petrograd, who Papa said had lived in Russia since England expelled its Jews back in 1290. So often she wished that her mother and father had lived to know Michael.

"I've made a list of what I'd like to find for Christmas presents," Sara said. "I've promised myself I'll never again wait until the last minute to choose presents. I've been saying this ever since I can remember," she laughed, "but this year I'm doing it. I think it's your good influence, Vicky. Daniel's always amazed at how organized you are."

"I would never have guessed he felt that way." Vicky smiled faintly. It always infuriated her when he replied to something she said as being "out of the mouths of babes." But several times, Gary reported, her father-in-law had adopted some suggestion she had made regarding the business. He wouldn't admit, of course, that a woman could have a brain in her head. He was outraged that women had just been given the right to vote.

Sara explained that Vicky was to shop for gifts that she and Gary would give to family members, and that the gifts were to be charged to what was known as "the family account."

"I can't wait to see Michael's eyes when he sees the Christmas tree and all the decorations," Sara said sentimentally when they'd finished their shopping and were having tea in the beautiful tea room at Miller & Rhoads. Smoking these days, Lily was outraged that the tea room refused to allow women patrons to smoke. "And next year we'll bring him down to see Santa Claus."

"Oh, yes," Vicky agreed, but her attention had been captured by the conversation between two well-groomed, middle-aged ladies at the table behind them. They were discussing plans for a family Hanukkah party.

"I remember when Gary was about three, and I took him to a children's Christmas party where there was a Santa Claus," Sara reminisced. "Oh, he was so excited!"

Those two ladies talked so openly about Hanukkah, Vicky thought enviously. She remembered quiet, secretive Hanukkah celebrations at the Veronsky Palace in Petrograd. Mama banished the servants and went into the kitchen herself to make Hanukkah donuts. Mama lit the Hanukkah candles, each year inventing amusing stories for the servants to explain the candle lighting.

"I think Michael adores that teddy bear Daniel brought home for him last week," Sara decided. "His little face just lit up so when he saw it."

"I'm sure he does," Vicky said, part of her attention remaining with the ladies at the table behind them. They were talking now about a Hanukkah party being planned at their synagogue.

Vicky marvelled at the religious freedom for Jews in this country. *Michael must know he was Jewish. He must understand his heritage.* The old fears—Papa's admonitions—lingered with her. She remembered Daniel Barton's warnings that even here it was not wise to parade your faith if you were Jewish.

She knew about Henry Ford and his newspaper, the *Dearborn Independent*, in which he published scurrilous attacks against the Jews. From Gary's angry tirades on the subject she was aware that some of the finest universities set quotas for the admission of Jewish students and for the number of Jewish faculty members. And now the Ku Klux Klan was spreading its hatred against Jews, Negroes, Catholics and the foreign-born in alarming strength. Yet here in beautiful Richmond, she thought, there were Jews who lived their lives openly and worshipped as they believed.

"Vicky, do you think Gary would like a cashmere sweater like the one I bought Daniel?" Sara asked.

"He'd love it," Vicky guessed.

"Then let's go see if they have it in his size. Then I'll have all the

Christmas presents bought except for Lily's and Stephanie's. They're always the most difficult.''

Vicky entered into the festive spirit that permeated the house with the approach of Christmas. However, she still secretly celebrated Hanukkah. She bought a china elephant-shaped bank for Michael and each night of Hanukkah dropped change into the slot.

On a private shopping trip in Richmond she'd discovered a store that sold menorahs, and each night she lit the proper number of candles. And she envied those Jews in Richmond who attended their synagogues regularly, observed their holidays without fear—and thumbed their noses at the dark clouds of anti-Semitism that invaded the "land of the free and home of the brave."

Ten days before Christmas, Gary's cottage was finished. Sara arranged for his piano to be moved there. She went with Vicky to Richmond to choose a rug and drapes and a second club chair, because sometimes Gary invited Vicky and his mother to hear him play, though he always refused to play the opening segment of his symphony-in-progress.

"Not until it's right," he told them firmly while Vicky and Sara exchanged frustrated glances. Both knew that Gary was a perfectionist.

But on the day that Vicky and his mother took him into the new cottage—which he had not been allowed to enter until now—he played a new lullaby he'd composed for Michael.

"Next week we'll bring Michael here, and I'll play it for him," Gary promised.

"Michael's first Christmas," Sara said lovingly. "He's such a happy baby."

And Michael's first Hanukkah, Vicky told herself. He didn't understand about the festival of Hanukkah now—but one day he would.

There was a mellow feeling at Barton Manor on Christmas day. Even Lily and Stephanie seemed less flighty and contentious. Sara's parents and brother were charming and eager to join in the holiday spirit, yet Vicky sensed that they were not entirely comfortable with their daughter's family. It was as though they lived in another world, now long past. She suspected, too, that they felt intimidated by Daniel.

Michael basked in all the attention bestowed on him. Gary seemed less tense than usual. Vicky herself felt touched by the warm feeling of family that filled the house.

Late that evening—after the Warrens had returned to Richmond, Lily and Clark to their own house—the others settled in the double drawing room for coffee and additional servings of rich plum pudding. Michael had long been asleep in the nursery. Now Daniel announced that Gary would spend the first six months of the new year in the New York office.

"It's time for you to learn about merchandising and advertising," he told Gary. "Advertising may be the most important element in the business. You'll learn from Frank Leslie. He's as shrewd as they come."

"You mean, live in New York for six months?" Gary was unnerved, yet Vicky saw a glint of anticipation in his eyes when they met hers for an instant.

"Consider it a post-graduate course," Daniel said expansively. "Except this time you won't be living in a dormitory. Frank will make reservations for you at a good hotel. You'll—"

"Surely we'll be able to find an apartment," Vicky broke in. "A hotel is hardly the place for a baby." Her heart was pounding as she spoke. Her sweet smile gave no indication that she realized he meant for Gary to go to New York alone. *She wouldn't allow that to happen.*

"Vicky, you don't want to go chasing up to New York with Gary and the baby," Daniel protested. "You'll hardly see him. He'll be all tied up with business."

"I wouldn't dream of our being away from Gary all that time," she said softly.

"He'll be home for a few days each month," Daniel dismissed this. "Before you know it, the six months will be over."

"Michael and I will go with Gary. I couldn't bear our being separated that way." Vicky kept her voice soft and respectful, but her eyes warned Daniel not to pursue this.

The atmosphere in the drawing room was suddenly electric. Vicky was conscious of Stephanie's open-mouthed shock at her defiance. She thought she detected a glint of amusement in Sara's eyes.

"Well, if you're going to be upset about it," Daniel said after a moment, as though he was giving in to one of Lily or Stephanie's whims, "then you and Michael will go along with Gary. Take Mattie

Lou with you. And cut the New York assignment to three months. I'll tell Frank I expect him to work you like the devil, Gary.''

Maybe this would be their real escape from Bartonville, Vicky thought in soaring excitement. In three months' time Gary would be able to get a feel of how they could manage on their own in New York. She'd look around to see about an inexpensive little apartment, about work for herself as a translator. This would be a whole new life, she told herself—and then Daniel's voice brought her back to the moment.

"I'm going to miss seeing Michael every day," he said with an unexpected, and uncharacteristic, wistfulness in his voice. "That's going to be a long three months."

Daniel had cut the trip from six months to three months, Vicky realized, because he didn't want to be separated from Michael. She was oddly uneasy at this indication of his affection. Never—*never*—must Michael fall into his grandfather's trap.

On a cold, early January afternoon Vicky boarded the New York–bound train with her small entourage of husband, son, and nursemaid. She felt that they were halfway to freedom, though she felt guilty about Mattie Lou. If she were able to persuade Gary to disassociate himself from Barton Tobacco and remain in New York, then they would have to send Mattie Lou back to Bartonville. They'd hardly be able to afford a nursemaid.

"You're looking forward to New York," Gary guessed when they were seated at a beautifully appointed table in the dining car and waiting to be served lunch. "You didn't see much of the city when we were there before."

"It was thoughtful of Mr. Leslie to find us an apartment." Vicky guessed that it would be an expensive apartment, and that the company would pay for it. "I hope it's near the office."

"A ten-minute bus trip," Gary told her, reaching for her hand across the table. "I can probably walk it in twenty minutes. These three months will be like a second honeymoon."

Already Gary felt a whiff of freedom, Vicky thought with pleasure. Oh yes, this could be their road to a new life.

At Pennsylvania Station they were met by Frank Leslie, whom Gary knew from the New Yorker's visits to Bartonville for business conferences, but who was a stranger to Vicky. A middle-aged man with a warm, courtly air, he had a car waiting to take them to their apartment.

"It's on the West Side of town in the Sixties. Not very fashionable," he apologized, "but it was available immediately. And it has a fantastic view of Central Park."

"Vicky will love it," Gary said.

Vicky gazed in delight as the car moved north over a blanket of snow and past skyscrapers brilliantly illuminated against the night sky. So many cars here!

"How beautiful the city looks! Michael, you're in New York," she said with a rush of love for her small son.

"I never seen such tall buildings!" Mattie Lou whispered in awe. "There ain't even one that tall in Richmond."

As Frank Leslie told them, the seven-room apartment looked down on Central Park, which tonight was a winter wonderland. Though it was furnished in the cluttered Victorian style that she detested, this did nothing to dispel Vicky's pleasure at being in New York.

While Mattie Lou whisked Michael off to bed, Vicky went into the kitchen to heat up the dinner prepared earlier by Althea, the woman Frank had hired to come in five afternoons a week to cook.

Soon, Mattie Lou emerged to report that Michael was already asleep.

"I'm going to bed, too, Miz Vicky," Mattie Lou announced, covering a yawn. "I'm so excited about being in New York."

"What about your dinner?" Vicky asked.

"I just want to sleep," she declared. "You all sleep well now."

Vicky relished being alone with Gary this way. It would be so wonderful to have a house—or an apartment—of their own. When they finished dinner, Gary insisted on helping her clear the table and wash and dry the dishes. She knew he was impatient to be alone with her in their bedroom.

"It's like I told you," he teased while they prepared for bed. "Our second honeymoon." He reached for the comb in her hand. "Let me do that." He swung her around with her back toward him and moved the comb over her lush, dark hair.

She stood demurely in one of the delicate pink chiffon-over-lace nightgowns that he liked her to wear, feeling the warmth of him against her back, aware of his arousal and her own. Then he tossed the comb onto the dresser and spun her around to face him.

"It scares me when I think I might have missed you that day in Paris," he whispered, his hands at the shoulders of her nightgown. "How would I have survived?"

She lifted her face to his while he slid the length of chiffon and lace to the floor and his hands fondled the provocative spill of her breasts. How could Lily talk the way she did about making love, as though she were doing Clark a favor?

"I love you so much," she whispered as he lifted her from her feet and carried her to the bed. Gary switched off the lamp and undressed in the dark, dropping his clothes to the floor in his impatience to be with her. The ornate brass bedstead seemed to give off a glow of light.

"I'm so lucky to have you." Gary's mouth was at her ear while his hands moved over her velvet skin. "I can endure anything as long as we have each other."

And then they abandoned talk to touch and kiss and then to merge into one. They clung together, reluctant to relinquish these precious minutes.

Their first morning in New York, Vicky awoke with a start. Her eyes sought the clock she'd set on the bedside table last night. It was late, she thought in alarm. Then she heard Gary talking in the dining room with Mattie Lou. He was up and dressed already!

The pleasing aromas of fresh coffee and bread drifted down the hall to the bedroom. She'd meant to get up early and make breakfast for Gary. She reached for her robe that lay across a slipper chair by the window, pulled it about her, and raced down the hall to the dining room.

"You let me sleep," she scolded Gary. "And I was going to make you breakfast."

"Mattie Lou has everything under control," he said soothingly.

Vicky smiled as Mattie Lou came into the dining room with a platter of golden scrambled eggs and another of fluffy biscuits. "Oh, Mattie Lou, everything looks so good!"

Gary ate with one eye on the Wellington clock that stood on the cluttered buffet.

"I don't want to be late my first day," he said anxiously.

"Mr. Leslie will understand," Vicky said. "I gathered he was surprised that you meant to come in today."

"What will you do?" he asked in sudden curiosity.

"I'll spend the morning with Michael while Mattie Lou straightens up the apartment," she said. "Then the three of us will have lunch. In the afternoon I'll take the *Métropolitain*—the subway," she corrected herself, "and go to see the big department stores that your mother told me about."

"By yourself?" He frowned in concern.

"Gary, do you know how many times I traveled by subway in Paris?" she jeered good-humoredly. "Alone."

"I worry about you going about alone in the city," he confessed, his eyes serious. "I told you about that article in the *Literary Digest*. The one that talked about the terrible crime wave in New York and Philadelphia and other large cities. Just recently a Fifth Avenue jeweler was murdered in broad daylight in his office. A man was robbed and murdered right at a city subway entrance. It went on and on."

"Gary, I'm not going to be a prisoner in this apartment," she said calmly.

"The deputy police commissioner in New York blames a lot of the crime wave on drugs. Addicts go out on the streets and rob and murder to keep up their habit."

"I'm just going downtown to see B. Altman and Lord & Taylor and Best and Company," Vicky said, "like thousands of other women will be doing today. Stop worrying about me," she ordered. "Anyhow, I can't run up staggering bills," she laughed. "We don't have a charge account in any of the stores up here."

She was astonished at her eagerness to see the city. After growing up in Petrograd, and living in Paris, she'd found herself for almost two years now in quiet little Bartonville, with only occasional trips to nearby Richmond—which was a beautiful city but hardly Petrograd or Paris or New York. Oh, yes, she was impatient to see this exciting, temporary home.

Chapter Fourteen

AS SHE HAD planned, Vicky left the apartment house immediately after lunch. Mattie Lou was already putting Michael down for his nap. The air was crisp and cold, the sky a brilliant blue. Last night's blanket of snow was quickly disappearing, though the barren winter tree branches in Central Park still bore a pristine, white edging.

Vicky walked west to Broadway and paused at the subway entrance. For an instant she remembered Gary's report of the man who was robbed and murdered recently at such a locale. But those who hurried down into the darkness of the subway seemed little different from those who'd made their way down into the Paris *Métropolitain*. For a few moments she was caught up in nostalgia, remembering Paris. While they were here, she would buy a small gift to send to Simone, she promised herself. That she could afford.

When the train pulled into the station at the next stop, Vicky impulsively joined the emerging throngs and followed them up the stairs and out into early afternoon sunlight. It was a glorious day. She would walk downtown to Fifth Avenue in the Thirties, where fabulous New York department stores were located.

At Fifty-seventh Street and Fifth Avenue she hesitated again, remembering how Gary and Mr. Leslie had talked last night about Carnegie Hall. Mr. Leslie said it was at the corner of Fifty-seventh and Seventh Avenue. After asking directions at a newsstand, she headed west toward this temple to music.

Arriving at her destination she stood in awe before the neo-Italian Renaissance structure. Here had appeared the greats of the musical world. Gary told her that Tchaikovsky himself had conducted his own works at the gala opening in 1891.

One day, she promised herself, she would sit in the audience at Carnegie Hall with Gary at her side and hear his symphony performed. That day would come. His talent mustn't go unrecognized.

She'd hoped that having the studio would make him less unhappy, allow him to compose. But he was frustrated that he could give so little time to his music. And now he'd be away from the piano for three months. But, she thought, he didn't have to be away from music.

With a surge of excitement, she read the billboards that announced coming events. Rachmaninoff was to appear at a piano recital on Tuesday evening, January 18. All at once her mind hurtled back through the years. She was ten years old and beside herself with excitement because tonight she would join the grown-ups at a concert in the Palace. Rachmaninoff was going to perform.

Knowing little about music, she'd nevertheless understood that Sergei Rachmaninoff was a great pianist. He was a composer, too, Mama had whispered to her while the guests applauded his performance. Gary felt such reverence for Rachmaninoff, she recalled. He'd be so happy to know that the maestro had escaped the Russian Revolution.

In sudden decision she opened her purse to see how much money she carried with her. When he left the apartment this morning, Gary had given her several bills. "*If you get lost, you can always take a taxi home.*"

She would go to the box office and buy a pair of tickets for the Rachmaninoff concert. Gary would be so surprised and pleased.

With the tickets tucked away in her purse, Vicky abandoned her plans to walk all the way downtown to the stores. That would be for another day. She reveled in being part of the city. It was sufficient today to walk without direction, feeling the beat of Manhattan. Each large city had its own rhythm, she thought, recalling her years in Petrograd and in Paris. New York was the city where Gary needed to be—where he could write his music, earn the success he deserved.

She longed to go down to Greenwich Village. Gary had talked so much about it in Paris. That was where musicians and artists and writers with very little money gathered to nurture their talents. That should be their ultimate destination. Like other young musicians and artists and writers, that should be Gary's world.

She mustn't rush him, she warned herself. He must make the choice to break away from Barton Tobacco—and Barton Manor. But while he was working at the New York office, she would try to help him find his way to the Greenwich Village way of life.

At the end of their first week in New York, Vicky decided to invite Mr. Leslie, a bachelor, to dinner the following Friday evening. Instinct told her that Gary was not quite comfortable with his current superior. He liked Mr. Leslie, but he was tense and self-conscious about the relationship.

"Are you sure this is a good idea?" Gary asked her on the eve of the dinner while she brought an arrangement of hothouse crocuses to the table. "I keep worrying that Frank's annoyed at having me in the office. He's so efficient, Vicky. I'll never learn what Papa expects him to teach me."

"He's not annoyed at having you there," Vicky said. "You need to relax with him, that's all. And I suspect that sitting with him at the dinner table will help." She smiled encouragingly.

Frank Leslie was almost diffident, Vicky thought when he arrived— bearing a cherished bottle of French champagne in this era of Prohibition. He knew what Daniel expected of him and was determined to fulfill that expectation.

During Althea's superb dinner, Vicky drew Frank out on various aspects of the tobacco industry. He reacted with pleasure to her show of interest. Vicky realized he was surprised that she knew as much as she did about the business. She felt a recurrent sense of guilt that she was fascinated by the processes that carried the simple tobacco leaf into the form of a finished cigarette, when Gary found the whole process to be totally uninteresting.

"There's no denying it," Frank said, smiling. "I've long been enchanted by everything to do with tobacco. It induces a special kind of commitment in people in the industry."

Frank talked with a messianic zeal about the future Daniel visualized for Barton Tobacco.

"The reason Camels has taken off the way it has is great merchandising," he pointed out. "The Camel blend isn't responsible for its sales. It's how they've merchandised their cigarette. You know," he mused, "tobacco people are like those in no other industry. The Indians worshipped tobacco as sacred. The Southern planters and manufacturers are pretty close to that."

Gary worshipped music. Finally he was living in New York—the mecca for musicians and composers. If he couldn't bring himself to walk out on his father's business now, he never would.

Instinct cautioned Vicky against rushing Gary. These first three or four weeks she would focus on helping him to relax, to enjoy the city. She bought tickets to more concerts, persuaded Gary to take her to the theater.

They saw Marilyn Miller in the hit Ziegfeld musical, *Sally*. They saw *The Passing Show of 1921*, with Marie Dressler at the Winter Garden. They saw Ina Claire in *The Gold Diggers*, and Ruth Chatterton in *Mary Rose*. After much hassle they were even able to get seats for the hit musical, *Irene*.

Vicky was enamored of the glitter of Times Square and the elegant movie palaces that lined Broadway—the Rivoli, the Strand, the Capitol, which was billed as the "world's largest and most beautiful theater." They saw Lionel Barrymore in *The Adventure*, Mary Pickford in *The Love Light*, and Ina Claire in *Polly With a Past*. Theater stars were being drawn into the Hollywood scene.

On some afternoons Vicky went downtown to roam about the elegant department stores. B. Altman, Lord & Taylor, Best and Company, and Franklin Simon were all within four blocks of one another. She shopped for a beautiful present for Simone and another for Sara—ever mindful that their funds were quite limited.

In B. Altman, a charming older saleswoman—delighted by her warmly expressed admiration for the store—told her a bit about its history.

"Mr. Altman—the nicest gentleman you can imagine," she said reverently, "died in 1913. He didn't live to see the store expand to the full city block he imagined. The original store was down on Sixth Avenue. When he began to build this one in 1905, there was a terrible outcry. Families in the neighborhood resented seeing a store rise among their fine mansions. But Mr. Altman got around that," she continued. "You noticed how beautiful the outside of the building is? Mr. Altman hid the store behind that Florentine mansion exterior. He didn't even put the name of the store outside."

On unseasonably warm mornings, Vicky took Michael to Central Park, where he was fascinated by the squirrels. She took him to see the ice skating in Central Park. She felt uncomfortable having Mattie Lou take on cleaning the apartment as well as caring for Michael much of the time, but Mattie Lou insisted she was having a wonderful time in New York.

Now Vicky began to study the "Help Wanted" columns in the newspapers. She was disappointed by the poor prospects of finding work as a translator. But she could be a clerk in a store like B. Altman, she told herself with shaky determination. She was shocked when she read the ads for apartments and realized what their apartment in the "unfashionable West Side" must be costing the company. But they didn't have to have a large apartment, she told herself. They'd find a little place down in Greenwich Village, the kind Gary used to dream about.

Reading in the *New York Times* about a production of *The Beggar's Opera* at a small playhouse in Greenwich Village, she suggested to Gary over dinner that they go to see it. Up until now he'd avoided a visit to Greenwich Village, though she had dropped wistful hints about exploring this unknown segment of Manhattan.

"Why do you want to see that old thing?" he chided humorously. "Do you know anything about it?"

"No," she confessed. "Except that a reviewer in some newspaper said it was very gay and 'with more charm, satire, and sweet tunes than anything that reached Broadway in six seasons.' "

"Sounds extravagant," Gary mused. "Actually it's a racy old opera written back in 1728. It was written by an English poet named John Gay. Every once in a while it gets revived."

"Why can't we go?" she asked. Why did Gary keep avoiding Greenwich Village? "You told me once that there were little cafes down there that were great fun and cheap."

"All right," he said after a moment. "We'll go. I'll call for tickets. I remember my roommate at college talking about a basement cafe called the Brevort. It's a place to go after the theater. Before the performance we'll find a little Italian restaurant with red-and-white checkered tablecloths and candles on the tables. And low prices."

On the Saturday they were to see *The Beggar's Opera*, they left the apartment in the late afternoon. Mattie Lou would give Michael his dinner and put him to bed. Vicky and Gary traveled to West Fourth

Street by subway, both caught up in an air of youthful festivity. The winter sun was setting by the time they walked from the subway station to Washington Square Park.

The late afternoon chill discouraged sitting on the park benches, but young people—and an occasional more mature man or woman—strolled in the dwindling daylight. Hand in hand Vicky and Gary walked around the perimeter of the park. The trees were winter-bare, gaunt, yet there was an intangible air of expectancy here, Vicky mused—as though greatness lurked in the months ahead for a fortunate few.

Vicky admired the elegant Greek revival houses on Washington Square North—most of them red brick with slate or metal roofs. Versed in Village lore, Gary told her that the beautiful marble Washington Arch had been designed by Stanford White, an architect murdered by millionaire playboy Harry Thaw back in 1906.

With an eye to curtain time at the playhouse, they left the Washington Square park area and strolled south in search of an inexpensive Italian restaurant. They settled for a little cafe off Grove Street. The narrow, crooked streets of the West Village reminded Vicky of sections of Paris.

Though the restaurant was nearly empty when they arrived, every candle-lit table was occupied when they rose to leave, and a line of prospective diners waited to be seated. The spirit here was young and ambitious and confident, Vicky thought. This was a different world from the one they inhabited up in the West Sixties.

As the reviewer had said, the production of *The Beggar's Opera* was gay and charming and rich with laughter. Vicky and Gary left the playhouse with an air of conviviality and walked up to Fifth Avenue and Eighth Street. The two-roomed basement Cafe Brevort was already thick with cigarette smoke and noisy with conversation. The atmosphere was heady, defiantly bohemian, with women dressed in odd necklaces, bracelets, and earrings, and flamboyantly colored smocks.

Vicky and Gary sipped wine and held hands under the table. Tonight she didn't feel like a married woman with a child. She was not even nineteen—younger than most of the girls seated at the tables around them. Gary was twenty-five. They were too young to deny their dreams.

By the time Vicky and Gary left the Brevort, Vicky was fighting yawns. On the northbound subway she dozed, her head on Gary's shoulder. But deep in her subconscious she knew that tomorrow she and Gary must talk about their future.

After Sunday morning breakfast Vicky went into the temporary nursery to play with Michael while Gary went down for the Sunday *Times*. Last night in the Village had been a beautiful time, she thought. Gary had enjoyed every moment. There was a special feeling down there that brought out a rare joyousness in him.

Now was the time, she told herself with mounting excitement, time to talk to Gary about their leaving Bartonville behind to start a new life here. They were young and strong—they could manage. She must make Gary understand that.

"Miz Vicky, why don't I take Michael over to the park for a little while? He sure loves the squirrels." Mattie Lou stood in the doorway with a bright smile. "It's real nice out."

"Fine, Mattie Lou," Vicky agreed. "But remember, it's cold. Don't stay too long."

"I'll bundle him up so he won't know it's cold," Mattie Lou chuckled and reached for Michael.

Vicky was grateful that Mattie Lou was taking Michael to the park. She and Gary would be alone in the apartment. They could talk freely.

She was standing by a living room window and watching Mattie Lou cross the street to the park with Michael when the doorbell rang. Her face lit up. That would be Gary with the Sunday *Times*. She hurried to the foyer to open the door for him.

"I saw Michael heading for the park," Gary said, his eyes full of love. "He's sure taking to the squirrels."

"Wasn't last night fun?" she asked softly.

"I enjoyed every minute." He placed an arm around her waist as they walked into the living room.

Gary dropped the newspaper onto the coffee table and began to thumb through the sections.

"I suppose you want to see all the ads for pretty dresses," he teased.

"We can't afford that," Vicky said good-humoredly. "I'd rather spend on concerts and theater tickets. Remember, we're hearing Toscanini and the La Scala Orchestra at the Hippodrome next Sunday."

"I won't forget," he promised, pulling out the music section of the *Times*.

"Gary, wouldn't it be wonderful if we could live here in New York?"

"That's not likely." His smile was wry, his eyes wary.

"Why can't it be?" she pursued. "You hate working for the company. And in Bartonville you have so little time for your music."

"I'd have less time here," he said.

"The time would mean more," she pressed. "You'd be with other composers and musicians, learning from them. You could find a job playing the piano instead of sitting behind a desk. You—"

"Vicky, no," he rejected, but his voice was deep with affection. "I know what you're trying to do for me, but it won't work. We have to think of Michael. In New York we'd live on the edge of catastrophe."

"It doesn't have to be that way," she said. "If you have a job playing at some restaurant—or a 'speak'—and I have a job as a salesgirl in maybe Macy's or Gimbel's, then one of us would always be home to take care of Michael. He's such a good baby—you'd have time to sit down at the piano and compose—"

"What piano?" he broke in.

"We'll buy a cheap secondhand piano. We'll live in a cheap apartment. We'll manage!"

"What makes you think I could get a job playing the piano?" he countered. "How long would our savings last?"

"I could get a job in a department store right away," she said.

"What would that pay? Do you know? I'll tell you. You'd probably earn twelve dollars a week—in New York that's starvation wages."

"You've told me yourself how many cheap apartments there are in the city," she said, reaching for the *Times*. "Let's see what's here." She pulled out the real estate section and pored over the listings. Her face showed her dismay at what she read.

"Five rooms at one thousand dollars," Gary pointed out, leaning over her shoulder. "New York is for the rich—unless they live in cheap furnished rooms. We can't move with Michael into something like that!"

"Here's a three-room apartment at University Place for $115."

"We couldn't afford that." Gary was grim. "Here's four rooms on Washington Square for $700."

"The cheap apartments aren't advertised," Vicky said. "But they're out there! You've told me so dozens of times!"

Gary sighed, pulled her close.

"Vicky, you don't want to face the truth." His face mirrored sadness and compassion and resignation. "We can't live with Michael in what we just might be able to afford. Would you want to take him into a hovel? Do you want to worry every time he sneezes that we won't be able to afford a doctor if he gets sick? Worry if we'll have the money for new shoes, warm clothes?"

"I don't want to see your talent waste away," she whispered.

"When we go back home, I'll make myself work at the music," he vowed. "I have that beautiful cottage now. I'll go there every night after dinner. It'll make a difference. I'll write something that satisfies me. And then I'll fight for a performance. Thank you for believing in me, my love." His voice was soft and caressing. "That's why I can survive."

Chapter Fifteen

VICKY WAS astonished to realize that she was glad to be back in Bartonville after the three months in New York. She loved the quiet beauty of the house and its surroundings. She loved the serenity—which had been missing from their lives in New York. She felt almost a traitor to Gary in this, yet she knew that he, too, enjoyed the slower pace of the South.

Gary was tense about the new responsibilities his father was foisting on him now.

"How much did he expect me to learn in three months?" he said desperately while they dressed for a small dinner party at Barton Manor.

"You've learned a lot about merchandising," she said, seeking to bolster his confidence. "You came home every night, and we talked about what had happened during the day."

"You learned more than I did—even though most of it was secondhand," Gary said sheepishly. "Frank said you have the business head of a man—and one twice your age."

"Why do people insist on thinking women can't understand anything about business? Except Frank," she conceded laughingly.

"Anyhow, nobody'll be talking business at dinner tonight," Gary said. In addition to family, two Richmond men—deeply involved in the gubernatorial race—and their wives, would be attending the dinner. Daniel wanted to manipulate the political situation.

"We'd better get downstairs," Vicky said. "Your mother looks on us as co-hosts."

It would not be a gay evening, she surmised. The conversation would revolve around state politics. Lily and Stephanie would be bored and chatter between themselves about clothes and parties. But Daniel had masterminded the dinner to deal with points he wanted to get across to the two men.

Vicky was relieved when their guests left. At the first opportunity Stephanie escaped upstairs to her own room. Daniel insisted that Gary and Vicky join him in the library for a glass of wine.

"I'm thinking about cutting wages the beginning of next month," Daniel announced with a glint of triumph in his eyes. "That'll up the annual profits a sizeable chunk."

"How can you do that?" Gary was startled. "Tobacco workers are the lowest paid in the state."

"Down in Winston-Salem, Reynolds just announced he's cutting salaries by twenty percent. Why shouldn't I do the same?" Daniel said.

"That's terrible!" Vicky gazed at him in dismay. The tobacco growers were suffering from dropping prices, and now the manufacturers wanted to see the workers suffering, too. "How can you lower wages at a time when you've said yourself that profits are soaring?"

"Because I'm in the driver's seat," Daniel pointed out complacently. "It's smart business."

"No, it isn't." All at once Vicky knew how to fight this. In her mind she remembered Frank's eloquent summation about the value of advertising and publicity. Now she dropped her voice to a tone of quiet confidence. She ignored Gary's pantomimed plea for silence. "First of all, if you cut wages, the workers will be angry and unhappy. Quality will drop. Production will fall off. But if you *don't* cut wages—when Reynolds does—then Barton Tobacco can pick up publicity that money can't buy." She saw the glint of interest in Daniel's eyes. "You'll be showing up Barton Tobacco as the humane company that protects its workers at the very time the Camels people are inflicting suffering on theirs. You'll condemn Reynolds for their actions," Vicky pushed ahead, exuding excitement. "Talk about never subjecting *your* workers to such tactics. The newspapers and magazines will play it up. Barton Tobacco will be the talk of the industry!"

Daniel's eyes narrowed as he absorbed what Vicky had said.

"Damn it, out of the mouths of babes comes pure gold," he chuckled, and Vicky clenched her teeth to keep back a furious retort. "We'll do it! It'll be a front-page story in tomorrow's *Bartonville Herald*. Our ad agency will see to it that other newspapers and national magazines pick it up." His face exuded triumph. "Reynolds will turn green."

Stephanie was pleased that she and Lily had persuaded Clark to accompany them for a five-day visit to New York, yet it rankled her that Lily seemed so smug at having a husband in attendance while she herself had to draft Mr. Leslie from her father's New York office to be her escort. Mr. Leslie was weird, the way he kept talking about how smart Vicky was. Didn't he know women weren't supposed to be smart? That killed their sex appeal.

Still, she relished these runaway trips to an exciting city like New York. The four of them sat at a table in a fashionable "club"—as the speakeasies preferred to be known—on the ground floor of a brownstone in the West Fifties. She knew that Mr. Leslie was uncomfortable being here. But he wanted to accommodate Papa's family, she told herself with a gloating smile, so he'd agreed to come with them.

It was ridiculous that there wasn't even one speakeasy in Bartonville or Richmond. Folks had their liquor delivered to their house or office. Some made their own in their basements, Papa said.

At intervals Stephanie's eyes met those of a young man at the next table. He was so good-looking, she thought with a familiar stirring low within her pelvis. He was with a group celebrating somebody's birthday, she gathered—but he was bored. At cautious moments she allowed herself to smile at him.

When Mr. Leslie excused himself to make a phone call, she knew this was her chance to make contact. She reached into her purse for the tiny pen she always carried and wrote down her name and the Plaza Hotel phone number on a scrap of paper. Now she demurely murmured to Lily and Clark—arguing about how late they would stay here—that her make-up needed freshening.

"Shall I come with you?" Lily offered.

"No need," Stephanie said and left the table. Passing the table of the young man who'd caught her interest, she managed to prod the scrap of paper into his hand while their eyes met for a heated moment. He'd call for sure, she promised herself.

Lily sulked when Stephanie agreed with Clark that they should return early to the hotel.

"We're tired," Stephanie said. "We had to get up so early to catch the train this morning."

Back at their suite at the Plaza Stephanie settled herself on her bed with a copy of *Vogue* and waited for the good-looking man at the "speak" to call. When she was about to dismiss this venture as futile, the phone rang.

"Hello." She contrived to sound both sweet and sexy.

"Stephanie?" a male voice inquired somewhat self-consciously.

"Yes," she drawled. "Who're you?"

"Jeffrey," he told her. "Jeffrey Nelson. I got away from the 'speak' as soon as I could."

"What do you do when you're not at 'speaks'?" she asked.

"I'm interning at Bellevue Hospital," he explained. "That is, for now. In June I start my residency at a hospital down in Virginia."

"Where in Virginia?" she demanded avidly.

"Richmond," he explained. "You're from the South," he suddenly recognized. "Your voice drips magnolias and honeysuckle."

"I come from Bartonville," she told him. "About nine miles out of Richmond." This was perfect!

"What about dinner tomorrow night?" he pursued and hesitated. "Something down in the Village. Interns' salaries don't allow for fancy places like tonight. That was a party."

"Pick me up in the hotel lobby at seven-thirty," she ordered. "Oh, I'll tell my brother-in-law you went to college with a girlfriend's brother. He might not understand."

At seven-thirty sharp Stephanie was down in the Plaza lobby. For the first time in her life, she wasn't late for a date. She was aware of furtive male glances at the shortness of the skirt of her fashionably low-waisted bright yellow taffeta dress. She knew her sheer black silk stockings emphasized the length of leg on display.

She tapped impatiently with one high-heeled brocade sandal. Where the devil was Jeffrey? Then she spied him striding through the lobby in her direction. Oh, he was much better looking than Clark, she gloated. A lawyer was dull. A doctor sounded exciting.

They took a subway to Greenwich Village. She'd never been in a subway before. It was not her favorite mode of transportation, she decided; but for tonight it would do. It was clear that Jeffrey knew

his way around this part of town. He piloted her south toward a favorite Italian restaurant, his arm about her waist, his eyes bright with
promise.

She pretended to be charmed by the tiny Italian restaurant. The
food, she admitted grudgingly, was good, the atmosphere acceptable—though she'd prefer dinner at the Plaza or the St. Regis. But
Jeffrey Nelson was unlike any man she'd known. Maybe because
she'd only gone out with Southern boys, Southern men, she corrected
herself. She was twenty-one years old. She was a woman now. She
could even vote—not that she'd bother.

She wasn't surprised when—while they dallied over espresso and
he talked about the grimness of interning at Bellevue—he suggested
they go up to his apartment to listen to his jazz records.

"Do you like jazz?" he asked. "I've got records of the Original
Dixieland Jazz Band," he said reverently.

"We'll go up to your place," she said. But not to listen to his old
jazz records.

Jeffrey lived in the tiniest two-room apartment Stephanie had ever
seen. If you fell down drunk in the middle of the living room, she
thought, your head would be in the bedroom.

"I don't have anything to drink," he apologized, his arm about her
waist as she gazed about the closet-sized living room.

"Do you have a condom?" she asked, lifting her face to his in
provocative invitation.

"I don't think so," he stammered. Then his eyes lighted. "But you
don't have to worry—"

"I have one in my vanity," she interrupted, strolling into the un-
lighted bedroom. All the girls in their crowd made a point of that, or
at least the smart ones.

"Then we're in business," he murmured hotly and reached to pull
her close.

"Wait," she said after a moment. "I don't want to get my dress
all wrinkled."

She heard Jeffrey's involuntary grunt as she pulled the dress over
her head and tossed it across the chair. She stood there in black lace
teddy, with an expanse of milk-white skin between teddy and black
silk stockings and felt a surge of pleasure. He was so excited!

"Come here, baby," he ordered, his mouth opening as it reached
for hers.

She closed her arms around his shoulders with a sense of power. She was driving him right up the wall!

He stripped away the teddy in one swift gesture and lifted her onto the bed. In the spill of light from the living room she saw the passion in his eyes. This was going to be sensational, she promised herself.

She murmured encouragement as his hands fondled her breasts, then moved down to her hips. His mouth tugged at a nipple. She frowned when he lifted himself above her in sudden impatience and began to probe between her thighs. She really liked the other part best, but men never understood that.

She whimpered softly when he thrust with increasing intensity. Most times she just pretended, but this was different. Her whimper became a low, urgent cry. Her hands dug into his shoulders while they moved together in explosive passion.

"Oh, wow!" she gasped, reluctant to relinquish the heady excitement of those last explosive moments. "Wow!"

She'd marry this one, she told herself complacently. It was weird how things happened! He'd be a resident at a Richmond hospital. It'd be so easy.

Wouldn't Papa be impressed when she was a doctor's wife? He said all lawyers were crooks—but Lily said Papa meant to see Clark on the Bartonville City Council in another three or four years. Eventually he meant for Clark to be mayor. Sure, she thought arrogantly— Clark was married to a Barton.

What would Papa do for Jeffrey? He was always saying the town needed a real hospital. Maybe Papa would build one—and appoint Jeffrey chief-of-staff. Not right away—but before Clark was elected mayor.

In August the family became caught up in Stephanie's engagement to Jeffrey. Vicky knew that Daniel was disappointed that Stephanie was not marrying a Virginian but a first-generation American from New York City—the son of immigrant parents who'd moved doggedly into the middle class. Vicky was aware of some temporary hostility between Lily and Stephanie. She'd heard Lily scold Stephanie: "How could you marry beneath yourself—like Gary?"

Nevertheless, a splashy late January wedding was planned. Daniel promised to build a house on the family estate for Stephanie and Jeffrey, close to the one occupied by Lily and Clark. Again, Vicky was aware of Stephanie's barely veiled resentment of the fact that one day Gary and Vicky would own Barton Manor.

While Vicky disliked Clark, she found Jeffrey a warm, likeable man. She suspected he was pleased at the prospect of living the leisurely life of an upper-class Virginian—his status through marriage— yet he was candid about his dedication to his profession.

Then Stephanie's engagement and approaching wedding took a backseat when Lily announced she was pregnant. She basked in her father's attention. He hovered about his "little girl" constantly, ordering her to give him a second grandson. By the time she approached her fifth month—and decided she looked too awful to be her sister's matron of honor—she vowed she'd never get pregnant again.

"Clark never gets near me again after this baby is born, unless he's wearing a condom," she announced to a startled gathering at a baby shower.

Vicky watched hopefully through the passing months for signs that Gary was less resentful of his job, more satisfied with his music. He was spending many of his evenings at the cottage—which his father preferred to ignore. He talked passionately to Vicky about the symphony he was trying to write. It had evolved through his war experiences, especially those final agonizing weeks at the front lines in France when he was surrounded by death and destruction.

"Vicky, it's going so slowly," he complained. "But here and there I hear bits that I like."

"You'll finish it," Vicky assured him. "And it'll be wonderful."

He wouldn't allow her to hear what he had written of his symphony so far. But at regular intervals he took her and Sara to the cottage to hear him play because he knew how much they enjoyed his "little concerts." Daniel always pretended to be unaware of the existence of the cottage.

Stephanie's wedding at the end of January was a major social event of the season. After the ceremony Stephanie and Jeffrey left for a three-week honeymoon at The Breakers in Palm Beach. Yet, even on Stephanie's wedding day Lily managed to be the center of drama. After a minor fall down several stairs her doctor insisted she remain in bed until she gave birth.

Early in March, Lily went into labor. Amid screaming declarations that she would never go through childbirth again, Lily was informed by the attending physician that her newborn child was a girl.

Daniel was disappointed at not being presented with a second grandson but rejected Lily's insistence that she'd never give him another grandchild.

"My little girls will give me at least two or three grandsons between them," he predicted. "Why else am I building a tobacco empire?"

Three months after Lily's daughter Kara—the image of Sara—was born, her mother and her aunt Stephanie were preparing to leave for a vacation in Paris.

"After what I went through I deserve it," Lily said airily.

Vicky assumed that Daniel was paying for the trip for his "two little girls." Neither husband could afford such an extravagance. Vicky herself dreamt wistfully of a trip to Paris, a chance to see Simone—but that seemed unlikely to happen.

Both Vicky and Sara were shocked that Lily was leaving her infant daughter in the hands of servants.

"I know you, Mama," Lily cooed when Sara reproached her for this. "You'll keep an eye on Kara for me. I just have to get away. And we won't be traveling on a 'dry ship.' " She giggled in anticipation. "We'll be drinking the minute we're beyond the three-mile limit—and they unlock the liquor closet."

Vicky knew that Sara worried about Lily and Stephanie in the changing times of the very early Twenties. Both were enraptured by the postwar changes. Like most small-town Americans, Vicky and Gary were not part of the new scene. They were not guzzling bathtub gin, were not fascinated by Freud's sexual theories, nor were they part of the new hedonism adopted by the most publicized of their generation—which Lily and Stephanie were determined to emulate.

In the coming months Vicky and Sara were shocked by the shorter and shorter skirts being worn by Lily and Stephanie and their friends. Sara forced herself to be silent because, after all, her daughters were married women now. She confided to Vicky that she was upset about their frequent trips to New York and their involvement in the new world being called Cafe Society.

Lily and Stephanie talked condescendingly to Vicky about the fascinating speakeasies in New York with their circular, revolving bars and their lush decor. They argued about the superiority of one cocktail over another. Lily was partial to the Goldfish—concocted of Goldwasser, gin, and French vermouth, while Stephanie praised the Zani

Zaza—a mixture of gin, apricot brandy, the white of an egg, lemon juice, and grenadine. They gloried in their new monthly allowance from their father, who was even more generous due to Barton Tobacco's soaring profits. Though this arrangement was supposed to be secret, Lily made sure it was leaked to Vicky.

"Wouldn't you think Clark and Jeffrey would make the girls behave?" Sara demanded of Vicky in exasperation. But Vicky suspected she knew the answer: like the portion of their generation written about in magazines and newspapers, Lily and Stephanie would do whatever they pleased.

When Stephanie announced in mid-1923 that she was pregnant, Daniel predicted this third grandchild would be a son. Now there was a fresh competition between Lily and Stephanie. To produce a son would be a personal triumph.

Gary grimly continued at his job at Barton Tobacco, clinging to the hours he could spend composing—but Vicky sensed his growing dissatisfaction.

"Composing isn't like chopping off cigarettes," he told her in constant frustration. "The work isn't developing right—I have too little time to give to it."

Still, Vicky knew Gary would not walk out on his job. He was afraid to throw away the security their lifestyle assured Michael. At Gary's urging—and surprisingly with no rejection from Daniel—Vicky began to spend three or four hours a day at Gary's office. Supposedly she was Gary's secretary. Another desk was moved into his large corner office on the floor that housed the crew of executives that ran Barton Tobacco.

Gary tried to be efficient, to do what was required of him, Vicky conceded, but his mind just wasn't attuned to business. He ruefully teased that she was the businessman his father wanted him to be.

When Daniel decided that it was time Gary acquired an understanding of buying tobacco, it was tacitly agreed that Vicky would accompany him to auctions.

"He knows I'll mess up," Gary told Vicky when they were en route to his first buying deal. "I'll be there, but you make the decisions."

For Vicky, the auctions were exhilarating. Through the years she had absorbed much of what Daniel had expounded on buying tobacco leaf. And while he didn't comment on what she and Gary bought, she sensed that he was pleased. Of course, Gary told her with ironic amusement, his father would never admit to knowing it was Vicky who was making the decisions.

Early in the new year—1924—Daniel announced that Gary was to go to New York for ten days to sit in on conferences with the company's new advertising agency.

"Take Vicky with you," he said casually. "Have her sit in with you and Frank on the conferences about the new campaign. So many women are smoking these days. Let's hear the woman's viewpoint."

Neither she nor Gary smoked, Vicky thought with amusement. Still, she looked forward to a trip to New York. And there was no question in her mind—or Daniel's—that Michael and Mattie Lou would accompany Gary and herself.

Along with Michael and Mattie Lou, Vicky and Gary arrived in New York on a gray February afternoon. Michael had been thrilled by the train trip. Now he gazed with wonder about the Roman temple that was Pennsylvania Station.

Vicky was delighted with the suite Frank Leslie had reserved for them at the fashionable Plaza.

"Tomorrow morning," she told Michael as he gazed out a window at the vast sweep of Central Park, "Mattie Lou will take you to play in the park. We'll buy a bag of peanuts so you can feed the squirrels. Would you like that?"

"Yeah!" His face was radiant in anticipation.

"Should we call Frank and find out about our appointment schedule?" Gary asked tensely.

"I'll call," she offered, knowing he dreaded these meetings. "And they won't be too bad."

Vicky and Gary were delighted to learn that they would have most of their evenings free. Tonight they would have dinner at the hotel with Frank, and one other evening there was a dinner meeting planned with account executives from their ad agency. The other nights, Vicky resolved, they'd go to concerts or to the theater.

At breakfast the following morning in their suite, Gary spied an ad in the *New York Tribune* for a concert at Aeolian Hall.

"Paul Whiteman and his orchestra are giving a concert on Lincoln's birthday." Gary's voice was electric. "At three o'clock in the afternoon. We don't have any meetings on that day, do we? It's a legal holiday."

"We're clear," Vicky confirmed. "Let's go over and pick up tickets this morning.'' She scanned the newspaper—folded back to the ad—which Gary passed across the table to her. The ad announced that Paul Whiteman and his Palais Royal Orchestra were presenting ''An Experiment in Modern Music,'' assisted by Zez Confrey and George Gershwin. Tickets were from 55¢ up to $2.20.

''Confrey wrote 'Kitten on the Keys,' didn't he?'' Vicky asked.

''That's right. I remember reading about the concert—before I knew we'd be here in the city. It's a special project of Whiteman's. He's invited a distinguished panel to pass judgment on 'What is American Music?', including Sergei Rachmaninoff, Jascha Heifetz, Efrem Zimbalist, and Alma Gluck. Irving Berlin is writing a syncopated tone poem. Victor Herbert will present an American Suite, and a musician named George Gershwin is going to play his own jazz concerto.''

In the course of the next few days they saw two chamber music concerts and stage performances, but Vicky knew Gary waited eagerly for the Paul Whiteman concert. He searched the entertainment pages of the newspapers for comments.

''Whiteman's increased his orchestra from nine men to twenty-three. Everybody important in music will be there.'' Gary's voice was hushed. ''He's making musical history.''

On the day of the concert snow began to fall shortly after noon. Still, as Vicky and Gary emerged from their taxi at just before three, it was clear that the snow was not discouraging concert goers. Crowds were filing into Aeolian Hall on West Forty-third Street.

Inside the auditorium Vicky and Gary made their way down the aisle to their seats. The chatter that filled the air was vibrant with expectation.

''Gary, there's Rachmaninoff,'' Vicky whispered in excitement. She remembered hearing him play a dozen years ago at the Veronsky Palace, remembered the Rachmaninoff concert at Carnegie Hall they attended three years ago.

''Up front, Vicky.'' Gary's face was aglow. ''Walter Damrosch and Leopold Stokowski.''

Now they studied with candid astonishment the array onstage. In addition to the pianos and every kind of wind and percussion instrument, they saw a collection of frying pans, large tin utensils, and a speaking trumpet. The lighting picked up the golden sheen of the brass instruments and spilled it against an Oriental backdrop.

"It certainly is a modern music concert," Vicky joked.

Consulting the program, Gary pointed out that the frying pans and similar "instruments" were probably to be used by the five-piece band opening the concert with jazz of an earlier decade.

Now every seat was filled. Standees lined the rear of the auditorium. A silence fell over the audience as the opening number—a lively rendition of "The Livery Stable Blues," with barnyard sound effects—began. After this, the Palais Royal orchestra—the musicians all wearing gray spats—came onstage to give a "melodious jazz" treatment to "Mama Loves Papa."

As the program continued, Vicky reminded herself that this was a musical experiment. Still, she realized that she was not alone in being restive. The crowded auditorium was hot, despite the snowy weather, and the program was uninspired, monotonous. Vicky spied standees slipping out through the exits.

After intermission, it was clear that the audience had thinned. Not even Victor Herbert's *Suite of Serenades*—written especially for the concert—created much excitement. Vicky glanced surreptitiously at her program. There were twenty-three numbers—only two more, she realized with guilty relief.

She smiled reassuringly at Gary, who was striving to conceal his disappointment. He'd expected so much of today's performance.

"The pianist named Gershwin is next," she whispered. He was to play his own composition, she recalled.

George Gershwin walked briskly across the stage, sat down at the piano, and glanced for a moment at Whiteman. The conductor lifted his baton, gave the downbeat. The audience was electrified by an exuberant and unexpected clarinet solo that wailed to the heart of every listener.

Soon Gershwin's hands were flying over the keyboard, his body moving in a natural counterpoint. Everyone on the stage performed with an urgency that brought a hushed expectancy over the audience. Every listener sat transfixed, caught up in Gershwin's *Rhapsody in Blue*.

When *Rhapsody* ended, the audience was silent for a few seconds, then burst into tumultuous applause. Most of the audience—including Victor Herbert, Vicky noticed—leapt to their feet, continuing to applaud, cheering wildly. Again and again, Gershwin was recalled to the stage.

Clutching one of Vicky's hands in his, Gary drew her with him through the packed aisle, out of the auditorium into the street. He was silent, too emotionally wrought up for speech. They emerged into the sharp chill of the late afternoon and walked toward Fifth Avenue.

"We've witnessed the birth of a classic," he finally broke his silence. "Gershwin will be one of the greats of this century."

"I'm so glad we were in New York for this," Vicky said tenderly.

"Do you mind if we walk back to the hotel? You're not too cold?" Gary asked.

"I'm fine," she told him.

For much of the evening—except for his play time with Michael—Gary was unnaturally quiet. Vicky understood he was still caught up in the magic of the Gershwin music. He was impatient to see the reviews.

Early next morning—after a night of restless sleep—Gary rushed from their suite and downstairs to buy the morning newspapers. He was impatient to see the reviews of the concert. Over breakfast in their sitting room, he read the reviews to Vicky. He was alternately jubilant and angry.

Olin Downes hailed Gershwin's work—"this composition shows extraordinary talent." Gabriel of the *Sun* wrote that, "Mr. Gershwin has an irrepressible pack of talent." Deems Taylor wrote in the *World* that the Rhapsody is "genuine jazz music, not only in its scoring but in its idiom," and added that it "hinted at something new, something that had not hitherto been said in music." But then there were some, such as Lawrence Gilman of the *Tribune*, who derided Gershwin's talent, calling it "lifeless, stale, inexpressive."

"How dare anybody say one derogatory thing about the *Rhapsody*!" Gary railed. "Oh, how I wish I might have written that." His voice dropped to a reverent whisper. "And no greater compliment could any composer offer."

Not until late in the evening—with Gary suddenly depressed—did Vicky realize the torment that had imprisoned him.

"I'll never write a *Rhapsody in Blue*," he told her, his voice taut. "It's over for me, Vicky. I learned that this afternoon. Oh, I won't stop composing—it's an obsession with me. But from this day forward it'll be just for my own diversion. Somewhere along the line I missed the boat. No major orchestra will ever play a Gary Barton composition. I'll never make musical history."

"Gary, don't say that." All at once she felt encased in ice. "You're just at the beginning of your musical career."

"I have a small talent, Vicky. It's better to recognize that now than to fight a futile, endless battle. Sitting there this afternoon I knew I could never soar to the heights that a George Gershwin will reach. And anything less won't do for me. But it's not the end of the world," he said with spurious serenity. "I have you and Michael. I don't need anything else."

Chapter Sixteen

VICKY FOUGHT to pull herself out of painful despair. She knew she must accept Gary's decision that from this time forward his music was to be no more than a personal diversion. It was as though part of him had died.

On Sundays he went to the cottage. He was writing music to Michael's best-loved nursery rhymes.

"My favorite audience," Gary laughed when he and Vicky brought Michael to the cottage to hear the latest. "My favorite critic."

Daniel was elated when Stephanie gave birth to a son in March. He was baptized Douglas Warren Thompson and immediately called Doug. It was amazing, Vicky thought tenderly, how much tiny Kara and Doug resembled each other. They might have been brother and sister.

Lying in Gary's arms after they had made love on a hot May night, Vicky was pleased that he still found such joy with her in moments like these. The only times she felt he was fully alive was when they made love and when he was with Michael.

Perhaps, she thought with sudden eagerness, it was time for them to have a second child. Perhaps then Gary would be able to accept this compromise with life he'd forced on himself. Still, she was upset that he had abandoned his symphony. He had a wonderful gift. It shouldn't be squandered.

Vicky watched impatiently for the signs that she was pregnant. She

was filled with happiness when she realized she was carrying her
second child. As with Michael, Gary was solicitous, hoping for a
daughter but assuring her a second son would be most welcome. He
worried that she insisted on coming into the office when she moved
into the late months of her pregnancy, even while he was relieved that
she was there.

"I like being here with you, Gary," she insisted.

"You like being part of the business," he told her, and Vicky was
startled that he realized this. "It's a fascinating game to you."

"It—it's kind of a challenge," she admitted, unsettled by Gary's
sharpness. It was almost a gentle accusation, she thought. "I'm not
the party type," she said cajolingly. "I'd rather be at the office with
you than dashing about to volunteer luncheons and bridge parties and
mah-jongg clubs."

A week after Doug's first birthday Vicky gave birth to a second
son, to be named Adam in memory of Daniel's father. Tiny Adam—
even at birth—was a replica of his paternal grandfather. Daniel
crowed about this constantly, infuriating his two daughters. But the
resemblance was remarkable.

"My God, Sara, it's like looking into a mirror," Vicky heard him
say endlessly.

He was devoted to Michael because this first grandchild promised
him a continuation of his empire, but it was clear already in those first
weeks after Adam's birth that Daniel saw Adam as his true successor.
Vicky found this disturbing. She was grateful for the Stutz-two-seater
he gave her on Adam's birth, though she knew that the reason for this
had little to do with sentiment but was designed to expand her business activities. Now she was in the office eight hours a day.

As with Michael, Vicky told Sara that Adam was not to be baptized.
While she was not publicly practicing her faith, she maintained within
the household that she was Jewish, as were her sons. In silence she
rebelled against the restraint placed upon her by Daniel—even while
she remembered her father's fears about being a Jew in an intolerant
world.

But for all the talk about anti-Semitism, Jews worshipped openly
in Richmond. Beth Ahabah, which boasted of a membership of two
hundred seventy-five, catered to Reform Jews of mainly German or-
igin. Richmond Jews of more traditional thinking worshipped at the
Russian Sir Moses Montefiore synagogue or the Polish Kenesseth Is-

rael. But Vicky Barton—born Viktoria Gunsburg—worshipped within the confines of her bedroom, she taunted herself.

Three weeks after Adam's birth she drove herself to the Hebrew cemetery. She found her way to the fence-enclosed plot reserved for Jewish Confederate soldiers. Often she remembered her brief encounter here with Mr. Ginsberg. As she approached the site of his brother's grave, she was startled to see a new grave with only a marker.

Her heart pounding, she leaned forward to read the name. Mr. Ginsberg had died; he was buried beside his brother. In the Jewish tradition a headstone would not be in place until a year after his death. Tears filled her eyes. It was as though she had lost a friend. She wished that she had seen more of Mr. Ginsberg, but that would have meant being part of the Jewish community of Richmond.

The Ku Klux Klan was spreading into a formidable organization—its membership now over four million. Gary—who hated all forms of bigotry—was becoming embittered. Even as a small child, he'd confided to Vicky, he had been uncomfortable with the treatment of the Negroes. He pointed out that Bartonville—like Richmond—was proud of its good relations with their colored folks.

"Remember, the Negro Elks are holding their national convention in Richmond this year. It'll be the first in the South. They expect eighty thousand uniformed Elks to march in the parade. Segregation ordinances will be suspended during the convention," he said. "No riding in the back of the buses, no restrictions in the restaurants. I hear that white residents on the parade route are inviting Negroes to watch from their front porches." He paused. "That's a start."

A month after Adam's birth Vicky returned to the office. She wanted to enlist the support of other company executives in her current battle with Daniel over installing air-conditioning at the factories. By now all the Reynolds facilities, she'd managed to learn, were equipped with what was being labeled "manufactured weather." She brought the subject up at the next executive meeting. Immediately Daniel began to shake his head.

"We've got the figures on the Reynolds operation," one executive brought up tentatively.

"It's expensive and bad business," Daniel said. "We all know Vicky's ideas about the employees," he jeered. "She'd like to send them all down to Palm Beach for a month in winter and to Bar Harbor for a month in summer."

"Air-conditioning saves money," Vicky said with her usual enforced calm. "I've got the figures to substantiate this."

"You spend all that money on electricity and you're saving?" Daniel shot back.

"Reynolds didn't do it for their employees," Vicky told Daniel. "Air-conditioning reduced the dust down to a minimum. It cuts back on waste. I had a man involved with Camels do some sleuthing for me." She saw the glint of interest in Daniel's eyes. "Here—" She thrust a sheaf of papers toward him. "Here's the kind of savings we can expect." There was no point in talking about comfortable working conditions. Daniel was concerned only with the bottom line: *What do we save?*

Adam was a fretful baby—totally unlike Michael. Frequently Vicky felt guilty that she was not constantly at his side, but Sara scolded her for this.

"Every child is a little different," Sara told her. "And Mattie Lou is always right there beside Adam every minute you're away, or I am. He's surrounded by love and attention."

Sara was pleased, Vicky thought lovingly, that this year the first woman governor in American history had taken office. Nellie Ross of Wyoming. Sara was appalled by F. Scott Fitzgerald's new novel, *The Great Gatsby*, and the people it portrayed.

"I don't know what's happening in this country," she told Vicky. "But I know I don't like it."

Vicky knew she worried about the lifestyle favored by her two daughters. It seemed to Vicky that she and Sara saw more of Kara and Doug than their mothers did. They were either running up to New York or down to Palm Beach—or to Southampton or Newport or Bar Harbor when the hot weather descended on Bartonville. While neither husband was sufficiently affluent to support this dashing about the country, their father enjoyed constantly enlarging their "allowances."

"They're not Daniel's 'little girls' anymore," Sara fretted. "Giving them all that money doesn't change the situation."

But nothing seemed to be enough to satisfy Lily and Stephanie. At a dinner at Barton Manor in celebration of Daniel's fifty-eighth birthday, Lily sulked about the so-called modesty of her house.

"We live like we were poor," Lily complained. "Barbara Lee down in Richmond just had a whole room brought over from a chateau in France. They have a phone system set up so there's a phone in every room—and they have thirty-four rooms.''

"You don't need thirty-four rooms,'' Sara said caustically.

"Next time we're in Paris we ought to pick up some paintings,'' Stephanie said. "And I keep telling Jeffrey he ought to invest in the stock market. He knows Clark made a killing last month,'' she added before Lily could point this out yet again.

"I don't trust buying on margin.'' Daniel shook his head in disapproval. "You don't buy unless you've got enough stashed away to bail yourself out if troubles come up—and that's not the way the game's being played these days.''

"Oh, there's Adam wailing his head off again,'' Lily said. "He's always carrying on.''

"Sit down, Vicky,'' Sara ordered as Vicky pushed back her chair. "He's just spoiled to death. He thinks he has to be the center of attention every minute. You just stay here and finish your dinner.''

Before his first birthday Vicky realized that Adam was not the warm, sweet child that Michael was. Kara and Doug, too, were loveable little ones. She fretted that there might be a medical cause for Adam's querulousness, his fits of baby rage.

"He's a healthy baby,'' Jeffrey comforted Vicky after she had consulted a New York pediatrician. "Just of a different temperament from Michael.''

"I can't help worrying about him,'' Vicky admitted. "I keep on thinking I'm doing something wrong.''

"Don't punish yourself for things that aren't your fault,'' Jeffrey said, his eyes bitter.

Vicky suspected that his marriage was not going as well as he would have liked. She knew he resented Stephanie's frequent absences from home, and she remembered the caustic jibes Stephanie had thrown at him on occasion about their financial state. Stephanie was pushing him to set up a practice in Richmond where he'd have a chance to attract affluent patients. He enjoyed his practice in Bartonville, liked serving the community.

In May of 1927 the whole world was electrified by news of Charles Lindbergh's nonstop flight from Roosevelt Field, New York City, to Le Bourget Field near Paris. He'd traveled three thousand six hundred miles in thirty-three and a half hours. At Le Bourget Field he was welcomed by one hundred thousand cheering Frenchmen. The following October Lindbergh was to fly to Richmond in the *Spirit of St. Louis* for the dedication of the city's new Richard Evelyn Byrd Municipal Airport.

The citizens of Richmond and the surrounding area threw themselves into making this an historic visit. Daniel arranged for a table at the dinner given for Lindbergh at the elegant Jefferson Hotel, considered by many to be the finest in the South.

Michael was fascinated by the story of Lindbergh's flight, begged his grandfather to repeat every detail available to the public. Daniel took him to the airport so he could see the planes at the new municipal field at close range.

"I'm gonna fly an airplane when I grow up," he told his mother with determination when Daniel brought him home from the airport. "How old will I have to be to learn?"

While Michael was earnest about learning to fly, he was also absorbed in Gary's efforts now to teach him to play the piano. Vicky was ambivalent about the Sunday morning sessions when Gary took Michael to the cottage. She cherished the prospect of Michael's learning to play, but to her this was a disturbing indication that Gary had erased all thoughts of a career as a composer from his mind. She'd harbored a hope that the charming little bits of music he wrote for Michael from time to time would blossom into the symphony that had haunted him for so long.

Gary was pleased to see a real talent in Michael, but he was overwhelmed when Doug—four years Michael's junior—clamored to join Gary and Michael for their Sunday morning music session. Doug had heard Michael at the piano in the rarely used music room at Barton Manor and had been captivated by the sounds.

"You wouldn't believe Doug's ear for music," Gary told Vicky. "He's a baby, but if Michael hits one wrong note, he knows it!"

"Don't let on to Stephanie," she warned wryly.

"When does Stephanie see Doug?" Gary's voice was caustic. "You and Mama are raising him—not his mother."

Both Vicky and Sara found pleasure in bringing the children together. Michael—the oldest by two years—was the leader. Kara adored Michael. Together the two of them were tender and solicitous toward Doug, the next youngest of the four.

The three of them tolerated Adam, but by the time of his third birthday they began to rebel. He fought viciously, biting and scratching. Once he tore a gash in his mother's arm. Only Daniel seemed to have control over Adam.

"Daniel spoils Adam rotten," Sara said flatly. "And young as he is, Adam knows he can twist his grandfather around his little finger. I wish I could make Daniel understand it's not good for Adam. In a way they're very much alike . . ."

With the approach of Passover—the Jewish holiday celebrating the exodus of the Jews from Egypt, where they had been slaves—Vicky determined it was time to begin to teach Michael Jewish history. Adam, of course, was too young to understand. She debated about how to handle this without confusing Michael.

In time he would be told that since his mother was Jewish, he, too, was of that faith. For now she'd explain about the need for tolerance in the world. He knew something about Christian holidays. Now she would teach him Jewish history and holidays, stressing that Christianity is based on the Old Testament. She would teach him about Islam—the faith taught by Mohammed—and point out that Islam, originating in the seventh century, was built on both Judaism and Christianity. *Let him understand that the world must learn to respect all faiths.*

Vicky worried that Gary seemed to be removing himself from all social life not within the immediate family. Occasionally they went to Lily's or Stephanie's for dinner, but he refused to attend other dinner parties, the theater, concerts. Still, she told herself, he enjoyed being with the children. He was pleased that Kara and Doug were often underfoot.

She and Gary spent long hours at the office, though the inner circle of company executives understood that Gary had become just a presence in his office. They respected and answered to her. Gary spent his days reading the local newspapers, national magazines, allowing Vicky—the sole woman executive in the company—to handle business. Dutifully he accompanied her to auctions, on brief business trips, and to twice-a-year conferences with Frank Leslie and their ad agency in New York.

It was Sara who prodded them later in the year to consider a trip to Paris to celebrate their tenth wedding anniversary that coming April.

"You need to get away from the business," Sara told Vicky for the dozenth time. "Take the children and Mattie Lou," she said. "I know you—you wouldn't have a moment's peace if you didn't take Michael and Adam with you. And it'll be good for Gary, too,'' Sara added.

"I'll talk to him about it tonight," Vicky said in sudden decision. Sara, too, worried about Gary's state of mind.

Vicky waited until she and Gary were in bed to bring up the subject of their going to Paris.

"It would be wonderful to see Simone and Henri." It seemed incredible that it was almost ten years since Simone and Henri had been witnesses at their marriage. All at once she was flooded with memories of their flight from Petrograd to Paris. Without Simone she would not have survived.

She and Simone exchanged letters several times a year. Simone had knitted beautiful sweaters when each of the boys was born. And at intervals she wrote wistfully that she hoped one day to see Vicky and Gary and the children.

"Then we'll go to Paris. I presume Papa will foot the bill," he said with a touch of irony. "Mama will see to that."

Immediately they began to make plans for the trip next April. Mattie Lou was terrified at the prospect of spending five days aboard a ship, yet simultaneously she was awed by the thought of going to Paris.

"Miz Vicky, I never been on a ship," she said solemnly. "My folks just won't believe it!"

Gary took charge of making the arrangements for the trip. They would spend one night in New York City at the Plaza before boarding the *Aquitania* for the trip to Cherbourg. He'd given way to sentiment in choosing the *Aquitania*. He remembered traveling to England with his mother aboard this ship before the war.

From Cherbourg they would take the train to Paris. Gary decreed that they would stay at the Crillon, where he and Vicky had met. Simone and Henri would come into Paris from their small farm to spend a day with them.

Vicky allowed herself to be caught up in the excitement shared by Michael and Adam as the departure date arrived, though she worried that the pleasure of seeing Paris again might be a bitter reminder to Gary that his dreams for a musical career had been buried. Ten years ago in Paris he had been so confident of his future, so dedicated to his music.

Lily gave a family dinner party the night before Vicky and Gary were to leave. Though she and Stephanie gloried in their frequent trips to London and Paris, they appeared somewhat irritated by Vicky and Gary's imminent departure.

"Just everybody's running to Paris these days," Lily said distastefully. "Once they started calling steerage 'Third Cabin,' all those nobodies started traveling to Europe."

"Vicky and Gary won't be traveling third cabin," Sara assured Lily.

In the morning Vicky and Gary and their small entourage left from the Richmond depot. The following evening they were ensconced in their luxurious first-class suite aboard the four-funneled *Aquitania*. Vicky was relieved when a steward promised her this would be a comfortable crossing.

"Not like some Aprils," he said ebulliently. "You picked a good year, young lady."

Michael was fascinated by the ship. He insisted his father report every detail of the earlier crossing on the *Aquitania*. When they arrived in Paris, he wanted to be shown the house where his mother had lived. He knew already how his father and mother had met in the midst of an air raid.

What would he think, Vicky asked herself whimsically, if he knew she'd worked as a maid in that same hotel? What would he think when he saw the shabby building where she had lived with Simone? But he knew that she'd lived in the Veronsky Palace in Petrograd—which was now known as Leningrad. He knew his maternal grandfather had been a fine doctor and his grandmother a beautiful lady.

After their first day onboard, Adam became restless and demanding, embarrassing Vicky in front of the other passengers with his ugly outbursts. She blessed Mattie Lou for being patient with him. Michael's familiar retort was, "Adam, stop being a baby!" But Adam was only four, and Vicky tried to excuse his behavior.

Their first days in Paris were joyous. Vicky felt as though time had raced backward. They'd been so very young and so in love. The day spent with Simone and Henri—beginning with breakfast in their suite at the Crillon—was fraught with sweet recall and the pleasure of being together again.

"Vicky, the boys are so handsome," Simone said lovingly, though Vicky suspected she considered Adam dreadfully spoiled. "Michael's the image of you, Gary. I don't know who Adam resembles."

"His grandfather on my side," Gary chuckled. "The spittin' image of my father."

Yet when she and Gary were alone in their bedroom, he abandoned the light façade he managed the rest of the time. He was remembering the war years. He was remembering his lost dreams.

"Gary," she whispered while she lay content in the curve of his arms. No matter what, in bed together they were the same lovers as on their wedding night. "Do you remember the night we went to dinner at Larue's and you suddenly got up and played the piano?"

"Chopin's *Minute Waltz*," he recalled, and his face was suddenly taut. "That was another lifetime."

They shouldn't have come to Paris, she reproached herself. For Gary it was a reminder of what he had lost. How could she ease his pain?

"Gary," she reached out a hand to him, her eyes eloquent.

"You're impetuous tonight," he joshed, but she knew he was pleased.

She would comfort him in the only way she knew how.

Chapter Seventeen

IN THE EARLY FALL of 1929 the mood of the nation was optimistic. There were mergers and expansions, booming sales in luxury items. The car industry appeared strong. Steel was going up at record pace—and the saying was that "as steel goes, so goes the country."

The tobacco industry was thriving. Down in Winston-Salem, Reynolds was building a twenty-two-story office building. In Richmond, Tobacco Row was enjoying record sales. In Bartonville, Daniel had just finished a huge addition to the factory complex, and rows of tiny houses destined for new Barton employees were being completed.

Then on Thursday, October 24th, panic hit the nation. Stock prices were plummeting. Brokers were calling for more margin—or investors would be wiped out. By afternoon there was some slight recovery. But on Monday, October 28th, disaster hit again. Investors frantically rushed to get out of the market. The orders went out to sell. By Tuesday morning it was clear—the bubble had burst. Across the country, investors—small and huge—became penniless overnight. Shocking news of suicides headlined the tabloids.

Vicky was aware of what was happening in the stock market. But her world consisted of family and Barton Tobacco—neither of which was affected by the crisis in the stock market. Or so she believed.

On this Tuesday morning she had been absorbed by a heated business conference with Daniel and top company officials, had lunched at her desk, and was now going over the records of Barton Tobacco purchases during the recent auction season. At a desk across the room from her own Gary was reading the current edition of *Literary Digest*.

All at once raised voices punctured the usual quiet in the executive wing of the floor of offices.

"What the hell are you talking about?" Daniel yelled. "Why should I give you forty thousand dollars?"

"I'll be wiped out!" Clark's voice was shrill. "I'll lose everything if I don't come up with more margin!"

"You dumb bastard! I warned you to stay out of the market! I'll—" All at once a strange gurgling sound emerged from Daniel. Vicky turned to Gary in alarm.

"Daniel? Oh my God!" Clark's voice telegraphed disaster.

Without a word between them Vicky and Gary darted from their office, across the hall to Daniel's. Gary pulled the door wide and charged inside. His father lay on the floor, his face contorted and drained of color. Clark hovered over him in alarm.

While Gary dropped to his knees beside his father, Vicky phoned the Richmond hospital and summoned an ambulance, then called Jeffrey.

"I don't think you should move him," Vicky cautioned Clark, who was making an effort to raise Daniel to a sitting position. "Wait until the ambulance comes."

Within a dozen minutes the ambulance—its siren screaming— pulled up at the entrance to the office side of the building. Simultaneously, Jeffrey arrived. Along with the intern on ambulance duty, he charged into the office.

"What happened?" Jeffrey demanded while he pulled a stethoscope from his pocket.

"We were talking," Clark stammered, "then he keeled over."

"He was upset and yelling," Gary said tersely. "Jeffrey, what happened to him?"

"We won't know until we get him into the hospital. Offhand I'd say he suffered a stroke." Jeffrey looked up at Vicky. "You'd better get to the house and tell Sara."

Gary went with his father in the ambulance while Vicky drove to Barton Manor. Sara was about to leave for a committee meeting when Vicky arrived. Instantly she knew that something terrible had occurred.

"Vicky, what is it?" she asked, her face ashen. "Something's happened to Daniel!"

"He's at the hospital," Vicky said quietly. "Gary's with him."

"Zachary is just bringing the car around—" Sara seemed in a daze.

"I'll drive you," Vicky told her, reaching for her arm. "He's going to be all right. He'll get the best of care."

In silence they drove to the hospital. When they arrived, the main floor receptionist left her desk to come to them.

"Mr. Barton's on the third floor," she told them sympathetically. "The doctors are working over him now—"

"Thank you, Katherine." Sara knew everybody at the hospital, Vicky remembered. She served as a volunteer two days a month.

When they emerged from the elevator, Vicky saw Gary at a window in the reception area. He was staring outdoors but with an air that told Vicky he saw nothing.

"Gary, how is he?" Sara asked, rushing to his side.

"We won't know for a while," he told her gently. "It was a stroke, they believe."

They waited for what seemed hours before Jeffrey came out to join them.

"He'll make it," Jeffrey told them, his eyes guarded. "It was a serious stroke. He'll be here for at least three or four weeks. He—" He hesitated.

"How bad is it?" Sara asked. She was terribly shaken, Vicky thought. At one time she must have loved him very much. "I want you to be honest with me, Jeffrey."

Jeffrey hesitated an instant.

"We doubt that he'll ever walk again. But with care—therapy— he'll be able to get around in a wheelchair. At the present he's having difficulty with speech, but we expect that will clear up in time. What he needs most now is total rest."

"Daniel in a wheelchair," Sara whispered in anguish. "He'll be so angry. So rebellious. For him it'll be a living death."

Sara was at Daniel's bedside constantly in the days ahead. Vicky was touched by the way he clung to Sara's hand, followed her movements with his eyes when she was not beside his bed. Gary, too, spent long hours each day at the hospital.

Vicky carried on at the office, ever conscious of the questions in the minds of the company executives. Who would take over until Daniel could return to the business—if he could ever come back at all. It was understood among the others that Gary was only a figurehead. Vicky felt the hostility aimed toward her. She was a woman and at twenty-seven far younger than any of the male executives.

By the end of Daniel's first week in the hospital he was able to speak to them—slowly, with difficulty, but his mind was clear and sharp. He ordered Gary to bring Vicky over that evening.

"We've got a company to run," he said with agonizing slowness. "Until I can take over again, I want Vicky to be in charge. Jointly, of course, with you, Gary," he said with an unexpected glint of humor in his eyes. "You'll have to front for her, you know. The others will try to make mincemeat out of her."

"Not likely, Papa," Gary assured him. "Vicky's tough."

"We'll make decisions," Daniel told him. "Vicky and I. And you'll convey our decisions to the staff. Your wife has the sharpest head in the family, after myself. She—and I—will run the show."

In the weeks that followed, it seemed to Vicky that Daniel had little patience for his daughters' prattle. He seemed to find comfort only in Sara's presence. It were as though, she thought, he was amazed that Sara was there for him.

Daniel was grim and silent when he arrived home in a wheelchair. He knew there was little likelihood that he would ever walk again. An elevator was installed for his use. He brushed aside the suggestion that a male nurse be hired to care for him. Zachary—who had been with him for fifteen years—would do whatever was necessary.

"Damn it, I can't walk—but I can get around on my own! That's what the chair's for!" Reluctantly he agreed that Zachary be coached by Jeffrey in how to cope with these new duties.

At intervals, Daniel sent terse messages to the staff. By the beginning of the new year, he said, he expected to be in his office for two or three hours each day. He brushed aside Lily's injured entreaties that he bring in Clark to run the company.

"*I'm* running my company," he told her with unfamiliar harshness. "You tell Clark to concentrate on his lawyering. And you see that he gets to church every Sunday. There are a lot of votes sitting there in the pews. Especially now," he said with grim humor, "that you women have got the right to vote. He'll need those votes when I decide it's time for him to run for city council.'' He understood that Lily and Clark thought that this decision was long past due.

It soon became clear that Daniel's convalescence would be prolonged beyond his expectations. He was cantankerous, restless, demanding constant attention. He waited impatiently each night for Michael and Adam to be sent up to their rooms after their time with their mother so that he could cross-examine Vicky about the day's activities.

Vicky sympathized with his need to feel in command of the business, his feeling of humiliation at being tied down to a wheelchair, at having to fight to speak coherently. Still, he was determined and gradually improving in this capacity. And Vicky admired Sara's devotion to him. His illness had brought them together.

At Barton Manor no one felt the insidious Depression that was moving over America. By spring of 1930—six months after the collapse of the stock market—four million Americans had been thrown out of work. Families were suddenly homeless. Breadlines appeared. Yet Bartonville—like Richmond—still appeared to be untouched by the deepening Depression. The stability of the tobacco industry was remarkable.

That same spring—when Daniel was now appearing in his office for an hour or two each afternoon—Vicky began to battle with him about improving labor relations with their employees.

"A waste of money," Daniel scoffed. "Unemployment's high in the country—they're glad for their jobs."

"When employees are happy, production goes up," she insisted. "And what I'm suggesting won't cost us more than a piddling amount. I want to set up lunchrooms—one for white and one for colored—where employees can eat at cost. They'll be rested, instead of tired from chasing around at lunch time for a place to sit and eat out on the streets somewhere. We'll provide a decent hot lunch at cost."

Vicky argued with Daniel for weeks. Finally he agreed. Then she began to press him to move into radio advertising. She brought Frank Leslie down from New York to back her up.

"Damn it, we spend a fortune on billboards, newspaper ads, magazine ads," Daniel grumbled. "We have to stop somewhere!"

"Look how well Camel is doing with their radio show," Frank said with the deference he always displayed toward Daniel. "The rumor around the ad agencies is that they're setting up two more. And Lucky Strike is hopping on the bandwagon.''

"How soon before sales start dropping way off?'' Daniel countered. "Everybody knows how bad the economy is right now. And you two want us to blow money like it grows on trees. We should be retrenching.''

"I ordered a survey to be taken,'' Vicky began and Daniel grimaced. "I know, it was expensive,'' she agreed calmly, "but the truth is business for the average tobacco company isn't dropping. It isn't jumping the way it was five years ago—but so far this year there's a mild increase. It's only one percent,'' she conceded, "but the Top Three are doing well. This is the time when we can move right up there with them if we handle ourselves right.'' She paused, gearing herself for one more push while Frank was in town to fight with her. "And I think it's time we put out a 'roll your own' package—for smokers who're feeling a financial pinch.''

Daniel squinted in thought. Vicky exchanged a hopeful glance with Frank. The two of them—like Daniel—were obsessed with moving the company into a higher position.

"All right,'' he agreed. "Run with it.''

Gary sometimes teased Vicky that her world traveled two miles— between Barton Manor and Barton Tobacco Company. Occasionally, Vicky worried that her new role was disturbing to him. He felt shamed that it was his wife—not himself—who had stepped forward to run the business in a crisis situation. And she was aware, too, of Lily's rage that her father continued to refuse to put Clark at the head of the company.

In her battle to make their factory complex more efficient, their advertising more powerful, their tobacco buyers the shrewdest, Vicky was able to hide her fears that her marriage was slowly disintegrating. She was unhappy at the way Gary was drawing within himself. It frustrated her that she couldn't reach over the wall he was building between them. Only when they made love—and that was less frequent these days—did she feel that this was the Gary she had married.

Like Kara and Doug, Michael went to a private school in Richmond. When Adam started kindergarten, Sara was sure that he would calm down now that he was in school, too.

"The poor little fellow has felt left out,'' Sara said. "He saw Michael going off to school every day, and then Kara and Doug. Now he's one of them.''

"He's such a charmer sometimes," Vicky said tenderly. "He can smile at you and just win your heart over. Then he turns fretful and rebellious, and I wonder what I'm doing wrong.''

"I think it's tough being the youngest among our little brood. Sometimes he even wins over Kara—she's the softy among them.'' Now Sara was somber. "But I don't ever want you to feel guilty about how you handle Adam. You're a fine mother. I wish Lily and Stephanie were as devoted as you are.''

Like Sara, Vicky was upset that Lily and Stephanie were so cavalier about their maternal responsibilities. Kara and Doug were such warm, sweet children, she told herself. She and Sara always tried to involve them in family activities at Barton Manor. Perhaps Sara was right. Now that Adam was in school, also, he'd be less belligerent toward the other three children.

Vicky was ever astonished at the passage of time, as months sped into years. But at painful intervals she was conscious that while the business brought her closer to Daniel, nights in Gary's arms were becoming increasingly rare.

Sara always observed the children's birthdays with a family party. Michael's twelfth birthday brought Vicky face to face with the problem she had thrust in the back of her mind. She knew that Daniel would be upset; but this he would have to accept, she vowed. She would not deny her son his bar mitzvah on his thirteenth birthday. She could delay no longer in bringing him together with his faith.

She had taught the children about the major religions of the world, always stressing the importance of tolerance. Sara had closed her eyes to the fact that Michael and Adam rarely attended church service, did not go to Sunday school. But it was time her sons were told of their Jewish heritage—and for Michael to be tutored for his bar mitzvah.

To her astonishment Gary tried to dissuade her from this.

"I don't know if they can handle this," he objected. "All right, Adam is little—you may eventually make him understand. But Michael's twelve years old. How can you come out and tell him—out of the blue—that he's Jewish." He hesitated. "Half-Jewish.''

"Gary, are you ashamed that I'm Jewish?" Vicky stared at him in painful suspicion.

"Vicky, no. My God, no!" he lashed back. "But with what's happening in the world, I wonder if this is the time to tell him."

"Michael knows about the Ku Klux Klan. He thinks they're the scum of the earth." She reveled in Michael's liberal feelings, forgetting that these were a reflection of her own and Gary's beliefs.

"I'm talking about Germany. About that maniac Hitler." A vein pounded at his temple. "He and his rotten Nazi party are agitating hundreds of thousands of Germans against the Communists and Jews—particularly the Jews." He paused. Unexpectedly an ironic smile lifted the corners of his mouth. "I know how you feel about the Communists, but you don't want to see them massacred. As for the Jews, we know what they've endured through the centuries. I'm afraid for them, Vicky—"

"Germany is across the ocean," Vicky defied him. "The Nazis will never dare invade this country. I want my sons to know their faith. Their heritage. Especially now. I want to have Michael tutored for his bar mitzvah. It's not too late—he has almost a year. I'm not asking you to convert," she reminded. "I'll join a synagogue in Richmond and arrange for Michael's tutoring—"

"Papa's going to carry on," Gary warned unhappily.

"That won't change the situation," Vicky said. "I'll join a Richmond synagogue. My sons will have their bar mitzvahs."

A few days later Vicky left the office early. She brought the two boys together in the library. Quietly she told them it was time they understood about their religion. She explained why this had never been brought up before.

"Your grandfather Barton felt that this could wait until you were old enough to understand," she fabricated. "You both know about the Ku Klux Klan and the terrible things they do. And I've told you about the pogroms in Russia. About how Grandfather Gunsburg sent me away for fear of what would happen to me in Russia—" She paused, touched by the solemnity on Michael's young face.

"I don't want to be Jewish!" Adam screeched, his face flushed. "I won't be! I won't!"

"Adam, shut up!" Michael ordered and turned to his mother. "Does this make us any different? I mean, what happens to us now?"

"When you're thirteen, you'll have your bar mitzvah. That's a very special occasion for Jewish boys. Next week you'll begin to have private tutoring by a very nice rabbi. He'll teach you what you need to know for your bar mitzvah. That's a ceremony in the synagogue where—on the Saturday after your birthday—you'll be honored as coming of age. In the Jewish faith at thirteen a boy becomes a man.''

"I don't want—whatever you call it!'' Adam rejected shrilly.

"You're too young,'' Michael said, though he seemed uneasy. "What will I have to do at the synagogue?''

"You will have learned a little Hebrew,'' Vicky told him softly. "You'll recite a prayer before the Ark. The rest the rabbi will explain. It's a beautiful ceremony. I only wish your grandfather and grandmother on my side could be here to see it.''

Late that evening Zachary came to Vicky's bedroom to say that Daniel wished to speak with her.

"I'll be right there,'' Vicky promised.

"What the hell's the matter with him?'' Gary complained. "Can't he discuss whatever's on his mind tomorrow?''

"You know your father,'' Vicky said, expecting Daniel to want to argue some business decision. "I won't be long.''

Minutes later Vicky approached Daniel's bedroom, knocked lightly.

"Come in,'' he ordered. He was in a rotten mood, Vicky guessed.

She pulled open the door and walked inside. Daniel maneuvered his wheelchair to face her.

"What's this garbage you've been feeding Adam and Michael?'' he demanded. "Adam's all upset.''

"It isn't garbage,'' she said quietly. "I told them they were Jewish, and that it was time for Michael to be prepared for his bar mitzvah. That's—''

"I know what it is.'' He glared at her, she thought, as though she'd committed treason. "Why do you have to start up with that now?''

"Because I was too stupid to start earlier,'' she flared.

"Why do you have to expose those kids to the trouble that brings? God knows—the way Gary is carrying on about that man Hitler—you're aware of what's going on over there. Isn't that enough to make you understand that Michael and Adam can be spared that kind of trouble?''

"We don't live in Germany or Russia.'' Vicky spoke with deliberate calm. "This is America. I'm Jewish, therefore my sons are Jewish. They have a right to know and practice their faith.''

"You are the most stubborn woman I've ever encountered!'' Daniel shouted. "Why do you have to do this to them?''

"I'm doing it for them," Vicky corrected him.

"It'll be all over Bartonville," he pointed out.

"That doesn't bother me."

"Stubborn woman," he grumbled again. "I knew that from the first minute I laid eyes on you. Gary might benefit from some of that," he said with an unexpected grin. "Marrying you might be the best thing he ever did for this family."

"I'll take that as a compliment." She managed a wisp of a smile. She had never expected to hear something like that from Daniel.

"Now get the hell out of here and let me get some sleep," he ordered. "Find Zachary and send him to me."

For Vicky the beautiful part of the next year was Michael's involvement in his coming bar mitzvah. He was so earnest, she thought with pride. She promised herself that when Adam was older, he'd want to have his bar mitzvah, too—because he always wanted what Michael had.

She was grateful that her joining the synagogue was accepted casually, though she suspected this belated expression of her Jewishness must have created much talk. She attended only occasional services—despite intentions to the contrary—because of the demands of business and family. For the same reason she rarely socialized with the members of the congregation.

But on the morning of Michael's bar mitzvah, she sat proudly in the synagogue—Sara beside her—as the services began. She was disappointed that Gary had not come with them. Tears filled her eyes when Michael was brought up before the Ark to recite the chosen prayer. How handsome he was! How in love with life!

After the services Michael went home to the small family party arranged by Sara. To the family it was Michael's slightly delayed birthday party. But to his mother it was a magnificent victory.

The ugly part of this year was what was happening in Germany. In April of 1933, shops owned by Jews were boycotted. A month later books written by Jews were burned. Jews were already forced to wear yellow badges and were being brutalized by Hitler's Brownshirts.

Late in the summer Lily and Stephanie—whom Jeffrey now called the Bobbsey Twins—went to Europe for three weeks. They returned to gush about the Wagner festival at Bayreuth and seeing Hitler at a restaurant in Munich.

"We're sure all those terrible things they're saying about Hitler in the newspapers are wrong," Lily effervesced at a welcome-home dinner at Barton Manor. "Everybody says he's absolutely charming."

"I'll take any odds," Gary said grimly while his father grunted in rejection of Lily's declaration, "that within five years Hitler will lay the groundwork for a war that'll make the last one look like a scene from Gilbert and Sullivan."

Vicky gazed at him in anguish. Her mind hurtled back through the years to the horrors of the World War. She remembered death and destruction—and the vows that something so awful could never happen again.

In five years Michael would be eighteen. Old enough to fight. No, she told herself. It was time the world learned to live in peace. But would the new Nazi chancellor of Germany—a former corporal in the World War—allow this to happen?

Chapter Eighteen

T HOUGH the Depression deep-
ened on a national level, Bar-
tonville—dependent on Barton Tobacco for its economic health—felt
none of the hardships afflicting most of the country. Under Vicky's
leadership the company was expanding. Now she began a campaign to extend the company's operations into other fields. As a
result of the stock crash back in Twenty-nine, real estate specula-
tors were in serious trouble. Farm land was up for sale at stagger-
ingly low prices.

"Daniel, they're giving farms away in the South," Vicky argued
with him at one of their nightly sessions early in 1934. "We can buy
land for almost nothing!"

"What'll we do with it except pay property taxes?" he asked.

"One day we may decide to branch out into raising our own tobacco. We—"

"Nobody's doing that," Daniel said.

"I'm not saying we ought to invest a fortune in buying up land,"
Vicky continued. "But when something is available at such a low
price—and we know that in time prices are going to move upward—
then we ought to buy."

"I'll give it some thought," Daniel said after a moment. "We'll
talk about it again."

But Vicky knew she'd won. Barton Tobacco Company would extend itself to buying up farm land. The prospect cheered her. Yet later,

lying sleepless in bed while Gary snored gently beside her, she asked herself why——at moments like this—she felt as though life was passing her by.

When a group in Richmond had campaigned two years ago to launch a symphony orchestra—and actually brought it about despite the Depression—she'd prayed that Gary would become involved. But he wouldn't even attend performances. He was isolating himself from the world, even from her, she forced herself to concede, except on those occasional nights when he turned to her in the dark and tried to reclaim the passion they'd shared in earlier years.

Now she sought to relive in memory precious moments in the past. But that was wrong! She was thirty-two years old—much of her life lay ahead of her. *She needed something more.*

To their workers she appeared to be blessed. She lived in a beautiful house, had a handsome husband and two handsome sons, no financial worries. Most of their workers' waking hours were spent at dull, repetitive tasks. They pushed away those hours each day, she guessed, waiting for the brief times that belonged to them alone. They had no real hopes of lifting themselves above the daily drabness that colored their existence. This was the way it would be forever.

She remembered her shock on that traumatic trek from Petrograd to Paris—when she came to understand that most people didn't live in a palace with maids to cater to their needs, with no concern of what it cost to buy food and clothes and other necessities of life. In Paris she came face to face with the way of life endured by most people— a hassle from birth to death, with tiny rewards to see them through this journey.

She turned on her side and reached an arm out to Gary.

"Are you asleep?" she asked quietly. "Gary?"

"Hmmm?" He stirred without opening his eyes.

"I can't get to sleep tonight," she whispered.

"Sorry, honey," he mumbled. A moment later, while she rested her face on his chest, he spoke again. "You work too hard," he said and shifted about so that he could bring her into his arms.

"Maybe we could go away for a couple of days," she said. His hands were maneuvering beneath the fragile chiffon of her nightgown. "Just the two of us." Like their wedding night in Paris.

"No kids?" he teased, his mouth at her throat.

"They won't miss us for one night," she said after a moment. It

would be the first time she'd be away from them overnight. Sara
would be delighted to take charge so that she and Gary could go away.
All at once it was terribly important to be alone with Gary for a swatch
of time.

"This weekend?" Gary asked.

"We can't," she said. "Frank is coming down to discuss the new
ad campaign. The following weekend," she decided. This would be
like the old days, she thought.

"You have a real estate closing down in Roanoke," he remembered. "I'm your designated driver."

"We'll stay overnight in Roanoke," she murmured, feeling young
and romantic at the prospect. "At a hotel."

"Unlike Lily and Stephanie," he drawled, "we won't have to
worry about a hotel detective." So he knew about his sisters' extra-
marital affairs, she realized subconsciously. Did everybody—except
their husbands—know?

Then there was no more thought of conversation. Both felt a need
to seek comfort in the other. But too soon Gary relinquished these
heated moments and withdrew again. It wasn't like Paris, after all.

Vicky and Sara were both upset when Lily mentioned at a family
dinner in the spring that she was corresponding with several boarding
schools.

"What about?" Sara asked sharply. Kara's pretty little face was
stormy, her eyes downcast. Michael and Doug appeared unhappy.
Vicky surmised they'd been told about this latest development and
sympathized with Kara. Adam wasn't at the table. He was being pun-
ished for putting a mouse in a drawer in the kitchen and scaring Lula
Mae into near hysteria. "For whom?"

"For Kara, of course." Lily's voice brought Vicky back to the
moment. "She's old enough for boarding school, Mother." In the last
three years she and Stephanie had declared that "Mama" and "Papa"
were gauche terms. They now addressed their parents as "Mother"
and "Dad."

"Lily, she's just passed her twelfth birthday," Sara said. "She's
far too young for boarding school."

"She'll have a wonderful time." Lily's devious smile told Vicky
there was no changing her mind. Was Kara's presence interfering with
Lily's affairs, Vicky wondered, or was a twelve-year-old daughter an

affront to Lily's image of herself as twenty-two? "I always wished I'd gone off to boarding school."

"Bullshit," Daniel said brusquely. "You were seventeen, and you wouldn't stay at Ward-Belmont." He ignored the fact that Lily had been ordered to leave.

"If I'd been sent to boarding school at Kara's age, I would have been used to it. I would've stayed. You're more adaptable at twelve." Lily smiled, pleased at her retort.

"It's a rough age to send a little girl away," Vicky said. At that age they were just beginning to develop. Already Kara was unhappily conscious of her budding breasts, Vicky thought in sympathy.

"It's easy for you to talk," Lily bristled. "The maids are raising your children. All you think about is the business."

"Be damn glad that she does," Daniel shot back. "Without Vicky at my side we wouldn't be making the progress we are. We're giving the 'Big Three' real competition," he said with satisfaction. "If Vicky wasn't there with me, I wouldn't be increasing your allowance the first of the year." He grinned at his daughters' sudden euphoria.

"Oh, Dad, are you really?" Stephanie cooed. "Lily, isn't that just wonderful?" Her eyes warned her sister to abandon the present conversation.

"Dad, you are just the sweetest thing!" Lily jumped up from her seat and hurried to hug her father. "That means Stephanie and I can go to Paris in June. We were worrying about how we could handle it." Though Clark was now on the city council—thanks to Daniel's maneuvering—that did little to swell their income.

Lily and Stephanie lived in a world of their own, Vicky thought. They were constantly rushing up to New York, to sleep away the days in a suite at the new Waldorf-Astoria and to spend the evenings at El Morocco with its zebra upholstery and starry ceiling, or at one of the red and white check clothed tables in the backroom bar at "21," or listening to Eddy Duchin at the Persian Room.

Every year they ran off to Paris, enjoying cocktails at Fouquet's, dinner at Maxim's or the Ambassadeurs, and evenings at the bistros with their Cafe Society friends. Before coming home they'd go with their new friends to the Riviera or the Lido. In January—for once with husbands in tow—they were off to Palm Beach.

Bartonville was surviving with little signs of the Depression that was bringing such pain to most of the country, but Richmond—

despite its flourishing tobacco companies—was suffering. Gary said that over seventeen thousand people in Richmond were on relief. The jobless—with no money to buy fuel to heat their houses—were being allowed to help themselves to coal from strip deposits in Chesterfield. How could Lily and Stephanie ignore what was going on in the world?

The following September Kara was sent off to boarding school. Sara confessed it broke her heart to see her only granddaughter shipped off to the care of strangers.

"Lily and Stephanie are my daughters," Sara said, her eyes reflecting her anguish, "but I'll never understand them."

"I told Kara to phone us collect whenever she likes," Vicky confided. "Poor baby, she seemed so scared and unhappy."

At regular intervals Kara telephoned Barton Manor to talk with her grandmother and Vicky. She was already counting the days until the Thanksgiving holidays. She'd been told that, as usual, the whole family would gather at Barton Manor for Thanksgiving dinner. The following morning her parents were flying to Charleston for a house party at a nearby plantation.

"Can I stay with you, Grandma?" Kara asked.

"Of course, darling," Sara told her. "And Doug will be here with us, too."

"Oh, that's right," Kara remembered. "Aunt Stephanie and Uncle Jeffrey are going, too."

Jeffrey's new practice in Richmond was thriving. Sara wondered if his wealthy women patients were drawn by his medical expertise or by the fact that he was as charming as he was handsome. She had tried to dissuade Jeffrey from giving up his local practice, but the effort had been futile.

"I would never have believed that Jeffrey would change so," Sara told Vicky over a Sunday morning breakfast. For months now Gary had been sleeping late on Sunday mornings, rising only in time for lunch and the afternoon music lesson for Michael and Doug. This was the only time he used the cottage now. "Remember what he was like when he first married Stephanie? Daniel was unhappy that Stephanie had not married a Southerner, but Jeffrey had been sweet and so dedicated to his profession. Now all he thinks about is how much he can charge his patients." As close as she was to Vicky, she still refrained from discussing her suspicions that some of Jeffrey's patients were more than that.

At Thanksgiving and again at Christmas Kara cried and pleaded not to be shipped back to boarding school. Lily was adamant. Already Stephanie was talking about sending Doug to military school. There was never a thought of boarding school for Michael or Adam.

Vicky worried constantly about Adam's rebellious ways, though he could be utterly ingratiating when he chose. Lily and Stephanie were forever making snide remarks about Adam's behavior. The implication was that if *she* were not so involved in the business, Adam would behave differently.

"Really, Vicky, you don't understand that child," Lily told her with a superior smile. "He's just screaming for attention."

He got attention, Vicky told herself guiltily. Adam was her son—she loved him the way she loved Michael. Lily and Stephanie were deliberately baiting her when they spoke that way about Adam. From the first day she'd come to Barton Manor they'd resented her presence. They were even jealous of her closeness now to Daniel.

For her, Vicky thought, Barton Manor was a velvet prison.

In September—protesting as Kara had a year ago—Doug was sent off to military school.

"He's the last child in the world that should go to military school," Vicky said to Gary in the privacy of their bedroom. "He's shy and sensitive. He needs nurturing, Gary. Your mother's so upset that he's off at school."

"Not my father." Gary's eyes were bitter. "He thinks military school is 'exactly what Doug needs to make a man of him.' He has such talent, Vicky. It hurts to see that stifled."

Gary had talent, too, Vicky thought angrily. His father had contrived to stifle that. It mustn't happen to Doug. Somehow, she and Gary must see to that.

Vicky was shaken when she read in the Richmond *Times-Dispatch* about the passing of the Nuremberg Laws in Germany. This excluded Jews from citizenship, public office, the professions—from participating in the intellectual and artistic life of the country. The new law also decreed that those they considered "half-Jews" would be included in this ostracism. For now "one-quarter Jews" were accepted as Germans.

"And this is happening," Gary pointed out in biting frustration, "at a time when Jews have only a meager chance of getting out. The immigration laws are so damn tight—both here and in European countries. Only a few are going to escape."

In the next months—in addition to her anxiety about the Jews in Germany—Vicky was caught up in a battle with Daniel over his insistence on slashing wages.

"What the hell's the matter with you?" he yelled. "Are you working for the company or for those lazy bastards?"

"They're not lazy. They work hard. They're conscientious and loyal. Daniel, they *are* the company."

He was further outraged when she decreed that the coming Christmas the company would give out bonuses.

"Reynolds is doing it," she pointed out. "It's good business." Daniel claimed to base every decision on this. "It pays off in production."

She was able to get Daniel to agree to the Christmas bonuses— which were greeted with gratitude by the employees—because Daniel seemed to be losing some of his old fire. She knew that Sara worried about his health. They'd all accepted the fact that he'd be forever confined to his wheelchair, but now he'd developed a chronic cough and seemed to be experiencing shortness of breath.

As always Daniel chain-smoked. After he suffered a bad coughing spell on New Year's Day, Vicky brought up the subject of his smoking as a cause for his coughing. Sara had tried on repeated occasions to talk him into curbing his smoking.

"You sound just like Sara," he complained. "I'm not coughing because of the cigarettes. It's some germ floating around, that's all." He rummaged around in his jacket pocket until he came up with a rumpled pack of cigarettes. "Get me matches, Vicky. I'm stuck in this damn chair—at least, let me enjoy a smoke."

"Daniel hasn't been truthful with me," Sara told Vicky anxiously when they sat down to Sunday breakfast early in the new year. "Dr. Gordon—and Jeffrey as well—thinks he should go into the hospital for tests. He didn't say a word to me about that. Dr. Gordon asked Jeffrey to talk to me about it. Daniel's going to be furious," Sara predicted, "but I'm going to insist he go in for those tests."

Three weeks later Daniel was in the Richmond hospital undergoing extensive tests. Vicky waited with Sara to hear the results. When Dr. Gordon approached them, his demeanor prepared them for a devastating report.

"I'm sorry," Dr. Gordon said gently. "Daniel has lung cancer."

"Oh, my poor darling," Sara whispered, her face devoid of color. "I was so afraid of that."

"I'll tell him," Dr. Gordon said gravely. "It'll be easier that way."

Despite Daniel's objections he was scheduled for surgery. On the morning of the operation, Vicky left the office to sit with Sara and Gary in the waiting room. Lily and Stephanie were in Palm Beach.

"I promised the girls I'd call as soon as Daniel comes out of surgery," Sara told Vicky and Gary. "They both sounded almost hysterical."

"But they're staying in Palm Beach." Gary made no effort to conceal his cynicism.

While they waited, Sara talked about the early years of her marriage. She lived in those memories, Vicky thought with compassion. A few years of her life had to nurture a lifetime.

She didn't want to spend the rest of her life remembering the early years of her marriage to Gary, Vicky thought. There had to be more *now*. She was a success in the business, she acknowledged bitterly; but as a wife and mother she was a failure.

The Gary she had known in those first years had disappeared behind a wall she couldn't scale. She would never learn how to handle Adam. Thank God for Michael, she thought with a rush of love. With Michael she didn't feel herself to be a failure.

At last Dr. Gordon emerged from surgery.

"The surgery went well," he reported, though his voice was guarded. "I can't make any long-term promises, but he should have some comfortable years ahead." He paused. "He's going to have to take it easy now. For God sake, Sara, try to keep him away from the office. He needs a lot of rest."

"He'll rest," Sara promised and turned to Vicky. "You'll have to handle the business from this point on. I know you can do it alone. Daniel knows it, but forgive him if he's cantankerous now and then."

Vicky lay sleepless far into the night. It wasn't that she was frightened by the responsibility of running the company on her own. She was frightened by the narrowness of her life. Gary used to tease her and say her world extended for two miles—from Barton Manor to the office. *But that wasn't enough.*

Gary had withdrawn from all social life. He refused to go into Richmond to the concerts or to the theater. He'd rejected so many invitations to parties and dinners that nobody invited them anymore. Hardest of all, he'd rejected *her*. The last few times she'd reached out to him in the night he'd pretended to be asleep.

He religiously continued Michael's piano lessons. When Doug came home from military school—which he detested—Gary took him to the cottage for lessons. But outside of family and employees at Barton Tobacco, she and Gary saw no one. His depression frightened her, yet she knew no way to fight against it.

The excitement of working to build the company, of making "The Big Three" sit up and notice them, was ebbing away. She used to relish the battle to push their sales figures to new heights, to work with the advertising agency for campaigns that made Barton cigarettes competitive with the fastest-selling in the field. She was disturbed to realize that the enthusiasm that had carried her through these past years was diminishing. But all she had in her life—other than the children, she conceded guiltily—was the Barton Tobacco Company.

Chapter Nineteen

THE FAMILY at Barton Manor settled in to deal with Daniel's convalescence. As Sara had warned, he was irascible. Within a month after surgery he insisted on smoking again. He brushed aside Dr. Gordon's orders that he cut cigarettes out of his life.

"For all we know," Dr. Gordon told him, "this whole business might have been brought on by your damn chain-smoking. You coated your lungs with tobacco."

"No way, Doc. The Indians smoked tobacco for hundreds of years. You never heard of them getting lung cancer."

Vicky suspected that Daniel was hurt that Lily and Stephanie never stayed longer than fifteen minutes on their daily trips to the house—when they were in town. She was astonished and touched to watch the closeness developing between Adam and his grandfather.

Adam came home from school and went directly to the library, where Daniel spent much of his time now. They talked about football and baseball and boxing. With the arrival of the baseball season they listened together to broadcasts of the games.

Vicky knew that Daniel was unhappy that Michael, who was crazy about planes, planned to become an aeronautical engineer. Michael had confided in Vicky that he meant to keep up with his music, but he considered it unrealistic to count on that as a career. Still, both she and Gary were pleased that he would enroll at Columbia College in

New York next fall, where he would also have the opportunity to study piano.

Disappointed that Michael harbored no desire to join the company, Daniel was convinced that Adam would follow in his own footsteps. He talked to Adam for hours about various phases of the business. Vicky began to feel that she had been unduly harsh in her assessment of her younger son. Adam's devotion to his grandfather filled her with tenderness and pride.

But within a year of his original surgery Daniel was back in the hospital again. He emerged from this second surgery with an increasing fragility. Now—in addition to Zachary—a private nurse was brought into the house to care for him.

In late August 1937, Vicky and Gary saw Michael off from the Richmond depot as he prepared to enter Columbia College in New York City. Oh, she would miss him, Vicky thought as she held him close before he boarded the train. Gary, too, was both proud and wistful about Michael's imminent departure.

"You'll be home at Thanksgiving," Gary reminded Michael. "And again at Christmas."

"Just think how often I could be home if I could fly from New York to Richmond," Michael joshed. He was eager to take flying lessons, but Vicky firmly rejected this. "I could make it in three hours."

"No deal," Gary said. Lily and Stephanie had boasted about flying from London to Paris in three hours, talked about the British socialites who were learning to fly.

Then the final call for boarding sounded, and Michael exchanged hasty final embraces with his parents and joined the last stragglers en route for points north.

"One down and one to go," Gary said wryly as he and Vicky headed back to the car. They continued to drive a seven-year-old Cadillac in addition to Vicky's aging Stutz. Lily had just acquired a new Dusenberg. "And that one is raring to take off, too." Gary shook his head in bewilderment. "Why does he think military school would be so great?"

"He's too young for college," Vicky pointed out. "He wants to do whatever Michael does—and military school would be as close as he could get." Her face softened. "But he's so good with your father. Daniel would miss him terribly if he was away."

Vicky had thought that with Daniel's growing fragility she would have no more problems with him in running the company. At intervals—certain that she was going to bankrupt Barton Tobacco with her employee benefits—he became vicious. She tried to tell herself that this stemmed from his ill-health, that she could handle the situation. Yet each new encounter left her more disenchanted with her role as head of the company. The excitement was gone, and it was just a job.

She looked forward to the times when Michael was home from college. Usually Kara and Doug spent most of their holidays and summer vacations at Barton Manor. Clark learned to fly, bought a plane—which Vicky suspected Daniel financed. He'd tired, she assumed, of Lily's frequent complaints that other people were flying down to the Greenbrier's new airport on their private planes while she and Stephanie had to sit on a dusty, dull train.

Despite her impatience with Daniel's inhumanitarian thinking, Vicky felt compassion for him as his health deteriorated. First there was a critical bout with pneumonia, then a shocking weight loss. The family knew he was in constant pain, though he shouted in denial of this.

Gary was feeling a terrible guilt that he had disappointed his father. By August of 1939 it was clear that Daniel's time was running out fast. Gary spent hours at his bedside, occasionally escaping to listen to the radio newscasts. Remembering his own experiences in the last war, he dreaded seeing the world enmeshed in another conflict.

In March of the previous year, Hitler had seized and annexed peaceful Austria. He'd demanded that Germany be given the German-speaking part of Czechoslovakia—and the British and French agreed. A peace pact had been signed in Munich, with Italy joining Great Britain and France in consent.

This March Hitler seized the rest of Czechoslovakia, and took the small district of Memel from Lithuania. There was talk now of a non-aggression pact with Russia.

"Why doesn't somebody stop Hitler?" Vicky blazed. Only with Gary could she discuss what was tearing Europe apart. Sara thought only of trying to bring comfort to Daniel; Lily and Stephanie and their husbands were unconcerned about world affairs.

"Hitler, Mussolini, and the Japanese," Gary said grimly, "they're all guilty of aggression. Of course, Neville Chamberlain can't see that. The great British prime minister thinks he can negotiate peacefully.

There are those in Britain who believe that the Nazi atrocities against
the Jews are grossly exaggerated. They say, 'Oh, the Jewish problem
is one the Germans have to solve among themselves.' "

"They don't believe *Kristallnacht*?" Vicky asked. On the ninth of
last November the Nazis had embarked on a nationwide pogrom. They
burned synagogues, Jewish homes, beat and imprisoned Jewish men.
Then they fined the Jewish community one billion Reichsmark to pay
for the damages *they* had committed.

Over Labor Day weekend Vicky and Gary found it difficult to leave
the radio. Nazi troops had invaded Poland—ignoring Chamberlain's
threat to support Poland if they resisted a German attack. The following day Great Britain and France declared war on Germany.

Was Gary right, Vicky asked herself. Would the world be engulfed
in a second world war? She wished desperately that Michael was
home with them instead of settling in for his junior year at Columbia.
With war clouds hovering over the world, she yearned to have him
safely within her sight.

Late the following Friday—while Vicky and Gary huddled before
the radio and listened to yet another broadcast—Daniel lapsed into a
coma. The following morning he died.

Sara summoned the strength to make the arrangements for Daniel's
funeral.

"This is the last thing I can do for Daniel," she told Gary when
he and Vicky tried to relieve her of this painful responsibility. "This
I must do for him."

Michael was summoned home from college, Kara and Doug from
their respective boarding schools. An elaborate funeral was arranged.
Pallbearers would be high-ranking executives from the Bartonville and
New York offices. Two senators, three congressmen, and a judge
would attend. Floral tributes flowed into Bartonville from all over the
country.

At the church services and at the cemetery Sara handled herself
with a stoic calm while Lily and Stephanie sobbed dramatically. Vicky
wished that Daniel's long-time attorney had not insisted on having
the will read the evening of the funeral.

"The grandchildren are included," he'd pointed out. "They must
be present, and the three older children have to return to their
schools."

At eight that evening the family gathered in the double drawing room for the reading of the will. Zachary, his eyes swollen from weeping, moved about the room to open the avenue of tall, narrow windows, hoping to ease the humid heat of the evening. A ceiling fan whirred softly.

Daniel's attorney, Martin Woodstock, seated himself behind the desk that had been moved into the drawing room for this specific gathering. Vicky noted an air of wariness about him. He had been Daniel's attorney for thirty years, but there'd never been a question of friendship between the two men. Mr. Woodstock was an elegant Southern gentleman who'd probably recoiled from Daniel's deliberate crudity.

Sara sat between Gary and Vicky on one sofa. Lily and Stephanie—in smart black Paris frocks and exuding the sultry fragrance of Chanel No. 5—shared a second sofa with their husbands. Lily was outraged that Mr. Woodstock, not Clark, had drawn up her father's will. It had been a matter of dissension through the past years, though Clark had outwardly expressed his understanding of this decision. Kara and Doug each sat stiffly in a lounge chair—not quite sure what was expected of them. Adam had pulled up a hassock close to the desk where Mr. Woodstock sat. Vicky sensed a disconcerting air of exhilaration about him.

Tension escalated as Mr. Woodstock—who was co-executor of the estate with Sara—began to read the will. Lily and Stephanie exchanged an annoyed glance when the initial bequest was a fairly modest sum to go to Zachary. Sara nodded in approval. There were additional small bequests to other members of the domestic staff.

Lily and Stephanie gasped in shock that their own substantial bequests—like Gary's—were in trust funds, to be passed along to their descendants in the same form. That had been wise of Daniel, Vicky approved in silence. He knew his daughters' penchant for uncontrolled spending.

Vicky was startled that a lesser—but still substantial—trust fund had been willed to Adam. He was the sole grandchild to be remembered in Daniel's will. Involuntarily she turned to Adam. She saw the glint of triumph in his eyes before he dropped them to the floor.

Adam had known this would happen, she told herself. Had he been playing up to his grandfather all this time just to bring this about? But immediately she was ashamed at her suspicions. She must stop this habit of always expecting the worst of Adam.

"There's a stipulation that goes with this bequest." Mr. Woodstock looked up from the will for a moment and gazed in odd contemplation at Adam.

Then he began to read again. Adam's trust fund was based on his transferring to a military academy at the beginning of the next school year. Vicky understood; Adam knew his grandfather was leaving him a trust fund and had asked for this stipulation because she and Gary had rejected his pleas to go off to military school.

The remainder of Daniel's estate went to Sara. He'd made a point of stating that Vicky remain in charge of the Barton Tobacco Company—"because there's not a man in the company who can match her."

Mr. Woodstock was barely out of the drawing room before Lily and Stephanie began to express their wrath over their inheritances.

"How could Dad do this to us?" Lily shrieked. "We can't ever touch a cent of the money except for the income!"

"Clark, can't we do something?" Stephanie demanded. "How much can that income be?"

"Shut up!" Sara's voice rang out, laden with contempt. "When I go, you'll receive stock in the company. I don't have to tell you how successful the business is. There's a lot of money involved. This is the way your father wanted his fortune handled. If you cause any nastiness, or let people know that you're unhappy about the will, then I promise you I'll cut you out of my will entirely. Remember that," she said, rising from the sofa. "Now if you'll excuse me, I've had quite enough for one day."

Vicky was relieved that Sara seemed able to cope with her widowhood. Oddly she worried about Gary. He seemed so restless, unable to deal with his grief. She knew that he was suffering from insomnia. Still, she was unprepared two weeks later for what he proposed when he came up to their bedroom after listening to the late evening war news on the radio.

"Gary, what are you talking about?" She stared at him in bewilderment, his words echoing in her brain: "*Vicky, let's get out of Bartonville. Let's move to New York.*"

"What I just said." His eyelid fluttered in agitation. "We don't have to stay here now that I have the income from the trust fund. We have some savings. We can be comfortable, see Michael through college. I want to get back to my music, Vicky!''

"But we can't leave now," she protested. Without her the company would fall apart. She couldn't do that to Sara. And in time a chunk of the company would go to Michael and Adam. She had to keep the company healthy for them. "Gary, you can compose here in Bartonville. You'll have total freedom now," she said earnestly. "Forget about coming into the office. Work at your music on a full-time basis. You can—"

"You don't understand! I can't work here! I have to get away!''

"Gary, I have a responsibility to run the company. I have to do that for your mother's sake. For Michael and Adam. You can give all your time now to composing. Forget about the office—"

"I can't work in this town.'' He paused, his eyes strangely cold. "You don't understand, do you?''

"Gary, be realistic,'' she pleaded. "The company needs me. And there'll be no demands on you. You'll be free to work as you please.''

"You won't come with me to New York?''

"No,'' she said after an anguished moment. This was fifteen years too late. "I can't walk out on the company.'' Her heart began to pound. *Was Gary leaving her?* She couldn't envision a life without Gary.

"Lily and Stephanie are right,'' he said savagely. "All you care about is the company.''

"That's not true!'' What was happening to Gary and her?

He spun about and reached into his closet for an armful of clothes.

"I'll move the rest of my things into a guest room tomorrow. I've lost my wife to her ambitions.'' He charged from the room and out into the hallway, leaving the door to close slowly on its own.

Vicky stood motionless, white and stricken. It wasn't his music Gary wanted to pursue, she thought in sudden comprehension. He thought he could run from Bartonville and escape the past, escape the death of his dreams.

Gary would remain in Bartonville, but her life with him was over. It was as though part of her had died.

Chapter Twenty

VICKY KNEW that Sara was upset at the estrangement between Gary and herself, though Sara refrained from questioning this. The whole domestic staff knew Gary had moved into one of the guest rooms. There were few secrets in this household.

Gary made no effort to leave Bartonville, nor did he make any effort to pursue his music again. While Michael and Doug were away at school, the cottage remained closed, though both boys still expected Gary to work with them at the piano when they were in Bartonville.

With the approach of Christmas Sara began to talk with Vicky and Gary about a memorial to Daniel.

"I'm not sure just what," she said as the three of them settled themselves in the library after dinner. Gary, as always, gravitated toward the radio, in search of news of the fighting in Europe. "I just want something that will say that Daniel Barton made a contribution to this town."

"A real hospital," Vicky said immediately. "The town's population has quadrupled in the past fifteen years, and the health station is woefully inadequate. When accidents happen at the factory, we often have to call for an ambulance from Richmond. And the workers' families need access to local hospital care." She hesitated now. Gary had disassociated himself from their conversation. He was listening to reports of the recent Russian invasion of Finland, which violated a non-aggression pact between the two countries. "It'll be expensive," she warned.

"Daniel made his fortune with the help of people in this town," Sara said carefully. "I'd like to give something back. I've already checked on his stock portfolio. I'll sell and put that money into a fund to build the hospital. The Daniel Barton Memorial Hospital. Vicky, will you please work with Martin Woodstock on this? I have no head for business."

Vicky appointed herself, Gary, and Martin Woodstock to a committee to handle the building of the hospital. Almost immediately they realized that the war in Europe would have an effect on the construction. The country was moving into a stronger economy. Prices were escalating. Manpower was less available.

Vicky was pleased that Gary was involved in the project. He made the contacts with the various firms to be involved in building the hospital and came in with necessary figures. He made a point of stressing that decisions were to be made by Vicky and Martin.

"You two are the business heads on this committee," he said frankly. "I'm just bringing you the information." Still, Vicky knew he was happy to be part of the project. And Sara was pleased.

In mid-January Vicky began to see the need to expand Barton Tobacco in order to keep up with the changing economy. She remembered Daniel's boasting about General Pershing's cable to Washington, D.C. during the World War: "Tobacco is as indispensable as the daily ration; we must have thousands of tons without delay."

Daniel talked about how the use of cigarettes had increased during the war—and these days the consumption was even higher. It was time to expand, Vicky told herself, to prepare for what lay ahead. She immediately arranged for a quick trip to New York to confer with Frank Leslie. She trusted his instincts more than those of any of her executive staff.

She took an early morning train from Richmond, which would give her the afternoon and evening to confer with Frank. She'd sleep over in New York and leave in the morning.

By mid-afternoon she was closeted with Frank in his large, comfortable private office.

"We know the demand is going to increase," she said, a glint of challenge in her eyes. There were those who insisted the market had reached its saturation point. Already the war was disproving this.

"They're feeling shortages in England. Prices on machinery will go sky-high—"

"If this war keeps on, we may find it impossible to buy machinery at any price," Frank pointed out. "Steel will go for armaments."

"Then you agree with me that we ought to buy as much machinery as we can handle—and expand the plants to contain it?"

"Absolutely."

"And we should stockpile as much tobacco as we can buy at decent prices," she continued.

"It's already rising," he reminded. "You've heard the grumbling among the growers—"

"I just wanted you to confirm my feelings about this." She smiled in relief.

"We need to talk about the advertising," he told her. "I've got some people from the ad agency meeting with us for dinner. With so many American young men being called up by the draft, we've been talking about reslanting our advertising. Replace the beautiful young girls with handsome young men in uniform."

As was their custom they jumped from subject to subject, each stimulated by the ideas of the other. Shortly before seven they left the office for Toot Shors—for dinner and the conference with Barton's advertising men.

"Cigarettes are not only big business," Frank said with pride. "They're necessary for the morale of our armed forces. We provide a public service."

Up until early spring, Sara managed to keep the proposed hospital under wraps.

"We'll have to tell the others now," Sara said as she waited with Vicky and Gary for "the girls" and their husbands to arrive for a Sunday evening dinner. "We're breaking ground next week."

As often happened, dinner was held up almost half an hour because Lily and Stephanie and their husbands were late in arriving.

"I was waiting for this call from our ticket broker in New York," Lily explained as they all went into the dining room. "I wanted to be sure we'd be able to see *Life With Father* when we're up in New York next month."

"You called your ticket broker on a Sunday?" Gary raised an eyebrow in surprise.

"He's always open on Sunday evenings," Stephanie said coldly. "That's a big night for theatergoers. Of course, you never go to the theater."

"You never go anywhere." Lily's smile was malicious. "Really, people in Richmond think you're weird."

"I don't care what people in Richmond think of me," Gary said.

"What do you hear from Kara?" Vicky said, attempting to change the subject. Lily still insisted on bickering with Gary—as though they were ten and six instead of forty-five and forty. "Isn't she due home for spring vacation any day now?" Vicky knew Kara was due home the coming weekend. She'd talked with her on the phone for half an hour last night. Kara was upset that her mother insisted she apply for admission to a socially prestigious college in New York in the fall—"where you'll meet the right young men." Michael, too, was due home, Vicky remembered. She and Gary were so eager to see Kara and him.

"Kara's arriving on Saturday," Lily said, annoyed at being derailed from her attack on Gary. "She's carrying on about going to college here in Richmond. That's tacky." She shuddered in distaste. "Only unimportant people go to a local college."

"I'm going to military school in September," Adam said with a triumphant smile. He'd been outraged, Vicky remembered, when he discovered he wouldn't control the income from his trust fund until he was twenty-one. He was so impatient to grow up. "We'll all be away at school next term."

Vicky waited tensely for Sara to bring up the announcement of the hospital. They were both uneasy about the girls' reaction. It meant less money in the estate they anticipated inheriting one day.

When dessert and coffee arrived and Sara showed no indication of making her announcement, Vicky surmised she'd decided to wait until after dinner.

"Mother, when are you going to drop that ridiculous rule about our not smoking in the dining room?" Stephanie asked petulantly. Since Daniel died, the rule had been extended to include the library. "I just never enjoy ending a meal without a cigarette."

"You and Lily smoke like chimneys," Jeffrey told her. "It won't hurt either of you to have one less cigarette. In fact, it might do you good."

"You say that because you don't like to smoke," Lily said. "The whole world smokes today. I remember Dad saying that every year more people become smokers."

"I have news," Sara began after Adam had excused himself to go up to his room to listen to some sporting event on his radio. Now she told her daughters and their husbands about the ground-breaking for the Daniel Barton Memorial Hospital.

A stunned silence followed.

"Mother, that's going to be awfully expensive!" Lily said finally. High color stained her cheekbones as she exchanged an agitated glance with her sister.

"It's a fitting memorial to your father." Sara ignored her daughters' startled reactions. "Earnings of the company have jumped unbelievably in the past ten years. I can afford it."

"Daddy wouldn't want you to throw away money on strangers!" Lily said. "You know he wouldn't!"

"Lily, be quiet," Clark ordered. He knew Sara was determined to carry out this memorial to Daniel. Neither Vicky nor Sara genuinely liked Clark, but they conceded he was shrewd.

"You'll need somebody to handle staffing the hospital," Jeffrey said cautiously after an awkward pause. "A chief administrator who'll look out for the family interests."

"I've thought about that," Sara acknowledged. "Of course, I know your practice takes up much of your time—" Vicky noted the glint of cynical humor in her eyes.

"I could handle both," Jeffrey rushed to reassure her. A quick exchange between himself and Stephanie told Vicky they would try to salvage what they could from this new development. "You can't just leave this in the hands of an attorney." He was pouring forth the charm that did so well, rumor hinted, with his women patients. A charm, Vicky suspected, that was no longer potent with his wife.

"We'll talk about it," Sara stalled. "It'll be months before the building is completed, of course." But there was no doubt in Vicky's mind that Sara would succumb to Stephanie's entreaties and put Jeffrey in charge of the hospital. A handsome salary would naturally be part of the deal.

Over the next weekend Michael, Doug, and Kara arrived home for their spring breaks. On Monday, Lily and Stephanie and their husbands flew to Bermuda in Clark's plane for a ten-day visit with island-hopping friends. Doug and Kara were to stay at Barton Manor for the balance of their vacation time.

Barton Manor resounded with the young voices of the Barton cousins. For Vicky, Gary, and Sara, their presence was a joy. After dinner each night—except when the young people were involved in some social event—the family gathered in the library.

Tonight was unseasonably cold. Gary took on the task of starting a fire in the fireplace grate. Vicky and Sara relaxed on a sofa while the four cousins settled in another corner of the room to talk avidly about their plans for the next school year. Adam triumphant at being one of them now. Kara still teasing Michael about having skipped a year in elementary school so that he was three years ahead of her rather than the two years dictated by their age.

"It's incredible to me," Sara said, radiating affection, "how by just looking at them anybody would know they were cousins. Not Adam," she conceded. "He's the image of Daniel. But Michael and Kara and Doug all look like Gary at that age."

The four of them—Gary and the kids—looked liked Sara, Vicky thought tenderly. They all had the same dark hair, the same fine features, the same eyes that seemed to change with their moods from blue to green. Sometimes Michael's mannerisms reminded her of her father—the way he listened to fine music, the way he lifted his tea cup.

She knew that Gary was anxious about the war in Europe, terrified that this country would be drawn into the conflict. He worried about Michael and Doug and Adam if this should happen.

"We've got to stay out of the war!" Gary said repeatedly. "I don't want my sons involved!"

This evening—as the four young ones talked about school—the war seemed far removed. Michael was intent on making Kara understand that New York was a great place to go to school.

"Look," he said soothingly, "if you have problems, I'm right up there at Columbia."

"I really don't want to go to college," Kara said, tossing her long dark hair. "I want to go to dramatic school." At boarding school she'd discovered the drama club and had become enthralled by the theater. "I want to go to the American Academy of Dramatic Art. That's in New York, too." She giggled, then sighed. "Mother and Dad think I'm nuts. But at least, in New York I'll be able to go to see the Broadway plays."

"When you get out of college, you'll decide what you want to do," Michael encouraged. "You'll be grown then."

Sometimes it startled her, Vicky mused, to realize she had a twenty-year-old son. She didn't feel like a thirty-eight-year-old matron. Sara was always saying she looked a dozen years younger than her age. But Gary never set foot in the bedroom they'd shared for so many years—not since that night she'd refused to move to New York. Sara worried about that, too.

The fire a healthy blaze now, Gary crossed to turn on the radio. He adjusted the volume so as not to disturb the others, but Vicky strained to listen. The war news was upsetting. Nazi forces were smashing the Norwegian resistance despite the help of British troops.

But what about *their* lives, Vicky asked herself. She was still young. She wanted her husband back in her bed.

On May 10, 1940, Nazi troops invaded Belgium, Luxembourg, and the Netherlands. Every night Vicky and Gary rushed from the dinner table to sit before the radio to hear the latest war news, both ever conscious that their own country could be drawn into the war at any time, both terrified that Michael might have to fight.

In late May the whole world listened to the news that German armored columns were arriving at the English Channel and trapping four hundred thousand British and French troops around Dunkirk. Now a hastily assembled armada of destroyers and small civilian craft sped across the Channel to retrieve the stranded soldiers from the beaches and transport them to England.

On June tenth, Italy declared war on Britain and France—at a moment when France was desperately fighting a losing battle against the Nazis. Vicky was distraught. Mail was not coming through from Simone and Henri. *Were they all right?*

In June the world learned that the Nazi armies were parading through the streets of Paris.

"Marshal Pétain surrendered in the same railway car at Compiègne where the Germans signed the armistice in 1918," Gary said bitterly.

Compiègne was just outside of Paris, Vicky remembered. Once— when Gary had had the staff car at his disposal—the two of them had driven there for a picnic. But now it was France who had been defeated. Simone and Henri were out in the countryside, Vicky told herself. Please, God, let them survive this horror.

This summer an air of gloom hovered over Barton Manor. The uncertainty about Simone and Henri made the war intensely personal for Vicky. Adam had only faint recall of Simone and Henri, but they had made a deep impression on Michael, who was five years older than Adam. From time to time since their visit to Paris, he'd asked about "Aunt Simone and Uncle Henri."

In early September, Michael and Kara left together for New York and their respective schools. Seeing them off at the Richmond depot, Vicky found some comfort in Kara's pleasure that her roommate in her last year at boarding school would be her roommate again. Texan-born Betsy Canfield had spent a week with Kara at Barton Manor during the summer. Betsy was a lovely, warm girl, Vicky had discovered. She and Kara would be good for each other.

A few days later Vicky was again at the Richmond depot to see Adam off to his school. He'd refused to go to the same school as Doug, but the one he'd chosen was close to Bartonville. Gary had not come to the station with them. He was upset that Adam was going to military school—he hated anything that reeked of war.

"Call us, Adam," Vicky entreated. The house would feel so empty with both boys gone. "We're almost always home on Sunday nights."

"Sure, Mother." Adam kissed her goodbye and headed for the train. Except for a small weekender, his luggage had been sent ahead of him.

Vicky stood and watched until the train began the slow chug out of the depot. In a window seat Adam waved an ebullient farewell. All the children would be away until Thanksgiving, Vicky thought wistfully. But she'd be working long hours at the office, she reminded herself. The months would fly past.

Early in the new school year Michael decided to go on to graduate school at Columbia. Vicky was relieved. As long as he was in college, he wouldn't be subject to the draft.

Adam was doing well at his military school and thrilled to be on the football team. Kara was enthralled with New York. She and Betsy saw every new play that came along, she wrote Vicky. "Sometimes when we're almost broke we climb up to the second balcony for twenty-five-cent seats. We've seen *There Shall Be No Night* and *Time of Your Life* and—oh, just everything!" Secretly Vicky sent Kara a generous check—"*an advance birthday present, so you don't have to climb up to the second balconies.*"

Doug was excited about going to college next fall instead of boarding school. He wrote that this last year wasn't so bad because he had a new roommate—a young French boy whose parents had managed to get him out of Paris and to the United States only weeks before Paris fell to the Germans last June. Like Doug, Paul was dedicated to music. They talked about writing a musical together one day. They'd both decided to apply to New York University, and both were accepted.

"I feel as though we're living in two places," Vicky said at a family dinner at Barton Manor. "Bartonville and New York City."

"New York isn't what it used to be," Lily said scornfully. "But of course, Paris and London are out this summer."

The cigarette industry was booming. Understandably, Gary remarked. "The soldiers want their nicotine tranquilizers," he drawled. For no reason she could understand, Vicky was disturbed by his remark. Perhaps, she thought later, she remembered Dr. Gordon's offhand suggestion that Daniel's lung cancer might have been brought on by his chain-smoking.

But that was ridiculous. Other doctors all said that though cigarette smoking didn't do any good, it did no harm, either. They were wrong about smoking doing no good, Vicky thought. Many millions of people found cherished relaxation in smoking.

Vicky looked forward to attending Michael's graduation from Columbia College late in May. She, Gary, and Sara went up to New York with shared enthusiasm. Frank Leslie had arranged a suite for them at the Plaza, a three-bedroom suite, she noted self-consciously. Gary had made the arrangements with Frank.

She was delighted to see Doug and Kara as well as Michael. They spent a joyous first evening together, with dinner at the elegant Le Pavillon—which Lily insisted was New York's sole cause for fame. Yet, strangely, this trip to New York was traumatic for Vicky.

Lying sleepless the first night, she tried to dissect her feelings. She'd made countless quick business trips to New York in the past years for meetings with Frank Leslie and the New York staff or conferences with their Manhattan ad agency. But this was a family trip, laden with ghosts.

Two days later Vicky and Gary, along with Sara, Kara, and Doug, attended the graduation exercises at Columbia. That evening Michael took them to a concert at Carnegie Hall. Settling in her seat beside Gary, Vicky's mind raced back through the years. She remembered with fresh anguish—as though it were only days past—that night at

Aeolian Hall when Gary heard George Gershwin play his *Rhapsody in Blue* and declared his own musical career was over. He'd been afraid, she thought compassionately, that he couldn't measure up to Gershwin's genius. How sad that he refused to compromise. Sad for both Gary and herself.

Chapter Twenty-one

I N THE MIDST of an early summer heat wave Vicky received a phone call at home from Frank. Instantly she was on the alert. Frank only called her at Barton Manor when confronting a serious problem.

"Have you seen the July *Reader's Digest*?" he asked.

"No." Her voice was sharp with anxiety.

"All hell's breaking loose in the cigarette industry," he said grimly. "The *Digest* is tearing down the whole industry with complaints our advertising is more fiction than fact. They've run tests in a lab and have come up with the report that there's little difference between any of the major brands."

"We know that, Frank." Long ago Daniel had instilled in her the understanding that great merchandising and advertising sold cigarettes.

"There're rumors around town that some of the companies will sue. I don't believe it," he admitted.

"That would be stupid," Vicky said flatly. "Why all this fuss now?"

"Good for circulation," Frank guessed. "They're claiming that we're guilty of lying to the public about what's special about each of the major brands. They say the chemical differences are slight, we all use a similar method of manufacturing, so it all comes down to flavor. But Consumers Union claims in blindfold tests even heavy smokers can't tell one cigarette from another."

"Frank, I don't think we have anything to worry about. Look, the

A.M.A. has accepted us, and all of the major brands, for advertising in the Journal of the American Medical Association. If they thought we were deceiving the public, they'd say so."

"I know," he conceded, "but it bothers me that the *Digest*'s five million readers are going to read this tripe. Of course, they admit their lab research focused on such a small number—twenty-four cigarettes from each brand. How could that be conclusive?"

"We all know that there's no great difference between any of the top brands. We learned long ago that it's how we merchandise that sells cigarettes. I don't think we need to be upset about it," she reiterated. "The public loves to smoke. It provides pleasure—at low cost—for millions of people. They'll read that article, and see that it really has nothing to say. So they don't like the industry's claims in advertising. Everybody knows that most of what goes into advertising is myth."

"We'll have to revamp our new campaign," Frank said thoughtfully. "We don't want any problems."

"Talk with the agency and get back to me," Vicky told him after a moment. "I know you feel the *Digest* is smudging the image of the whole industry. But it's like Daniel always said—we're providing a service."

It soon became clear that the *Reader's Digest* attack was causing no harm to the cigarette industry. The few leaders who'd predicted a year or so ago that the market was reaching its saturation point and would level off were wrong. Cigarette sales were soaring. In one of his weekly phone conversations with Vicky, Frank was jubilant.

"People have more money to spend," Frank pointed out. "And there's war nerves," he added on a suddenly somber note, "and the quickening pace of our daily lives. You were right last year when you decided we should expand."

"I wouldn't have gone ahead without your approval," she told him candidly.

"We're using the military angle in the next campaign," he reported. "No more beautiful girls. Handsome young men in military uniform. Everybody's jumping on that bandwagon. Lucky Strike's and Chesterfield's radio show band leaders are going to do goodwill stints in the army camps—"

"Let's move into that area, too," Vicky said, but her heart pounded as she envisioned Michael as a draftee. Let him be able to stay in school. Let the fighting be over before American boys were involved. "And work out some kind of special deal for men in uniform—I mean, price-wise."

Now they settled down for earnest discussion of what to take up with their ad agency. That was the most important cog in their selling machinery.

In September there was the usual rush of getting the four young people off to school. Again, Barton Manor seemed painfully empty. Only at Thanksgiving did the house become alive again with the usual gathering of the clan for Thanksgiving dinner. Doug brought Paul Giraud home with him. Paul's parents were trapped in France, but they'd managed to transfer funds to New York to see Paul through college. They were adamant about his not becoming involved in the fighting.

This year, Vicky thought, Kara and Doug didn't seem to mind that their parents left right after Thanksgiving dinner for a house party at a Charleston plantation. Barton Manor was home to them. It was Vicky who was their sympathetic confidante. Only she knew that Kara and Doug meant to remain in New York after college graduation, Kara to break into the Broadway theater and Doug to work with Paul on a musical they hoped to have produced in some experimental playhouse in Greenwich Village.

On Saturday of the Thanksgiving weekend the Daniel Barton Memorial Hospital held its formal opening. Vicky knew that Sara was hurt that the girls and their husbands were not present.

"Jeffrey will be there to receive his weekly checks as chief administrator," Sara surmised in a rare moment of overt bitterness. "For their father's sake they should have been here!"

"Everybody's so pleased," Vicky whispered consolingly as the ceremonies began. "The hospital provides a real service for the community."

She'd never loved her father-in-law, Vicky acknowledged as the mayor began a long-winded eulogy to Daniel. She'd never really liked him. But she'd respected his shrewdness, his uncanny knowledge about the cigarette industry. And he'd come to respect her. She'd been grateful for that. And she'd learned everything she knew about the industry from Daniel.

With the arrival of December, Vicky was already anticipating the college winter break. Michael would be home for a long stretch, along with Kara and Doug. Adam had a shorter vacation, but that didn't concern him. He was eager to return to school to try out for the basketball team.

On Sunday afternoon, December seventh, Vicky settled herself in her bedroom to write a letter to Michael. It pleased her that he saw much of his cousins in New York. Of course, music was a bond between Michael and Doug. Michael had written enthusiastically about going to the theater with Doug and Paul to see *Let's Face It*, the Cole Porter musical with Eve Arden and Danny Kaye. He'd told Kara to be sure to see it.

Then suddenly the Sunday afternoon silence of the house was broken by an agitated summons from Gary. His voice filtered up to the second floor and into her room with an eerie urgency. "Vicky! Get down to the library!"

Vicky put aside her pen and rushed into the hall.

"I'll be right there, Gary—" *What was he so upset about?*

She hurried down the stairs, reaching the foyer just as Sara came back from a church luncheon.

"What a beautifully warm day for December," Sara began.

"Something's happened," Vicky broke in. "Gary sounded terribly upset when he called me."

Now Gary appeared at the library door.

"Pearl Harbor is being attacked by the Japanese!" he said grimly. "I'd just turned on the radio to wait for the Philharmonic concert—"

"Pearl Harbor?" For a moment Sara was bewildered.

"Our naval base in Hawaii," Gary told her, white with shock. "Around eight AM Hawaii time—one-thirty here—more than three hundred Japanese planes attacked our Pacific Fleet units at the naval base and our Army aircraft at Hickam Field."

"Oh, my God!" All at once Vicky's mind hurtled back through the years to the bombings of Paris. She remembered her terror at the first bombings. "Has there been a lot of damage?"

"They're not coming through with much specific information," Gary said while the emotional voice of a radio announcer reiterated news of the attack. "But it sounds as though our planes are being destroyed while they're still on the ground!"

Shaken but refusing to lose her poise, Sara summoned Zachary and asked that coffee be brought to the library.

"It's going to be a long afternoon," she predicted, joining Gary and Vicky before the radio.

"You know what this means," Gary said agonizingly. "We're at war. The draft is going to be accelerated. I prayed that Michael would never have to see what I saw in France."

"He'll be allowed to finish the school year—" Vicky clung to this. She recoiled from the vision of Michael in military uniform, Michael fighting in a war. "By then the war will be over," she said.

"Vicky, don't be naive!" Gary lashed at her. "It'll be a long and bloody war. Worse than we saw the last time. What's the matter with this world? Does every generation have to see its young butchered in battle?"

For the rest of the afternoon they sat huddled before the radio and listened to the meager news that was coming through. Sara ordered that dinner be served on trays in the library. Already, the nation was preparing for local defense. Finally, at close to ten PM, Sara rose to her feet.

"I might as well call it a night," she said tiredly. "They're just repeating the same things over and over again." There were no definite figures about casualties, but it was obvious they were heavy. Naval ships and aircraft had taken a rough beating.

"Japan hasn't lost a war since 1598." Gary's eyes glittered ominously. "I've read that their planes are better than anything we have in the sky. But we'll beat them. At what cost in lives I don't want to guess. Nobody truly wins a war."

"I'm going up to bed, too," Vicky said. She'd finish the letter to Michael tomorrow. No, she corrected herself, she'd phone him tomorrow night.

"I'll listen a little longer." Gary leaned forward to lower the volume. "It won't disturb you."

The whole world had changed in these last few hours, Vicky thought as she walked into her bedroom. She'd worried for years about what was happening in Germany. She'd worried about the invasion of Poland and the outbreak of war in Europe. But now the war had moved onto their own territory.

Numbly she prepared for bed. She was exhausted from anxiety. Michael was twenty-one, his life just beginning. Adam, thank God, was only sixteen. Would it be a long and bloody war, as Gary predicted? She'd lived through one war—she hadn't expected to see another.

As she brushed her hair, her eyes fastened to the cluster of snapshots of Michael and Adam on her dressing table. She started at a knock on her door. That would be Sara, she guessed.

"Come in—" She laid aside her hairbrush and rose to her feet.

The door opened. Gary walked in.

"I can't believe what's happened." His eyes were bleak as they met hers. "I don't want Michael fighting in this war! Nor Adam nor Doug. I don't want to see any American boys dying because of a few maniacs loose in the world! Why should anybody have to die that way?"

"I'm so scared, Gary." She abandoned her usual façade of strength. "I remember what it was like in Paris—the wounded coming back from the front, the soldiers without arms or legs, those with their faces blown away by shrapnel. I've seen what most American mothers haven't seen—" She closed her eyes as though to shut out those memories.

"Vicky, we came through it," he reminded. "We have to be strong now—because there is no other way."

His arms pulled her close, and she buried her face against his chest. Now it was Gary comforting her, Gary murmuring soothing encouragement. Vicky lifted her face to look into his eyes.

"Gary, how can it happen to us again this way? How many wars must we see in our lifetime?"

"I prayed it would never happen again," he murmured, smoothing her hair. "Early on I told myself, 'We have the League of Nations now—we can keep peace in the world.' But who can foresee the likes of the Nazis and the Fascists—and the Japanese? We'll see this through together—"

He kissed her tenderly on the cheek. Then all at once she felt his hands tighten at her shoulders. She lifted her face to his, her eyes questioning, her heart pounding. His mouth reached for hers. They clung together, the years seeming to rush backward.

It had been so long, she thought. In comforting each other they had rediscovered passion. As he swept her off her feet and carried her to the bed, she remembered their first night together at the Ritz in Paris.

For a little while they forgot the rest of the world in each other's arms. She murmured in heated encouragement when he lifted himself above her and began the passionate journey they had not shared for almost two years.

"Oh!" She cried out again and again while they moved together. For now the intervening years were swept away. For now.

As had become the custom, Vicky observed Hanukkah by lighting the Hanukkah candles and by giving gifts to both Michael and Adam, though Adam always pretended to ignore the holiday. Last year she attended the Hanukkah party given at the synagogue, but this year she was too anxious about the United States' entry into the war to feel in a mood to celebrate.

She cherished Michael's Hanukkah gift to her—a copy of last year's Pulitzer Prize novel, John Steinbeck's *The Grapes of Wrath*, which she had mentioned wanting to read. Michael was so like Gary in his capacity for compassion, she thought lovingly.

Michael's homecoming for the college winter recess held a special poignance this year. He was in graduate school—but would that keep him out of uniform? She felt recurrent guilt that she prayed—along with Gary—that Michael might not have to fight.

The Japanese had already invaded the Philippines. Guam surrendered to Japanese forces. On the day Michael was to arrive, news came that Wake Island in the Pacific had fallen to the Japanese.

Much of Europe was in the hands of the Nazis. Russia was fighting ferociously against the advance of Nazi armies. Great Britain had long been under attack.

In Bartonville and Richmond—as in towns and cities across the nation—a system of air raid wardens was set up. There were practice blackouts, and they were urged to acquire black cloth to cover windows at night. Sirens were to be installed in key areas. Already air raid spotters were assigned positions to search the skies for enemy planes.

On the scheduled day, Vicky and Gary went together to the Richmond depot to meet Michael. Vicky was disappointed that Gary had not moved back into her bedroom. Still, they were closer than they had been in years, she comforted herself. There were nights when they forgot all their fears and anguish in each other's arms.

"The train's late," Gary grumbled as they waited before the tracks.

"Two minutes," Vicky said, but she shared his eagerness to see Michael. "Here it comes now!" She spied the train approaching in the distance.

Tomorrow Doug and Kara were both coming home, and the following day Adam would be here. But this afternoon the normal air of festivity that seemed to fill the depot when students arrived home was tainted with a covert apprehension. These were the boys that would be going into uniform. Dear God, let the war be over soon!

Minutes later she was clinging to Michael, grateful for his presence, listening avidly to his exuberant report of his activities since his last letter.

"You'll be sleeping till noon every day," Gary joshed. "I remember when I came home from college—"

"Look, make sure you don't say anything to Aunt Stephanie and Uncle Jeffrey about the concert Doug's giving in April at the music school," he warned his parents.

"Will it be the same week as yours?" Vicky asked. "Dad and I are coming up for it, you know."

"Yeah." He dropped an arm about his mother as the three of them walked toward the car. "Doug's so grateful for all those 'advance birthday checks' you've sent him. He couldn't have kept up the lessons without them."

Occasionally she felt guilty that she was supporting Doug's secret aspirations. But how could she not help him, she thought defiantly. If Gary had received outside help, how different his life would have been!

"Doug and Paul are working on a musical," Michael told them. "They don't have much time, of course, what with school—but they make a terrific team. 'Music by Douglas Nelson, words by Paul Giraud.' I may even get around to doing some composing for them," he added, all at once self-conscious. "How do you like that? An aeronautical engineer who writes music on the side."

On the drive to Barton Manor Gary plied Michael with questions about his piano coach. She knew that Gary would have liked to see Michael abandon his engineering studies to concentrate on music—to do, she thought with anguish, what he had not been able to do. But why couldn't Gary focus on his music now? *There were no barriers any longer.*

Vicky treasured every minute of Michael's time at home, though she listened with escalating alarm to the somber talk between Michael and Gary about the progress of the war. On occasion Adam joined in.

To Adam, fighting a war was an exciting adventure. He was vowing to enlist the minute he was old enough.

Michael knew the ugliness of war, Vicky tried to reassure herself. He'd listened enough to his father to understand that. But as his winter recess shortened, he was hinting at the possibility of his enlisting. He knew the urgency to stop the atrocities of Hitler and Mussolini in Europe—and the Japanese in the Pacific.

"Don't even think about enlisting!" Gary ordered Michael when they waited at the Richmond depot for the New York–bound train. "You have to finish school. By then this insanity should be over."

Even while Michael promised that he wouldn't enlist with graduation only a few months off, Vicky could read his mind. If he enlisted, he'd have a choice of branches of service. He was so enamored of flying—and the Air Force would give him that chance.

Only days before Vicky expected Michael home for the spring break he phoned to tell her that—along with a Columbia buddy—he'd decided it was time to enlist.

"I know how you and Dad feel about my hanging around until I get my master's—"

"Michael, it's only another two months," she interrupted frantically. But would the world change in another two months? "Please, let's talk about it when you come home."

"We'll talk, Mom," he agreed gently. He hadn't called her "Mom" since he was eleven. "But the way things are going I don't see how I can stay out. It's a matter of months before I'll be drafted anyway—and if I enlist, I'll have my choice of services. Dad's going to be terribly upset. You'll have to help me make him understand."

Chapter Twenty-two

MICHAEL CAME home to argue heatedly into each night with his father while Vicky and Sara watched helplessly. German submarines were taking a staggering toll in the Atlantic. While Michael was home, Bataan fell to the Japanese. For the Allies the situation was critical. Disaster followed disaster. Michael's mind was made up. He couldn't continue at school when the world was in chaos.

Michael returned to school only to wind up his affairs. He was not alone in deserting classes to enlist. He was jubilant when he was accepted in the Air Force and sent off to Texas for training. Thank God, Vicky told herself over and over again, Adam was too young to go into military service.

The day after Michael left for Texas, Vicky received a phone call at the office from Adam's school. He'd injured a knee in a basketball game.

"It's not serious," the physical education instructor assured her, "but surgery is required and your signature is necessary on the release form."

"Where is he?" Vicky asked. Any kind of surgery frightened her.

"At Madison Hospital here in town. But the doctors say that it isn't serious," he reiterated. "And Adam will graduate in June, right on schedule."

"His father and I will be there within—" she glanced anxiously at her watch, "within four hours. Just give me the address. And tell Adam we're on our way."

Vicky rushed to locate Gary, told him what had happened.

"Now don't be alarmed," Gary urged. "It's routine to require a parent's signature. I'm sure it's minor surgery. But we'll drive right up to the hospital."

Vicky and Gary arrived at Madison Hospital in three hours. For once Gary ignored the speed limits. They found an unfamiliarly sub-dued Adam in a private room arranged by his school.

"It wasn't my fault," he told his parents. "I was pushed."

"These things happen, Adam." Gary managed a calm that Vicky knew was a façade.

The surgeon scheduled to handle the operation pointed out that the surgery was hardly life-threatening, but there was a strong possibility that Adam's sports activities might be limited in the future. "He won't have a limp or anything like that, but that knee won't take rough treatment."

The operation was performed almost immediately. Adam would re-main in the hospital a week, be on crutches another three or four. He could return to classes as soon as he was out of the hospital but with limited activities.

"We'll do everything to make sure he's comfortable," the anxious physical education instructor promised. "We'll make sure he doesn't overdo it."

Adam was alternately rebellious and sullen. Vicky agonized over his state of mind. At the end of the second day after Adam's surgery, Gary insisted she return to Bartonville.

"You're needed back home," he rationalized. "Adam's going to be fine except for some stiffness in the knee. I'll stay here until he's out of the hospital." He managed a wry smile. "At least, we know he'll never be drafted."

With the first hot spell in June, Lily and Stephanie were searching frenziedly for a cottage at Virginia Beach.

"I don't know how you all stand this awful heat," Lily complained at dinner at Barton Manor the night before she and Stephanie were to leave. "I just don't have the constitution for it."

"As little as you're wearing, you shouldn't be aware of it," Clark drawled, inspecting Lily's backless white pique dress that barely skimmed her knees.

"Have you seen their bathing suits?" Jeffrey asked. "I know we're expecting cloth rationing, but these two have a headstart."

Lily ignored her husband and brother-in-law.

"Mother, we've taken this darling little house right on the beach. Why don't you come out for two or three days?"

"I'm busy with my volunteer groups." Sara smiled faintly. "I wouldn't want to shirk my duties at a time like this."

"Mother, nobody's going to attack us." Stephanie exchanged a superior smile with her sister. "All this nonsense about air raid wardens and blackouts."

"You've never seen war!" Gary shot back. "You never even think about this one." Vicky knew he had no patience with his sisters when so many American boys, including Michael, were laying their lives on the line.

"What good would it do for us to fret?" Lily asked.

"You might get off your rump and do some volunteer work," Clark told her. "I *am* on the city council. Folks here in town expect my wife to show some patriotic fervor."

"Don't be so stuffy, Clark." Lily frowned in annoyance.

"Anyhow, tomorrow night at this time we'll be sitting on our deck and enjoying dinner under the stars," Stephanie said smugly. She stared at the somber faces about the table. "Well, you can't be serious all the time."

Four evenings later—with the heat wave showing no signs of breaking—Sara decided dinner would be served on the side veranda of Barton Manor. When Vicky arrived from the office, she joined Sara and Gary there. Now Effie began to serve.

"There's a breeze from the river," Gary began with a sigh of pleasure, then stopped short at the sound of a car pulling to a strident crunch out front.

"Who on earth is that?" Sara asked.

"Lily and Stephanie," Vicky identified the light, agitated voices. "What are they doing in town so soon?"

"Mother, you won't believe what happened," Lily began dramatically as she charged toward them. "It was awful—we might have been killed!"

"What happened?" Sara asked, familiar with her daughters' frequent theatrics.

"We saw a German sub just offshore of Virginia Beach," Stephanie picked up breathlessly. "We saw it torpedo two American merchant vessels!"

"How close to shore?" Gary asked.

"Well, a few miles," Lily conceded. "But if it came a little closer, we could have been killed."

"When bombs rain overhead, then you worry," Gary said drily. "Not when a submarine is a few miles offshore."

Still, Vicky conceded, an attack just off Virginia Beach was a startling reminder that the country was at war, and that Michael was in the Air Force. They didn't know when he'd be shipped out. Or where.

"Gary, you never change!" Lily accused. "You're always trying to pick a fight with me or Stephanie. I don't think you'd care if a torpedo had come ashore and killed the two of us."

"Lily, stop that nonsense," Sara ordered. "You're forty-two years old—it's time you grew up."

"You don't have to throw my age at me," Lily sulked. "Nobody thinks I'm a day over thirty. Do you suppose we could have dinner? We just drove home without thinking of eating. We thought we'd find a little compassion."

Vicky ignored the dinner conversation. She was exhausted from the long hours at the office, striving to increase Barton's productivity, struggling to replace the workers who were going into military uniform. Demands for deliveries were soaring, with a huge amount going overseas.

She felt personally driven by the knowledge that American officers ranked cigarettes among the "Big Three" necessities of war—the other two being food and mail. The story filtered back to the industry about how General MacArthur had taken time off from his military duties to huddle with Prime Minister Curtain over a plan to allow Aussies to buy cigarettes at the U.S. PXs.

It seemed a matter of time, Vicky feared, before Barton Tobacco—and other firms—would have to ration cigarettes to their dealers. But she felt a compulsive need to be able to assign massive shipments to the armed forces. That was Barton Tobacco's patriotic duty.

* * *

In August Michael came home on a weekend pass. Suddenly the house exuded a festive atmosphere. There was a silent pact between Vicky and Gary and Sara to conceal their fears for his safety. They knew it was a matter of weeks or months before Michael would be shipped overseas.

For Vicky there was the painful recall of her own years of living with German bombings over Paris. Like women all over the country, she contrived an air of optimism, of patriotic pride—but ever since Michael had enlisted, her nights were fraught with insomnia. She knew, too, the anguish that afflicted Gary.

While Sara had been born almost ten years after the end of the War Between the States, she had grown up in the shadows of a devastating war. Daniel had not been drafted in World War I because he was married and a father of three, but her parents never ceased to talk of the horrors of war. Vicky knew Sara's air of serenity was only a façade. She, too, worried constantly about Michael. The three of them worried about all the young men and young women whose lives were at stake through no fault of their own.

Though Adam talked excitedly about going up to New York City to college, Vicky knew he fumed about the injury to his knee that would keep him out of military service. He'd always wanted to do whatever Michael did—except study music. He was angry, too, that he had not been accepted at Columbia College, like Doug. He was following Kara to NYU and talked about going on to Columbia Law.

"You'll have to settle down and work for good grades if you're thinking of law school," Vicky warned him. Adam was so bright, she thought in frustration, but he ignored whatever didn't interest him.

"I'll make Columbia Law," he bragged. "Or Harvard."

Subconsciously she remembered that Harvard Law had a quota system for Jewish students. But then Adam had always rejected his mother's faith.

On a Saturday morning early in November, Michael called to say he was coming home that evening on a pass.

"I'm catching a ride on an army plane flying into Richmond," he explained. The Byrd Airport had become the Richmond Army Air Base. "I have to report in early Monday morning."

"Tell us when you expect to arrive," Vicky said, her heart pounding. He couldn't tell her over the phone, of course—but she guessed he was being shipped out. "Dad and I will be there to pick you up."

Almost an hour before Michael was scheduled to arrive, Vicky and Gary waited at Richmond Army Air Base for his plane. Vicky remembered Michael's excitement when they'd brought him here back in 1927, when he was only seven, to see Charles Lindbergh, who'd come to Byrd Field for the airport's dedication. From that point on he'd been fascinated by flying. Still, he'd clung to his music, she remembered tenderly. His dual loves.

"He's going to be shipped out," Gary said, interrupting her introspection with fatalistic calm. "He may not be able to tell us—but it's happening."

"He's going to be all right." Vicky reached for Gary's hand. "Let's just pray the war's over fast."

"The tide's turning in the Pacific," Gary admitted. "We beat the Japs at Guadalcanal." His face tightened. "I don't want to think about the price."

Michael's plane landed right on schedule. Gazing into his eyes Vicky knew this was the last time they would see Michael on American soil until the war was over. Like Gary, she gave him no inkling of her anguish at this realization. They talked almost gaily about local happenings.

"It's supposed to be top secret," Gary told Michael, "but the *Times-Dispatch* is launching a campaign next week to advocate the abolition of segregation on streetcars and buses."

"Hey, that's great!" Michael's face lighted. "I'm proud of Richmond."

"Lula Mae's making a big dinner," Vicky said. "Everything you especially like."

"How's Grandma?" he asked.

"Dying to see you." Vicky smiled. "She won't admit it, of course, but you're her favorite grandchild."

Despite the chill of the evening, Sara was waiting on the veranda to welcome Michael.

"You look like a movie star in your uniform," Sara told him after they'd embraced. Her fingers brushed the lieutenant bars at his shoulder. "I'm so proud of you. But let's get to the dinner table. Lula Mae will never forgive me if the roast beef has to stay in the oven too long."

Since the night was cool, Vicky asked Zachary to prepare a fire in the library fireplace. They'd have their after-dinner coffee in there, she decided. Tonight and tomorrow night belonged to the three people closest to Michael. She was relieved that Lily and Stephanie were visiting friends in Charleston—she didn't want to share Michael with anyone else these brief hours.

Over dinner he talked calmly about being shipped out.

"We don't know where we're headed, of course. There's all this talk about a Second Front—possibly Egypt or Malta." He smiled wryly. "We'll know when we get there—and you'll know when you receive a card with my APO number."

Over coffee in the library—with an aromatic blaze in the fireplace grate—Michael talked about Doug and Kara, up in New York.

"Doug's writing some beautiful music," he said. "He and Paul are a great combo." He hesitated. "You know what I'd love to do tonight, Dad?" He turned to his father. "That is, if the old piano in the music room is in tune—"

"I have it tuned every year," Sara told him.

"What would you like to do, Michael?" Vicky prodded.

"I'd like to play a duet with Dad. The way we used to do when I was a kid." His eyes rested on his father with deep affection. "How about it?"

"Sure." Vicky thought she saw tears in Gary's eyes. "Let's go."

Sara sat beside Vicky on the sofa in the music room while Gary and Michael played a series of duets. Both women became caught up in the beauty of the music.

"I failed Gary," Sara murmured, the sound of her voice covered by the music. "I failed my obligations to my son. I should have fought Daniel and saw to it that Gary had every chance to fulfill his dreams."

She had failed him, Vicky thought in anguish. But how could she have walked out on the company when Daniel died? She, too, had obligations—to Sara and to the children.

Why couldn't Gary pursue his music here? Why was it important to go to New York? But she knew the answer to that, as she had three years ago. Gary thought he could run from Bartonville and escape the past. Escape the death of his dreams.

After some anxiety about a return flight to his base, Michael worked out arrangements. He would fly out at dawn. Vicky insisted that she and Gary would see him off.

"Dad and I will sleep when you leave. So I'll go in to the office late one morning," she shrugged, and Michael's eyes lit with tender laughter.

"You'll sleep two hours, feel guilty, and rush to the office," he teased.

They sat over endless cups of coffee and talked while the fire in the grate mellowed into ruddy, gray-edged embers. Sara remained with them until close to midnight when she conceded she was falling asleep on the sofa. Michael walked with her to the staircase, exchanged a warm farewell.

Time seemed to stand still in the library while Michael talked about small incidents in his growing years that Vicky had thought he'd forgotten long ago.

"If I'm sent to Europe, maybe I'll get a chance to see Aunt Simone," he said. "I haven't seen her since the time we all went to Paris together. I remember you showed me the rickety little house where you lived with her in Paris. She brought Adam and me the most wonderful cookies—"

It was still dark when the three of them settled themselves in the car for the short drive to the airport. A few stars flickered overhead in the night sky. As they drove, the first hints of dawn appeared.

"When I come home again," Michael promised, "I'll take the two of you up in a plane. I can't believe you've never flown!"

"Clark's offered to fly us down to Palm Beach," Gary recalled, "but neither your mother nor I ever quite trusted him. You," he joshed with a playful poke at Michael, "we'll trust."

The sky was faintly pink when the plane on which he was "hitching a ride" came down on the runway. Suddenly there was time for no more than a quick embrace. Then Michael ran toward the plane. Before he climbed aboard, he swung around and waved to his parents. His smile was warm, radiating enthusiasm and confidence.

Vicky and Gary lingered until the plane was a speck in the sky. There would be no beautiful sunrise this morning, Vicky thought while the gray morning chill wrapped them in discomfort.

"You'll catch a cold standing here this way," Gary said softly, a hand at her elbow. "Let's go home."

Where was Michael going, she asked herself in silent torment. To fly against the Japanese in the Pacific? To fight the German planes over England or France or even in Germany? How would she survive, knowing her precious child was fighting a war?

Chapter Twenty-three

Each day seemed to drag end-lessly until the postcard that provided Michael's APO number arrived and Vicky and Gary knew now that he was somewhere in England.

"Michael's going to be all right," Gary told her. It was as though he was trying to convince himself as well as her, she thought. "I came through my war—he'll come through his."

Gary threw himself into volunteer war work. He arranged salvage drives, worked with War Bond committees, volunteered at the Richmond armories that had been set up to provide sleeping quarters for servicemen on leave. And—like Vicky—he waited anxiously for Michael's letters.

Since June much of the mail from servicemen overseas consisted of the new V-Mail. Though V-Mail allowed a minute amount of space for writing, it arrived with commendable speed. In between, Michael promised, he'd write longer, conventional airmail letters.

"Gary, look how tiny he's trying to write," Vicky said tenderly when Michael's first V-mail arrived. Normally Michael's handwriting was large and sprawling. "So he can say as much as possible."

Late in February Michael and his crew were given a weekend pass and headed for London. Along with his navigator—a high-spirited young Texan named Bert Winston—Michael settled into the first available hotel room, then set out to celebrate.

"I want to eat like a pig," Bert told Michael as they searched for the restaurant they'd particularly liked in those first restless days in London. "If it's still standing."

"And afterwards let's go to the theater," Michael said with a surge of anticipation.

"Something with a lot of girls and *leetle* costumes." Bert grinned, gesturing eloquently.

"The music has to be good," Michael stipulated. His eyes were nostalgic as he remembered the Broadway musicals he'd seen during the years at Columbia. One thing the Air Force had accomplished for him, he thought. He knew now that engineering school was out. When he got home from this bloody war, he just wanted to concentrate on writing music.

"Hey, it's still standing!" Bert chortled as their destination came into view. "Remember the great roast beef we used to get there?"

It had only been a matter of weeks since they'd been here, Michael thought as they strode inside the restaurant, but it seemed like months.

"There's a little table in the back." Bert prodded him toward the left. "God, the place is mobbed already."

"You don't need ration coupons to eat in restaurants," Michael reminded. "I'll bet the same thing's happening back home." He chuckled unexpectedly. "You should have heard my aunts scream when they found out about shoe rationing."

"An aunt of mine—she's a school teacher back home—was here for ten days about five years ago. She's mad about anything English. I told her she probably wouldn't recognize London today."

"Oh, sure she would," Michael said, smiling wryly. "If she could overlook the scars from all the bombings, the anti-aircraft guns in Hyde Park, the sandbags, the barrage balloons, the signs everywhere pointing to day and night shelters."

"Some of these English gals—" Bert said, staring at an attractive brunette across the room. He whistled softly. "We ought to be able to find ourselves some action for the night. Some of them sure like Yanks. Especially Air Force," he added smugly.

"Take it easy." Michael chuckled. "You hear the complaints about us from the less impressed. We're 'overpaid, oversexed, and over here.' "

A buxom blonde waitress in her forties approached to take their orders. Bert immediately asked for her advice. For a few moments they concentrated on dinner fare.

"Honey, how am I going to eat potatoes without butter?" Bert reproached when the waitress suggested potatoes in lieu of wartime bread. "With just that pence-size chunk of margarine—"

"Well, for a pair of good-looking Yanks the margarine might be spread out a bit," she said with a wink. "I'll bring your coffee to get you started." She shook her head in good-humored curiosity. "I don't know how you Yanks can drink that bilge. That's one thing I can't understand about Americans—"

"There's more?" Michael asked humorously. Right away he'd developed a strong admiration for the British. Despite the constant bombings, the shortages on every side, the devastation, they were able to accept whatever came along without hysteria. Even the heaviest raid they'd encountered in London had elicited no more than "we had a bit of trouble last night" from a waiter who had served them the next day.

"I'm not sure I ought to be saying this—" Their waitress hesitated.

"Say it," Bert pushed.

"I don't understand about the way you Americans run your Army. I mean, why are your colored troops separated from the others?"

Michael sighed. How could he explain to this Englishwoman what he didn't understand himself?

"You might call it our blind spot," he said finally. "But something tells me," he added with quiet intensity, "that once this bloody war is over, that'll change."

Kara hurried from her final class of the day, across still winter-bare Washington Square, en route to the subway. Jimmy was waiting for her in his studio apartment on West Seventieth Street. How could he have dropped out of school this way, just three months before graduation, she asked herself yet again. At least, he could have had his degree before he enlisted—even if he never used it.

These past months—ever since she'd met Jimmy at that evening drama class—had been wonderful. Both of them were intent on making careers in theater, while they satisfied their parents by taking degrees in English. They'd never shared a class, never knew the other existed, until they'd signed up for an off-campus evening class in improvisation.

At the West Side IRT, Kara pushed her way into the rush-hour mob, which normally she avoided. But tomorrow morning Jimmy had to show up for induction. He'd warned her that for the next thirteen weeks he'd be lucky to get a phone call through to her.

"The way the war is going," he'd told her, "we'll probably be shipped right out after basic training."

She wasn't going back home after graduation. She'd move into Jimmy's studio over this weekend. After graduation she'd find herself a daytime job and take evening classes at the Neighborhood Playhouse or the American Academy. When the war was over, Jimmy would come home and they'd get married and look for work in the theater.

"*Hey, maybe we'll be the next Lunt and Fontanne.*" His words darted across her mind, eliciting a warm glow.

They weren't a pair of crazy kids dying to be movie stars, she thought. They loved theater, loved bringing life to a role, connecting with an audience. They found a beautiful satisfaction in acting that nothing else in the world could give them.

She left the subway at Broadway and Seventy-second Street, headed south. Nothing was going to happen to Jimmy, she told herself. They had their whole lives planned. And Jimmy was so good. Sometimes in class she watched him with tears in her eyes because she knew he had a special gift.

She hurried across West Seventieth to the graystone townhouse where Jimmy had a fourth-floor furnished studio. The instant she buzzed he buzzed back to open the door. He must have been standing there waiting for her, she thought lovingly, and began the long climb.

"I have to be out of here by six-forty AM tomorrow morning," he told her as he drew her into the softly illuminated room. "I figured we'd have dinner here—so we'd have more time alone."

"Yes." Her smile was tremulous. Jimmy had placed a pair of candles on the tiny maple table, and a bunch of hothouse pansies—her favorite flowers—sat between the silver candlesticks. "Oh Jimmy, I wish you didn't have to go into the Army."

"The sooner I go in, the sooner I'll come home," he said. "I'm going to help them win this war fast."

"You and my cousin Michael," she said.

They sat down at the table and pretended the cold cuts Jimmy had bought at the delicatessen were a gourmet feast. He'd bought a bottle of inexpensive champagne and apologized that it wasn't something grand. She knew it had taken some scraping on his family's part to see him through NYU. His spending money was limited.

It was only in the last month that they'd made love. But why shouldn't they, she asked herself defiantly. The whole world was upside down. They knew that Jimmy would be going into service after graduation—and then suddenly he wasn't waiting. He'd enlisted.

"If I wasn't so damn broke," he said ruefully, "I'd have rented a suite for us tonight at the Waldorf."

"Jimmy, we don't need that." She reached a hand across the table to cling to his. "Just any place where we can be alone."

The last weeks of school were drudgery for Kara. Jimmy had been sent to boot camp in Louisiana. All kinds of rumors were flying, he wrote, but he suspected he'd be shipped out to the Pacific as soon as his company was ready for action. *"The fighting is fierce there. The Allies need every able-bodied man possible in the Pacific."*

Kara became addicted to radio newscasts—remembering how Vicky and Gary were similarly addicted. She read everything she could find about the war in the Pacific because Jimmy was so sure that was his destination. She was terrified by what she read of the fanatical Japanese code of *bushido*—which ordered Japanese soldiers to fight to their death. They preferred suicide to surrender.

As graduation approached, Kara geared herself for a battle with her mother. She had no intention of returning to Bartonville. She'd find a job in New York—there were plenty to be had in the middle of the war. And she'd take acting classes in the evening.

When her mother wrote that she would not be able to attend graduation exercises—*"Daddy and I have to be in Richmond for an important political dinner"*—Kara wrote back to say that she was staying in New York after graduation. Immediately her mother phoned her from Bartonville. Kara was relieved that her mother had never questioned the change in her phone number when she'd moved into Jimmy's apartment.

"Kara, what is this craziness?" Lily demanded without any preliminaries when Kara answered the phone. "I won't have you living alone in New York!"

"Mother, I'm twenty-one years old," Kara said. "It's time I took charge of my own life. I'll have no trouble getting a job—"

"This has something to do with your being so stage-struck," Lily interrupted. "I'm sure Vicky's been encouraging you in this all along!"

"I don't need any encouragement, Mother." She refrained from admitting that her aunt was supportive, both emotionally and financially. Years ago—with Vicky agreeable and her mother outraged—she'd dropped the formal "aunt" to use Vicky's given name alone. Though Vicky was only two years younger than her mother, she seemed so much closer to her own age.

"Your father's upset," Lily warned. "It'll do nothing for his political career for word to get around that his daughter's trying to become an actress. You won't receive one cent from us, Kara, if you don't come home."

"I'll manage." Kara struggled for calm. "Betty's joining the WACS."

"What on earth for?" Lily was astonished. "With all that oil money in the family?"

"She's enlisting because she wants to be part of the war effort." It was so hard to be patient with her mother. "She has two brothers in the service."

"I think you've lost your mind!" Lily shrieked. "Both you and Betty. Girls today have no sense of tradition."

The following day Kara received a call from her grandmother.

"I just want you to know that Vicky and I are coming up to New York for your graduation," Sara said fondly. "We wouldn't miss it for the world."

"Oh, Grandma, that's so sweet. I'll look forward to seeing you."

She knew that her grandmother disliked traveling these days and that Vicky was interrupting a hectic work schedule to come here. Mother must have told them she wasn't coming, Kara thought, touched by their solicitude. They wanted her to know they'd be here. And Doug and Paul, of course. She wished wistfully that Jimmy could be here, but that seemed highly unlikely at this point.

Graduation day was a festive occasion. Right away Kara sensed that her grandmother and Vicky were annoyed that Adam didn't show up for the graduation exercises. He was such an arrogant jerk, she thought distastefully. But Doug and Paul were here. She relished being surrounded by family.

In the evening Vicky took them all—including Adam—to dinner at Sardi's. For that Adam made himself available. Vicky always did such sweet things. She realized Sardi's would be special to *her*, with its walls plastered with caricatures of Broadway personalities. She and Jimmy dreamt about one day going to Sardi's after the opening of their first Broadway play—to wait for the reviews. Later the whole family went to The Blue Angel to see a marvelous comic named Leonard Elliot.

Kara was delighted when both her grandmother and Vicky presented her with checks in lieu of more conventional graduation gifts.

"You're both so understanding!" She kissed each with candid gratitude. "And it's been such a wonderful evening."

In the morning her grandmother and Vicky would take the train back to Bartonville—but it had been so good to see them. Doug and Paul were taking summer jobs at a hotel in the Catskills—what was called "the Borscht Belt," she remembered. They'd be part-time entertainers—most of the time busboys, Doug had admitted humorously. But like her, they wanted to be independent. Paul's money was being rationed, she remembered. His parents were caught in Nazi-occupied Paris. At regular intervals Paul threatened to drop out of college and join the Free French. So far Doug had managed to persuade him to stay on at school until graduation—or until he himself was drafted.

Ten days after graduation she received a phone call from Jimmy.

"I'm being transferred to Camp Edwards," he reported jubilantly. "That's near Boston—I'll be able to get down to see you on my first leave!"

"Jimmy, I can't wait," she whispered. "It's been such a long time."

"How's the job situation?"

"I start working next Monday," she told him. "As a receptionist in a law office. Betty leaves for induction on the same day."

"Don't you get any such ideas," he warned. "I want to know just where you are all the time."

"I'll be here waiting for you," she promised. *Why hadn't they got married before he enlisted*? But she knew the answer to that. His parents were looking forward to a big wedding for their only son. They'd just have to wait until after the war.

Vicky was about to leave the office for the day when her special line—held open only for calls from the New York office—penetrated the stillness of the office floor. As always she was the last to leave.

"Hello—" Her voice was eager yet wary.

"I figured you'd still be at the office," Frank Leslie chuckled affectionately.

"What's happening?" Any call from Frank was motivated by something important.

"It doesn't actually affect us," he told her, "but the new issue of *Reader's Digest* is after the industry again. The issue won't hit the newsstands for a few days, but I got my hands on an advance copy through my special sources."

"They're slamming industry advertising," she guessed.

"They claim cigarette company advertising is out to hoodwink the public. The Federal Trade Commission has issued complaints against Lucky Strike, Camel, Old Gold, and Philip Morris. They say the great quotes from growers, warehousemen, and auctioneers don't mean a hill of beans—sometimes the so-called quoters didn't even know they were being quoted. They said what we all know—that these guys do business with all of us. They'll let us all quote them."

"What else did the FTC complain about?" Vicky asked. Sometimes she had battles with their ad agency about the copy it set up for Barton cigarettes. She knew the ad execs thought she was terribly naive to insist they not make extravagant—phoney—claims.

"For one thing, the article mentioned the Old Gold ballyhoo about the nicotine content of their cigarettes—when everybody in the business knows the difference between all the leading brands—including Barton—are negligible. And they brought out that old bit where Old Gold claimed that people with coughs were cured when they switched to Old Gold. The tests were all a farce." Vicky's mind was suddenly assaulted by memories of Daniel's heavy cough—which he'd always denied came from smoking four packs of cigarettes a day.

"But we're not listed in the FTC complaint," Vicky pinpointed, yet she felt the article would damage the entire tobacco industry.

"Not us or Ligget and Myers," he said with relief. "Still, I don't like it."

"Sometimes it seems to me that cigarette advertising is all sleazy. We all know that basically there's almost no difference between one brand and another. It's how we promote our product that sells it."

"Don't get philosophical, Vicky," he teased good-humoredly. "Just remember—we're performing a public service. The government's screaming for us all to turn out as many cigarettes as possible. It gives pleasure to our service men and women. I just wish it wasn't so damn hard to buy all the leaf we need." He was serious now. "I know you'll be chasing around like crazy at the auctions next month. It's damn crazy the way the government puts mandatory restrictions on how much tobacco can be grown while they're after us to deliver more cigarettes! Hell, they've dropped restrictions on other commodities since the war began. Why do they keep up the restrictions on tobacco?"

Vicky knew it was a rhetorical question. Still, she replied.

"Because it's supposed to make sure the tobacco farmer gets a fair shake," Vicky reminded. She remembered with a rush of sympathy how badly the tobacco farmers fared before the Depression era brought in regulations and price support. The tobacco companies had been paying next to nothing because so much was available. "And the tobacco-growing states have powerful senators and representatives who'll fight like mad to keep those supports in place."

Frank sighed.

"All that doesn't make our job any easier. There's talk now that the price of leaf will go up again when the new crop comes in."

"We're still making a damn good profit, Frank. We can't complain."

"Nobody's ever satisfied making a *good* profit. Everybody wants to make record profits. Especially in the middle of a war when almost everybody's raking in huge profits."

"That bothers me, Frank," Vicky confessed. "When so many people are dying, where do we get the gall to worry about profits?"

"It's the nature of the beast," Frank said quietly. "Let's pray the war's over soon."

When Jimmy called early in July, Kara knew immediately that he was being shipped out.

"I'll be in town some time tomorrow afternoon," he told her. "I have a twenty-four-hour pass. Can you get off work?"

"I'll call in sick," she promised. "Tell me when your train arrives. I'll be at the station to meet you."

She was exhilarated by the prospect of seeing Jimmy after all these months of separation—and she was terrified that he was going overseas. Not the Pacific, she guessed, if he was on the East Coast. But, of course, even if he knew, he couldn't tell her. Maybe he'd run into Michael, she thought wistfully. He and Michael would like each other.

In the morning she called in sick—though she suspected that her boss would understand if she'd told him the truth. An hour before Jimmy's train was to arrive she was at Penn Station, which was always a hectic scene in war time, with every branch of service represented at both arrival and departure points.

Her heart pounding, she saw him searching among the crowd for her. She'd never seen him in uniform. His hair cut so short.

"Jimmy!" she called, a hand held high.

Jimmy's brief leave seemed to fly past with incredible speed, yet she felt such relief at being with him again, seeing for herself that he was all right. And then—with shattering suddenness—she was at the station again, kissing him goodbye at his train.

"Write me," she pleaded, fighting tears. "And don't try to be a hero," she said with shaky laughter. "I want you to come home to me."

"We've got a date with the marriage bureau and a Broadway marquee," he told her softly. "I have to be all right."

Chapter Twenty-four

KARA HADN'T BEEN surprised when her monthly allowance checks stopped arriving. Her mother had warned her there'd be no more allowances. Why should there be, she asked herself—she was working. Still, it was a wrench to attempt to live on her salary.

Jimmy had teased her about never having learned to budget, she remembered. No more shopping at Saks and Bergdorf, she warned herself. No more buying the best theater tickets. No more lunches at Schrafft's—from now on it would be the Automat.

Her graduation gift checks had been deposited into a savings account—they were to pay for her evening drama classes, starting in the fall. She'd written Jimmy—now somewhere in Sicily—about her plans to sign up for classes. He was pleased.

Then with shattering suddenness she was thrust into emotional and mental chaos. She was dizzy with shock when she realized she was pregnant. She couldn't write Jimmy—what could he do when he was fighting a war? Why couldn't Betty be here?

For two days she wrestled with this devastating situation. She was so *alone* in New York now that she was out of school. She couldn't go to some creepy abortionist—she'd heard terrible stories about what happened to girls who did that. This was Jimmy's baby—their baby. She was suffused with tenderness as she imagined holding the baby in her arms. Would the war be over by the time it was born?

On a steamy July afternoon—walking into the apartment after being crammed into an airless subway car for twenty minutes—Kara told herself she'd have to go home. Just until the war was over and Jimmy and she were married. If her parents threw a fit about her being pregnant, Grandma and Vicky would be there for her. Dropping onto the studio couch, she debated about phoning her grandmother. Grandma would be shocked, she rebuked herself in discomfort. Vicky had fallen in love with Uncle Gary in the middle of World War I. Vicky would understand.

She reached for the phone. Call Vicky at the office, she told herself. Vicky kept long hours—she wouldn't be home yet. She called, waited impatiently for Vicky or her secretary to respond.

"Mrs. Barton's office."

"Mollie, it's Kara," she identified herself. "Is Vicky there?"

"No, she's out in Pittsburgh," Mollie told her. "Trying to buy some machinery."

"I'll see her when I come home," Kara told Mollie, hiding her disappointment.

She sat immobile for a few moments, trying to settle on her next move. All right, stop looking for someone to hold my hand, she ordered herself. There was no way out but to go home for a while. This didn't mean she and Jimmy weren't going to make it in theater. The career would just have to wait for now.

With a need for action she pulled valises from the closet, began to pack in a haste born of panic. They could tell folks back home that she and Jimmy were married just before he was shipped out. That happened all the time these days.

Then, forcing herself to be realistic, she conceded that she couldn't just pack up and leave tonight. There were details to be handled. She had to tell her boss she was going back home, give up the apartment, withdraw her money from the bank. And she must go to the post office to arrange for her mail to be forwarded. Jimmy had to know where to write her.

All at once she felt a surge of homesickness for Barton Manor and her grandmother and Vicky and Uncle Gary. Barton Manor had always been more of a home than the house she shared with her parents. Doug was in the Catskills and Michael was flying missions over Germany. She wished they were all home together at Barton Manor.

All right, she thought. It was only fair to give a week's notice to her boss. But then she'd be on a train bound for Richmond.

A faint breeze drifted into her mother's bedroom, alleviating the torpid heat of the day, as Kara haltingly explained why she had decided to come home. Lily had abandoned her nightly beauty ritual in shock.

"How the hell did you let yourself get pregnant?" Lily screeched.

"The usual way." Kara's smile was wry. "We're getting married when Jimmy comes home. We'll just tell everybody we got married before he was shipped out."

"I'll arrange something," Lily told her with an air of martyrdom. "I've heard about this very discreet private sanitarium just on the other side of Richmond—"

"Mother, I'm having the baby," Kara interrupted.

"Oh, no you're not!" Lily snapped back. "With your father preparing to run for mayor of Bartonville? We can't afford a breath of scandal."

"There won't be a scandal," Kara refuted. "My husband's in Sicily fighting with the Allies. He—"

"You don't have a husband," Lily brushed this aside. "Your father's competition would dig that out fast enough. How would it look to the family, Kara? Your grandmother would just die of embarrassment."

"Nobody would have to know—" Kara was trembling now.

"Don't be naive! The redneck crowd that's fighting your father would dig up the truth. He'd never be elected. Oh, God, I can just hear the snickering! I won't let you do this to the family, Kara."

"Nobody has to know," Kara repeated. But she knew her mother was winning.

"It's late, but I'll make some phone calls. You and I will drive to the sanitarium in the morning. You'll stay there overnight. I'll drive you home the following morning. And don't talk about putting it off for a day or two," she warned. "Stephanie and I are leaving day after tomorrow for a month at Newport."

Vicky left the office earlier than usual today because this latest heat wave was setting records.

"It's been another scorcher," Zachary greeted her when she crossed to the waiting car. "But we're gettin' a little breeze from the river right now."

"Thank goodness for that, Zach."

Gary was reading on the veranda at Barton Manor when Zachary pulled up before the house. Most days he was involved in a War Bond drive or scrap metal collection or helping at the town's victory garden. Vicky had tried to get him to volunteer as a pianist at a Richmond canteen for service men from the Army base. But with Michael overseas and Doug away he'd withdrawn entirely from his music.

"I figured you'd be home at a more civilized hour in this weather," Gary greeted her. Sometimes she wasn't sure that he wasn't being sarcastic about her involvement in the company. "Lily and Stephanie left this afternoon for Newport. Of course, they're stopping off in New York to buy clothes. Oh, Lily said Kara's home."

"For a vacation?" Vicky sat in a rocker beside Gary, startled by this news.

"She didn't say. She just said Kara had a bad cold and she'd be staying in bed today, but she'd probably be coming over here tomorrow."

"No mail from Michael?" she asked automatically.

"If there had been, Mama or I would have called you." His face grew somber. "When does he have time to write when American bombers are blanketing Europe?"

"I wonder what brought Kara home," Vicky said uneasily.

"Miz Vicky, would you like a glass of lemonade?" Effie asked from behind the screen door, a tall, frosty glass in one hand. "I heard the car coming up the driveway."

"Oh, Effie, yes," Vicky said with a smile.

Vicky listened while Gary reported on the progress of the five million dollar Army hospital under construction at Broad Rock Road and Belt Boulevard. The new hospital was to accommodate 1,750 wounded. Still, in a corner of her mind she worried about Kara's having come home.

She couldn't believe Kara had abandoned her plans for a career in theater. Kara wasn't some impressionable young girl caught up in the glamour of being an actress. She loved theater the way Michael and Doug loved music. As Gary had once sworn to dedicate his life to writing music.

After dinner she debated about calling Kara, then remembered that Lily said she had a bad cold. Better let her sleep, poor baby, she decided. Nothing was better for a bad cold than bed rest.

She was in her room, studying reports that Frank had sent down to her from the New York office—which predicted that the U.S. government was about to allow tobacco to be shipped to Great Britain again, though only for its armed forces—when Kara called.

"Kara, how're you feeling?" she asked solicitously.

"Rotten." Her voice a forlorn whisper.

"Are you running a fever?" Vicky asked. "Summer colds can be treacherous."

"I don't have a cold—"

Vicky listened—with intermittent murmurs of sympathy—while Kara told her about Jimmy, about her pregnancy and abortion.

"I shouldn't have listened to Mother," Kara said in self-reproach. "I should have gone straight to you and Grandma. But she made it seem so awful—that I was disgracing the family."

"Darling, there's a very strong chance that I would have become pregnant by Gary if it hadn't been for Simone. You remember my telling you about her. She was strict. It could have happened to us the way it happened to you and Jimmy."

"I was just so scared. And you know Mother."

"Yes, I know your mother. But aside from remorse, do you feel all right?" Vicky asked. Lily, of course, would have known where to take Kara for an abortion. Lily had been through that at least twice, she suspected from snide remarks that had passed between Lily and Clark. Kara's father very much wanted a son.

"Just a little shaky. And worried about Jimmy. Vicky, you'll like him."

"I'm sure I will," Vicky comforted. "Let's just pray the war's over soon and Michael and Jimmy are both home." She was ever fearful now that Doug would soon be drafted.

"Can I come over for dinner tomorrow night?"

"You never have to ask, Kara," Vicky chided gently. "Just come."

It seemed to Vicky that the times Gary and she were the closest were when they hovered before the radio to hear the latest war bulletins. In the Pacific, American troops were pushing the Japanese into a slow, tortuous, and costly retreat in the Solomon Islands. In Europe,

Allied forces conquered Sicily and on September 3, 1943, invaded the Italian mainland. Five days later Italy surrendered unconditionally.

On a humid mid–September day Vicky came home from the office to find both Gary and Sara absorbed in a newscast.

"Sit down," he told her, impatient to hear the radio report.

"Gary, they're just repeating what they've been saying all along," Sara said indulgently.

"What's happening?" Vicky asked, collapsing into a chair. No matter how hard they tried to cool the plants, there were days—like this one—that were almost unbearable.

"This newscaster is summing up the new air front," Sara said, her voice low. *Air front meant Michael.* "He talked about how the U.S. Air Force is bombing the daylights out of the Germans. Literally. You know our Flying Fortresses were designed for daylight precision bombing. They're avoiding civilian areas," she said. "Well, some of our Flying Fortresses were over Paris yesterday. By the time they started home, it was dark already. For the first time they landed in England by flare path."

"Our planes are extending their operating hours," Gary said with pride, but Vicky knew he shared her apprehension. How many planes didn't come home?

"We both worry about Michael," Vicky said to Sara on a balmy late October evening when they sat on the veranda after dinner. They could hear the drone of the radio in the library, where Gary was fiddling with the radio in search of newscasts. On October thirteenth, Italy had declared war on Germany. Gary was convinced it was a matter of weeks before the war in Europe would be over. "But for Gary it's a full-time vigil," Vicky said. "He's obsessed. How can he listen to those same news reports over and over again?" She shook her head in bewilderment. "I know he feels guilty that he's not out there fighting, too. He remembers his war," she said with fatalistic calm. "I don't think he's ever been able to forget what he saw in England and in France—"

"Everyone feels the war can't go on much longer," Sara comforted. "The Japanese are on the run in the Pacific and the Germans in Europe."

"But Sara, it's so slow," Vicky reminded her desperately. "How many more lives will be lost before it's over?"

Again, Sara planned a family Thanksgiving dinner. Doug and his friend Paul were coming in from New York, Adam from his school. Kara was home. The house would seem lively—almost normal— Vicky thought. But Michael would be sorely missed. What would Thanksgiving mean to him, she asked wistfully. Just another day of flying missions over Germany?

Kara made it clear she would not leave Bartonville until the war was over and Jimmy was safely home. She filled her time with volunteer work—growing close to her uncle in these wartime months. It was as though, Vicky thought, that time stood still for Gary and Kara. Each would begin to live again when the fighting was over.

This year Doug and Paul were scheduled to stay at Barton Manor. Doug had been hurt when his mother expressed annoyance at having Paul as a houseguest. *"I suppose you'll want to bring him home with you at Christmas again."*

Everything annoyed Stephanie and Lily, Vicky thought when Sara told her about the invitation she'd offered to Doug's friend. To them the war was no more than a personal inconvenience. They contrived to spend time in Palm Beach and Newport and Nassau. They kept a residence in Bartonville, but they lived in their private world of the Cafe Society.

Two days before Thanksgiving, Kara returned from an afternoon at the Bartonville Red Cross with an eagerness to inspect the day's mail. It had arrived late today, she noticed, as she said goodbye to the fellow volunteer worker who'd driven her home. She hadn't had a letter from Jimmy in over three weeks—but Vicky kept reminding her about how the American troops were on the move in Italy. They had no time to write.

Kara hurried into the large entrance foyer, the house quiet except for the faint sound of singing in the living room. Elvira always sang when she was washing windows, Kara thought.

She reached for the pile of mail on the foyer table and flipped through it impatiently, hoping for a V–mail, or better still, a long, rambling airmail from Jimmy. All at once she froze, for a moment bewildered when she saw the envelope with her own large scrawl, addressed to Jimmy. Then she saw the ugly rubber-stamped words at one side of the envelope.

"Oh, my God—" She was cold with anguish. *Jimmy dead?*

"Miss Kara—" Elvira hovered at the living room entrance. "The postman—he says not to write to that person no more," she said.

"Yes, Elvira—" Kara clutched the edge of the table to steady herself. "I'll remember."

Dropping her purse on the table, Kara crossed to the door and hurried out into the afternoon sunlight. Her mind in chaos, she headed for the woods. They'd let themselves believe this couldn't happen. They were *special*. But that beautiful life they'd planned together would never be. Jimmy had been killed in action.

He'd died without knowing about the baby. And she'd killed the baby. The baby they both would have loved so much. *Now she had nothing.*

Chapter Twenty-five

VICKY AWOKE EARLY on Thanksgiving day. It was the American holiday she most cherished. Thanksgiving meant a coming together of family.

It had become a tradition for her to have breakfast with Sara on Thanksgiving morning—usually in the library, with birch logs crackling in the fireplace grate. Sara enjoyed reminiscing about earlier Thanksgivings, when the children were young.

After breakfast she and Sara would go out to the kitchen to talk with Lula Mae and Effie about the dinner, to be served in the early afternoon—after which the domestic staff was off to their own family dinners. After dinner she and Sara and the children would clear the table and go out to the kitchen to do the dishes. Lily and Stephanie disdained such activities. *"Mother, why can't the servants stay and clean up after dinner? You always spoil them so."* This was Lily or Stephanie's usual post-Thanksgiving dinner reproach.

But this Thanksgiving Michael wouldn't be at the table, she thought wistfully. Would Kara come? Yesterday Kara had phoned to tell her in anguished whispers that Jimmy had been killed in action. Immediately she'd invited Kara to come to stay at Barton Manor—to be comforted by herself and Sara.

"I just want to be alone," Kara had insisted. "I can't see anybody now. But I wanted you to know—" Her voice had trailed away. "I need some time alone—"

Vicky threw aside the comforter and left her bed. She ached to comfort Kara. She was so young to know such grief. And thinking about Jimmy, she felt fresh apprehension for Michael. But this was a special day, she exhorted herself. A day for giving thanks.

All at once she was impatient to be downstairs. Adam would sleep late, she guessed. He probably wouldn't surface until dinner was about to be served. He'd arrived late last night—that was to be expected. He spent most of his time at home sleeping, she thought while she dressed. Why did Adam always make her feel defensive—as though, somehow, she had failed him as a mother? But Doug and his friend Paul would probably come downstairs early, she told herself with anticipation.

Sara was in the library, sipping fragrant coffee before the fireplace. Logs were piled high in the grate and ablaze in brilliant color. "I told Lula Mae we'd have breakfast as soon as you came downstairs," Sara greeted her with a welcoming smile. "It feels good to have the young folks here." Now her smile grew somber. "We'll miss Kara, poor baby."

Effie brought Vicky coffee and went off to tell Lula Mae to prepare breakfast. Vicky sat and listened while Sara reminisced about earlier Thanksgivings. Gary would be downstairs in another hour or two—and the radio would be on until they went in to dinner.

Where was Michael today? What kind of Thanksgiving dinner was the Air Force serving? Would they fly missions on Thanksgiving day?

As Vicky had anticipated, Gary arrived downstairs while she and Sara dawdled in the breakfast room over second cups of strong, chicory-laced coffee. He greeted them warmly and settled at the table for breakfast. Gary was always so considerate, Vicky thought while he listened with seemingly absorbed attention to one of his mother's favorite Thanksgiving stories, yet she was troubled by a feeling that only part of Gary was here at the table with them.

She yearned for the closeness and the passion she'd shared with Gary in the first years of their marriage. She'd thought they'd found that again when he'd come to her the night of the attack on Pearl Harbor, but his visits to her bed were infrequent.

After breakfast Gary left the table to go into the library to listen to the radio newscasts. "I want to hear more about the meeting of Roosevelt, Churchill, and Stalin in Teheran," he said tensely. "It'll deal with future war operations."

In silent agreement Vicky and Sara transferred themselves to the drawing room. Gary's obsession for listening to newscasts was sometimes unnerving to both Vicky and his mother. In the rare hours when she was not involved in business, Vicky tried to relax, but this morning she worried about Kara.

While Sara flipped through the pages of *House Beautiful* and Vicky scanned an article in *Business Week*, Doug and Paul arrived downstairs. Sara's face lighted at the sound of their voices in the breakfast room.

"How sad for Paul that he has no word of his family," Sara said softly. "But, at least, they know he's safe in this country."

After their breakfast Doug and Paul joined the two women in the drawing room. How sweet Sara was with Paul, Vicky thought tenderly. She asked him about his music—knowing that music was his escape from the ugly realities of the war. Soon Gary joined them. Immediately he drew Paul into talk about Paris.

"It's a matter of weeks—months at the most," Gary predicted encouragingly, "before Paris is liberated."

Gary and Paul exchanged nostalgic stories about Paris, with Vicky drawn into this exchange. She was always anxious about Simone and Henri, on their farm close to Paris. Then, with the scheduled dinner hour approaching, Adam appeared. It was incredible, Vicky thought, how Adam could exude such potent charm one moment and turn cold and antagonistic a moment later. Doug and Paul always seemed to bring out the worst in him.

While she intervened in a verbal battle between Adam and Doug, Vicky heard the voices of Lily and Clark in the foyer. Zachary was shyly congratulating Clark on his recent election as mayor of Bartonville. Moments later Zachary was greeting Stephanie and Jeffrey.

Sara rose to her feet.

"We'll go right in to dinner," she told the others in the drawing room. "Thank goodness I told Lula Mae not to expect to serve until almost three. It's a physical impossibility for Lily and Stephanie to be on time."

As always, no one sat at the head of the table. Sara decreed that would remain unoccupied in memory of Daniel. Gary and Vicky flanked the empty chair. Sara sat at the foot of the table, flanked by Lily and Stephanie and their husbands. The young ones filled in the other empty chairs.

"Where's Kara?" Doug asked Lily in surprise.

"Home sulking." Lily uttered a small sigh of impatience.

"She's upset," Vicky told Doug, straining to hide her annoyance with her sister-in-law. "She just learned a friend has been killed in action."

"Jimmy?" Doug gasped. Vicky nodded. So Doug had known Jimmy. "That's rough," he commiserated, exchanging a pained glance with Paul. "We'll go over after dinner."

"She won't see you," Lily warned aggrievedly. "You know how melodramatic Kara can be."

"She'll see us," Doug said quietly.

To dispel the pall that had fallen over the dinner table, Vicky asked Clark about his new duties as mayor—a part-time job but one he'd long coveted.

"It's not really an important position," Lily broke in before Clark could respond. "I mean, if Clark had been elected mayor of Richmond, then we could celebrate." Still, Vicky knew Lily was pleased.

"You forget how this town has grown in the last ten years," Clark shot back.

"Of course," Lily said scathingly, "that article in the *Times-Dispatch* about abolishing segregation on buses and street cars doesn't make life easy for elected officials."

"Aunt Lily, since when did you ride on buses or street cars?" Doug teased.

"I just think our Negroes should know their place." Lily glared at her sister. "Really, Stephanie, where does Doug get all his weird ideas? All his talk about 'interracial harmony.' And just remember," she pounced before her sister could reply. "I adore 'Amos 'n' Andy.' And I'm as proud as I can be that Freeman Gosden is a native Richmonder." The white Gosden played Amos on the radio show that attracted four million listeners.

Now table talk shifted to business in Bartonville—which centered, of course, around Barton Tobacco.

"You can't complain, Vicky," Clark said in that tone of mild condescension that she had never learned to accept without silent rebellion. "You can sell every cigarette the factory can turn out. Sometimes I can't even find a pack to buy."

"Business is very good," Vicky conceded, "but profits are not keeping pace. The cost of tobacco has tripled since the war. Labor costs are spiraling.''

"If you'd stop being a philanthropist, Vicky, profits would be stronger,'' Stephanie said. Vicky knew that Stephanie was concerned about protecting her future inheritance. ''When are you going to become more realistic toward the company employees?''

"I don't understand all this talk about a booming wartime economy,'' Lily sulked. ''If business is so good, why don't we see higher returns from our trust funds?''

All Lily and Stephanie thought about was spending money, Vicky thought in distaste.

"Zachary, you tell Lula Mae this is the finest turkey she's ever sent in to the Thanksgiving table,'' Sara said briskly. ''You all go off to your dinners now. Miss Vicky and I will serve the dessert and coffee.''

Vicky had hoped that Kara would pull herself out of her grief and return to New York to study drama. But by the beginning of the new year she realized this would not happen. Without Jimmy to support her, Kara was beset by doubts about her talents. And Vicky sensed, too, that for Kara New York was full of ghosts.

On January twenty-second, American and British troops made landings at Anzio and Nettuno, Italy. At home Americans waited anxiously for the Allies to invade Western Europe. In the Pacific—early in February—Allied troops set foot for the first time on prewar Japanese territory. By February twenty-second, all the Marshall Islands were under Allied control.

At home, living costs were escalating at an alarming rate. Unions were demanding raises to offset the higher prices. And always the cry was out to increase the volume of cigarettes to go to servicemen overseas.

Vicky was startled when union organizers approached her own workers. Just recently she had set up a retirement plan that had been met with much approval. Rumors warned that the unions were being infiltrated by Communists.

It was an obsession with Vicky to know that she was a good employer. In earlier years Gary used to tease her, saying she ''saw into the working man's soul and felt for him.'' True, she conceded. She would forever remember the young *midinettes* in Paris, who had gone on strike to raise their earnings by a few sous. She would never forget the years when she had been a maid at the Crillon in Paris.

Early in March, Vicky and Gary were euphoric when they read the latest V–mail from Michael.

"Guess what! I've got just two more missions to complete my tour of duty. Then I'm scheduled to come home for thirty days of 'rest and recuperation.' It'll be wonderful to see you all, and home."

"Oh Gary, I can't wait to see him." Vicky felt herself enveloped in relief. Michael was coming home. He'd be home for his twenty-second birthday! "Maybe by the time he has to return to duty the war will be over."

"From your lips to God's ear," Gary said softly.

"We'll have his bedroom repapered and painted," Vicky decided. "We'll have a party—" Her mind was absorbed by the compulsion to make his homecoming memorable. "Oh, I hope he's here by the time the boys are home from spring vacations. It'll be like old times— with Michael and Adam and Doug and Kara all staying here at the house."

"Hey, Doug and Kara do have homes of their own," Gary chided, but his eyes were bright. "But they'll want to be here when Michael is home."

At this same time news came through that Berlin had been attacked by eight hundred Flying Fortresses. Over two thousand tons of bombs had been dropped on the German capital.

"At this rate the war in Europe can't go on much longer," Gary declared while he and Vicky listened to an impassioned newscast about the massive attack on Berlin. "Maybe Michael won't have to return to his squadron."

Vicky waited impatiently for mail from Michael that would tell them his missions had been completed. Or perhaps he'd just phone from wherever he landed in this country. Then on a stormy midweek morning she was summoned from a meeting with her top executives to take a phone call from Gary.

"He said it was important," Mollie, her long-time secretary, apologized as she interrupted the top-level meeting.

"Thank you, Mollie." Vicky excused herself and hurried from the meeting room to her office. A letter had arrived from Michael, she thought with a surge of anticipation.

"Hi, Gary."

"Vicky, come home." His voice was a stunned monotone. "Something terrible has happened—"

"What is it?" All at once she was ice cold. "Gary?"

He'd hung up. She reached for her coat, dug car keys from her purse, and rushed from her office—not hearing Mollie's anxious voice. She left the building and rushed to her car, frightening questions darting across her mind.

She drove with unfamiliar speed, silently berating Gary for not explaining his call. His words echoed incessantly in her mind. "*Something terrible has happened.*"

Fighting against panic she turned into the long, winding driveway that today seemed endless. Then, approaching the house, she spied Gary slumped in a rocker on the veranda. His head was in his hands.

She pulled to a sharp stop before the house, left the car, and darted toward the steps to the veranda.

"Gary!" Her voice sharp with anxiety. "What's happened?"

Only now did Gary seem aware of her arrival. His face was drained of color, haggard.

"We have a telegram from the War Department," he told her. "Michael's gone—"

"Missing in action?" She grasped at the lesser of two devastating possibilities.

"He's dead." Gary's voice was hollow, disbelieving. "His plane was shot down over Berlin."

Chapter Twenty-six

VICKY STRUGGLED for strength. She knew that her life would never be the same again. Nothing more terrible than losing Michael could ever happen to her. Barton Manor was a house engulfed in mourning. She and Gary and Sara were three wraiths, moving about in an anguished daze.

At intervals she closeted herself in Michael's bedroom, freshly wallpapered and painted, with new draperies hanging at the windows. This was the refurbished bedroom he didn't live to see. Yet, somehow, here she felt an intense closeness to Michael.

Why? Why did he have to die?

Sharing their grief, Kara came to Barton Manor to manage the household, to deliver messages from Vicky to the office. Vicky was observing the Jewish rite of *shivah*, a week of mourning when she remained in the house. Vicky longed to seek comfort from Gary. Gary hid himself away in his cottage, refusing to see anyone.

Still encased in shock, Vicky forced herself to return to the office. She had obligations—to family and workers. The company must not falter because of her anguish. She was touched by the outpouring of sympathy from the workers.

Adam came home from NYU on spring break—unfamiliarly quiet and solemn. Doug and Paul arrived from Columbia—after Kara had asked permission for them to stay at Barton Manor. Vicky was ashamed of her initial secret recoiling at the prospect of their presence at the house.

"Of course, Doug and Paul must come here to us," she told Kara. She knew how upset Doug had been that his parents resented his bringing Paul home on school holidays. "We need them here," she said tenderly. Michael and Doug had been so close.

Vicky sought to pull herself out of her grief through long hours in the business. In the weeks ahead she came to realize that Gary meant to live alone in his cottage now. He'd come to the house only once—when she'd sent Zachary to the cottage to tell him they'd received a letter of condolence from Michael's Group Commander. Michael was being recommended posthumously for a Distinguished Service Cross.

Sometimes at night, Vicky stood at an open window in the sultry summer heat and heard the faint sound of piano playing in the distance. In his grief, Gary sought to lose himself in his music.

Both Vicky and Sara worried about Gary's mental state. They'd finally persuaded him to come to the house for Sunday dinners. He spoke little, obviously shrouded in a deep depression. Except for Sunday dinners at the house, he refused to leave his cottage. Zachary carried food trays to him at mealtimes. Late in May he sent word with Zachary that he'd like a radio for the cottage. This was immediately provided.

Prodded by Sara, Vicky geared herself to go to the cottage. Approaching the entrance she heard Gary at the piano. The music was unfamiliar, hauntingly beautiful. She knocked lightly and waited. A moment later Gary opened the door.

"May I come in, Gary?"

"I'd rather you didn't," he said brusquely. "I don't feel much like company." *She was company?*

"Gary, your mother and I worry about you. We—we want you to see a doctor."

"No," he shot back, almost antagonistic. "Please. Just let me be."

Vicky flinched as he closed the door with a jarring note of finality. In that moment she knew beyond all doubt that her marriage to Gary was forever dead.

On June 4, 1944, Allied tanks pushed the German troops out of Rome. Since it was Trinity Sunday, the Allied troops didn't occupy the city until the following morning. On June sixth—D day—four thousand ships, three thousand planes and one hundred seventy-six thousand Allied troops began the invasion of Normandy. In the days ahead, the world would learn that those troops would increase to over four million. The long-awaited invasion—under the command of General Eisenhower—was on.

Later in the month, Kara dropped by Barton Manor—as she did on frequent occasions—to have dinner with her grandmother and Vicky.

"A friend will be picking me up later," she told them over dessert and coffee. "If he picks me up at the house and Mother is there, she'll bombard him with questions—"

"Someone we know?" Sara asked interestedly.

"No. He's just out of architectural school and working in Richmond." Kara hesitated. "He's not in the service because he has a punctured eardrum. He feels very self-conscious about not being in uniform."

"Adam will never be in uniform, either," Vicky reminded gently. By now the college campuses were almost devoid of male students. Even fathers were being drafted. It was a miracle, she thought, that Doug had not been drafted.

"I think you'll like Derek." Kara gazed from Vicky to her grandmother. "He's sweet and sensitive and caring."

"You make it sound serious." Sara smiled in approval.

"Do you think it's terrible that I'm going out with someone? I mean, so soon after Jimmy?" She had told her grandmother that she'd been in love with a soldier who died in action.

"No, Kara," her grandmother reassured her.

"Jimmy would want you to be happy," Vicky said. She was disappointed that Kara had abandoned her dreams for a career in theater, but still hoped she would find what happiness she could in life. Happiness came in such short bursts.

"I think I'd like to get married." Kara smiled. "And have a baby right away. Well, ten months later," she said with shaky laughter.

"Kara, darling, I can't wait to be a great-grandmother." Sara glowed. "As I couldn't wait to be a grandmother." Now she reached out to take Vicky's hand in hers—knowing Vicky was remembering those precious months when she carried Michael.

"Kara, be sure the father you pick out for your baby is the right man for *you*." Vicky worried that Kara would rush too quickly into marriage, because she had lost Jimmy and their baby.

But almost from the first few moments of talking with Derek, Vicky decided Kara was choosing wisely. It was obvious that Derek was in love with Kara and that he was a warm, caring young man. Michael would have liked Derek, she thought involuntarily. But Michael would never know him.

In the weeks ahead Vicky and Sara learned that Derek Reeves—like Kara, an only child—came from an old Atlanta family. His parents died—several months apart—while he was a college freshman. They left a small estate.

When Lily learned that Kara was serious about Derek she was furious. She screamed that Derek was after the Barton money. "He knows we're becoming one of the richest families in the country! He'll be waiting for your grandmother to die and for me to inherit a third of the Barton fortune. But you tell him for me—if you marry him, you won't receive one cent of my inheritance."

Late in August Kara and Derek were married in the rose-scented drawing room of Barton Manor with only her grandmother, Vicky, Adam, Doug, and Paul present. Her mother and father were not there. They were attending a lawyers' convention in Boston. Stephanie and Jeffrey were spending August in Newport. Gary refused to come. A wedding was a celebration of life. He couldn't celebrate when his older son was dead. The Barton domestic staff—who had watched Kara grow up—hovered lovingly at the drawing-room entrance.

Doug and Paul had given a week's notice on their summer jobs when Kara phoned to tell them she was marrying Derek. No question in Doug's mind that he must be there for Kara. He and Paul automatically came to Barton Manor. That same day word came through that Paris had been liberated by American troops.

Vicky knew that while Sara loved all of her grandchildren, Michael—the first-born—held a special place in her heart. Her grief was deep. In earlier years, Vicky remembered, Sara had attended church more as a social function than from religious fervor. But when Daniel died, she had sought solace there. Now—grieving for Michael—she was finding comfort there again.

In September, with the Jewish High Holidays approaching, Vicky's thoughts turned to the synagogue she had joined when Michael was twelve. With the nation's entry into the war she had abandoned her own attendance.

Perhaps in the synagogue, she thought desperately, she might learn to accept Michael's death. Of course, she didn't want to forget him because that could never happen, but she needed to learn to live with the knowledge that he would never come home to her again.

On a Friday evening when Sara was going to visit her reclusive brother—their parents both gone now—Vicky decided to go to Friday evening services at the synagogue. She had never been involved in the active social life of the congregation. She had merely attended services. She suspected she appeared somewhat of an oddity to the others. She was a woman—married to a Christian—who was head of a major cigarette company. One son had his bar mitzvah at the synagogue—the other had not.

A certain shyness—that disappeared in her business dealings—made her appear reserved, almost aloof. She understood that the other members of the congregation harbored a covert curiosity about her.

Since the incident over twenty years ago—when she unmasked the phony Count Veronsky—they had known she was Russian-born. Gossip traveled fast in Bartonville and Richmond. She still spoke English with an accent more of London than Richmond. Then she had startled Richmonders by joining a synagogue. Nobody had realized that Daniel Barton's only daughter-in-law was Jewish.

This Friday evening was hot and sticky, the air sweet with the scent of honeysuckle. She wore a simple black and white pique dress. Through the years Sara had encouraged her to dress smartly. Even while Daniel was alive she'd drawn a substantial salary.

Vicky drove herself to the synagogue. She always insisted that Sara had first call on Zachary's service. Arriving at the synagogue, she was conscious of friendly stares. She was astonished and touched when—one after another—fellow congregants came over to offer their sympathy. She hadn't realized so many of them knew of Michael's death. But he was a Barton—and in Richmond that was a powerful name.

She fought against tears when a woman about her own age approached to tell her gently that she, too, had lost a son in the war.

"We're not alone, you know," the woman said with painful acceptance. "Not that this makes it any easier to bear. But it's a help to share your pain."

Before they settled themselves for the services, Vicky learned that the woman with whom she had been speaking was Lisa Feinberg, a

widow who had operated a catering service for the past eleven years—
since her husband's sudden death.

Surprising herself, Vicky accepted Lisa's invitation to come over
to her house for coffee after the services.

"There'll just be a few people there, but I think you'll enjoy being
with them." Lisa mentioned several names she vaguely recognized,
then added that she had also invited a new couple in town, Marc and
Anita Roberts. They hadn't attended services because Marc had been
tied up at a meeting earlier, Lisa explained.

"Marc came down to Richmond last spring to join the faculty at
the university. He teaches courses in English lit." Her eyes glowed
with amusement. "I think half his women students have a crush on
him—he's thirty-eight and very good-looking. Anita's a beautiful
woman who bears up remarkably well in tragic circumstances. She's
been in a wheelchair since three years after their marriage. A drunken
driver ploughed into their car," Lisa explained.

"How sad," Vicky sympathized. Did anybody on this earth escape
tragedy in the course of living?

With a sense of guilt that she was socializing when Michael was
dead only six months, Vicky drove to the charming small colonial
where Lisa Feinberg lived alone since her daughter's recent marriage.
She felt drawn to this warm woman, who had also lost a son.

She sat for a moment in her car, her mind a collage of special
moments with Michael. Lisa had said she was grateful for the years
she'd had with her son. Lisa had lost her husband as well. Gary was
alive—but lost to her.

She fought off a sudden impulse to start up the car and drive away.
That would be rude, she reproached herself. She'd told Lisa she was
coming.

The front door was open. She reached for the knob of the screen
door and walked into the foyer. Lively voices filtered from the living
room. No one would know from these convivial sounds that this was
a household that had known double tragedies.

"Hi—" Lisa beckoned to her from the living room entrance. "I
was beginning to worry that you might have got lost."

"I'm not too familiar with this part of town," Vicky apologized.
"Gary and I haven't gotten around much these last few years."

Lisa introduced her to the three couples and an older woman who'd
been arguing with good-humored intensity about the failure of the

general assembly last year to introduce legislation for the abolition of segregation on street cars and buses.

"I don't know what's the matter with them," Lisa joined in. "It's clear most Virginians are in favor of it."

"It won't happen," Vicky predicted, "until there's legislation on a national level." She was quoting Michael, she realized subconsciously.

"Once the war is over," one of the men said, "we'll see some action. When our colored troops come home, they'll have plenty to say against a segregated Army. They're out there putting their lives on the line, but they can't eat at the same table with whites."

"Oh, Marc and Anita have just pulled up," one of the wives said. "Lisa, I'll go out to the kitchen and help you with things."

Through one of the windows facing the street Vicky saw Marc Roberts bring a wheelchair from the trunk of his car, then help the woman on the front seat into the wheelchair. Everyone seemed to be watching the tableau with affection. Marc and Anita were a special couple, Vicky understood.

All attention was focused on the arriving pair. Marc Roberts was a slender, handsome man with dark hair and expressive brown eyes, which belied his relaxed air, Vicky thought. Here was a man of intense emotions. Anita's ash-blonde hair—worn in a cluster of curls atop her head—lent her an air of ageless, fragile beauty. Her heavily lashed, gray-green eyes were serene, defying any feelings of compassion from strangers.

"Anita, that dress is gorgeous," one of the women admired. It was smart and expensive, Vicky recognized, and revealed exquisite taste.

"I couldn't resist stopping off for a couple of days in New York to shop," Anita confessed, "though I'm sure Marc was bored to death with it all."

Anita's eyes were candidly inspecting Vicky. Another guest rushed forward to make introductions. Vicky gathered that Marc and Anita had spent the summer at the Grand Hotel at Mackinac Island. Not on a university teacher's salary, she surmised. It was obvious that the Roberts had private funds at their disposal. To the others here, Marc and Anita were an exotic couple, Vicky mused—bringing a dash of glamour into otherwise prosaic lives.

Marc pushed Anita's wheelchair into the inner circle and settled himself at her side. Lisa and one of the wives brought in trays of coffee and a lavish arrangement of cookies and petit fours. Now the conversation focused on the newest books. Two of the women were fascinated by John Hersey's *A Bell for Adano*, while another confessed that she thought Kathleen Winsor's *Forever Amber* was "deliciously naughty."

"Hey, Marc, what do *you* think about the current crop of fiction?" one of the husbands joshed.

"Oh, Marc doesn't read anything more recent than Henry James," Anita answered for him. "He teaches English lit, but all he thinks about is the war. If he wasn't worried about leaving me alone, I'm sure he'd be off fighting somewhere in Europe or the Pacific."

"It's frustrating sometimes to be sitting on the sidelines," Marc said somberly.

"You're too old to be fighting, darling," Anita told him with a tender smile. Not true. He was registered for the draft. Anita's condition kept him out of uniform. "Besides, everybody's sure the war can't last much longer."

"Tell that to the British." Marc was somber. "Hitler's damned buzz bombs are killing thousands."

"No more talk of war," Anita ordered. "Did I tell you all that Marc and I saw *The Searching Wind* while we were in New York? It was much too serious for me, but Marc, of course, loved it. He likes anything by Lillian Hellman. I think he's prejudiced in favor of Jewish playwrights."

"You didn't stop raving about Montgomery Clift," Marc teased.

"Oh, he's gorgeous," Anita drawled. "And so sexy."

Soon the conversation was diverted into two groups. The women were dissecting an article in the current issue of *Glamour*.

"I suppose this all sounds trivial to you," Anita said to Vicky. "I mean, to a woman who runs a big corporation."

"I'm still a woman." Vicky smiled. "I admit to a touch of extravagance when it comes to clothes."

"I was at journalism school when I met Marc. I was so determined to make a career for myself. Then I capitulated to marriage. I'd thought, in three or four years—when we're settled in some university town—I'll pick up a job on some local newspaper." For a barely perceptible instant Anita's effervescence disappeared. "But, of course, that wasn't meant to be."

Marc and Anita play-acted their way through life, Vicky thought with compassion. Perhaps that was the only way they could survive. As the group prepared to disperse, Marc told her softly that he had just learned moments ago about her loss.

"I wouldn't have gone on so much about the war if I'd known," he apologized. "Lisa insists we don't monitor our conversation in her presence—it's almost an obsession with her—but I know it can be painful."

"The world goes on." Vicky fought against tears.

"I can't believe you could have a son old enough for military service."

"We were preparing for his twenty-second birthday. He had just two more missions before coming home on furlough. Instead—" Vicky paused. "Instead, we received a telegram from the War Department."

"In times like this you have to dig for strength you never thought you had," Marc said gently.

"Listen, everybody!" Anita's voice was convivial. "Tonight was such fun. Why don't you all come to our house for dinner tomorrow a week? Marc found us this wonderful cook, who says she just adores cooking for parties."

There was a general acceptance from those gathered in the foyer. Only Vicky hesitated.

"Vicky, do come," Anita coaxed ingratiatingly. "I finally feel as though I've discovered real friends here in Richmond. Marc's academic crowd is terribly stuffy."

"I'd love to," Vicky said. Meeting Anita—seeing how she coped with a life sentence in a wheelchair—was a silent rebuke. "Just give me the address."

Tonight had been good for her, she thought. At Barton Manor she and Sara seemed to wallow in their grief. Michael would want her to move ahead with her life.

She remembered what Lisa had said. "*I cherish every minute of every year that I had with my son.*"

Chapter Twenty-seven

MARC TURNED into the driveway to the rambling, one-level Tudor that had been their home for the past four months. The lights in the master bedroom suite told him that Martha had returned from her evening at the movies and was waiting to prepare Anita for bed. He hoped that the current nurse-therapist would continue to please her. They'd been through a dozen since the accident.

"You're awfully quiet tonight," Anita scolded. "Are you annoyed that I decided to give a dinner party?"

"Why should I be annoyed?" he countered. "You'll be doing all the work." Their domestic staff would be doing all the work.

"I want to talk a bit after I'm in bed," she told him. "Don't go to sleep yet."

"Sure." He contrived his routine smile, though his mind was replaying those few moments when he and Vicky Barton had carried on a private conversation. It was difficult to believe that such a lovely woman—who looked no more than thirty—was the head of a major tobacco company. "Shall I bring you a glass of wine?"

"Not that awful white wine you brought home last week," she murmured in distaste. "A glass of champagne, I think. That always helps me sleep."

Marc pulled up before the garage and left the car to go to the specially constructed wheelchair that fitted into the trunk. Anita could walk a few steps but refused to acknowledge this except within the privacy of their house. This ritual had become automatic through the years. He would help Anita from the car, push the chair up the side ramp into the house, then Martha—or the current nurse-therapist—would take over.

Tonight Anita wanted to talk. Once again, she was envisioning herself as presiding over a salon of adoring acquaintances. God, let them stay here a few years. He was so tired of playing the nomadic professor.

"Martha—" Anita called as they entered the house through the study. "I hope you've drawn a bath for me. I'm just exhausted."

"It's waiting for you, Miss Anita." Martha's voice preceded her ample, white-uniformed body. "I'll just run a little more hot, and you can get right in."

With a subconscious sigh of relief, Marc settled himself in a lounge chair in the study. Anita was in a good mood tonight, for which he was grateful. After twelve years he had still not been able to shake off the guilt that he had allowed Anita—at her own insistence—to drive the night of the accident. He knew she blamed him for not being quick-thinking enough to seize the wheel in time to avoid the oncoming drunken driver.

He reached to turn on the radio, fiddled with the dial until he located a news program. Allied troops were sweeping up the Rhine Valley from the south of France. It was clear the plan was to join the Third Army near Dijon. How much longer could the war drag on?

Involuntarily he thought about Vicky Barton. She was so lovely and so vulnerable. He'd yearned to pull her into his arms and comfort her, or even more than that, he forced himself to recognize. She'd evoked feelings he'd forced himself to deny for a dozen years. God, he hoped they could settle down and stay in this town. He was tired of playing the college circuit—he wanted roots. Anita beguiled people for a while—until she got bored and began the slow, startling disenchantment.

It didn't bother Anita that with the constant moves he couldn't earn his way up the academic ladder. She didn't care that he was always the low man on the totem pole. Her inheritance supported them in the style she demanded. Occasionally he wrote and sold an article. That pleased her. It was something she could talk about with her acquaintances. Anita never had friends—they were her vassals, members of her salon.

He waited a while, then went out to the kitchen to open up a bottle of champagne and pour a glass for Anita. He was putting away the champagne when Martha appeared at the door.

"Miss Anita would like you to come to her, sir," Martha told him.

"Thank you, Martha." So far Martha seemed to worship Anita, but that wouldn't last long, he thought. Once she was bored with playing the beautiful martyr, Anita could be a bitch to the servants.

Marc left the kitchen, walked down the hall to the master bedroom. Martha had left the door ajar. He walked inside, knowing he'd find Anita propped against a mass of white satin pillows and looking ethereally beautiful, her hair cascading about her shoulders.

Sometimes he was convinced she deliberately tried to arouse him. The doctors had said when she was released from the hospital that they could enjoy an almost normal sex life, but Anita berated them as unfeeling liars. They had never shared a bed after the accident. Not a kiss, not an embrace.

Eventually Marc had come to realize that Anita had never cared for sex. She had endured it as a requirement for marriage. She had found pleasure in knowing that she was desirable, that she made him passionate.

In truth, he mocked himself, he'd known that after the first year. He'd just hoped that the situation would change. He'd thought, "If we have a child, Anita will be different." But she hadn't wanted a child.

"It was a rather good evening," Anita greeted him, a hand extended for the glass of champagne. Her lace-trimmed chiffon nightgown revealed the high thrust of milk-white breasts that no longer elicited heat in him. "I don't believe Vicky Barton actually runs that company. People in Richmond are so gullible."

"I believe it." On occasion Marc refused to play Anita's game. "She's obviously intelligent. Lisa says she's been involved in the business for twenty years."

"The husband's strange, I understand. When he balked at going into the company, she took over. I'll bet Vicky Barton is invited everywhere." A hint of envy invaded her voice. "She's married to a Barton so they forget she's Jewish."

"Anita, Richmond is a remarkably well-integrated city," Marc said with strained patience. Anita was quick to see discrimination everywhere. She hated Atlanta—where she was born and raised—because the prestigious Capital City Club and the Piedmont Driving Club were closed to Jews.

"Oh, everyone is as sweet as pie," she drawled. "On the streets and in the stores. But I don't see us being invited into the homes of the Old Families."

"We don't know the 'Old Families,' " he pointed out.

"And don't overlook all the resort hotels that don't admit Jews," she pursued, her face flushed with rekindled rage.

"We don't need those hotels," he pointed out.

"I think I'd like to be friends with Vicky Barton," she said softly. "She's important in this town. You be nice to her, you hear? But not too nice," she laughed. "You're a married man."

Vicky was startled to realize she was looking forward to the small dinner party at the Roberts's house on Saturday evening. She was touched by Anita's gallant approach to life, by the blend of strength and tenderness she felt in Marc. He reminded her of Gary in those early days in Paris. Lisa said they'd been married fifteen years and were as devoted to each other now as the day they were married.

Marc hadn't failed his wife as she had failed Gary, she thought with recurrent guilt. But Gary had waited too long to pursue his dream. How could she have walked out when Daniel died? *She had obligations.*

As usual, business was making incessant demands on her time. While the tobacco crop had been excellent this season, every tobacco company was fighting to buy leaf. Prices were rising yet again.

Preparing to leave the office on Saturday afternoon, she thought about the articles Frank had recently sent to her. A psychologist had written that smoking had conditioned American lives. Younger brothers—and now younger sisters—wanted to smoke because older siblings smoked. Another psychologist warned that it was important to supply the nation with cigarettes: "If they can't get their cigarettes, they'll turn to drinking—and we don't want to see that."

As she walked out of her office, she heard her private line—the one held open for New York calls—puncture the late afternoon office silence. She hurried back inside to pick up the phone.

"Vicky Barton," she said briskly.

"I figured you'd still be at the office," Frank greeted her with a chuckle. "Is it hot as hell down there?"

"It's hot," she admitted and remembered Lisa saying that the heat was very uncomfortable for Anita.

For a couple of moments they engaged in small talk, then Frank explained his mission.

"I know you're in no mood to traipse up to Washington, even for a day, but this official down there wants an off-the-record meeting with the two of us."

"About what?" Vicky sighed impatiently. The government kept screaming at the tobacco industry to increase production, but the WPB did nothing to loosen the controls on how much tobacco could be planted.

"The usual outcry. They want to see higher production. They can't figure out why it takes three years from seed to finished cigarette," Frank said with sardonic humor.

"When do we have to go there and draw pictures for them?" Why couldn't they leave the business to people who knew what they were doing? There was no way to cut back on the time to produce acceptable cigarettes.

"Can you be there Monday afternoon?" he asked, resigned to this interruption in his work schedule.

"I'll be there."

"Unless you hear from me to the contrary, I'll have Tina make reservations for us at the Mayflower." Tina—his long-time secretary—had developed amazing skills in acquiring hotel reservations and railroad tickets in these trying times.

"I'll check in around noon," Vicky said, "and call you right away."

"We'll have time for lunch," Frank told her. "Then we'll shoot over to this bureau chief's office. There'll probably be a dinner meeting later with him and some associates."

Vicky left the office and drove home. Now she was ambivalent about having accepted the invitation to the Roberts's dinner. She always felt slightly self-conscious about appearing without Gary— though after all these years people in Bartonville and Richmond knew Gary refused to socialize.

She realized there were some wives in both towns who regarded her with wariness. She was closely akin to being a widow in their eyes—and youngish, fairly presentable widows were considered as potential husband-snatchers in some quarters.

She was grateful for the faint breeze that filtered into the house from the river as she changed into suitable attire for dinner. Sara, too, would be going out for the evening, she remembered. A fund-raising dinner given by a church committee to benefit families of overseas servicemen.

Mattie Lou had pressed the delicately flowered cotton she had chosen to wear tonight and laid it across the bed. None of the women would be wearing a long dinner dress, she assumed, not in these times. She hesitated, glancing at the clock atop the fireplace mantel. If she didn't dawdle, she would have time for a quick bath.

Lying in the tepid water—fragrant with the scent of lily-of-the-valley bath salts—Vicky found her thoughts dwelling on Gary. Often late in the evening while she struggled with insomnia, she heard the faint sounds of music drifting through the night. Gary was at the piano he had shunned for so long. Neither she nor Sara was able to penetrate the wall which he had built around himself.

Almost obsessive about punctuality, Vicky left the tub and prepared to dress. Now her mind focused on the trip to Washington on Monday morning. Frank was so good about finding friends in the right places in Washington, she thought gratefully. In turn they met their obligations to those friends.

The train from Richmond to Washington would be mobbed on a Monday morning, she guessed. If Tina was unable to get reservations at the Mayflower, there was no telling what hotel would be available. She'd become spoiled through the years, she chided herself—she expected elegant hotel accommodations when she traveled.

From the lack of cars in the driveway of the Roberts's house, Vicky realized she was the first arrival. The Southern trait of being casual about time had never touched her, though at Barton Manor neither she nor Sara ever expected guests to arrive as scheduled.

Feeling faintly self-conscious, she parked and left the car. By the time she arrived at the entrance Marc was already at the door.

"It's good to see you again." Marc's smile radiated welcome.

"I'm a little early," she apologized.

"You're right on time. That's an admirable trait these days. Come inside and I'll bring you a tall glass of ice-cold fruit punch."

Vicky was pleasantly surprised to find that the house was air-conditioned.

"Oh, this is delicious," she approved. "We haven't gotten around to air-conditioning the house yet, but it's a godsend at the plant."

"Let me get you that glass of punch—" He walked her to the living room, then headed for the rear of the house.

Anita's voice filtered down the hall from what Vicky assumed was her bedroom.

"Martha, not those shoes," Anita rejected, faintly imperious. "They're so *klutzy*. The high-heeled pale pink ankle-straps."

Vicky was touched by Anita's determination to appear at her best. There was something poignant about her wearing high-heeled shoes when she could take no more than two or three steps and that with effort. Marc returned with Vicky's glass of punch, settled down with her on the sofa.

"How do you like living in Richmond?" Vicky asked.

"I have loved this town from our very first week here." His eyes crinkled with laughter. "I think I was seduced by all the bookstores."

They became so involved in a lively discussion about the merits of current fiction that both started as Anita wheeled herself into the living room.

"Don't let Marc monopolize the conversation with his shop talk," Anita warned lightly.

"You're looking lovely," Vicky said in candid admiration. "That's a beautiful dress." She should have known Anita would wear a long dinner dress, she reproached herself, hoping that the others wouldn't do the same.

"This is one of my prewar Paris dresses," Anita shrugged, but Vicky knew she was pleased.

"Mainbocher," Vicky guessed, inspecting the flowing fullness of the delicate pink chiffon that dropped from a wide-necked gathered top.

"Yes." Anita was surprised that she recognized the designer, Vicky suspected.

Now they began to talk about Paris. Vicky reminisced about having been a maid at the Crillon after escaping from Petrograd. She was amused by the simultaneous shock and awed fascination this evoked in Anita. What other white woman in the South would make such an admission? She was disconcerted by the intensity of Marc's gaze as she replied to Anita's questions about her growing-up years in Russia.

Then in a rush of activity the other guests arrived, within moments of one another. The house echoed with convivial sounds that didn't grow serious again until after a superb dinner, when Lisa brought up the subject of the imminent High Holidays—and the horror that was facing the Jews in Europe was explored.

"For a little while I had hopes that the Hungarian Jews would be saved," Marc said somberly. Back in May the *New York Times* had reported that Hungarian Jews were being sent to "murder camps in Poland." That was translated into Auschwitz. The War Refugee Board had launched a desperate campaign to stop this, but conditions for Hungarian Jews remained critical. They were being beaten and murdered every day.

"Let's not dwell on such sadness," Anita cajoled. "Not tonight. Marc, bring me a cigarette," she ordered and continued while he rose to his feet. "We all need some light in our lives. I've decided that one night each month I'm giving a small dinner party. Just our little group here," she confided, her voice lilting. "I don't ever remember finding such a congenial group."

Vicky was puzzled—somehow, disturbed—by the flicker of resignation on Marc's face as he stood frozen beside Anita with a lighted cigarette in one hand.

"Your cigarette, Anita." He was almost terse.

Didn't Marc like Anita to give dinner parties? It seemed a harmless diversion for a woman deprived of so much.

Chapter Twenty-eight

VICKY BOARDED the Washington-bound train early Monday morning and was relieved to find a seat. Immediately she settled down to study reports that she had brought along to support her explanations to the Washington bureau chief she and Frank were to meet. But she couldn't keep her mind off Saturday evening at the Roberts's house.

She'd sensed a bottled-up intensity in Marc that reached out to her. She guessed that he harbored a painful guilt about the accident that had sentenced Anita to a wheelchair. But Anita had mentioned somewhere in the course of casual conversation that she had been driving when the accident occurred. Then later on, Vicky recalled, Anita had said she loathed driving. Had she been driving at Marc's insistence?

Did anyone go through life without collecting guilt? At dinner last night—the one hour a week when she and Sara saw Gary—she'd tried to bring up the subject of his seeing a physician. He'd been furious.

Each Sunday when she sat down to dinner with Gary, she felt as though she was being evaluated, and at any moment he might hurl damning accusations at her. She felt, she thought, as though she lived on the edge of an abyss and could—at any moment—be hurled into fresh disaster.

She'd been horrified when Adam had suggested before he left for school in New York that the family have his father committed for psychiatric care. How could she do that to Gary? He wasn't insane.

He was just grievously hurt—and neither Sara nor she knew how to
help him.

At Union Station she searched for an available taxi. Usually when
she traveled on business, she took Mollie with her so that she was
relieved of such routine tasks. At the moment, Mollie was spending
much time at the bedside of her terminally ill father—she would have
been nervous at being away from Bartonville overnight.

Vicky found a taxi after several frustrating moments and headed
for the Mayflower Hotel. It was a miracle that Frank was able to get
them reservations at the Mayflower, she thought, as the taxi pulled up
before the hotel's two great curved bays that lent such grandeur to
D.C.'s main shopping street. The Mayflower was the recognized head-
quarters of war contractors.

Frank was waiting for her at the reservation desk.

"We can't get into our rooms until later in the day," he apologized.
"We'll check our luggage and go on to lunch."

"I'm not surprised." Vicky was philosophical about this wartime
problem. She knew the management had set up the Intervals Club so
that businessmen waiting to check in could use its showers, lockers,
and writing desks. What about women? she thought humorously.

Vicky and Frank had lunch at the hotel, and then headed for their
appointment. Both knew nothing could really be accomplished at this
meeting—it was merely a matter of soothing tempers. At their destination they were given passes, then ushered to their meeting.

Frank's patience, Vicky thought, was phenomenal. She fought
against revealing her own irritation at the bureau chief's lack of acceptance of their statements.

"I'm sorry," she said at last with the quiet finality that served her
well in business dealings. "There is no conceivable way that we or
any other company can produce a finished cigarette in twelve to eighteen months. We understand how important it is to ship cigarettes to
our fighting men." In a corner of her mind she remembered that
Michael had never smoked. "We—"

"Damn it, Vicky, we can't even supply the men on the front lines,"
the bureau chief interrupted in frustration. "There's this Senate committee out there investigating the shortage, like I've told you. We're
committed to supplying each GI with about two and a half packs a
day, seven days a week. The men in the front lines are lucky to get
five packs a week; those behind the lines may see two packs. The

Senate committee suspects that the industry is working to control the market and kill off competition.''

''We would never do that!'' Vicky's voice was controlled but betrayed her anger. ''To give an American cigarette what the public expects requires twenty-four to thirty-six months of aging and mellowing. As it is, we're already dipping into 1945 and 1946 inventories to try to meet demand.''

Over and over Vicky and Frank defended their stand. They knew other major companies were receiving the same treatment, but there was no way that any of them could increase their production because the government wouldn't release controls on how much tobacco was grown. It wasn't a question of workers. Even though defense plants paid higher wages, they were finding workers. It was the lack of tobacco leaf that held them up.

Two hours later Vicky and Frank headed for the Mayflower. Another meeting was scheduled over dinner. There the same threats of Senate investigations were thrown in their faces. Couldn't these men understand that more people than ever, particularly women, were smoking in these tense times?

''Look,'' Vicky said, breaking into yet another accusation that the industry was putting profit ahead of patriotism, ''we haven't raised prices, even though leaf tobacco has tripled in cost in recent years. Does that sound as though a few companies are manipulating the market?''

Vicky was relieved when she was settled in her room at the Mayflower, even while she suspected sleep would elude her well into the night. The country would have to accept the fact that there was a cigarette famine. The magazines and newspapers repeated this regularly. In Chicago the newspapers reported a cigarette related killing and several sluggings.

How had the world survived before explorers in the New World discovered the Indians smoking tobacco leaves? Like James I—who tried with little success to ban smoking in England—she thought smoking was a detestable habit. But to listen to the War Department, supplying cigarettes was as important to the war effort as food and mail.

Vicky dreaded the approach of Thanksgiving—though usually this was the holiday she most enjoyed. There would be the customary family dinner at Barton Manor. Lily and Stephanie and their husbands would be at the table, as would Kara and Derek. Adam would be home from NYU, and Doug would stay at Barton Manor with Paul. But Michael would not be here.

She knew that Sara, too, dreaded the holiday. Then all at once it was Wednesday evening, and the house resounded with young male voices as first Adam, then Doug and Paul arrived for the long week-end. Even while she was delighted with their presence, she was ever conscious of Michael's absence.

On Thursday morning she was astounded when Zachary reported that Gary would not be coming to the house.

"Mister Gary said I'm to bring him a tray like every other day," Zachary told her apologetically. "He won't be coming to the house till Sunday dinner."

"Thank you, Zachary." Vicky was upset at Gary's decision, but she understood. He couldn't bear to sit at the dinner table and not see Michael.

Sara came down early to have breakfast with Vicky. They made a shaky pretense of anticipating Thanksgiving dinner. As usual, Lily and Clark and Stephanie and Jeffrey were going away on Thursday evening for the rest of the weekend. It disturbed both Vicky and Sara that Lily made no effort to conceal her disapproval of Kara's marriage. It would be, Vicky thought as she sat at the breakfast table, a most trying day. How did you celebrate when part of your heart was dead?

Sitting at the dinner table, fighting back tears, Vicky tried to list those things for which she was thankful. She loved Sara and Sara's grandchildren. She felt only contempt for Lily and Stephanie and their husbands. She was pleased that Kara seemed happy in her marriage and so eager to have a baby. And she was grateful that Simone and Henri, like Paul's parents, were safe and well in liberated Paris. But how could she properly appreciate Thanksgiving when Michael lay dead somewhere in Germany and Gary was enveloped in a depression that shut her out?

In truth, Vicky thought later that night as she fought another losing battle with insomnia, she was relieved when Thanksgiving day was over. Tomorrow night she'd go to synagogue. Each time she sat within those walls she remembered how her parents had yearned to be free to practice their religion. Being there made her feel close to them.

Adam didn't talk about it, but she sensed that Michael's death had disturbed him deeply. He was unusually sweet and solicitous toward her. Since he'd come home for the Thanksgiving holidays, she'd felt a new and precious closeness to him. He was her baby, she thought with a surge of sentiment. Even when he was being his most difficult, she loved him so much.

After Friday night services at the synagogue the newly formed clique that Anita had brought into being went to Lisa Feinberg's for cake and coffee. This had become an extension of their monthly Saturday night dinners at Anita and Marc's house. It astonished Vicky that she so looked forward to these get-togethers.

On these occasions everyone seemed to be drawn into Anita's air of conviviality. But tonight Vicky could not thrust off the sense of loss that had hovered over her since the approach of Thanksgiving. Marc, too, she noted, seemed off in another world.

"These holidays can be depressing times," he said softly to her while the others listened absorbedly to one of Anita's slightly risqué stories about friends in towns where she and Marc had lived before.

"Yes." How sensitive of him to recognize that she felt that way, too, she thought.

"My parents were killed on Thanksgiving day nineteen years ago when their car skidded on an icy road in upstate New York. I was going directly to my grandmother's house from college." From the pain she saw in his eyes, Vicky knew he was reliving that day again. "I think that was what drew Anita and me together when we met two years later. Her parents had been murdered by robbers they'd surprised in their house down in Atlanta."

"How awful," Vicky commiserated.

"For years I hated Thanksgiving." His smile was wry. "Even now it's tainted for me."

"To me Thanksgiving was such a wonderful holiday." Until now. "We had nothing quite like it in Russia, nor in France, the little while I lived there."

"Now I try to think about the joyful Thanksgivings. When I was growing up, we always went to my grandparents' house up in Salem, New York. Even after my grandfather died, Grandma used to insist she would cook Thanksgiving dinner for us. My mother and father and I and my aunt and uncle never missed a Thanksgiving dinner up there. They're all gone now. I'm all that's left of the family."

"I have distant cousins in Russia," Vicky told him. "If they survived the Revolution."

"But you have family here," he said encouragingly. "That's very precious."

He never asked about Gary, Vicky thought. The others had probably told him. He was such a warm, understanding man. She was glad that he occupied a small corner of her life.

On Sunday morning—cold and gray and with a hint of snow in the air—Vicky awoke with an instant realization that Adam and Doug—along with Paul—were at Barton Manor. It gave her an odd comfort to know they were here. So often now Barton Manor seemed a haunted shell of itself.

The boys would sleep late, she guessed tenderly. She remembered how Michael used to love to sleep late when he came home from school. *"My big luxury,"* he used to say. They had to leave for school this afternoon. They'd all have an early Sunday dinner before Zachary drove them to the depot in Richmond.

It was hard to believe that Doug and Paul would be graduating from college this coming June—and Adam a year later. Where did all the years go?

With a frown she tossed aside the blankets and rose from the bed. She would not indulge in self-pity. She would dress, go downstairs, and have breakfast with Sara before she left for church. It had become a ritual through the years to have a leisurely Sunday breakfast with Sara. The other mornings she was always in a rush to get to the office.

The tempting aromas of fresh biscuits in the oven and coffee perking on the range drifted through the house, eliciting hunger in her. Most times since they'd lost Michael she ate from habit—because she knew she must to survive.

Approaching the dining room she was astonished to hear the sound of Adam's voice. He was at the table with his grandmother. Oh, he was changing, she thought affectionately. He was growing up.

"We're waiting to have breakfast with you," he greeted his mother gaily. "Of course, I allowed Grandma a cup of coffee."

"That was generous of you." Vicky picked up his light mood. "I'll bet you don't get coffee up in New York that's as good as Lula Mae's."

This morning—having breakfast with Sara and Adam—Vicky felt

a new serenity in her life. Adam could be so ingratiating at times. Had she been too demanding of him in his growing-up years? Too critical? She'd always loved him, of course—but he'd been a difficult child to raise.

When Sara declared she must not dawdle any longer or she'd be late for services, Adam rose from the table with her.

"I'll walk you to the car," he said, offering his arm to his grandmother, his smile gently teasing. "I'll be back for another cup of coffee," he told his mother. "Keep me company?"

"Of course." Vicky was conscious of a surge of love. She'd never given Adam credit for much sensitivity, she scolded herself. He understood her desolation since they'd lost Michael.

She reached for the silver coffee pot to pour for Adam and herself when she heard him approaching the dining room. Her eyes lit up when he walked into the room. How sweet of him to walk his grandmother to the car.

"It isn't snowing yet, is it?" she asked.

"No, though I wouldn't be surprised if we have an inch before nightfall." He sat down and reached for his coffee cup. "We'll probably really get it up in New York."

"I remember snow in New York those three months we lived up there—before you were born." She was caught up in recall—she and Gary and Michael in that apartment overlooking the park. "Central Park was glorious after a heavy snowfall."

"New York's a terrific city, but everything costs so much." Adam paused. She was aware that his eyes were appraising her. "I was thinking. I'm pushing so close to twenty-one—"

"Adam, don't push the time away," she laughed. "You won't be twenty until March."

"Twenty-one is breathing down my neck," he pursued. "I know I won't start getting money from my trust fund until then, but why can't I borrow on that? From a bank or from you," he said with elaborate casualness.

"Adam, you receive a substantial allowance." *He'd turned on the charm to pave the way for this, she thought in sickening comprehension.* "It's more than Doug receives. It's more than adequate."

"Doug's a jerk," he said impatiently. "All he cares about is his music. I'm broke half through the month."

"Then it's time you learned to budget." She struggled to remain calm. "You're a student, Adam. Not a member of Cafe Society."

"You act as though we were poverty-stricken!" he yelled and she glanced instinctively toward the door that led to the kitchen. She hated having the servants hear her fighting with Adam. "All I'm asking for is a loan. You know I can pay you back." There was a certain swagger in his voice now.

He had always been smug about the trust fund, Vicky remembered, since he was the only grandchild to receive one. He'd charmed Daniel into that. The day of his grandfather's funeral—when they gathered in the library to read the will—she'd recognized Adam's campaign to win himself a trust fund. When Sara was irritated with Adam, she always said, "He's Daniel all over again."

"There'll be no loans against your trust fund," she told him firmly. "And no bank will extend a loan to you at your age without my signature. Remember that, Adam."

"If Grandpa were alive, he'd increase my allowance," Adam spat at her. "He wouldn't expect me to live like we were one step from the poorhouse."

"He's not alive. You'll learn to manage on your allowance." She was trembling now. It was absurd to feel guilty that she was refusing Adam. But he had to learn the value of money. One day he'd be an extremely wealthy man. He must know how to handle his finances.

"I'll call the depot and see if I can get an earlier train out of here." He pushed back his chair and rose to his feet. "What's the point of hanging around?"

Vicky knew it was ridiculous for her to be upset because Adam had tried to borrow money against his trust fund. She'd said "no" and that was it. He was a student. He had no time to run to nightclubs and expensive restaurants. He listened to Lily and Stephanie carry on about "Elmo's" and "21" and the Stork Club, and he figured this was the scene for him.

Then again she was caught up in demands from Washington that the cigarette manufacturers increase their production. She was sent a memo reporting that General Eisenhower was threatening court-martial for any GI caught operating on the black market in cigarettes—where servicemen were handing out $2.00 to $2.75 for a pack of cigarettes. At a time when cigarettes sold in New York for seventeen cents a pack. Overseas cigarettes could be bartered for any-thing—including sex.

Frank sent her an item from the *New York Times* magazine, which stated that three out of four males and two out of five females over sixteen used tobacco—with ninety percent favoring cigarettes. People stood in endless lines to buy a pack of cigarettes. Almost a billion cigarettes a day were being smoked—and more were being demanded.

"It's incredible," Sara said when Vicky read her the statistics. "Cigarettes are just a nasty opiate. And think of all the time people waste on smoking," she added. "How many hours are wasted just reaching for a cigarette, lighting it, drawing on it? Add that up twenty to forty times a day."

Vicky knew that the Hanukkah season would be difficult for her. She would remember the Hanukkahs before Michael went off to school and how together they lighted the candles each of the eight nights of Hanukkah. For Michael it had been a beautiful ceremony, though Adam had always refused to participate.

There was to be a Hanukkah party at the synagogue, but Vicky would not be among the celebrants. Then Anita phoned to say that their Saturday evening dinner this month was to be switched to the second night of Hanukkah.

"Oh, I'll have to miss this month," Vicky apologized. "I have to be in Washington that day." In truth, she would be in Washington the previous day.

"But Vicky, I count on you," Anita cajoled. "You bring something special to our dinners."

"I enjoy so much being there," Vicky said. "I'll look forward to the next one. If I'm still invited," she said lightly.

"Of course you're invited, darling. But we'll miss you this month." Vicky sensed a faint reproach beneath Anita's cordiality. "Will you be at the synagogue party?"

"I doubt it. This is a terribly busy time at the office." She was self-conscious at lying to Anita.

"Oh, you working women," Anita joshed. "I so envy you. You're out there accomplishing things. I feel so useless. I've been thinking about having little 'Sunday evenings.' Nothing fancy, just a buffet and drinks, and folks can pop in and out whenever they like. You might enjoy meeting some of Marc's colleagues from the university."

"I'm sure I would." Why did Anita seem to try so hard to cater to her? Immediately the answer jogged into her mind: because of her success in business—and because she was a Barton. She felt uncomfortable in her cynicism. "I'll look forward to your 'Sunday evenings' if you decide to have them." She strived for a tone of sincerity.

"Not right away," Anita stipulated. "In the spring. I have to persuade Marc to let me do this."

They talked a few moments longer, and then Anita excused herself to call the others in their group about the dinner for the second night of Hanukkah. Why did she have the feeling that Anita was annoyed with her?

She realized she wished to remain part of what Marc had once laughingly called "Anita's salon." Because if she wasn't, she thought with candor, she wouldn't see Marc. She looked forward to those evenings when they seemed to find a conversational oasis of their own.

The realization was disturbing.

Chapter Twenty-nine

SHORTLY BEFORE Adam was expected home for the winter intercession, he wrote that he wouldn't be coming home.

"I have a job," he wrote, without elaborating on it. "I need the extra money." For what, Vicky asked herself. His allowance was far more than most college students received.

She tried to conceal her disappointment that Adam would not be coming home. It was as though the family was being torn apart, she thought at the approach of Christmas Eve. Gary, too, had said that he would not be at the house for the holidays.

She was grateful that Doug and Paul were at Barton Manor, and any moment Kara and Derek would be coming in from Richmond to stay over for two nights. Tomorrow Lily and Stephanie and the husbands would come over for the traditional early-afternoon Christmas dinner and to exchange Christmas presents. For a little while Barton Manor would echo with conviviality.

Vicky enjoyed having Doug and Paul here, though it disturbed her that Doug's parents still rejected Paul as a house guest. "It's unhealthy for Doug to be so close to that boy," Stephanie complained to her.

Perhaps Gary might be coaxed into a better mood at the Sunday dinners with Doug and Paul at the table, Vicky thought with a flicker of hope. He'd always been so impressed with Doug's talents—which Stephanie and Jeffrey preferred to ignore. Or would Doug's presence be a bitter reminder that Michael was not at the table?

As Vicky had subconsciously feared, Gary did not come to the house for his customary Sunday dinners until he was sure that Doug and Paul had returned to school. And when he did resume this routine, his conversation consisted only of morbid comments about the war. The world had learned about a meeting of Roosevelt, Churchill, and Stalin at Yalta in the Crimea. A meeting praised by both the American and the British press. But the American public was shocked by the press photos of Roosevelt at Yalta. He appeared frighteningly drawn and haggard.

On February 23, 1945, the American flag was raised on Iwo Jima, but not until March sixteenth—after thirty-six days of fierce fighting—did Iwo Jima fall to the U.S. Marines. More than four thousand Marines were killed and fifteen thousand wounded.

"The Japanese lost twenty thousand," Sara pointed out.

March was a traumatic month for Vicky—as it was, she knew, for Gary and Sara. March a year ago Michael had written that he was finishing his tour of duty and would be coming home for a month-long furlough. Two weeks after that joyous letter they'd learned that he'd been killed in action.

In her bedroom Vicky lit a *Yahrzeit* candle in Michael's memory. She sat far into the night rereading all his letters—which she had saved in a hand-painted sewing box he had made in a high school woodworking class. Through tear-blurred eyes she looked yet again at the collection of snapshots that dated back to his infancy and up to a snapshot he had sent to her from somewhere in England.

She knew that today Sara had gone to church to offer up special prayers. No doubt in her mind that Gary, too, was remembering Michael. She wished that she could go to him, be with him on this day. But she knew she would be rejected. There was room in Gary's heart only for memories of Michael and for his music.

On April twelfth the world was shocked to learn of the death of President Roosevelt. All over the United States people cried unashamedly. It was as though every American had lost a close friend. That evening Gary appeared unexpectedly at the house for dinner. He was pale and shaken. He talked agitatedly with Vicky and his mother about the nation's loss.

"It'll be a long time before we see the likes of FDR," he summed up with an air of exhaustion as they walked into the dining room.

"How sad that he couldn't live to see the end of the war," Vicky said quietly.

"He'd seen too much already." Gary's eyes were anguished. "I've seen too much."

Over dinner, Sara tried to draw Gary into conversation about Doug's approaching graduation from college, but now it was as though he sat alone at the table. His body was here, Vicky thought, but his mind and heart were somewhere else.

The talk at Anita's Saturday night dinner party revolved around the death of Roosevelt. As usual, Anita made an impassioned effort to direct the conversation into less somber channels.

"I think it's fascinating to hear about Paris since the liberation," she said effervescently. "Chanel may have closed up shop when the Nazis took Paris, but I've read that French women still dress beautifully—with none of the awful rationing we had to put up with here. Thank God, I have the dresses I'd bought in Paris the summer of '39."

Anita didn't understand that the women in their circle might buy a designer dress once in a lifetime, Vicky thought. She owned several, she remembered guiltily—but they had been bought for business trips, when she'd needed to appear chic and successful.

After dinner Anita talked with mocking good humor about the Old Families of Richmond.

"Is there something sacred about their houses that Jews are never entertained?" Anita appeared more amused than vindictive, yet Vicky sensed her underlying annoyance. "But you've made it, Vicky," she laughed.

All at once Vicky understood. Anita was angling for an invitation to Barton Manor. It had never occurred to her that she should offer to entertain in her own home. In her mind—even after all these years—it was Sara's home. But she'd accepted the hospitality of Anita and Marc on half a dozen occasions now—and Lisa Feinberg's just as often.

"Would you all like to have dinner at Barton Manor next Saturday evening?" she asked. "You can see for yourselves." Everybody knew that Sara had been a Warren—one of Richmond's "Old Families." Sara wouldn't object to her having a small dinner party. Gary wouldn't even know. It wasn't wrong to entertain, she told herself—Michael was gone for over a year now. Her precious son would be the last to expect her to shut herself off from life.

Subconsciously she was aware of the flurry of high spirits this invitation elicited. Except for Anita and Marc—who were obviously wealthy—these were all middle-class Jews who would never be extended an invitation into the home of one of the Old Families. She omitted herself from the list of wealthy Jews. To her the Barton money was a family matter—she never thought of herself individually as wealthy.

Her mind raced backward through the years to those minutes when she stood in the Jewish cemetery with Mr. Ginsberg. All these years later she could hear his voice: "*Forty years ago a Jewish gentleman was president of the Westmoreland Club. Today a Jew could not head a fine Richmond club. Oh, we meet on the street and in the stores, and we're treated with fine Virginian courtesy. But not many of us see the inside of the homes of socially prominent Christians.*" That would not be said of Barton Manor, Vicky promised herself.

As Vicky had anticipated, Sara offered no objection to her inviting the group to the house for dinner.

"Vicky, it's your home, too," Sara said. "You don't have to ask me if you may entertain."

On impulse Vicky asked Sara—who would be visiting her brother on the night of the dinner—if she would remain long enough to give the guests a guided tour of the lower floor of the house.

"Of course I will," Sara laughed. "But Barton Manor isn't an old colonial mansion. Daniel and I started off with a five-room cottage, and it just grew."

"Lisa Feinberg says it reminds her of Tara in *Gone With the Wind*," Vicky told her. "And they'll enjoy seeing your beautiful antiques."

Vicky left the office early on Saturday to have the time to check on dinner preparations and dress leisurely. Earlier in the day Zachary had brought in armfuls of flowering dogwood, which Sara herself had arranged about the lower floor of the house. Lula Mae had been cooking since early morning. She was determined to make this first dinner party at Barton Manor in many years—other than for family—a culinary event.

Before going downstairs, Vicky took a final inspection of herself in the cheval mirror. She had chosen the flowered silk Mainbocher that she'd bought at Mainbocher's salon in Manhattan. She knew that

Anita would be pleased that she'd dressed specially for this occasion. And Anita would be pleased, too, at meeting Sara.

As Vicky had suspected, the first arrivals were Marc and Anita. Like herself, Marc had a compulsion to be punctual. Anita set herself out to charm Sara. It was clear that she relished being welcomed into the home of one of Virginia's Old Families.

With her innate graciousness Sara explained that she had to leave shortly to visit her invalid brother but was delaying so that she could show Vicky's guests through the lower floor of Barton Manor.

"It's not really one of the fine old Virginia houses," Sara confided, "but we've tried to recreate an older period with some authentic touches."

Vicky and Marc exchanged a smile as the other two talked enthusiastically about such details as the fan lights and sidelights of the main doorways and the Greek Key design in the dining room.

"Anita is just enthralled," Marc whispered softly as Effie came into the room to serve white wine in exquisite stemware. "Thank you for having us here."

"It's a huge house for two women," Vicky said. "Only on holidays—or times like this—does it come alive." Again, she felt self-conscious that Gary wasn't here to serve as host.

"You have a special grace that belongs in a house like this," he told her. "I have such trouble accepting you as a hugely successful business woman."

"I came into the business of necessity." She brushed this aside with a casual gesture of slender hands.

"The talent was there." His eyes were admiring. "The quick brain. And all the while," he chuckled, "you look like a lovely Dresden doll."

Vicky was relieved that they were interrupted by Lisa's arrival. She was often unnerved by Marc's presence. It had been so long since she'd felt the way she did when they were together.

It was absurd to feel this way, she chided herself in a corner of her mind while she introduced Lisa to Sara. Marc and she were two long-married people—past the age of becoming romantically drawn to each other. Yet she knew that Marc, too, felt this air of excitement when they were in the same room.

The others arrived almost simultaneously. Sara charmingly showed off the lower floor of Barton Manor, then excused herself to go off to visit her brother. In the dining room the chair at the head of the table had been removed to accommodate Anita's wheelchair. Vicky was conscious of an air of triumph in Anita as Marc wheeled her into position.

Anita envisioned herself as the chatelaine of a fine southern mansion, Vicky thought, with all the accoutrements of wealth and social position. She was candid about having inherited a sizeable estate from her parents—though admittedly small compared to the ever-increasing Barton money. But Vicky sensed this candor made Marc uncomfortable. It was a constant reaffirmation that his earnings did not provide for their lavish lifestyle.

As she saw her guests off at the door, Vicky decided the evening had gone well. It was the first time in all these years that she had personally entertained at Barton Manor. It was good to relax among friends, she thought. This had been an evening pleasurably spent. Life shouldn't be all business and personal obligations.

Moments after her guests had departed, Vicky saw the family car pulling up before the house. Zachary was bringing Sara home.

"How did the evening go?" Sara asked, walking across the veranda.

"It was fine." Vicky smiled. "Would you like some coffee? Effie said Lula Mae just put up a fresh pot."

"I'd love it. Rob won't allow coffee in the house." She chuckled affectionately. "Neither coffee nor cigarettes. He considers both an abomination."

The two women sat in the library and discussed their respective evenings over Lula Mae's chicory-laced coffee.

"I don't really care for the woman in the wheelchair," Sara confessed. "What's her name? Anita something?"

"Anita Roberts," Vicky said, surprised at Sara's reaction.

"I wouldn't trust her from here to the door. She's one of those devious Southern women. So sweet and charming, but she'd cut the throat of anybody who got in her way."

"She's been through so much," Vicky protested gently.

"And she uses that, my darling. I feel sorry for her husband. He seems such a nice man. I'll bet she rakes him over the coals regularly. And don't tell me about his obligations," Sara said before Vicky could respond. "There are some people—and I suspect he's one of them—who take on obligations beyond the call of duty."

Long after she had settled herself in bed, Vicky found herself wide awake and thinking about Sara's remarks. *Did* Anita give Marc a rough time? He smiled a lot but his eyes often seemed troubled.

Marc enjoyed his teaching, she analyzed, but there was an air of resignation about him when Anita made small, thoughtless statements about his work. Not that anybody took them seriously, but Anita had a way of making Marc's teaching seem no more than an ambitionless pastime. *"Marc knows he doesn't have to work—but he enjoys playing on the university circuit. All those adoring young coeds."*

Vicky was pleased that Sara had liked Marc. The years had proved to her that Sara's instincts about people were quite accurate.

Tonight Vicky surveyed the gathering in the Roberts's living room with covert curiosity. This was Anita's first "Sunday evening"—to be a monthly rather than a weekly ritual. Anita was radiant, she thought.

She quickly realized she enjoyed meeting Marc's friends from the university. Their conversation was stimulating, she decided as she stood with three faculty members and Marc and dissected the United Nations Conference, which had just opened in San Francisco.

"Delegates from fifty nations are there," Marc said with relish.

"It seems so strange," she said, "to be talking about building an instrument for world peace when we're still at war."

"It's a matter of days," a professor of economics assured her, "before Germany surrenders. And how much longer can the Japanese hold out?"

"I know what Vicky means," Marc said compassionately. "Every day that the war continues, lives are lost. They're talking about a future peace, but that's so remote to families with men—and women—on the fighting fronts."

Involved in a lively conversation with Lisa and Marc and a pair of his colleagues, Vicky stayed later than she had planned. Tomorrow was a working day. She'd be at her desk no later than eight AM. But she was among the last to leave.

"It's raining," she said in astonishment. She'd been too absorbed in good-humored argument to notice earlier.

"Darling, don't worry," Anita trilled. "You won't shrink."

The lightness in Anita's voice was belied by a sudden hostile glint in her eyes. Perceiving this, Vicky was shaken. Marc, too, looked suddenly grim. He turned to her with a strained smile.

"I'll get an umbrella, Vicky, and walk you to your car."

"Thank you, Marc."

Driving home, Vicky replayed in her mind those few disconcerting moments with Anita. Was she reading too much into what appeared to be humorous raillery? No, that was a dig. Marc had felt it, too. Had anyone else noticed?

She knew Anita was vain about being tall. Of the women there tonight she herself was one of the most petite—a fact that caused her no anguish. Anita's cattiness had sneaked out involuntarily, she surmised. All the little mocking remarks that Anita had dropped with devious sweetness in the past seemed to leap into one huge, ugly collage now. Anita resented her being a successful businesswoman, resented her being a Barton.

She didn't want to break away from this new circle of friends, Vicky thought defensively. She'd miss them. *She'd miss Marc.*

Chapter Thirty

Events in Europe were happening with cyclonic rapidity. On April twenty-second, Russian troops marched into the suburbs of Berlin while other Russian troops drove into northern Germany. For this final assault on Germany the Russians had assembled more than four million men. Now from all directions Allied forces closed in on Germany.

On April twenty-fifth Russian and American troops joined forces at Torgau, on the Elbe River—and were sickened by the discovery of the slaughterhouses Hitler had built at Buchenwald, Dachau, Belsen, and other locations. The world listened as stunned war correspondents told of the horrors discovered there.

A few days later Italian partisans captured and killed Mussolini and his mistress. On May first, German radio reported that Hitler had died while defending Berlin and that Eva Braun had committed suicide the previous day. On May second Berlin fell to the Russian army.

In Bartonville Vicky and Sara were making arrangements to go to New York for Doug's graduation from Columbia. Vicky suspected that neither Stephanie nor Jeffrey would attend the graduation. Though terribly depressed at not becoming pregnant, Kara had said that she would surely be there for Doug's graduation. Then on an early May night Doug phoned from New York with more news.

"You'll be here in time to see the little revue in Greenwich Village that's featuring a song Paul and I wrote," he said jubilantly, speaking to both Vicky and his grandmother via phone extensions. "We're excited about it!"

"Doug, we're so proud of you," Sara murmured, and Vicky echoed this.

"Mother's having a fit. She's still got this crazy bug about me going into Barton Tobacco." Doug sighed. "I talk, but she never listens."

"You know what you want to do with your life," Vicky said firmly. "That's so important."

They talked another few minutes, then Doug had to go back to studying for final exams. While Vicky and Sara lovingly discussed Doug's pleasure in his music, Stephanie arrived at the house.

"I'm absolutely furious," she declared, her eyes darting accusingly from her mother to Vicky. "Doug came flat out and said he's been studying music all this time he was up at Columbia. Now who was paying for all this?"

"Perhaps he used our Christmas and birthday checks," Sara said carefully. "Checks are always more appreciated than sweaters or ties or whatever."

"I told him he won't see one more cent from his father or me." Stephanie's face was grim. "He's talking about going to Paris to study music there. You know he'd do well in the company if he'd just apply himself."

"This seems to be a musical family," Vicky pointed out. "Talent should be nurtured."

"Like Gary?" Stephanie taunted. "What did he ever do with his talent?"

"I failed Gary," Sara said, her face drained of color. "I should have supported him more strongly. As long as I draw a breath, I'll hate myself for not taking his side against your father. Don't fail your son, Stephanie."

"I've told him." Stephanie's face was icy. "Either he comes home to Bartonville after graduation and goes into the family business, or his father and I wash our hands of him."

It was Daniel and Gary all over again, Vicky thought tiredly. But Doug knew that she and Sara would always be there behind him.

The day began like any other business day. Vicky was at her desk by eight AM. She remembered hearing a newscaster say the previous evening that this would be President Truman's sixty-first birthday. She spoke briefly with Frank by phone shortly before nine AM. At nine AM—as usual—Mollie brought her a cup of coffee.

Twenty minutes later Mollie—whose brother was fighting in the Pacific—burst into the office again.

"It's over!" Her voice was shrill with a blend of excitement and incredulity. "President Truman just spoke on radio from Washington! The war in Europe is over!"

People were pouring into the hallway, welcoming the long-awaited news with noisy greetings. Moments later jubilant sounds emerged from the plant.

"Of course, they're still fighting in the Pacific," Mollie said. "But it's the beginning of the end."

Vicky immediately announced that work was over for the day. Employees streamed out into the street—where others were spreading the joyous message. Church bells rang. As Vicky left the building and headed for her car, she saw a bunch of teenagers dancing in the middle of the road. School was out. Other businesses were closing. It was a day of celebration.

She arrived at the house to discover that no one had as yet heard the news. "Thank God," Sara whispered when Vicky told her, and rose from the table. "Effie, please go find Zachary. I want him to drive me to church."

"I suppose Gary's heard," Vicky said hesitantly, pushing aside an instinctive impulse to go to him.

"He's listening to the radio by seven every morning," Sara reminded. "He's heard." Her face was somber now. "He'll be happy—but he'll be hurting, too."

"I know." For Michael the end of the war in Europe had come too late. "If he wants to talk to us, he'll come here."

Vicky saw Sara off to church, then settled in a rocker on the veranda to savor what was happening. It was a bittersweet occasion for those like herself who'd lost a loved one in the war. Then in a burst of restlessness she left the veranda to go to the library. There she clung to the radio as a newscaster excitedly reported the latest word from Washington. American servicemen and women would be coming home, she thought—but it was likely they'd be reshipped to the Pacific.

Vicky listened to reports of how the news was being received around the country. In New York people were dancing in the streets, throwing miles of ticker tape out Wall Street windows. Work was forgotten. There was dancing and singing in the Chicago Loop, on the streets of every hamlet, town, and city in the country. Impromptu parties broke out to celebrate the president's news. But they mustn't forget, Vicky reminded herself somberly, that death and destruction had not ceased in the Pacific.

Now the phones at Barton Manor—as in the houses throughout the nation—began to ring. Everybody wanted to share the good news. Kara phoned—tears in her voice because victory in Europe had come too late for Michael and Jimmy. Lisa called and talked for almost an hour because she knew that Vicky shared her ambivalence about today. It was wonderful that there'd be no more dying from the war in Europe, but this only emphasized their grief that their sons wouldn't be coming home with the others.

Shortly before eleven AM Marc called.

"School's out, of course," he said. "It's wonderful news, but I know where your thoughts are today. I just wanted to let you know that—that I'm here if you need to talk." He hadn't said "we," Vicky recognized subconsciously—he'd said "I."

"I'm trying to cope," she said shakily. "It seems so selfish not to be completely thrilled that it's all over. At least, in Europe," she amended.

"Let's pray it's over soon in the Pacific. It's not going to be easy," he reminded. "Not with every Japanese soldier convinced that to die for the emperor means guaranteed immortality."

On and off throughout the day Vicky's thoughts turned to Gary. She remembered Armistice Day in Paris, and how work had been abandoned when the news spread and Parisians poured into the streets. She remembered French girls dancing with soldiers of many nations on the Champs Elysées. The singing, the bands playing, the impromptu square dancing. She remembered how finally—late in the afternoon—Gary came to her. They'd been so happy.

Each time someone arrived at the house, this afternoon, she half-expected to find Gary at the door. But Gary had no room in his heart for joy, she reminded herself—only for grief and bitterness.

Just as any other day, Vicky sat down to dinner with Sara. Zachary left the house with a tray to go to Gary's cottage. Neither of the women was in the mood to eat, yet each made a pretense for the sake of the other. Effie was serving Lula Mae's superb red snapper when they heard Zachary calling as he rushed through the house.

"Miz Sara! Oh, Miz Sara!" His voice was a terrified wail.

"Zachary, what is it?" Sara demanded as he hovered breathlessly at the entrance.

"You better send for the doctor, Miz Sara," he gasped. "Mister Gary has shot himself!"

Vicky summoned an ambulance and the family doctor while Sara hurried to the cottage with Zachary. Then Vicky rushed along the path beaten down through the years, trying to brace herself for what she would find at the cottage. Her face white, etched with grief, Sara sat in a rocker on the small porch.

"Don't go in, Vicky," Sara whispered. "He's gone. You don't need to see. My precious boy, my firstborn. I failed him, Vicky. I should have been stronger."

Vicky called Adam to tell him the devastating news. She was not sure how deeply he would be affected, but she was shocked when he tried to weasel out of coming home for his father's funeral.

"What difference will it make to Dad if I come home?" he said. "I need to cram for finals."

"You come home so as not to shame your grandmother," Vicky told him, trembling with rage. "You'll come for the funeral, and you can go right back to school."

"Did Dad leave a will?" he asked. "I mean, I know he owned some stock in the company."

"The stock was held in trust for me," Vicky told him. "Our joint bank account and stock portfolio come to me. There is no inheritance, Adam." *What kind of a child had she brought into this world?*

"I thought it would be kind of nice to have his share of the company," Adam said awkwardly. "You know—for sentimental reasons."

"In less than a year you'll start receiving funds from your trust fund," she reminded him, ignoring the sentiment ploy. "You'll have an income of your own. Call and let us know what train you'll be taking," she said. "Zachary will come to meet you."

Now she called Doug and told him what had happened. She could hear the shock and pain in Doug's voice.

"He couldn't handle Michael's not coming home," he said gently. "Don't blame him, Vicky."

"I know," she whispered.

"Is it all right if I bring Paul with me?"

"I'd like that very much."

Kara moved into Barton Manor with Derek to see the family through this latest tragedy. She and Derek would handle the funeral arrangements. Lily and Stephanie came to stay at the house and played the bereaved sisters with a gusto that sickened Vicky.

Two days later Gary was laid to rest beside his father. It seemed that half of Bartonville attended the services at the church and at the cemetery. A contingent from Richmond came, as well.

For a few moments she spoke with Marc. Anita hadn't come; she'd sent a beautiful floral piece.

"She's having one of her bad days," Marc apologized for Anita.

"I'm sorry," she said. Anita had not come, she thought with fresh vision, because she wouldn't be able to dominate the scene here. "I hope she'll soon feel better."

Despite Doug's insistence that he wouldn't feel hurt if Vicky and his grandmother didn't come to Columbia graduation exercises, both women traveled to New York for the event. They persuaded Doug and Paul to come down to Barton Manor for a few weeks because the new graduates were having difficulty obtaining passage to Paris—either by ship or plane.

"We'd like to fly to London on one of Pan Am's DC-4s," Doug said wistfully. "They've been making the flight since January. Can you believe, in fifteen hours and fifty minutes?"

"We'll settle for a merchant ship," Paul said, his eyes somber. Vicky remembered that he hadn't seen his family since the summer of '39. "We'd walk if we could," he added with a grin.

Not until she was back from New York could Vicky bring herself to go to the cottage and prepare to close it up. Unable to face this, Sara had asked her to see which of Gary's possessions should be saved. Then Zachary and one of the gardeners would dispose of what remained.

On a sultry morning early in June, Vicky walked toward the cottage. She was grateful for the shade provided by the towering trees, for an occasional breeze from the river. Her mind was assaulted by memories: the day she'd discovered the cabin and vowed to have it provide a studio for Gary, the day they had gone into Richmond to buy Gary's piano, the sweetly exciting period when she and Sara waited for the cottage to be built.

All at once she emerged from her reverie. The pristine white cottage stood before her. Red roses climbed on a trellis at one side, along the railing of the veranda. The lush scent of honeysuckle was everywhere. For a moment she closed her eyes, remembering Sara sitting on the veranda that awful day and ordering her not to go inside.

Gearing herself to face the empty rooms that had been Gary's self-imposed prison, she walked up the steps to the veranda, and then to the door. She hesitated only a moment, then pushed the door open. She was conscious of an unexpected coolness inside, a deceptive silence.

She walked across the tiny foyer into the small but charming living room, flooded with sunlight. Her eyes fell to the spot on the Persian rug where someone had tried to remove the bloodstains.

This was where Gary had shot himself with a gun she never suspected he owned. He'd sat there on the piano bench and ended the life that had become too tormented to bear. It wasn't just Sara who had failed him. His wife had failed him, too.

Vicky sat at the piano, caught up again in memories. Gary playing Chopin's *Minute Waltz* at the piano in Larue's in Paris. Gary playing the beautiful lullaby he'd written for Michael. Gary's agony at hearing George Gershwin play his *Rhapsody in Blue* at Aeolian Hall in New York and convincing himself he'd never compose anything so magnificent. Gary playing a duet with Michael on this piano on Michael's last leave before shipping out. Now both Michael and Gary were gone.

Through her tears she gazed at the sheet music on the piano. She leaned forward to read the handwritten words above the bars of music: "Ode to a Beloved Son."

This was what Gary had been working on all these months. She reached out a trembling hand to touch the paper—as though this might bring her closer to both Gary and Michael. All at once she was impatient to hear what Gary had written. Bring Doug to the cottage, she told herself. Doug would play Gary's music for her.

Despite the heat she ran the distance to the house, sought out Doug, told him what she had discovered.

"Doug, please," she whispered. "Play it for me."

Now she returned to the cottage with Doug and Paul. She sat in a chair close to the piano while Paul took his place to turn the pages for Doug.

"It's a symphony in memory of Michael," Doug said, his voice choked.

In a few moments Vicky knew that the music Doug played was a small masterpiece. She saw the recognition of this on the faces of Doug and Paul. She had stood by and allowed that wonderful talent to be suffocated. Gary didn't die just a few weeks ago. He'd died when he denied his talent all those years ago.

Chapter Thirty-one

ON AN EARLY July morning at the Richmond depot Vicky saw Doug and Paul off for New York, where they would board a ship en route to Cherbourg. Both were excited about resuming their music studies in Paris, and Paul was impatient for a reunion with his family.

"You'll have trouble for quite a while getting accommodations out of Europe," Vicky warned for the dozenth time. "Every ship will be bringing home our troops."

"We're in no rush to come back," Doug laughed. "It's just so great to be able to study over there. Thanks to you and Grandma," he said affectionately.

His mother and Lily had left several days ago for a month in Newport without bothering to say goodbye to him, Vicky remembered in silent rage. His father was too busy with law clients and his mayoral duties to exchange more than a terse few words about his "total lack of responsibility." His parents would never forgive Doug for not coming into the business. They wanted Doug to be a watchdog, to protect their interests.

Sara had not come to the depot because of the heat, which she was not tolerating well this summer. But she refused to go off to the mountains even for a few days. Vicky guessed that this was because of her brother Rob. His hold on life was very tenuous.

Vicky saw the two boys off on their train, then drove to the office with a sense of loss. Instinct warned her that they would not be rush-

ing back to Bartonville for a long time. But Adam would be home
for the summer, she told herself. Though he'd probably spend all his
time sleeping or swimming in the new pool Lily and Clark had recently put in, it was comforting to know he would be at Barton Manor
until late in the summer. Then, ten days before school started he would
go back to New York so he could spend some time on Fire Island,
where a buddy at NYU had the use of his family's house.

Adam kept urging her to insist that Sara have the house air-
conditioned. *"She's got plenty of loot—why shouldn't she be comfortable?"* Adam was right, she thought. She'd talk to Sara about that.

When she arrived at the office, she learned that Mollie would not
be coming in. Her mother had just received word that Mollie's
brother—a Marine in the Pacific—was missing in action. For too
many families, Vicky thought compassionately, the euphoria of V-E
day had become a mockery.

The Japanese had surrendered at Okinawa little more than a week
ago—but almost thirteen thousand Americans had died and forty thousand were wounded. Word had just come through that General Mac-
Arthur had reported the liberation of the Philippines—but in the ten
months of fighting there twelve thousand Americans had been killed
in action. Nobody doubted that the invasion of Japan would be costly.

As always in traumatic periods, Vicky tried to submerge herself in
her work. She avoided services at the synagogue, understandably
missed Anita's June dinner and "Sunday evening." She spoke at intervals with Lisa Feinberg, who was always supportive and compassionate. From Lisa she learned that Marc and Anita had gone again
to Mackinac Island for two months.

Then the world learned that on August sixth—after last-chance
warnings—an atomic bomb had been dropped on Hiroshima—causing
unbelievable devastation. When the Japanese refused to surrender, a
second bomb was dropped on Nagasaki. On August fourteenth President Truman announced Japan's unconditional surrender.

On the morning he was taking the train up to New York, Adam
insisted there was no need for Vicky to go with him to the Richmond
depot.

"I'm a big boy now, Mother," he drawled. "Zachary will drive
me to the station, and I'll put myself on the train. You know you hate
missing a morning at the office."

Adam had such a way of making her feel guilty, she thought, as though her being a working woman had deprived him of mothering. It hadn't been like that at all.

"That's right." She tried for a flippant tone. "You'll be twenty-one in a few months."

"Yeah." He grinned. A triumphant glint in his eyes. "I'll see you at Thanksgiving." He gave her a perfunctory kiss. "I've already told Zachary I needed him to drive me to the station. He'll be out front with the car."

"Enjoy your vacation at Fire Island," she said. Why did she always measure her words with Adam? She wasn't like that with Doug.

Adam immediately spied Chuck Wheeler, waiting for him at the arrival gate at Penn Station.

"Hey, Chuck, you've been out there lying on the beach all summer," he jeered. Hell, he was almost as dark as Zachary. "If you got on a train below the Mason-Dixon line, the conductor would worry about which car to seat you in!"

"We have to grab a train to Bay Shore." Chuck checked his watch. "The train's probably pulling in right now. Let's scram."

On the Long Island Railroad train to Bay Shore, Chuck filled Adam in on his summer activities. Up till three days ago he'd been working in his father's law office, spending three-day weekends with his family at the Fire Island cottage. Now his parents were off for two weeks at a hotel in the Adirondacks. "Mom's tired of cooking." Chuck paused. "Did you tell your mother yet that you don't want to go on to law school?"

"Not yet," Adam drawled. "When she has to know, I'll tell her."

Chuck had been so impressed to learn that his mother was Vicky Barton, head of Barton Tobacco. The old boy in the New York office—what was his name, Frank Leslie—must have a crush on her, the way he kept building up publicity about her, Adam thought. It was a crock, her pretending she didn't like it, that she just went along because it was good for the company.

"Hey, there's a bunch of girls—plus one mother—who've just moved into the cottage across from ours. One of them's a real knockout. Long blonde hair, blue eyes, built." He whistled in approval.

"So?" Adam grinned inquiringly.

"So far I haven't got to first base," Chuck admitted. "But she hasn't told me to get lost."

"Watch a master at work," Adam bragged. "Watch the Adam Barton charm take over."

At Bay Shore they left the train and climbed into a taxi for the ride to the ferry. Adam stood with Chuck at the railing of the boat deck and asked himself if he really wanted to spend ten days on some God-forsaken island he'd never heard of. But Chuck's report of the blonde in the cottage across from theirs offered interesting possibilities. Before they left Fire Island, he promised himself, he'd be in her bed. Or she'd be in his, he amended—remembering the mother in residence at the cottage.

Arriving at the tiny dock at Ocean Beach, Adam regarded the scene with amused condescension. Chuck good-humoredly brushed aside the ten-year-old with a red wagon who wanted to cart Adam's valise to the cottage.

"Where do we eat here?" Adam demanded as Chuck prodded him away from the dock. "I'm starving."

"We eat at the cottage." Chuck's eyes crinkled in laughter. "This isn't Barton Manor." Chuck had been impressed, too, Adam remembered, when he'd seen pictures of Barton Manor. He lived with his parents in a four-bedroom house in Forest Hills. "Franks and beans for dinner."

"I start drawing from my trust fund in March," Adam reminded Chuck, privy to much of his personal life. "We'll be doing some celebrating when that loot starts coming in."

The cottage was on a walk just off the beach. To Adam's thinking it was very modest, consisting of only a living room, an eat-in kitchen, and three bedrooms. The furniture, he surmised, consisted of discards from the Wheelers' Forest Hills house. The Wheelers weren't poor, Chuck had made clear—but they weren't in the Bartons' class.

"Hey, there she is!" Chuck summoned Adam to a window. "I think I heard the others call her Eleanor."

Adam glanced out the window. A small, slender blonde with an ethereal prettiness was running gracefully from the cottage across the way and toward the beach.

"Hey, not bad," he conceded. "Great legs, sexy boobs."

"So let's see how far you can get," Chuck taunted.

"First we eat," Adam decreed.

They ate, dumped the dishes in the sink, changed into swimming trunks, and headed for the lightly populated beach.

"Ignore them," Adam whispered when they spied the cluster of four girls from the neighboring cottage lolling on a nearby stretch of beach.

"So what's that gonna get us?"

"Dumb," Adam said. "We have to wait for a strategic moment."

They collapsed on the sand and pretended to be absorbed in conversation. Seven minutes later the moment arrived. An exuberant Irish setter charged over the sand, into the water, and then out—shaking himself with abandon.

"Now," Adam whispered with an air of triumph and jumped to his feet.

While Adam romped with the setter, he watched the little blonde. She was a dog lover, he concluded with satisfaction, and he maneuvered his actions closer to her group—already watching the play with interest.

In a few minutes Adam and Chuck were exchanging lively conversation with the four girls. Young, he thought with a certain indulgence. Probably no more than seventeen or eighteen.

"You're not from New York," the little blonde—Chuck was right, her name was Eleanor—guessed shyly.

"Virginia," he told her. "Near Richmond. I go to school up here. I'll be a senior this year."

"Where do you go to school?" Eleanor asked. She was impressed, he decided, by his status as a senior.

"NYU. Chuck and I have an apartment in Greenwich Village."

All at once her face was suffused with pleasure.

"I'll be a freshman at NYU in September."

"Hey, swell," he approved. "Maybe we can see each other back in New York. I'll show you the ropes. The first few weeks can be kind of rough."

Adam quickly realized that Eleanor—a product of the all-girl Hunter High School—would not be as easy as the girls he'd known in the past. By their last day at Ocean Beach, she was happy to smooch—but she kept his hands in check. That would change, he promised himself with confidence.

For a moment when Eleanor told him her last name—Kahn—he'd thought, *"I don't believe it—she's Jewish."* Then he'd looked at her blonde prettiness and decided she must be German—one of Hitler's "true Aryans." Out of an uneasy fear that someone might discover that he had a Jewish mother, he'd avoided joining a fraternity. Everybody knew that Jews were accepted only in Jewish fraternities. His mother could live any way she wanted—but it wasn't going to interfere with *his* life.

"This is gonna be one hell of a year," Adam whispered as he and Eleanor stood together at the railing of the ferry that was carrying them to Bay Shore. "If you look at another guy, I'll break his neck," he said with a grin.

Early in September Vicky received a phone call from Anita, who had just returned from Mackinac Island.

"It's great to be back in Richmond." Anita's voice radiated pleasure. "But I just can't tolerate the summers here, even with an air-conditioned house. I want you to come to our Saturday night dinner next week," she said. "A couple of people from the university will be there, too. Darling, you need to socialize. I know how hard you work at the career—but take time out for fun."

"I'll look forward to it," Vicky said, startled at her acquiescence. But it had been so long since she'd seen Marc.

In the next few days Vicky was unnerved by the realization of how impatient she was to see Marc. There was a quiet strength and compassion in him that gave her a sense of well-being when she was with him. Yet she asked herself if it was wrong for her to be socializing so soon after Gary's death.

Leaving for the Roberts's house on Saturday evening, she apologized to Sara for going to the dinner party.

"Vicky, if anyone deserves some relaxation, it's you," Sara told her. "You hold this family together. Now go to that dinner and enjoy yourself."

Tonight Vicky made a conscious effort not to be the first to arrive. When she pulled up before the Roberts's house, she was relieved to see three cars parked in the driveway. She walked slowly up the path to the entrance—trying not to remember her last encounter with Anita, when she'd been startled by a casual remark that seemed spiked with cattiness.

The maid opened the front door. Vicky welcomed the rush of air-conditioned coolness after the steamy outdoors. Lively conversation filtered from the living room. Marc and Lisa were absorbed in a discussion of Richard Wright's new novel, *Black Boy*. She must find time to read it, Vicky told herself.

"Darling, you look beautiful," Anita called to her. "I am forever amazed that you're such a successful businesswoman."

"Thank you." Vicky managed a gracious smile.

"When Marc and I were first married, I was dying to be a career woman—but I didn't have the courage to divide myself off. I mean, we were both so eager to have a family—and that came first. But of course, I was denied both."

"Tell us about your summer," Lisa encouraged. *Didn't Lisa see through Anita's phoney facade?* "I've heard such marvelous stories about Mackinac Island."

In the midst of a fresh burst of conversation Marc managed a few moments off to one side with Vicky.

"You look tired. You must have had a rough summer."

"I've had better," she conceded.

Now for the first time she talked about the awful period after Gary's death. She told him about finding the symphony Gary had written in memory of Michael.

"It's beautiful," she told him, her voice uneven. "Michael would be so proud if he could have known."

"Why don't you have it performed here in Richmond?" he said gently.

"Could I?" She was startled by this simple statement. "Of course I can," she said with sudden determination, her mind already charting a course. "I could arrange with a symphony orchestra to give a performance. A benefit performance for the Daniel Barton Hospital!" She lifted her face to his. "Marc, what a wonderful idea."

"All right, everybody, let's go in to dinner," Anita ordered gaily. "Renee is serving us a typical French dinner." Renee was the Roberts's new cook. In a city where domestics were always colored, Anita had brought a white Frenchwoman to her household. "You've lived in Paris, Vicky. Tell us how Renee compares to the chef at the Crillon." Anita remembered her saying that she'd worked as a maid at the Crillon. To Anita that was degrading.

Sara had gone to bed by the time Vicky returned to Barton Manor. Vicky churned with a need to tell her about Marc's suggestion that they arrange a performance of Gary's symphony in Richmond. Leave it to Marc to come up with such a beautiful tribute to both Gary and Michael, she thought tenderly.

She knew that she would fight insomnia tonight. Her mind was in high gear, plotting this newborn campaign. Bless Marc for being so clear-headed and compassionate. *She* should have thought of the concert, she rebuked herself. No doubt in her mind that Sara would approve.

She was at the breakfast table earlier than normal in her eagerness to talk to Sara. The September morning was hot and humid. She was glad that Sara had agreed to have the house air-conditioned before next summer. Adam could be so practical on occasion.

She sat nursing a cup of coffee until Sara arrived at the table.

"There's not the slightest breeze from the river this morning," Sara said tiredly. "I can't wait for the cool weather."

"You should go away for a couple of weeks," Vicky urged yet again. But she understood Sara's reluctance to take herself into unfamiliar surroundings when she was in such emotional turmoil.

"I leave that to my daughters," Sara said with ironic humor. "I gather both Clark and Jeffrey are furious that the girls didn't come back from Newport with them. I don't know how they afford their lifestyle," she conceded. "Not while I'm still alive."

Vicky knew how, but refrained from giving Sara fresh worry. Mollie's oldest brother was an officer at the bank. Vicky had found out through him that both Lily and Stephanie had taken out loans against their houses. Sara's daughters were still angry that their mother refused to provide them with an allowance from the family estate in view of the fact that their father had left them substantial trust funds.

While they waited for Lula Mae to send breakfast to the table, Vicky told Sara about Marc's suggestion. Sara's face grew radiant as she listened.

"Vicky, I liked that man from the moment I saw him. What a beautiful thought!" Tears welled in her eyes now. "We'll do it, of course. I don't care how much it costs. Do you suppose—" She paused in thought. "Do you suppose we could have the concert on the first anniversary of Gary's leaving us?" Even now Sara could never bring herself to use the word "death" when she talked about Gary.

"We'll do it," Vicky promised. "We'll have a performance first here in Bartonville," she plotted. "A sort of invitational dress rehearsal." There were no facilities in Bartonville to accommodate a large-scale benefit. That must be in Richmond. "Both Gary and Michael would like that."

"And the funds from the benefit will go to Daniel's hospital," Sara said with quiet pleasure. "All the funds," she emphasized. "I'll pay all the costs."

Over breakfast they discussed the mechanics of arranging for the concert. They would have no difficulty in meeting their scheduled date, Vicky reassured Sara.

"Miz Sara—" Zachary hovered in the doorway. "We best leave for church if you're not to be late."

"Zachary, thank you. I'll be right there." There was a new lilt in Sara's voice. This project would do much to lift her spirits, Vicky told herself.

Vicky lingered at the breakfast table after Sara left for church. She'd be forever grateful, she thought, for Marc's idea for the concert. She must tell him how grateful both she and Sara were.

Sitting here in the stillness of the morning she allowed herself to dwell on her own troubled, personal feelings. She was only forty-three years old. She shouldn't have this conviction that her life was all but over, a lid clamped down on her emotions.

With an inner candor she'd tried for months to avoid, she faced the knowledge that she loved Marc with a terrifying intensity. He was a man trapped in a marriage she'd come to sense was a velvet prison. And she knew, too, that Marc loved her. But this was a love that must forever be denied.

Chapter Thirty-two

ADAM WAS WHISTLING as he emerged from the shower. He paused for a complacent glance at himself in the full-length mirror on the bathroom door. He liked having the apartment to himself this way. Chuck had left this afternoon with his family for his grandmother's house in upstate New York, where they'd stay until the day after Christmas. And with any luck at all, he'd have Eleanor here in his bed before the night was over.

They'd have dinner at that Italian restaurant around the corner, then head uptown to see *Oklahoma!* He grinned in reminiscence. Wow, Eleanor had been impressed when he told her he was taking her to see the hottest musical in town! Old man Leslie at the company's New York office had wangled the tickets for him. And after the show they'd go to Lindy's for cheesecake and coffee.

He dropped the sodden bath towel to the floor and trailed into the tiny bedroom to dress. He couldn't figure out why it was taking him so long to make out with Eleanor. She'd mess around just so far. He could get a hand under her sweater but not under her skirt. It was going to that all-girl high school, he thought contemptuously—and her stupid strict mother. Her father had died when she was four. There was just her mother and her.

He reached into a drawer for underwear, socks, a shirt, all the while envisioning success tonight. He'd never gotten so hooked on a girl before. Chuck said it was because she played hard to get. But a lot of guys at school tried to make time with her. Nobody got this far, he reminded himself with satisfaction.

He'd told himself to cut loose when he found out she was Jewish— but something about her kept him coming back. Like Chuck said out on Fire Island—she was a knockout. And she was mad about him.

Adam hurried through the sharp cold of the night to the little Italian restaurant where he was to meet Eleanor. A holiday air was every- where; every shop window was decorated for the Christmas season. He knew she'd be waiting outside for him. It would never enter her head to go inside and ask for a table for two. In some ways he enjoyed her candid lack of sophistication. He relished being the teacher. With him she'd learned to smoke, though he suspected she disliked it.

He turned a corner and saw her standing with shoulders hunched against the cold but with a look of eager anticipation on her face. He felt a surge of pride as he saw the male glances shot in her direction— though she never seemed aware that she was especially attractive.

"Hi, Gorgeous," he called. Her face lighted up, he thought, like the Christmas tree at Barton Square back home.

"Hi." She could make one little word say so much.

Adam and Eleanor hurried inside the restaurant. His hands lingered amorously at her shoulders for a moment while he helped her out of her coat. He was so hot right now, he told himself, he'd be satisfied to forget *Oklahoma!* and go straight up to the apartment. She'd never been there alone with him—only when others were around.

"I can't stand not being able to see you for almost a month," he said when the waiter had taken their order and left them. His eyes made love to her.

"I'll hate every minute you're away," she whispered. Under the table his knee found hers. "I even hated Thanksgiving this year," she confessed, "because you went home for the long weekend."

They enjoyed their meal but were ever conscious of the time. Eleanor was excited about seeing a hit Broadway musical. Her wid- owed mother was a pattern-maker on Seventh Avenue. She earned enough for them to have a tiny Manhattan apartment and to see Eleanor through college—but there was little money for theater or restaurants or good clothes.

They left the restaurant in high spirits. Adam insisted on splurging on a taxi to the theater. She knew he came from Virginia and that his family was in the tobacco business. She hadn't connected him with

Barton Tobacco Company yet. He liked her to think he was sacrificing when he took her out to dinner and to a Broadway movie or to the theater.

Despite the fact that Christmas Eve was only days away, there wasn't an empty seat in the theater. Eleanor was enthralled from the moment the curtain went up. She was content to remain seated during the intermission, her hand in his.

He was impatient that she insisted on waiting through all the curtain calls. To hell with going to Lindy's for cheesecake and coffee. They'd go back to the apartment. She didn't know Chuck had left already. She'd expect him to be there with that smart-ass senior he was messing around with.

"Let's grab a cab and go down to the apartment," he said while they fought their way through the emerging theater crowd. "We'll pick up danish and have it with cappuccino." He kept his arm protectively about her waist.

"I can't stay long," she cautioned. But she was happy at the prospect of prolonging the evening, he decided. She figured they'd have danish and cappucino, smooch a while, and then he'd take her home. Didn't her mother know that these days girls didn't worry about curfew on nonschool nights?

He kissed her in the darkness of the taxi, allowed a hand to fondle her breasts. This much was allowed. But tonight he kissed her in a way that startled her. She was as eager for it as he was, he thought in triumph. *Tonight was the night.*

In the apartment—suddenly aware that they were alone—Eleanor turned to him with a question in her eyes.

"Oh, didn't I tell you?" he asked casually. "Chuck's on his way upstate with his family."

"Adam, I think I'd better go." All at once she seemed frightened.

"Baby, no," he crooned. "We're not going to see each other for almost a month. Nothing's going to happen that you don't want to happen."

He reached to pull her into his arms and brought his mouth down to hers in the soft, persuasive kisses she welcomed. But moments later—their bodies nuzzling in soaring heat—he abandoned this. A hand moved to forbidden territory.

"It'll be great," he promised, his breathing uneven. "You don't have to worry about a thing."

"Adam, I'm scared," she wavered.

"Don't you love me?" he asked.

"You know I do," she whispered.

"Then prove it," he ordered amorously.

Hand in hand they walked into the dark bedroom. He'd waited a long time for this, Adam thought in triumph as he helped her out of her dress, but it was going to be worth it . . .

Vicky felt guilty about not being home for dinner on Adam's first night in town. She'd explained to him about the committee that had been set up to handle the benefit concert.

"We have a dinner meeting every other week. As chairman I have to be there," she apologized. How handsome he was, she thought. And he could be so charming.

"Grandma will have dinner with me." He seemed in high spirits, Vicky thought in relief. "And fill me in on all the family gossip. I gather Kara isn't pregnant yet? But still trying, no doubt."

"Kara and Derek are very eager to have children." She recoiled from the image he seemed to create. But young people today were so frank in comparison to her generation.

"You still driving the same old car?" he teased. "It'll soon be a candidate for an antique show."

"It's in good condition," she said defensively. "And it'll be a while before cars start rolling off the assembly line again."

Was he about to make a pitch for a car for himself? Perhaps as a graduation present, she thought tentatively. She was so relieved that he'd buckled down and became a good student. Often she chided herself for fearing the worst from Adam. She'd always measured him by Michael—and that was wrong. Michael and she had been kindred souls, she thought with pained nostalgia. She'd understood him. She'd never truly understood Adam.

"By the time I can afford a car—next March," he said pointedly, interrupting her introspection, "they should be showing up in the showrooms."

"Possibly." She forced a smile. He was still angry that she wouldn't advance him money against his trust fund. "I'd better dash. I don't want to be late."

Driving into Richmond for the committee meeting, she allowed her thoughts to sum up these past weeks. Everything was moving on schedule for the concert. It was Sara who'd suggested that Marc be asked to serve on the committee. Anita had been pleased—it indicated a certain acceptance by local society.

She appreciated what Marc brought to the committee. He was intelligent, sensitive, and he had an unexpected talent for soothing ruffled feelings among the committee members. Even in something like this, Vicky thought ruefully, there were those seeking personal advantages.

A meaningful glance from Marc had kept her from losing her temper on several occasions. Between problems in the company and the personal tragedies in the family she was sometimes dismayed by her lack of patience these days. She'd prided herself on always being in control.

Marc was already in the private dining room of the restaurant where they were meeting when she arrived. The others would drift in momentarily, she guessed.

"Adam blow into town on schedule?" he asked with a smile. He knew how eager she was to see Adam. Yet always, she thought uneasily, there was that air of hostility that detracted from her pleasure at having Adam home.

"He came this afternoon. I feel guilty at running away his first night back."

"Don't feel guilty," Marc said with unexpected intensity. "There are people who brush aside all obligations, and then there are those like you—" His voice was almost a caress. "You think you have to take the world on your shoulders. There has to be room in your life for Vicky."

"How's Anita?" She tried to be casual.

"Anita's fine. She's all excited about the concert. I gather she's planning a huge party afterwards. She'll tell you about it."

The other committee members arrived, and the conversation began with the jubilation that more wartime rationing was ending. In October, shoe rationing ceased, then late last month meat and butter rationing ended.

"Thank God, tire rationing is over," a committee member said appreciatively. "I was afraid I'd have to give up my car for a bicycle."

There was the customary wrangling about petty details of the ticket sales for the concert. Marc said that this happened on every level—

from ladies' sewing circle meetings to top-level government conferences—Vicky remembered. Again, she allowed him to restrain her with a cautionary glance from a candid outburst of contempt for what had just been proposed.

Tonight they were winding up earlier than usual, she noted. She'd sit down and visit with Adam a while before bedtime. If he was home, she reminded herself. It was time they talked about where he was going to law school.

Her face tensed as she remembered Clark's blunt warning that he had no intention of taking Adam into his own firm after law school. She'd never liked Clark. In the beginning she'd felt deep sympathy for Jeffrey, but through the years he'd become as arrogant and obnoxious as Clark.

Then the meeting was over. The committee members began to disperse. Marc fell into step beside her to discuss setting up special discounts on concert tickets for university students. Vicky knew this was a ruse to delay their going their separate ways.

Marc walked with her to her car, hovered there while she reached for the ignition. The hunger in his eyes reached out to her.

"I'm going to try to sit down tonight and talk with Adam about law school," she began, frowning as the car did not respond. "He's been so uncommunicative about the law exams—"

"Are you flooding it?" Marc asked solicitously as she tried again to start the car.

"I don't think so. Adam's been teasing me about the car being an antique—"

"Move over and let me see what I can do," he offered and she complied.

They sat in silence while Marc tried to get the motor to turn over. Nothing was happening. But Vicky was sharply conscious of Marc's nearness in the night darkness of the car.

"You'd better let me drive you home, then call a mechanic to come over and pick up the car," he said finally. "I don't know what's wrong."

"All right. But I hate to take you all the way out to Bartonville—"

"A big twenty miles both ways," he said humorously. "No problem."

They left Vicky's car and went to Marc's white Lincoln Zephyr convertible, the top of which was magically raised or lowered at the touch of a button. Vicky knew that Anita liked to drive with the top down. Marc preferred the privacy of the raised top.

Marc pulled open the door on the passenger side for Vicky, then hurried around to the other side to slide behind the wheel. Both made an effort to keep the conversation casual as Marc headed for the road that connected Bartonville to Richmond. They discussed the tragic death yesterday of General Patton in a car accident in Heidelberg.

"It's ironic, isn't it? Patton went through all those years of fighting in the war and then died in an automobile accident." He paused. "I know Anita has always told everybody she hated driving. The inference being," he said tersely, "that I insisted she drive the night of our accident. It wasn't like that at all."

"I suspected it wasn't," Vicky said quietly.

"I pleaded with her to let me drive. The roads were icy, and she was addicted to speeding. No car ever went fast enough for Anita. But she's never forgiven me for not grabbing the wheel and swerving out of the path of that drunken driver. There was no way I could have done that. I don't argue about it—it's easier just to let it ride. But I— I wanted you to know."

"I knew that if there was anything you could have done, Marc, you would have." She felt a rush of compassion for what she suspected had been years of torment.

"Thanks for listening," he said softly.

They drove in silence for a few minutes, both trying to cope with rebellious emotions. Then Marc pulled off at the side of the road and turned to her.

"Vicky, we have to talk," he said and reached to pull her in his arms.

"Marc, this is wrong," she whispered.

"No. It would be wrong to deny ourselves," he said urgently. "I've been in love with you almost from our first meeting. You came into my life—and suddenly there was beauty where there'd been only resignation, and sometimes, despair. I've been in prison since the day of that accident."

"Marc, we don't have the right—" Her heart was pounding as Marc's mouth reached for hers.

"We have the right." He kissed first with tenderness, then with passion.

They clung together, caught up in the power of their long reined-in emotions.

"I can't bear being around you but not with you, Vicky," he told her. "We can have such joy together. You were a widow long before Gary died. I haven't had a marriage for a dozen years. Let us take what we can salvage. No one has to know. We're not two impetuous kids. But life is passing us by. I've been Anita's prisoner for so long it's become a habit."

"Marc, I'm afraid—" Yet even stolen hours with Marc could be so precious.

"Anita will never know. No one will ever know," he promised. "I'll rent a little house outside of Richmond. Anita wants me to publish—I'll set up a place to work there. She knows how difficult it is for me to write at home. It'll be our other life, Vicky. Let's take what belongs to us."

"Marc, I have to think about it," she hedged, but she knew when he kissed her again that she only needed time to accept this new way of life.

"I'll start looking right away," he said with exhilaration. "Oh my darling, we'll begin to live again."

They lingered in the car, content for now to kiss, to touch, to know that tomorrow would be another world for them.

"Marc, I'd better get home," she said reluctantly. "You can explain that you had to drive me to Bartonville."

"We'll be careful," he promised, sensing her fears. "No one will ever know."

Marc left her before the veranda at Barton Manor and drove away. For a few moments she stood there and watched Marc drive away. That which she had told herself must never happen again had happened—and she knew she didn't have the strength to put a stop to an affair with Marc. She'd been so tired. She'd felt so empty inside. But tonight Marc had changed that.

She opened the door and walked into the foyer. She heard the sound of classical music coming from the library. Sara must be in there alone, she guessed. If Adam were there, the music would be what was popular on the jukeboxes. She felt a tremor of relief. She wasn't prepared to face Adam right now.

Sara glanced up with a welcoming smile when she walked into the library.

"I told Adam he could take the Caddy and drive into town," Sara told her. "He was going to that soda fountain with the jukeboxes."

"I think he can handle that," Vicky said with an effort at humor.

"There's a kind of radiance about you tonight," Sara said quietly. "I haven't seen you looking like that in twenty years."

"I have no right." Fresh doubts tugged at her. Sara guessed, didn't she?

"You have every right," Sara echoed Marc.

"Are we talking about the same thing?" she hedged.

"We're talking about you and Marc. I've seen the way you look when you've been in his company. I knew the first time I met him— here at Barton Manor—that he was in love with you."

"Does everybody know?" she asked shakily.

"No. Only someone who loves you the way I do. Don't be afraid, Vicky," Sara said with sudden conviction. "I know what your life has been with Gary, after those first few years. I can imagine what it's been like for Marc. Don't cheat yourselves out of what you've found together. The years go by so fast—we have to grasp at those parcels of happiness that are within our reach. I look at Lily and Stephanie and their husbands, and I know the poverty of their marriages. You and Marc have something precious. Don't squander it."

They could handle this, Vicky told herself in dizzying anticipation. No one—except for Sara—would know. Anita would never be hurt— that must never happen. For Marc and her this was a magnificent gift neither had ever expected to receive.

Sara was right—they must not squander this gift.

Chapter Thirty-three

Despite the housing shortage, Marc found a furnished cottage in ten days. It was isolated, in the middle of farm country, and unappealing to most tenants. There was no central heating, only a big pot-bellied stove in the large kitchen and fireplaces in the living room and bedroom.

He set about immediately to bring in his typewriter and books, to give the cottage the instant appearance of a work place. He waited impatiently for Adam to return to school because Vicky stipulated that their first meeting at the cottage must wait until this time.

"Now," he told Vicky with an effort at humor on this fog-drenched evening when she first came to the cottage, logs crackling in the fireplace grate, "I'll have to write publishable articles to justify the time I spend here."

"I should have put my car in the garage," she said in sudden apprehension.

"This fog hides everything," he said and reached to pull her into his arms. "Vicky, I've waited so long for you."

"It's like being born again," she whispered as they swayed together, his face against hers. "I thought that except for work, my life was over."

"It's a new beginning." His mouth reached for hers, and clung in voracious hunger.

It was so natural, she thought later, while she lay in the curve of

Marc's arms, a blanket pulled above them in the chilly bedroom. The fireplace seemed to extend its warmth only within a radius of a few feet. She felt simultaneously relaxed and exhilarated. It had been so long. In panicky moments she asked herself if Marc would be disappointed in her. It was clear he had not been disappointed.

"You've quenched a long, long hunger," he murmured. "You've made me come alive again."

Vicky cherished her swatches of private time with Marc, yet constantly battled a feeling of guilt. They were depriving Anita of nothing, Marc repeatedly comforted her. And they were being almost obsessively cautious. Vicky was grateful, too, that the escalating demands of the benefit concert brought them together in their public lives as well.

She was upset when Adam wrote he wouldn't be home for the approaching spring break. She worried about how he would handle himself with the income from the trust fund coming in on his twenty-first birthday. Such a lot of money for a college student suddenly to have at his disposal!

"Oh, he'll go berserk the first month or two," Sara guessed indulgently. "Then he'll settle down. He's bright, Vicky. And he has a lot of Daniel's practicality in him."

"He promised to be home for the concert," Vicky said. "He knows how important that is to us."

She'd tried to imagine how Adam conducted himself in that life away from home. He was so difficult to understand, she thought in frustration. She'd never truly known Adam the way she'd known Michael—and she worried that this was a failure on her part.

Eleanor tried on one dress, then another, discarded the second for a third. This was Adam's twenty-first birthday, and he was taking her to Larue's—a favorite of rich college boys. It was as famous now as the Stork Club, she thought with awe.

She'd never thought of Adam as rich until he told her about the trust fund from his grandfather. He'd always complained that his mother was so tight about money. "I have to fight every month for my lousy allowance." He talked a lot lately about the family business. He said he had no intention of going to law school. He was going to tell his mother at graduation that he wanted to come into the company. "But don't worry, baby—I'll be working in the New York office. We'll be able to see each other like now."

She pulled the third dress over her head and smoothed it over her slender figure. She wished wistfully that she owned something terribly smart to wear tonight. Still, she was grateful that she was able to shop at the showrooms of her mother's company and buy at big discounts.

"Eleanor, are you still fussing?" Her mother stood at the entrance to the bedroom they shared.

"I'm almost ready," Eleanor said with a cajoling smile. She knew her mother didn't like Adam. In truth, they'd only met twice for a couple of minutes on the rare times when Adam came uptown to pick her up. But Mom wouldn't like any guy she went out with who wasn't Jewish, she told herself defensively. "How do I look?"

"Very pretty," her mother conceded. "Is Adam coming up here to pick you up?" Her perennial question.

"He's busy cramming for exams," Eleanor told her. "I'm meeting him under the clock at the Biltmore." This was their classic meeting place. "I'd better run—I don't want to keep him waiting." She reached for her coat, slid into it.

"Take your gloves," her mother reminded her. "It's cold out."

"I have them," she said, checking her pockets. Her eyes strayed self-consciously to the pack of cigarettes that lay beside her purse on the dresser.

"Oh, yes," Rebecca Kahn said bitterly, "don't forget your 'coffin nails.' "

"Mom, that's an antiquated expression that's been disproved a thousand times," she said defensively. "Everybody smokes these days."

"You don't need all that junk going into your lungs," her mother shot back. Ever since she'd had double pneumonia when she was twelve, Eleanor thought, Mom had worried about her lungs. Sometimes she was so overprotective.

"Don't wait up for me, Mom." She leaned forward to hug her mother for a moment. Mom was wonderful most of the time. She just didn't understand Adam.

Out in the night cold Eleanor walked quickly to the subway. Adam would probably be late, but she wanted to be there on time in case he wasn't. He promised her he'd wangle a good table at Larue's. Wherever they were seated would be all right with her. She'd never been to a famous nightclub.

Out of the subway Eleanor headed for the Biltmore, where already other girls were waiting under the clock—a festive glow in their eyes emphasized by the brilliance of the hotel lights. The Biltmore doorman seemed unaware of the cluster of pretty young girls anticipating an exciting evening.

She stood with her shoulders hunched against the cold and thought about Adam. Twenty-one seemed so grown-up compared to eighteen, she thought wistfully. She yearned to be beautiful and sophisticated like Chuck's girlfriend, who was a senior and scoffed at the way so many girls her age couldn't think about anything except getting married and buying a house out in suburbia, now that the war was over.

Then she spied Adam striding toward her. Her heart began to pound. He was so good-looking and so smart. It still surprised her that he'd ever bothered to give her a second look.

"Hi, baby." He leaned forward for a quick kiss. "Let's get over to Larue's before the mob descends."

At Larue's Eleanor watched while Adam exchanged whispered conversation with the headwaiter. She saw a folded bill pass between their hands. Adam looked like one of those male models in *Esquire,* she thought with pride. He'd be at home anywhere.

Not until they left Larue's and headed downtown in a taxi did Adam tell her he had another special birthday present in mind for himself.

"Go to Paris with me over our spring break," he coaxed, a hand roaming beneath her dress to fondle a thigh in the protective darkness of the taxi. "I've got this wacky cousin over there who'll show us the real Paris."

"Adam, I couldn't," she gasped. "My mother would kill me if I even suggested it!"

"Don't tell her." His mouth moved to nuzzle her ear. "Say you're going with some girl at school to visit her family."

"No," she said quietly, but she was terrified at the prospect of losing him. "Adam, I can't do that. And how can you go to Paris over the spring break? There's not enough time." She didn't want to think about Adam in Paris without her.

"We'll fly," he said in triumph. "TWA just started this service from New York to Paris. They guarantee to make it in twenty-two hours."

"I'd be scared to death to fly," she confessed.

"Ellie, we'll have a ball," he cajoled.

"I couldn't do that to my mother," she said. "Please, let's not talk about it anymore."

For a while Adam sulked. After they'd made love in his apartment, he tried again.

"Okay, forget Paris," he said while they lay tangled together in the narrow single bed. "Let's spend a weekend at this ski lodge I know in upstate New York."

"Adam, I don't ski," she laughed.

"Neither do I," he said. Damn that business with his knee. "But they've got these little chalets where we can hole up for the weekend all by ourselves. The restaurant will even send over food," he laughed.

"Adam, you don't understand," she apologized. "My mother would just die if she found out." But in a corner of her mind she remembered that her friend Irene lived upstate. It wouldn't be unnatural for her to go up there with Irene for a weekend.

"She won't find out." Adam seemed to sense they'd manage a weekend. "You can phone from up there. We'll go up Saturday morning, come back Sunday night. It would be just for one night. You know I can't get married for at least a couple of years—until I'm earning a living. And you want to finish school—"

"I'll call my friend Irene," she whispered. *He meant for them to get married.* Mom would just have to learn to like him.

Vicky was caught up in the final arrangements for the concert. Adam had agreed reluctantly to come home for that weekend, though he complained that he was in the midst of finals. She had shamed Lily and Stephanie into promising to be at the concert. She suspected that the husbands had been helpful in this. After all, Clark considered the dress rehearsal in Bartonville as a civic event he personally had arranged—and Jeffrey could hardly refuse to be at the concert when the Daniel Barton Hospital was the beneficiary.

Vicky felt as though she were living in two worlds—the frenetic public world that included running Barton Tobacco and handling the memorial concert, and the private world she shared with Marc. Their hours alone were few but precious. And as Marc promised, no one knew.

Both the Bartonville and Richmond newspapers gave lavish space to the concert, and talked with pride about the talented Virginian who had served his country in one war and gave his son to another. Every seat to the concert was sold out weeks in advance.

The invitational dress rehearsal was enthusiastically received. The conductor and the members of the orchestra were impressed by Gary's music, and saddened that there would be no more.

Sara had arranged for an early family dinner at Barton Manor on the eve of the concert. She had decreed that the family would arrive at the auditorium *en masse*. Except for Doug in Paris, everyone was present and in formal dress, though Adam had rebelled at first.

Vicky had known that this would be a traumatic evening, but she hadn't realized its true impact until she walked into the glittering auditorium and was assaulted by memories. Tonight Michael and Gary walked here beside her. Tonight Gary would receive the tribute denied him in life.

She remembered Gary at the Gershwin concert in Aeolian Hall twenty-two years ago. She remembered Gary and Michael playing a duet together just before he was shipped out. She remembered the day eleven months ago when she'd walked into the cottage and found Gary's symphony, "An Ode to a Beloved Son."

Across the auditorium she saw Marc arrive with Anita. Marc wheeled Anita's chair down the aisle, then solicitously helped her from the wheelchair into her seat. After the concert Anita and Marc were hosting a party for almost a hundred. Sara had begged off attending.

"Tell her an after-concert party will be too much for me," Sara had instructed Vicky.

In truth, Vicky thought as the family took their seats, Sara looked exhausted. Adam would see her home after the concert. He was being very sweet, she conceded. Except for that minor struggle to make him understand formal dress at the concert was decreed, he'd been charming to his grandmother.

Sara had looked at him as he came down to dinner and said to her, "It's like seeing Daniel when we first met." Then she'd added in confidence, "My mother could never believe that I truly loved Daniel. She was convinced I married him because it was obvious he would be a rich man—rich enough to restore the old family mansion. And because I loved him, I closed my eyes to the stream of other women who came in and out of his life. You see, I knew that Daniel would always come back to me."

Throughout the performance Vicky fought against tears. In the semi-darkness of the auditorium she saw Sara lift a handkerchief to her eyes. At the conclusion of the performance there was an emotion-laden silence for a moment, and then the audience erupted into overwhelming applause.

"Vicky, why couldn't Gary be here to hear this?" Sara's voice broke. "Why couldn't Michael be here?"

After a night of restless sleep Vicky came downstairs to have breakfast with Adam before Zachary drove him to the Richmond depot. Moments later Adam joined her. Why was he taking such an early train, she wondered? Was there some girl up in New York that he was rushing back to see? Adam never talked about his life away from Barton Manor.

"You're coming up for graduation?" Adam asked as he slid into his place at the table.

"You know your grandmother and I wouldn't miss your graduation," Vicky said.

"There's something I want to talk about, Mother—" He hesitated and Vicky immediately braced herself for some unpleasant confrontation. "I don't want to go to law school. I've given it a lot of thought. What I really want to do is come into the company." He smiled as her eyes widened in astonishment. "I want to start up in the New York office," he continued before she could reply. "You've always talked so much about the importance of advertising. I want to learn about that side of the business."

"We'll talk about it when I come up for your graduation," she said slowly. "There's a lot to discuss," she emphasized. "Working for the company won't be a game."

"I know. But it's what I want to do. Not standing there working at a machine," he warned, "but being part of your team that keeps the company running."

"We'll talk about it when I see you in New York," she said again.

Later, when Adam had left for the depot, she went into the library and asked Effie to bring her coffee. Sara, exhausted from last night's excitement, was sleeping late this morning.

Why did she feel this apprehension about Adam's foregoing law school to come into the business? It wasn't a decision he'd just made, she realized. He'd allowed her to believe that he'd taken his law school exams, had been accepted at Columbia Law. She suspected that none of this had happened. What was bringing him into the business? Would he stay with it? He had settled down in college, earned good grades. He was Daniel's grandson—wasn't it natural that he should develop an interest in the business?

Sara would be pleased, she guessed. Adam was doing exactly what Daniel would have wished. Daniel would have a Barton to carry on the company. Sara always said that Adam was "Daniel all over again."

But there were quirks in Daniel's character that were not best for the company. She remembered the fights with him to get the plant air-conditioned, to set up employee lunch rooms. She remembered the battle over giving out raises and bonuses. She could mold Adam in her ways, she thought in sudden determination. He was so young— she could form his thinking, teach him what she had learned through the years.

Adam would be another Daniel—with his strength and shrewdness—but she'd teach him the importance of fine labor relations. And one day Adam would take over the company. Daniel used to say, "*As long as there's a Barton at the head, the company will prosper.*" He'd accepted her as a Barton in the course of time. He would be proud to know that his grandson was following in his footsteps.

She had failed Gary. She mustn't fail Adam.

Chapter Thirty-four

VICKY TRIED to persuade Sara not to go with her to Adam's graduation—even on the night before they were to leave.

"You're still recovering from that bad cough," she said anxiously. "You need to rest."

"I'll rest on the train. Vicky, don't fret about me. I'm fine. I was there when Michael graduated, when Kara graduated, and when Doug graduated. I'll be there for Adam. Did you talk to him yet about coming into the company?"

"No, I figured that could wait until we see him. But he'll have to understand he can't make a game of this. And I won't let him start out in the New York office right away. He'll have to spend the summer in the office here with me. In September—if he still wants to work for the company—then he can spend a year up in the New York office." She tried to stifle her unease at the prospect of a close association between Frank and Adam. She must make Adam understand that Frank was very valuable to the company. He could learn a lot from Frank if he wasn't brash or hostile.

"At last one of the grandchildren will be part of Barton Tobacco." Vicky saw sentimental tears fill Sara's eyes. "This is Daniel's dream coming true."

It was Marc who had suggested she bring Adam into the Bartonville office first—where she could judge just how Adam could fit into the company. She remembered Marc's warning that Adam's presence there might bring out hostilities on the part of Stephanie, and particularly Lily. Lily was still angry that she had not brought Clark in as the company attorney. Sara had refused to intervene on Clark's behalf. If Lily and Stephanie acted up because of Adam, she'd deal with it, she promised herself.

In the morning Vicky and Sara left for New York. Frank had reserved a suite for them at the Plaza. Tonight he'd have dinner with them—along with Adam—in the Palm Court. Before dinner, Vicky had confided to Sara, she would tell Adam her stipulations about his joining the company.

While Sara took a predinner nap in her room of the Plaza suite, Vicky talked with Adam. He listened with disarming seriousness as she explained her rules.

"That's okay with me," he said with a casual smile. "Though I'd kind of hoped I'd be getting a few weeks in Europe for a graduation present," he joshed, yet Vicky sensed it was a tepid hope.

"I've ordered a Cadillac convertible for your graduation present," she told him, "but you'll have to wait for delivery. This is not the time to go to Europe," she reminded. "The countries there are in dreadful shape."

"Doug's there," he shot back, his eyes wary.

"Doug is there to study. It's not a place for tourists these days."

Marc talked with much compassion about the postwar problems that Europe was suffering. So many homes had been destroyed. Hunger was everywhere. And some Americans who remembered Russia as a brave ally were beginning to be disillusioned about its current aims.

Dinner went well, Vicky thought afterwards. Adam went out of his way to be charming toward Frank—whom in the past he had labeled "slightly weird" for his courtly manners and conservative taste regarding the company's advertising campaigns. It was agreed he'd spend the summer in Bartonville and return to New York in early September to learn about advertising and marketing under Frank's tutelage.

The following day Vicky and Sara attended graduation exercises at NYU. The last of the grandchildren had earned college degrees, and Sara was proud of this record. After the exercises Adam pushed his way through the throngs to embrace his mother and grandmother. Clearly he was pleased with the way his life was going.

"What time do you have to be at Penn Station?" he asked them. "There's this big bash tonight," he said apologetically.

"Don't worry about us," Vicky told him. "Go on to your party."

"Adam!" A slim, very pretty young blonde was charging breathlessly toward them. "Oh, I'm sorry"—she stammered when she realized Adam wasn't alone.

"This is a friend from school," he said nonchalantly. "Eleanor Kahn. My mother and grandmother," he introduced them.

"I'll see you at the party," Eleanor told Adam. "It was so nice to meet you both." She smiled shyly at Vicky and Sara.

Was this some special girl in Adam's life, Vicky asked herself. Instinctively she knew Eleanor Kahn was in love with him. Kahn, she mused—was she Jewish? Perhaps Adam had gotten over that disturbing rejection of his mother's faith.

"I'll be home in three or four days," he said, seeming self-conscious now. That girl *was* somebody important in his life, Vicky decided and was pleased. "I want to hang on to the apartment, even though I'll be away for the summer. Nobody gives up an apartment these days."

There was a family dinner in Bartonville to celebrate Adam's college graduation. After dinner Sara announced that Adam was coming into the company. Instantly Vicky saw the hostile glint in Lily's eyes, but Lily refrained from comment until Adam left to meet friends in town.

"So Adam has wormed his way into the fold," Lily drawled. "But my husband might as well be a stranger."

"Clark is mayor of this town," Sara reminded. "And your father paved the way for that."

"There's no money in that," Lily flared. "At least, you put Jeffrey into the hospital."

"Lily, you're getting out of hand," her husband warned, his voice sharp.

"I was always Papa's favorite." Lily lifted her head in triumph. "But now that he's gone, I'm nobody in this family."

"Lily, we've had the same attorney for forty-one years," Sara said. "I'm not about to dismiss him."

"Then put Clark on your board of directors," Lily pushed. "He's *family*."

"We don't have a board of directors," Vicky pointed out.

"All right, we'll set up a board of directors," Sara said tiredly, and

Vicky was startled. "You and Clark, Stephanie and Jeffrey, will be on the board along with Vicky, Adam, and myself." She turned apologetically to Kara and Derek. "And later you two will be appointed."

"Grandma, there's no need for that," Kara said softly. "We're not involved in the company." Her eyes said that she saw no reason for her parents or her aunt and uncle to be on a board of directors.

When the others left, Sara explained her capitulation.

"Their being on the board of directors means nothing," she pointed out, "except we might see some peace in the family. After all," she smiled, "I hold controlling stock in the company. And whatever you decree meets with my approval. So once a year we can put up with their presence at a board of directors meeting."

Adam settled down to long days at the company office. He made a point of being ingratiating to everyone. One day, he told himself in triumphant anticipation, this would be his company. He'd make the rules.

After hours he infiltrated the Richmond social scene. He was young, good-looking, and from an influential family. He took it for granted that he would be invited everywhere now that he was home. He'd been away at school since the old man died—but during the summers, he always found some action, he reminded himself.

Only now that he was coming into the company, seeing himself as a future big wheel in the industry, he planned to be selective in the girls he took out. One day he'd own Barton Manor. He and his wife would entertain at important dinner parties. He enlisted his grandmother's help in seeing he was invited to the right parties.

Almost every day there was a letter from Eleanor: "Of course, I miss you so much, Adam." He'd written once, warning her he was working "sixteen hours a day, trying to soak up as much as I can about the business—no time for anything else."

At a party ten days after he returned to Bartonville, Adam met Melanie Lee, whose family on both sides dated back to the founding fathers. She was tall and willowy, with ash blonde hair and blue eyes. She had spent a year at a finishing school in New York, and made it clear she thought Richmond was dull.

"Are you going back to school in New York in the fall?" he asked, his eyes clinging to the daringly low neckline of her lilac organza dress.

"I never look more than a week ahead," she said with a provocative laugh. "I mean to enjoy one day at a time." Her eyes seemed
to be weighing him. "What do you say we leave this bash for something more exciting?"

"Let's go," he agreed. Damn it, when would his Cadillac convertible come down the line? For now he had to borrow his mother's
car or take the family car.

Before the evening was over he was making out with Melanie on
the backseat of her convertible—the top decorously up. This one knew
her way around, he told himself with admiration. She was game for
anything.

He knew others in their circle realized he was giving Melanie a
rush. Why not? She was good-looking, hot, rich—and she came from
a family of important lawyers and judges. Her grandfather had been
a congressman, an uncle was in the state assembly. And she couldn't
get enough of him, he gloated.

He hadn't planned on marrying right out of college, but Melanie fit
right into the picture he visualized for himself. His grandmother had
gone to school with Melanie's grandmother—both families went back
to the original colonies. The old man may have derided that kind of
background—but underneath, he sure as hell respected it. He never
let anybody forget that his wife came from an "Old Family."

He was annoyed that Eleanor was writing frantic letters because
he wasn't writing her. That was another world, one that was behind
him now. He'd go up to New York to start working with the
company office up there while Melanie went back for the second
year at that finishing school—and around Christmas they'd announce their engagement. Melanie would want a big June wedding,
he guessed.

On a mid-August evening Melanie took him out to her parents'
summer house—a lakeside showplace estate—with the smug assurance that they'd be alone. They drove in her convertible, Melanie at
the wheel.

"We'll go swimming in the moonlight," she promised. "Just us
and the frogs."

"I didn't bring swimming trunks," he warned good-humoredly, a
provocative glint in his eyes.

"Who needs them?" Her smile elicited a rush of heat in him.

"I have to leave for New York right after Labor Day," he reminded her, a hand on her knee. "You'll be heading back for school then."

"That's two weeks away," she scolded. "Let's just enjoy now."

"I'll be looking for another apartment up there, but it's tough as hell to find anything. Now that I've started drawing on my trust fund, I feel like something fancier." He shot a sidewise glance at her, expecting some response to his admission of having a trust fund. Nothing. "Anyhow, this little Greenwich Village place is all mine now. My roommate's moving back home to save money while he's pushing through law school."

"Is he good-looking?" Melanie asked, turning off the road into a long private driveway now.

"Yeah," Adam conceded after a moment. "He's the big, football player type."

"That makes two of you," Melanie laughed. Only he hadn't played football since that lousy accident to his knee, he thought with simmering bitterness. "Hey, maybe the three of us will get together some night up in New York." He heard a hint of excitement in her voice. "If he's as good as you, the three of us could have a ball."

"I'm not sure I'd want to share you," he said. Melanie was wild, he thought with a mixture of admiration and unease. He wouldn't want a wife who messed around. "I'm selfish," he murmured, a hand sliding beneath her short skirt. "I want it all for me."

"We'll go for a swim," she said, pulling to a stop before the sprawling summer house. "The second one naked has to go into the house afterwards for towels!"

They swam briefly in the still-warm water of the pond, then scooped up their clothes and headed together for the house. Both were exhilarated by this minor exercise and relishing their unconventionality.

"Wouldn't it be awful if I'd forgot the keys?" she giggled, fumbling in her purse as they hovered—wetly naked—in the spill of moonlight.

"I'll break a window and open the door for you," he offered, a hand tentatively fondling one huge, damp nipple. "If you insist on towels to dry us off first—"

Without waiting for a reply he pulled her to him. She squealed and pretended to be pushing him away. In triumph he drew her down to the grass, feeling himself totally in command.

"Can't you wait until we get into the house?" she mocked, but already she was responding.

"We'll do it in the house, too," he promised. "Just shut up—"

"No noise?" she reproached, her voice uneven.

"All the noise you like, baby. Just no talk—"

Adam waited until they had showered together, dressed, and were back in the car before bringing up the subject of marriage.

"We make a great team, you know," he said, dropping an arm about her shoulders as she reached for the ignition. "What do you say we get married? In June after you graduate from school—" He paused as he felt her stiffen.

"Adam, this is for fun," she reproached, her eyes straight ahead as she headed down the long, tree-lined driveway.

"Sure, I know we're young—" What was the matter with her all of the sudden? "But we've got a lot going for us. I'm moving into the family's company and—"

"Down, boy," Melanie said coldly. "I told you—this was for fun. I'm marrying Ted Harmon when he finishes law school. Of course, he doesn't know it yet—but I'll tell him in time." Ted Harmon, Adam remembered, was up at Harvard Law. He was spending the summer in Boston in some big wheel's law office.

"Oh, you won't settle for less than a lawyer?" he taunted, hiding his rage.

"Ted's smart, and he's got all the right connections. We could even end up in the White House." She turned to him for a moment, moonlight lending a deceptive innocence to her delicate features. He remembered her posing with an armful of Easter lilies for the society page of a Richmond newspaper last April. "Fun's great, but for the long haul I want quality."

"What the hell's that supposed to mean?" he reared.

"In our world connections mean everything. The Lees and the Harmons are both Old Family."

"My grandmother's Old Family!" he shot back.

"Your grandfather was white trash before he became so rich," she drawled. "I hear your mother's Jewish. For fun that's all okay. Not for marriage."

"You stupid bitch!" he yelled. "I wouldn't marry you if you were the last female on earth!"

"You won't have to, darling. I'm going off to school in two weeks. At Christmas Ted and I will announce our engagement. In June we'll have this spectacular wedding. But you and I could have had such fun until I got engaged. Pity you had to spoil that.''

Vicky was surprised when Adam asked to leave for New York ten days ahead of schedule, but she agreed. She was impressed by his ambition to move ahead. He'd done well this summer. He was shrewd, quick to absorb everything she threw at him. She'd made no concessions because he was her son. Daniel always used to say, ''blood would tell.'' Adam was, indeed, Daniel's grandson. He would be a real asset to the business.

His graduation present—a gray Cadillac convertible—was delivered two days before he was scheduled to leave. She remained at the house three hours later than usual to be able to see him off. She stood on the wide veranda and watched as he slid behind the wheel of the Cadillac and drove off with an insouciant wave to her.

She hadn't expected to feel so excited because Adam was working out well with the company. It was exhilarating to know that in the years ahead he'd carry on what she'd been fighting to build. She knew that Sara, too, was pleased.

The house would seem empty tonight without Adam. Of course, she remembered indulgently, he always disappeared right after dinner. She often wondered how he could be so sharp and alert in the morning on so little sleep. But before his stroke Daniel had been like that, too.

Behind the wheel of her car, she remembered that in another few days Marc and Anita would be back from their summer at The Balsams in New Hampshire. Anita had wanted to go to London. Marc had finally convinced her this was not the year to visit England.

At intervals Marc had managed to phone from New Hampshire. She'd cherished those calls. She had known she would miss Marc. She had not realized how much she would miss him. He'd become such an important part of her life. She could discuss anything with Marc. And she valued his advice—both business and personal. They couldn't share more, she thought involuntarily, if they were man and wife.

The cigarette industry was booming. All indications promised that this year would be the best on record. But she worried about Sara's health—not just the lingering, raspy cough. Though Sara tried to deny it, she often appeared short of breath.

She must take Jeffrey aside and urge him to insist Sara submit to a thorough checkup. It unnerved her to think that Sara might be seriously ill. Through the years Sara had become as close to her as her own mother would have been had she lived. Once a month Sara arranged for a family dinner. That would be the time, she promised herself.

With a family dinner scheduled in mid-September, Vicky decided to enlist Jeffrey's help in getting Sara to agree to a checkup. Sara's longtime family doctor had retired, but she'd avoided choosing a replacement. *"There's Jeffrey—I don't need another doctor."*

It took several calls before Vicky could reach Jeffrey. In truth, she would have preferred any of a dozen other doctors she knew—but as family Jeffrey might be more persuasive.

"It's probably nothing," Jeffrey said with a touch of impatience. "Just one of those summer colds or coughs that hang on for a while."

"Jeffrey, talk her into going in for a checkup. Can't this be done at the hospital without her having to stay overnight?"

"I can schedule it," he agreed with a martyr-like sigh. "I'll talk to her when we come over for dinner on Friday evening."

She'd alert Kara, Vicky decided. Kara was devoted to her grandmother. They'd work together with Jeffrey. She wasn't being hysterical, she told herself. Sara was failing.

Chapter Thirty-five

TOGETHER Vicky and Kara persuaded Sara to go into the hospital for a checkup. Jeffrey arranged for her tests. A few days later he phoned Vicky rather than reporting directly to Sara.

"It's more than a summer cough," Jeffrey said. "She's suffering from emphysema. She doesn't smoke, does she?"

"Jeffrey, you know she doesn't!" Vicky was sharp. Lily and Stephanie were forever complaining because their mother didn't allow smoking anywhere in the house since Daniel died. Still, she suspected that Adam smoked in his own room. "What about treatment?"

"I've set up an appointment with a Richmond specialist," he told her. "Make sure she keeps it. He's a very busy man."

"She'll keep it," Vicky promised. "I'll see to that."

It was unnerving to think that Sara wasn't well. She had never been one to coddle herself, but now she must. She and Kara would watch over Sara, Vicky promised herself. She didn't expect any real concern from Lily or Stephanie. They always shut their eyes to unpleasant realities.

The one bright spot right now, Vicky acknowledged, was that Marc was back. Three or four times a week they managed a couple of hours together at the cottage. In addition, she saw him along with Anita at social gatherings—and at Anita's monthly dinner parties and her "Sunday evenings."

Again, the unions were fighting to organize at all the cigarette plants. She wasn't against the union coming in, Vicky reasoned—but unsavory reports leaked about Communist infiltration in the union. She went on record as being against this particular effort and was pleased when her own workers voted against joining the union.

Frank wrote that Adam was sopping up everything the advertising agency executives were throwing at him about the new Barton Tobacco ad campaign.

"He's sharp, Vicky. He asks the right questions. He seems to have an instinct for smart advertising and marketing."

After the rough growing-up years Adam was becoming what Lisa called a *mensch*, Vicky thought with pleasure. She hadn't been wrong. She was grooming a successor to Daniel at Barton Tobacco.

Adam was whistling when he said good night to Roger Owens—the account executive who handled the Barton account—after a lengthy dinner at Toot Shor's. He'd made it clear that if Roger left the agency to form his own with two other admen, then *he* would make every effort to swing the Barton account to the new agency. He'd also made it clear that he expected a personal reward for this effort.

He hadn't gone home for Thanksgiving—pleading a heavy work schedule. He knew he'd have to go home for a few days at Christmas to keep the peace. He seethed as he remembered Melanie's plotted engagement announcement, which she'd scheduled for Christmas. *That stupid bitch.*

He'd picked up with Eleanor where they'd left off. She was mad about him, he reminded himself with a surge of satisfaction. Maybe he'd make an announcement of his own at Christmas. Eleanor was gorgeous to look at, his adoring slave—and sensational in bed. Marry her. Go home for Christmas with his bride. Jump the gun on Melanie.

He'd had enough of New York. He'd made his connections. If Roger set up the new company, he needed to be close to his mother to push her into making the switch. A hundred to one Frank would fight it. But *he* could handle his mother. And there'd be a fat bonus in the deal for him. He'd open a bank account here in New York—too much chance of leakage in Bartonville or Richmond.

He stopped at a phone booth to phone Eleanor.

"Hi, baby," he murmured amorously. "I need to see you tonight. Something's come up that we have to talk about."

"Adam, I'm working like crazy on a paper for school," she protested. "And it's late—" Meaning her mother would argue with her about her leaving the apartment at almost nine at night.

"Take a taxi. My car is in for a tune-up." He didn't feel like driving all the way uptown. "I'll be waiting in front of the house to pay."

"I have the money—" He could sense she was wavering now.

"Sugar, this is urgent," he coaxed. "We have to talk."

"All right, I'll leave in a few minutes." She was dying of curiosity, he thought. *Wait till she heard what he had in mind.*

Twenty minutes later he was welcoming Eleanor in the manner they both relished.

"Adam, what was so important that it couldn't wait till tomorrow?" she asked while his hands roamed about her curvaceous breasts, his pelvis thrusting against hers.

"You have to know right this minute?" he teased, already envisioning them locked together on his bed.

"Yes," she said breathlessly. God, it made him hot to see her getting all worked up!

"I have to go home for Christmas. Let's get married first—"

She was suddenly immobile. Her eyes searched his.

"Adam, *next week*? You said we'd have to wait a couple of years—"

"What's wrong with next week? Besides, my mother wants me to come into the Bartonville office," he lied. "I don't want to leave you up here."

"My mother," she stammered, but he knew she was joyous at the prospect of getting married right away. "I'll need time to make her understand. She'll be upset that I'm dropping out of school. That— that I'm marrying out of my faith."

"I'm an agnostic," he drawled. He couldn't deal with the religious crap. He never even *thought* about it. "We'll be married at City Hall next Friday, honeymoon over the weekend at that ski lodge upstate. Then we'll go home."

"Where will we live?" She was simultaneously excited and unnerved. Worrying, he surmised, about her mother's reaction.

"We'll stay at Barton Manor until the cottage can be renovated," he decided. No need to push his mother into building a house for them. In time he'd inherit the family house. Wouldn't Lily and Stephanie be pissed, he thought with amusement. "Sugar, you'll love Bartonville."

"I need time to make my mother understand," she said again.

"We'll talk about that later." He slipped an arm about her waist and prodded her toward the bedroom. "Right now, let's rehearse for the honeymoon."

Everything was going to work out great, he told himself. Melanie would look at Eleanor and know he could get along just fine without her. He'd take Eleanor over to Saks before they left for home and buy her some knockout clothes. Everybody would see what a gorgeous wife he'd snagged.

In the not too distant future, he promised himself, he'd be head of Barton Tobacco. How much longer would his mother want to keep up her crazy pace in the company? Once she realized how well he could handle things, she'd be glad to step aside.

Eleanor stared in anguish as her mother's face drained of color. Why couldn't Mom understand that she and Adam were in love?

"Nothing good comes of marrying outside of your faith," Rebecca Kahn reproached. Eleanor was relieved that she wasn't saying how she disliked Adam. "And why this rush? Next week," her mother mimicked in distaste.

"Adam's mother insists he come back home to work in the company office there. He's doing so well, Mom. We'll have a wonderful life. Except," she said wistfully, "I'm going to miss you so much. But Adam says I can come up often to visit."

"Not even a real wedding with a rabbi," Rebecca mourned. "What about children?" she demanded now. "I know you're young. So young to marry. But someday you'll have children. What about them?"

"They'll be raised Jewish," Eleanor promised. "Adam understands that." He'd just shrugged when she'd brought that up. He hadn't said no.

"Ellie, baby, you're so young." Tears filled Rebecca's eyes as she reached to pull her daughter into her arms. "I'd hoped to see you finish college—"

"You'll never have to worry about me, Mom," Eleanor said softly. "Adam earns a big salary, and he has a trust fund. We'll be just fine."

Eleanor and Adam suddenly became caught up in wedding preparations. They rushed for their blood tests, their marriage license, scheduled the City Hall wedding. Eleanor was touched by Adam's insistence on taking her to Saks to buy clothes and luggage. The saleswomen were all impressed by him, she thought tenderly. He was so good-looking and so charming.

On Friday afternoon Eleanor and Adam were married in a fast, impersonal City Hall ceremony. Her mother and Adam's friend Chuck—whom he saw only occasionally since graduation—were their witnesses. Her mother took them for a wedding dinner at Lindy's, after which they headed for the ski lodge in upstate New York. Eleanor was giddy with happiness. She'd known, of course, that she and Adam would marry—but he'd said they'd have to wait a couple of years.

"Take good care of my baby," Rebecca told Adam with an effort at lightness when the wedding party prepared to go their separate ways. "She's very precious to me."

Vicky had just settled in bed for the night—with a batch of sales figures to go over before succumbing to sleep—when her phone disturbed the stillness. Probably Adam, she guessed. He had a habit of calling at this hour.

"Hello."

"Hi, Mother. I didn't wake you, did I?"

"Darling, no. How are you?"

"Fine," he told her.

"Will you be driving down or taking the train?"

"Driving." He paused. "Is it all right if I bring someone home with me? A girl."

"You know it's all right, Adam." Was it that lovely girl she'd met briefly at Adam's graduation?

"I've been debating about the work situation," he continued with an air of self-consciousness. "Don't you think it's time I came home and settled in at the Bartonville office?"

"I was waiting for you to make that decision," she confessed. She'd been afraid he might want to stay in New York for a year or two. "I'll be glad to see you in our home office."

"Is there any need to delay? I'd like to start there right away."

"That'll be great," Vicky agreed. Had he been involved in some disagreement with Frank, she asked herself, then guiltily dismissed this. Frank would have told her. "If you can wind things up in New York that fast."

"One of the secretaries can handle closing up the apartment for me," he said casually, then hesitated. "I know this is going to be a shock to you," he apologized. "I got married this afternoon at City Hall. Eleanor hated the idea of a big wedding, and so did I."

"Adam, you never gave us a hint." Her voice was deep with shock, her mind in sudden chaos. *Adam married?* "Is she that very pretty girl we met for a moment at your graduation?"

"That's right." He cleared his throat in a telltale gesture of unease. "Don't make a big fuss about our getting married. I mean, don't call in an item to the society editor or plan a splashy party."

"Whatever you like," she told him. She managed a convivial tone. "I can't wait to welcome you and your bride to Barton Manor!"

"I thought maybe we could renovate Dad's old cottage and live there," Adam said. "If you don't object—"

"That'll be fine," she said, yet she was taken aback. How could Adam plan on living in the cottage where his father killed himself? But then, Adam was always practical. It was actually a perfect choice. "When will you be home?"

"We'll drive down on Sunday. Expect us around dinner time. Oh, you'll tell Grandma, won't you?"

"I'll tell her." She was still reeling from Adam's news. *Her son was married.* She hadn't expected that to happen for years. She still saw Adam as a boy. But he was a man, she thought with pride—and doing well in the business already. "Grandma will be so pleased." For Sara it would seem the continuation of a dynasty. And in a corner of her mind she realized that Doug would never give his grandmother a great-grandchild. Doug's life would be dedicated to music. No room there for a wife.

Tonight Vicky encountered difficulty in falling asleep. Her mind churned with the news of Adam's marriage. She remembered her own marriage—over twenty-seven years ago—at a brief civil ceremony in Paris. That seemed to be in another lifetime.

She thought about Adam's bride. A sentimental smile lighted her face. Her daughter-in-law. Eleanor Kahn—the named jogged into her memory. *Was* she Jewish? Had Adam said nothing to her about his having a Jewish mother?

The possibility troubled Vicky. She knew that Adam had a way of closing his eyes to situations he was reluctant to face. All these years later she remembered his rage when she'd sat him down—along with Michael—to explain to them that he was Jewish on her side. She could hear his voice now: *"I don't want to be Jewish! I won't be! I won't!"*

He'd refused to come to Michael's bar mitzvah. He'd closed his mind to his being Jewish. Yet she strongly suspected that his sweet young bride was of their faith. Perhaps, she told herself optimistically, Eleanor would change Adam's way of thinking about that. Vicky's own mother and father would have been pleased that Adam married a Jewish girl.

In the morning, Vicky told Sara about Adam's unexpected marriage.

"He'll settle down now," Sara predicted, her face radiant. "I might even live to see my first great-grandchild."

"You'll watch him—or her—grow up," Vicky said. "You'll give a lot of birthday parties."

She phoned Kara to tell her that Adam was bringing home his bride. She knew that Kara would provide a warm welcome. Neither Lily nor Stephanie had ever shown any love for Adam—they'd hardly be interested in his wife. But she and Sara and Kara would make Eleanor understand that she was accepted with genuine affection.

"Shall I ask Kara and Derek to have dinner with us?" Vicky asked.

"That's a lovely thought," Sara said. "Call her and tell her we want the two of them here when Adam and Eleanor arrive. It's a very special occasion, and we want them to share it."

On Sunday afternoon Kara and Derek were at Barton Manor almost an hour before the scheduled time.

"In case Adam and his bride show up early," Derek explained.

Vicky prodded them into the library.

"I'm glad you could come early," she assured them lovingly. "We'll have coffee while we're waiting. But no advance dessert," she teased Derek, known for his love of sweets.

"How's Grandma?" Kara asked. She and Derek shared Vicky's concern over Sara's health.

"She's holding her own." Vicky was serious now. "You know your grandmother—she won't ever admit to feeling less than perfect. But I make sure she takes her medication." She glanced up with a smile as Effie came into the room with the coffee tray. "Effie, will you please ask Miss Sara to join us for coffee?"

Moments later Sara came into the library, to be greeted warmly by Kara and Derek. Vicky hadn't been sure that Kara loved Derek when they were first married, but there was no doubt that she loved him now. They were so good for each other. And both so eager for children.

"We wanted you and Derek to be here to welcome Adam's bride," Sara told Kara. "First impressions are so important."

"It'll be nice to have a cousin close to my own age right here in Bartonville," Kara said. "I'll introduce her around town." She hesitated. "Mother and Dad aren't coming today, are they?"

"No, she'll meet the rest of the family on Christmas day. It'll be strange to sit down to Christmas dinner without Doug at the table," Vicky added wistfully.

"Mother's sure that Adam's wife married him to get her hands on the family money," Kara said humorously. "All Mother and Aunt Lily think about is money. Thank God, Derek and I don't run in that rat race." She exchanged a warm glance with Derek.

"I hope that Adam and Eleanor will be as happy as you two," Sara said softly.

"We'd be happier if Mother and Dad would stop trying to run our lives." All at once Kara was grim. "They expect us to go into debt to buy a big house we can't afford—"

"And don't want," Derek added. "We don't even know if we're going to stay in Bartonville."

"Oh, we'd miss you two so much!" Vicky gazed from Derek to Kara in dismay.

"It won't be too far away," Kara said quickly. "Derek has a possible offer coming up in Atlanta. But it'll be at least a year before we'd make a move. Maybe by then I'll be pregnant," she said wistfully.

They heard the sound of a car pulling up out front. The four of them hurried from the library and down the hall to the front door. Watching Adam charge up the front steps with his slender young wife, Vicky felt herself speeding back through the years. She saw in Eleanor's eyes the uncertainty and shyness *she* had felt when Gary brought her to Barton Manor all those years ago.

She accepted a quick kiss from Adam, then turned her attention to his wife.

"Welcome to Barton Manor," Vicky said gently, reaching to embrace her. She saw the relieved glow in Eleanor's eyes. She must have been so afraid of this meeting, Vicky thought—and remembered her own arrival here. She, too, had been terrified. "I remember you from the graduation exercises. I had thought then, 'What a lovely, sweet girl.' "

When Eleanor began to try to stifle yawns rather early in the evening, Adam insisted she go up to their room. Tiring easily these days, Sara had excused herself an hour ago.

"It was a long drive," he told his mother with an air of indulgence, "and we were up early."

"Of course," Vicky sympathized, "you two run along. I'll be turning in soon myself." She was pleased by Adam's show of solicitude for his bride.

"I'll have another cup of coffee before I go up," Adam said leisurely and leaned forward to kiss Eleanor on the cheek.

"I'll get it for us. I'm sure Lula Mae left a fresh percolator on the stove." Vicky glanced at her watch. They wouldn't linger too long. She was in her office by eight, and Adam knew she expected the same of him.

Over coffee they talked about the state of the tobacco industry. Each year sales figures increased.

"This past year topped all other years," Vicky said with satisfaction. "Not just for us—for all the big companies."

"And 1947," Adam predicted, "will be even better. It all comes down to one thing—what company runs the strongest ad campaign. Oh, I had dinner the other night with Roger Owens. I was upset when he told me—though this is not for public consumption yet," he warned, "that he plans to leave the agency and set up his own with two other execs from the agency. He's done great for Barton."

"He's done well," Vicky conceded. "But I wouldn't be upset that he's leaving the agency. They have a great team there. We won't suffer."

"Roger's sharp—and he's young," Adam pursued enthusiastically. "He has fresh ideas for the industry. We could do worse than switch to his firm when it gets moving."

"We haven't made a change in over twenty years," Vicky pointed out. "Not because we're stick-in-the-muds, but because we get top-drawer service. I'm not ready to dismiss that."

"We need to push somebody out to become one of the Big Three." Adam leaned forward, a messianic glow on his face. "We've never gone as high as we should."

"We're a privately owned company," Vicky reminded. "We can't spend the way the Big Three spend."

"Did you ever consider going public?" Adam challenged.

"Barton Tobacco will never go public," Vicky said quietly. "We'll never put ourselves in a position where we can be controlled by stockholders."

"There are ways to manipulate that, too."

"Adam, don't try to make over the company in one huge swoop," she laughed. "We're doing extremely well. Our earnings are soaring. We must be doing something right."

Was she going to have trouble keeping Adam's feet on the ground? She approved of his ambition. But ambition must be guided by experience. There was no way she would change advertising agencies. No way she'd consider taking Barton Tobacco public.

She nurtured a disquieting suspicion that she and Adam would have bitter battles in the years ahead.

Chapter Thirty-six

IT SEEMED to Vicky as the new year rolled along that she was busy every waking moment. She maintained her usual long hours at the office, though she occasionally escaped to make sure the crew appointed to renovate the cottage was keeping to schedule. She personally saw to it that Sara kept her medical appointments. She was fighting with Adam to provide some social life other than family for Eleanor.

She cherished the interludes she managed to share with Marc, even while she struggled with guilt about the relationship. Somehow, the presence of Adam at Barton Manor had intensified that guilt. She told herself this was irrational, yet she'd feel more relaxed once Adam and Eleanor were living in the cottage.

On a late February evening when Adam and Eleanor had gone to a small dinner party at Kara and Derek's house, Vicky hurried to meet Marc at his hideaway. He was already there when she arrived. Chunks of wood were piled high in the fireplace grate and beginning to crackle.

"It'll be warm in a few minutes," he promised, helping her out of her coat. "The stove in the kitchen is sending out tons of heat, and I've got a fire going in the bedroom." He pulled her close, his face against hers now. "All day long I thought about being here with you this way."

Silently, arm in arm, they went into the bedroom. How wonderful, she thought, that she and Marc had found each other. How had she survived these last dark years without him? Sara was right, she thought yet again. Let them not squander this precious gift they'd found together.

After they'd made love, Vicky lay in Marc's arms under a blanket, and they talked. The firelight casting a warm glow about the room. She could talk with Marc—as she had with Michael—about subjects she couldn't discuss with anybody else. Like Michael, Marc shared her compassion for the Southern colored folks. He applauded her insistence on promoting worthy colored employees to supervisory positions. Sara supported her in this, yet she sensed that her mother-in-law didn't truly understand the need for change.

"We're always good to our coloreds, Vicky. And you know that Lula Mae and Effie and Zachary and Mattie Lou are like family. When Lula Mae was so sick with pneumonia, I helped nurse her."

This evening Vicky and Marc talked about the devastating problems in England and on the continent. This had been a terrible winter over there, with the temperature sinking well below zero for weeks on end. England was paralyzed by piled-up snow. Food shortages throughout Europe were alarming. Regularly Vicky sent parcels to Simone and Henri.

Now they talked about the company. Local newspapers had exposed union infiltrators as Communists. The union problem—never serious at Barton Tobacco—had been laid to rest.

"How's Adam working out?" Marc asked.

Vicky tried to ignore her conviction that Adam and Marc—who had met casually at a charity affair—shared a covert dislike of the other. "Adam's always impatient to see the company expand," she said indulgently. "I suppose that's part of being young."

"He takes after his mother," Marc teased.

"I was ambitious, yes." Vicky was thoughtful. "But I wasn't in a mad rush like Adam. Maybe he just wants to show his new wife that he can be a huge success. I like Eleanor. She's sweet and considerate—and she adores him."

"I'm going to give a paper at a school in upstate New York," Marc told her. "Early next month. I could stop off for a day and night in Manhattan." His eyes were hopeful.

"Marc, do we dare?" All at once her heart was pounding.

"Schedule a meeting in New York." His voice was a tender caress. "I'll meet you that evening. We can have a whole night to ourselves. You'll return on one train, and I'll take the next."

"We'll do it." Her face was luminous. "Oh, Marc, I love you."

She waited impatiently through the next weeks, setting up the meeting with Frank only a few days ahead of her anticipated arrival. She'd talk to him about the ad agency's new campaign. Adam kept saying it lacked sparkle. He was sure Roger Owens could come up with something much stronger, something more appealing to women. More and more women were smoking.

Marc took off for his date at the college. The following morning Vicky left for New York. She contrived not to mention this to Lisa or any of the synagogue circle. Only the office staff—and Sara and Eleanor—knew she was off on a short business trip. Anita would never know, she reassured herself uneasily. Nobody would be hurt.

Marc had made reservations at a modest hotel—under an assumed name. He met her at Pennsylvania Station, took her to dinner at a charming Greenwich Village restaurant. Then they went to their hotel. It was the first time they'd spent a whole night together.

"I wish we could be together every night," he whispered. "I wish we could belong together in the sight of the world."

"Be grateful for this," she murmured. "It's a small piece of heaven."

The next morning Vicky awoke with an instant, glorious awareness that Marc's arm lay protectively about her shoulders. Her eyes swept to the clock on the night table. She wouldn't wake him for another half hour, she told herself in a surge of tenderness. She'd never seen him asleep before, she thought. He looked so vulnerable. So young. She enjoyed teasing him about being four years younger than she.

But as though feeling the weight of her gaze, he began to stir. His eyes opened, met hers.

"We're really here," he murmured. "It wasn't just a wonderful dream."

He reached to draw her close.

"Marc, I have to make a train," she reminded.

"There's plenty of time," he soothed, his mouth closing in on hers.

All the while her train rolled over the tracks en route to Richmond, Vicky relived in her mind the beautiful stolen hours with Marc. As arranged, Zachary was at the depot to meet her. She instructed him to drive her to the office. She was back in the old routine again.

Adam was full of questions about her meeting with Frank. He was still fighting with her about changing agencies. He'd done his homework, she acknowledged. He laid out a report he'd ferreted out about the coming advertising campaigns of their competitors.

"Frank agrees with me, Adam," she said, fighting against impatience. "This is not the time to make a change."

"We have a board of directors meeting coming up," he pointed out. "Shall we discuss it with them?"

Vicky stared at him in astonishment.

"Adam, you know that board of directors deal was arranged just to shut up Lily and Stephanie. Your grandmother holds controlling votes. What they say means nothing. What do they know about the business?"

"Yeah, I guess you're right," he shrugged. "But I think we're missing the boat in not switching to Roger Owens's new firm."

The following morning Adam appeared at the breakfast table with an air of exhilaration.

"I've got news," he said, sliding into his chair. "Eleanor thinks she's pregnant."

"Adam, how wonderful!"

"She's not positive," he cautioned. "She talked to Kara last night. Kara's taking her to this doctor in Richmond. Anyhow, we'll know soon."

Three afternoons later he walked into Vicky's office with a jubilant grin.

"I just had a phone call from Eleanor. She's definitely pregnant. You'll be a grandmother sometime in October."

"Adam, I'm so happy." She rose to hug him. "And your grandmother will be out of her mind with joy."

"It looks like we'll be needing another room at the cottage," he said tentatively.

"That'll be my gift," she told him. "A nursery for the baby plus a bedroom for its nursemaid. I'll talk to Derek right away about the plans."

It seemed to Vicky that with Eleanor's pregnancy she was reliving her own. Because she realized that Eleanor was homesick for her mother, she insisted that Adam take his wife to New York early in May—while she could still travel in relative comfort. It disturbed her to realize that he disliked his mother-in-law.

So anxious to become pregnant herself, Kara spent much time with

Eleanor. Vicky enjoyed seeing the two of them together. They were good for each other, she thought. Neither cared much for the hectic social whirl of Richmond.

With the approach of school vacation, Marc and Anita were preparing to take off for the summer. Vicky and Marc dreaded the separation, though they knew Anita would insist on leaving Richmond for much of the hot weather. At her monthly dinner party in June, Anita blithely announced that she and Marc would leave early in July for six weeks in London.

"London's the only civilized city in the world," she said. "And now we can fly to Paris for a weekend."

"Take plenty of canned goods with you," Lisa Feinberg urged. "And boxes of biscuits."

"I know people wail about the shortage of food over there," Anita conceded, "but you can be damn sure the choice restaurants will have everything. We'll stay at the Savoy in London and probably at the Crillon in Paris. It's quite lovely, isn't it, Vicky?"

"Yes, it is." Vicky managed a strained smile. Anita was obsessed with mentioning the Crillon whenever the subject of Paris came into their conversation. It was as though, she thought, to remind her that she had once been a lowly maid in that hotel. "I remember staying there with my mother when I was a little girl," Vicky said, all at once caught up in nostalgia. "We had a beautiful two-bedroom Louis XV suite with a balcony that looked down on the Place de la Concorde. I remember the high curving ceilings, the crystal chandeliers—"

"I'm sure Marc and I will love it." Anita's smile lost some of its spontaneity. She hadn't heard of this earlier time at the Crillon.

Vicky was grateful that the summer seemed to be rushing past. She was impatient for Marc's return to Richmond. The cigarette industry was thriving; it was clear that 1947 would surpass even the banner year of 1946. And she waited eagerly for Eleanor to give birth to what would be her first grandson or granddaughter.

In the last week of August, Eleanor went into labor. Adam was out of town at a tobacco auction. Vicky and Kara went with her to the hospital.

"It's too early," Eleanor whispered in terror. "Am I going to lose the baby?"

"Lots of babies come early," Vicky soothed. "This baby is going to be fine."

But she waited anxiously in the reception area of the maternity floor with Kara until the obstetrician reported at last that Eleanor had given birth to a daughter.

"She's a little small," he conceded good-humoredly. "Just over five pounds. But she's doing fine. You can see the mother and the baby in just a little while."

"Adam's going to be annoyed," Kara whispered when they were alone. "He was sure the baby would be a boy."

"He'll just have to make do." Vicky was involuntarily sharp. She *knew* Adam wanted a boy—an heir to the throne, Kara had teased earlier.

Vicky was entranced by her new granddaughter. Everybody declared that tiny Jill was the image of her. Adam might be disappointed at having a daughter rather than a son, but both grandmothers were delighted. At Vicky's insistence Eleanor urged her mother to come down to Richmond to see her new grandchild. Vicky decreed that Rebecca Kahn would stay at Barton Manor for the three days she planned to be in Bartonville.

Adam contrived not to be able to meet his mother-in-law at the train station. Vicky left the office in mid-afternoon to drive to the Richmond depot. At Eleanor's instructions Adam had provided a snapshot of Mrs. Kahn. She would recognize her, Vicky told herself nervously as the train pulled into the depot.

The third person off the train was a rather tall, athletic woman with salt-and-pepper hair. She had Eleanor's face. Vicky moved forward with a warm smile as she saw uncertainty in the other woman's gaze. She'd been expecting Adam.

"Mrs. Kahn?" Vicky asked as the neatly clad woman waved away a porter to carry her small valise herself.

"Yes." Her smile was quick, showing relief.

"I'm Vicky Barton, Adam's mother," she explained. "Adam is at a tobacco auction—I've been delegated to meet you." She saw initial astonishment give way to respect. She had not expected the head of Barton Tobacco to be here to greet her, Vicky interpreted. "I'll drive you to the hospital first. I know you're dying to see our new granddaughter—and Eleanor, of course."

"How nice of you to meet me, Mrs. Barton," Rebecca said, almost shyly.

"Vicky," she said with an ingratiating smile. Rebecca Kahn was uncomfortable at staying at Barton Manor, Vicky thought. She must change that. Eleanor had told her—with such love—how her mother had brought her up alone since her father died when she was four. Rebecca Kahn hadn't had an easy life.

"Jill is just adorable," Vicky told her, walking with her to the car. "She and Eleanor will be coming home from the hospital early next week. She's going to be the most spoiled little girl in the state of Virginia!"

Not until they arrived at the hospital and were emerging from the car did Vicky notice the necklace Rebecca wore. A gold chain with a Star of David. She'd been right all along. Eleanor was Jewish. *Why all this secrecy?* And almost immediately she knew that Adam had said nothing to Eleanor about his own Jewishness.

"Rebecca, would you mind if we stopped for coffee in the hospital cafeteria before you go up to Eleanor's room?" she asked after a fleeting inner debate. She wasn't an interfering mother, but this was a situation that needed clarifying. "There's something I think we should discuss. It isn't anything unpleasant," she said hurriedly as she sensed Rebecca's alarm.

"Eleanor and the baby are all right?" Rebecca asked.

"They're fine," Vicky reassured her. "I just think there's something that needs to be said."

Over coffee in the hospital cafeteria Vicky told Rebecca Kahn that she was Jewish, but that Adam had long ago closed his mind to this.

"Perhaps it's my fault. I allowed my father-in-law to frighten me in the early days into being silent about my faith. I was only out of Russia for two years. I was born there—I knew about the horrible pogroms, though my family was safe from this. But I knew. I came to this country—and my father-in-law told me about the Ku Klux Klan, about the problems of being Jewish in this country. I didn't tell Adam until he was seven that he was Jewish, that in Judaism a child assumes the faith of his mother. With my older son Michael there was no problem." For a moment Vicky fought against tears. "I was so proud at his bar mitzvah. But there was no question of a bar mitzvah for Adam. He'd closed his eyes to his faith."

"But he married a Jewish girl." Rebecca was bewildered. "Eleanor doesn't know—"

"We'll go up and explain to her," Vicky said gently. "Perhaps I created the problem for Adam in not telling him sooner—" Why was she making excuses for Adam, she asked herself involuntarily. He was a man—a husband and a father.

After Rebecca had exchanged a tender greeting with Eleanor and had seen her granddaughter, Vicky haltingly told Eleanor what had to be said. For a few moments Eleanor was silent. She seemed to be trying to digest the news.

"Let's say nothing to Adam about this." Her smile was apologetic. "Let him tell me in his own time."

On October fifth—in the first telecast from the White House—President Truman campaigned for voluntary food rationing, based on the mounting food crisis in Europe. Sent on a twenty-four country fact-finding tour by the president, Herbert Hoover reported that many were on the verge of starvation. Truman proposed meatless Tuesdays, no eggs or poultry on Thursdays, and one less slice of bread a day per person. He urged distilleries to shut down for sixty days to save grain.

In the days ahead the public was assaulted by an advertising campaign to save food, use leftovers. The slogan flashed around the country: "Don't start World War III in your garbage pail." And Vicky began to think about diversifying the interests of Barton Tobacco. At one of their clandestine meetings at Marc's cottage she talked about this with him.

"A dozen years ago—in the middle of the Depression—I persuaded Daniel to buy up huge tracts of acreage. Land that had been reclaimed by the banks and was available for almost nothing. It's part of Barton Tobacco holdings. It's good farm land, Marc. It could produce a great amount of food."

"You can't pick that food and ship it to Europe," he said humorously, but Vicky knew he was sympathetic.

"My thought was to set up a segment of the acreage as an experiment, grow produce and sell it to a cannery. If it works out, we'll expand the program."

"I should have known you'd be practical. That shows good thinking. Both for the business and from the humanitarian angle."

"It'll take time to organize." But already her mind was racing ahead to sort out the technical problems. She was exhilarated by the potential of moving into farming. "But by next spring we should be able to put in the first crops. I think it's wise to diversify the company's holdings. And this will be a small contribution to the world food crisis," she said softly. "It's awful to know that so many people go to bed hungry at night, when in this country we have so much."

"I'm intrigued about the way people are pushing for freezing food," Marc said seriously. "Fish is being marketed frozen—"

"One day," Vicky predicted, "we'll be freezing instead of canning. But that'll require refrigerated units aboard ships. Whenever you read anything about freezing of food, Marc, please save it for me."

"I keep an active 'Vicky bag,' remember? Don't I always bring you all these clippings I cut out for you? You're a lady who never gets enough of learning," he teased. "That's one of the things that fascinates me about you."

"What else?" she challenged in high spirits.

"Come here and I'll show you."

On a Saturday evening in late October Vicky and Sara went to the cottage to have dinner with Adam and Eleanor. Vicky knew there would be pain in this. The memories of the day she and Sara rushed to the cottage to find Gary dead were agonizingly fresh when they walked up the steps to the veranda. Vicky sensed that Sara was fighting—as she was—to mask this anguish.

Eleanor rushed forward to welcome them. They were taken to the nursery to spend a little time with Jill before dinner would be served. Vicky and Sara listened with rapt attention to Eleanor's report of Jill's progress.

"She's so sweet," Eleanor crooned while she hovered above her tiny daughter. "She wakes up in the morning with this beautiful smile, as though she can't wait to greet the new day."

With candid reluctance the three women left Jill in the hands of Della—her proud nursemaid—when Adam called to say that dinner was about to be served.

"God, you'd think the father didn't exist anymore," Adam derided, "now that the baby's born."

"Adam, you're not being neglected," Eleanor said anxiously, then laughed. "You're teasing me again," she scolded. "I'm never sure when you're serious and when you're making fun of me."

They sat at the table in the small but charming dining room that had been added to the cottage along with the originally planned bedrooms. Vicky was touched by Eleanor's eagerness that her first dinner party go well. Over delicious "Country Captain"—Adam's favorite chicken dish—Vicky talked about her new plans for the land the company had owned since Depression days.

"I'd cherished the thoughts about perhaps our growing our own tobacco one day," she told the others. "But the war came along, and there was no time for that."

"How much land does the company own?" Adam's voice was charged with excitement.

"I don't have the exact figures, but it's a lot of land. It was available for almost nothing."

"Where is it?" he persisted.

"Virginia, North Carolina mostly," she began, but Adam interrupted her.

"Near large cities in those states?" he asked.

"Not far from them—ideally located for shipping," Vicky said with satisfaction.

"Then it would be crazy to waste it on farmland!" Adam's eyes swept from his mother to his grandmother. "Let me talk to some real estate developers. If the land is near big cities, it'll bring a fortune! The whole country's mad for housing. Developers are crying out for huge tracts that are suitable for commuting communities."

"This will be farmland." Vicky felt herself become tense. "I mean for us to grow produce that'll help alleviate world hunger. We—"

"Mother, you're out of your mind. You'd be throwing away millions of dollars. Look at what that man Levitt is doing up in the Northeast. People are standing in line all night to be able to sign up in the morning for one of his houses. Let me contact him about what we have to offer down here in the South!" A vein was distended in his forehead. "I'll contact other developers too."

"Adam, I know the housing problem is serious. And that a lot of money can be made in real estate." Adam, she thought with subconscious irony, was not concerned about the need. He envisioned the money the land could bring to Barton Tobacco—which he would one day inherit. "But Barton Tobacco will raise food, not houses."

"Grandma, are you going to let her do this?" Adam swung to Sara in soaring rage. "It's stupid!"

"Your mother makes the decisions for the company," Sara told him with icy calm. "She has my blanket approval."

"She's throwing away a fortune." He lapsed into sullenness now. Eleanor had been frantically signaling him to back down. "Grandpa never would never have allowed her to pull something so dumb."

"You don't talk that way to your mother," Sara reproached him, her anger obvious. "And let me tell you, Adam. Your grandfather had the greatest respect for your mother's judgment. If he were alive today, he'd go along with whatever decisions she made. She's built Barton Tobacco into twice the company it was twenty years ago. Don't you forget that, Adam."

"Times are changing. This isn't the same world it was twenty years ago," Adam blustered. "You'll both be sorry about this one day."

"Eleanor, did Adam ever tell you about the sports trophies he won at boarding school?" Sara redirected the conversation. "We were all so proud of him—"

Vicky made a pretense of listening to Sara's deliberately light chatter, but in a corner of her mind she tried to deal with the ugly encounter with Adam. Was she to spend the rest of her life battling with him on how she ran the company? It was a distasteful prospect.

Chapter Thirty-seven

VICKY WAS impatient to launch the produce arm of Barton Tobacco, but demands of the cigarette industry delayed this until early in the new year. Again, cigarette sales were eclipsing those of the previous year—and retail prices were rising.

She knew she'd startled her executive staff with a brief announcement of the new project. They were uneasy that she was diverting funds into other channels, and fearful that this might somehow jeopardize their own positions in the company.

From Frank Leslie in the New York office came strong approval.

"I think diversification is the way to go," he told her enthusiastically. He wasn't talking about the humanitarian aspect, Vicky knew—Frank saw this as a shrewd commercial move. "We're moving into highly competitive times. It's smart not to have all our eggs in one basket."

Now Vicky threw herself into exploring every facet of the new enterprise. She was too cautious to jump in without making herself thoroughly knowledgeable about the new field. Without discussing it even with Frank, she began a low-keyed survey of canneries that might be coming up for sale.

Yet, with all the demands on her time, she managed to spend a little while each day with Jill. She loved this tiny grandchild with an intensity that sometimes startled her. It was as though, she thought, she were reliving Michael's babyhood. In so many ways Jill reminded her of Michael. And always she salvaged hours to spend with Marc.

This would have been such a happy period in her life, she thought as she headed for a meeting with Marc, if she hadn't been so anxious about the state of Sara's health. She could deal with Adam's disapproval, his pointed remarks about the soaring value of real estate—but it unnerved her to see Sara's physical decline. Sara's only joy these days was spending time at the cottage with Jill.

Marc was at his typewriter when Vicky arrived at the cottage. He abandoned the article on which he'd been working to come forward to greet her.

"I saw the item in this morning's newspaper about the Bartonville library being opened up to colored people," he said, his smile approving. "The Vicky Barton influence at work," he surmised. "I didn't expect it to happen so fast."

"Sara got behind the drive," Vicky explained. "She pointed out that the Richmond library had recently done this. You know Bartonville always follows in Richmond's tracks."

"I've sold an article to a magazine up in New York," Marc told her with an edge of excitement in his voice. "It's just a small literary magazine, but Anita's delighted." His smile was ironic. "She can talk about her husband the author. But they want to talk to me about doing three or four articles a year. I should go up to meet with the editor personally, don't you think?" His eyes sent an eloquent message.

"When?" she asked, her mind focusing on a conversation with Frank a few days ago. He'd talked about a private meeting with her—away from the office. He saw a new development taking shape in the industry—so new he didn't want to discuss it over the phone or with the New York office staff until they themselves had considered it. "Your timing is uncanny. I've been trying to figure out when I could squeeze in a quick trip."

"It's up to you," he told her elatedly. "I'll go up on a Thursday evening, see the magazine people Friday morning. I'll come back sometime on Saturday."

"I'll go up on Thursday morning, meet with Frank in the afternoon. Oh, Marc, we'll have two nights together!" She was radiant with anticipation. "It'll be beautiful." She and Marc were cheating no one, she told herself defensively. He had no marriage with Anita, only an obligation to appear the devoted husband.

"Next Thursday?" He reached for her hand, brought it to his mouth.

"Next Thursday."

The following morning she phoned Frank to tell him about her arrangement to be in New York.

"I'll take a very early train. If you meet me at Penn Station, we can go somewhere for a long lunch. I'm dying to know what's on your mind," she laughed. "Don't I get even a hint on the phone?"

"Let's keep it totally private. Perhaps I'm being a bit paranoid, but in this business that's good."

On Thursday, Frank was waiting for her when she emerged from her train at Penn Station. They checked her valise and headed for the street.

"We'll have lunch at my club," he said. "A private corner where nobody will be seated close enough to hear a word we say."

"Is there some reason we shouldn't talk at the office?"

"I'm suspicious of a leak," he admitted. "Until I locate the source—and I will," he said grimly, "I figure this is more prudent. I want Barton Tobacco to have a headstart on what I think will be the next major trend in cigarettes."

Not until they were seated in the dining room of Frank's club and the waiter had taken their orders did Frank confide what was on his mind.

"For years, Vicky, I've wondered about the sales potential of filter cigarettes. The first ones came on the market back in 1936—"

"Viceroys," she said, "from Brown and Williamson. But they didn't go anywhere." She was bewildered.

"You know the old biblical saying—'To everything there is a season'? Well, I suspect this might be the season for filter cigarettes."

"Why?" Vicky challenged, though convinced that Frank must have put in much research to reach this point.

"You know the tremendous increase in women smokers. And women, I gather, dislike the wet end of a cigarette but don't know how to avoid it. And therein," he added in triumph, "lies a powerful new Barton Tobacco ad campaign."

"Frank, we need a stronger incentive than that to go into filter cigarettes," she said. Normally she had enormous respect for Frank's marketing skills.

"We have it," he told her. "You know Benson and Hedges?"

"They're a small company operating out of New York," she pulled from her memory. Their cigarettes were filter-tipped. "They do little advertising or marketing. Their sales don't make a dent in the picture.''

"We have our spies, too," he chuckled. "I wondered why some very selective people in the city are buying at the Benson and Hedges Fifth Avenue shop with such regularity. Vicky, their sales figures have jumped unbelievably in the past six months. Filter cigarettes are catching on. They're the wave of the future.''

"But why?" she probed again. "There has to be more to it than the wet ends annoying women.''

"We don't have to know why," he said, brushing aside her question. She'd never known Frank to be evasive, but she understood his mind was focusing on the increased volume that he was sure was out there for filter-tipped cigarettes. "And I know you're caught up in your produce deal. By the way, how's that doing?''

"It's moving along. I wish I had more time to give to it," she confessed. "I think it might even be wise for us to invest in our own cannery. It'll mean taking out loans—''

"If you're convinced of the practicality of it, go ahead," he urged. "This is a good time for you to push Adam into a stronger position in the company. Let him work with me on our bringing out a filter-tip. I know he's young and—" he hesitated, "sometimes headstrong. But he has a real flair for business. Let him spend a few days each month up here with me, then handle the retooling necessary for the plant. You'll have all the time you need for planning the produce venture. And the cannery.''

"You think I should go ahead with the cannery?" She would not be comfortable with bank loans, yet there would be no problem in acquiring them. Daniel had borrowed in the early days, she reminded herself. He had faith in the company's potential. She had faith in the potential of diversifying.

"You will even if I say no," he joshed. "I can see the determination in your eyes.''

They were the last diners to leave the room, Vicky noted. But she felt exhilarated by what she had learned. As always, Frank had explored the situation in depth. The report he'd given her to take home to study was thorough. And Adam would be so elated, she thought. He'd been churning for more responsibility for months now. He wanted to be the Boy Wonder of the tobacco industry, she thought indulgently. And why not? He was Daniel Barton's grandson.

After their long luncheon, Vicky went to the office with Frank
for a meeting with the staff. Instinctively she guessed—as the meeting progressed—that the new young executive who'd been with the
company barely six months was Frank's "leak." She saw the glint
of astonishment in his eyes when she told the staff that the company was contemplating diversification. He'd expected some new
development within the field that he could take to his private
source, she guessed.

He'd known Frank was onto something hot. All those conferences
with the research people told him that. And the secrecy at the office,
she pinpointed, had put him on alert.

Vicky and Frank remained in the conference room after the others
returned to their offices. Frank rose from his chair and crossed to close
the door.

"Fire Weatherby," she told him when he returned to the table.
"He's your 'leak.'"

"That's what I figured. I wanted to hear you confirm it. He was
dying to ferret out what's behind my meetings with the research people. Weatherby's working for anybody who'll pay him for information," he summed up. "I'll fire him tonight. I don't want him coming
into the office tomorrow morning."

Vicky glanced at her watch.

"I have to leave for an appointment with the broker who's repre-
senting Royal Foods, Inc. As long as I was coming here, I thought
I'd discuss a deal on their Roanoke cannery."

"It's up for sale?" Frank lifted an eyebrow in surprise.

"I heard a rumor they're having financial problems. I checked
around, learned the broker is making some quiet inquiries about prospective buyers. But the truth is, I still don't know much about the
field," she confessed. "I'll have to do a lot of learning."

The appointment with the broker went well, lasting longer than she
had anticipated. She knew she had lengthy negotiations ahead, but it
was a start. By the time she arrived at the hotel Marc had already
checked in. He was in a jubilant mood.

"I'll never make a fortune out of magazine articles, but it's great
for my academic career. I enjoy doing them—and they're a great
cover for us." He reached to pull her close. "Do you realize we have
two beautiful nights all to ourselves?"

"Plus all of tomorrow—except for your meeting with the editor—

and Saturday morning.'' She felt twenty years old and carefree. "Not
for one minute am I going to think about business!''

"That I don't believe,'' he joshed, his eyes tender, "but right now
I have one thing on my mind—''

"Me too,'' she whispered. "I feel so wicked, making love before
dinner.''

At dinner with Marc, Vicky talked about Frank's urging her to
elevate Adam's place in the company.

"You know how impatient he is to move up.'' She used Marc as
her private board of directors, she often told Sara.

"Vicky, he's a kid.'' Marc seemed uneasy about this.

"I know he's awfully young. But he's so sharp—and he's not afraid
of hard work. And at his age he's malleable,'' she said confidently.
She wouldn't think about the ill feelings this move would create in
the company. A mother had a right to promote her own son's career.
Sara was the major stockholder—and she'd approve. "I want Adam
to learn to think the way I do.''

"You're asking a lot,'' he warned. "Adam's not a little boy—he's
set in his thinking right now.'' His smile seemed forced. "Follow
your instincts, Vicky. They've always been good.''

On Monday morning Vicky called Adam into her office to brief
him on the direction the company was to take. Later she'd discuss it
with the executive staff. There'd be some initial grumbling—but that
was good because they might bring out something she'd overlooked.

This new move meant a major push up the ladder for Adam. Still,
the others must realize that Adam was being groomed to become
second-in-command in a few years. She was good to her executives,
she thought defensively—there'd be no defections because her son
was moving fast.

"What's up?'' Adam asked, dropping into a chair beside her desk.
It was uncanny the way he always knew when something important
was in the air.

He listened with an air of mounting disapproval as she talked about
her meeting with Frank.

"He's off his rocker,'' Adam interrupted finally. "We'll cut way
back on profits if we start with filter tips!''

"No!'' Vicky shot back with a victorious smile. Adam, like Daniel, always thought in terms of profit. "Frank has worked out the finances with our research people. We can manufacture filter tips for less than the standard cigarettes. The filter material—which replaces some of the tobacco—is cheaper. Plus by using filters we can do well with cheaper-priced tobacco—there's no loss of taste. Adam, we'll be ahead of the game price-wise."

"Are you sure Frank and the research people are right?" Adam remained skeptical.

"Nobody is more thorough than Frank." She paused. "I want you to go up to New York next week and go over this whole picture with him. As a matter of fact, Frank suggested that. You'll be his right hand—his liaison with the team that comes into the plant for the retooling. Take Eleanor and the baby along—she'll enjoy spending some time with her mother."

"I'm going on business." He was annoyed by this suggestion. "Later she'll go up to see her mother."

Alone in her office, Vicky reviewed her brief meeting with Adam. He was excited about being part of this new development, she recognized and was pleased. And she shouldn't reproach him for plying her with questions, not accepting even Frank's study of the situation. He wanted to see everything for himself. He might be very young, but he would be a real asset to the company in the years ahead.

Adam was impressed that Frank met him at Penn Station on his arrival and took him to lunch. He was impressed, too, at being taken to Frank's club for lunch. That indicated a certain equality, he told himself. And why not, he thought smugly—one day Barton Tobacco would be his company. Doug would never come back from Paris— he loved his life over there, with that character Paul. Didn't the family understand he was queer?

At first tense in the Old World elegance of the club's dining room, Adam began to relax over a preluncheon martini.

"I have to think there's something more that's drawing people to filter tips than a dislike for the wet end of a cigarette," he said, his eyes overtly probing. He'd dropped this "Mr. Leslie" shit now, he told himself. From now on he'd be "Frank."

"There is, Adam." All at once Frank was somber. "I didn't want to discuss it with your mother because I knew she'd be terribly upset.

Mind you, I think it's all hogwash—but the industry's in for some rough bashing.''

"Why?" Adam demanded.

"More and more scientific papers are circulating. Not to the general public,'' he conceded, "but that's bound to follow. Some well-placed researchers are carrying on about cigarettes being harmful to the health—''

"That old bullshit that cigarettes are 'coffin nails'?" Adam interrupted derisively. "That goes back to the last century." He'd heard his grandfather scoff about that. "Nobody's ever paid any attention to those crackpots.''

"Doctors are listening these days. Some of them. They're telling their patients to smoke filter cigarettes because less tar and nicotine goes to the lungs.''

"A handful of people," Adam guessed. Was the old boy off his rocker—or was there something to this? He had a reluctant respect for Frank Leslie because of his track record.

"Now it's a handful, but this could grow into a real explosion. I see that happening, Adam. I want Barton Tobacco to be there up front with what the public wants. Back in 1938 some professor at Johns Hopkins University came up with a major study that claimed smoking was responsible for shortening lives. Fortunately for the industry it was buried somewhere in the back of the *New York Times*. Then *Time* came out with a report on the study and said it was 'enough to scare the life out of the tobacco manufacturers and make tobacco users' flesh creep.' ''

"But it went nowhere," Adam pointed out triumphantly.

"Because war was brewing in Europe. World War II saved our hides. But now the war is over, and we'll be seeing more such studies. Like I said before, I think it's all hogwash. But the public can be terrified by medical studies. We must be prepared to deal with that. Step number one is to offer filter-tip cigarettes.''

"Okay, I can see that." Adam's mind was charging ahead. This old boy was sharp. Together they'd have to keep news of any sensational medical reports from his mother's eyes. That shouldn't be rough. She was all wrapped up in the produce and cannery venture. He and Frank would carry the ball with the filter tips. He felt a surge of satisfaction. "And that means we'll need a whole new concept in our advertising,'' Adam pursued. He could pick up a terrific bonus if he could steer the account into Roger Owens's hands.

''That's eight or ten months down the line, at least. But yes, we'll need a strong ad campaign to introduce the Barton filter tip.''

For the next three days Adam was Frank Leslie's shadow. He absorbed everything that was told to him, asked endless questions. He felt himself shifting into a power position. In five years, he vowed, he'd be running the whole show. *Nobody could stop Adam Barton.*

Chapter Thirty-eight

IT SEEMED to Vicky that she'd hardly greeted one season when the next was upon them. With Marc she always welcomed each new season, though she dreaded the summers when he was away from Richmond. She was in the process of buying the Roanoke cannery, and had set a staff to handle the produce division of Barton Tobacco. She toyed now with the prospect of reorganizing as Barton Enterprises, with Barton Tobacco and Barton Foods as separate divisions. However, she hesitated to discuss this with Sara, because Sara's health was so precarious.

The first huge crops from Barton Foods were of necessity sold to another cannery. She was exhilarated by the sight of vast tracts of Barton farmland offering healthy harvests. The next crops would be canned by their own company. Her involvement in this new venture helped her survive the summer without Marc, she told herself. Again, he and Anita were spending the summer in London.

She was taken aback when Lisa Feinberg mentioned that disenchantment with Anita was setting in among their crowd.

"I'll bet Anita gives Marc an awful time," Lisa confided. "I mean, behind all that charm and fluff—and I know, we should be compassionate—she's awfully controlling. Even among her friends. She's wary of you," Lisa decided. "You're an important woman executive. But I've seen her take digs at you, too."

"As you said, Lisa, we have to be compassionate," Vicky reminded gently. "Anita's built a fantasy life for herself. That's really all she has."

"If she comes back from London again and throws that crap about London being the only civilized city in the world," Lisa warned softly, "I'm going to ask her why she doesn't move there. She can certainly afford it."

People in this country were worrying about an influx of supposed Communists in important governmental positions. In February, Soviet forces seized Czechoslovakia. On June twenty-fourth the Soviets set up a blockade of Berlin, which the United States circumvented with an airlift that was to last for painful months. Governor Dewey of New York was campaigning as the Republican candidate for president. Vicky contrived to listen to election returns with Marc at his cottage. Anita banned political broadcasts and baseball games from their house radio.

By mid-1949 Vicky could declare that the Barton Foods division of the company was out of the red. Barton filter-tip cigarettes were on the market along with their standard brand. Thus far, sales were sluggish. Frank and Adam sided together to persuade Vicky to split up their advertising account, and to give the filter tip to the new agency headed by Roger Owens.

With January 1950 approaching, Adam received a late night phone call at home from Frank.

"Adam, as soon as the January issue of *The Reader's Digest* hits the stands in Bartonville, buy up every issue on sale," Frank ordered tersely.

"What's going on?" Adam demanded.

"An article you don't want your mother to read." Frank was grim. "Nor workers at the plant. One of the fellows at the ad agency got wind of it, managed to get a copy. The writer admits that medical men don't have a case yet, but some are claiming cigarette smoking causes serious health problems. They're even blaming it for the big rise in lung cancer. The damn article goes on for pages."

"It won't stop people from smoking," Adam predicted. "Maybe some might try it for a few days—but they'll be puffing again. They enjoy smoking—they're not going to believe that shit. Relax, Frank."

But early the following morning Adam headed for the three stores in Bartonville where residents might buy copies of *The Reader's Di-*

gest. He gave each the same instructions, knowing that, coming from a Barton—the town's main employer—they'd be respected.

"Whatever comes in, save for me. I'm buying. Don't reorder," he cautioned. "An article slandering the tobacco business is in the January issue. This is a tobacco town—we don't want that, you hear?"

Early in 1950 the Barton filter tips suddenly took off, fighting for a position beside Brown and Williamson's Viceroy. Vicky's pleasure in this was drowned out by her anxiety over Sara's health. When she wrote Doug—still in Paris—about the seriousness of his grandmother's illness, he flew home. He was touchingly attentive, spent a week at her bedside, filling her with stories about his life in Paris.

"Paul and I are working like mad on a musical. We have a producer interested. Once it's on the boards, you'll come and see it," he said with determined optimism. But he knew when Vicky drove him to the Richmond depot that he would never see his grandmother again.

Soon after Doug's visit, round-the-clock nurses were brought in to care for Sara. Now living in Atlanta, Kara and Derek came up every other weekend to visit with her grandmother. Lily and Stephanie made little concession to their mother's illness. In the summer they took off as usual for the resort circuit.

"You're here. Kara and Derek, Eleanor and Jill," Sara said weakly when Vicky protested at the absence of Lily and Stephanie from their mother's bedside. "That's all I need." Subconsciously Vicky was aware that she hadn't mentioned Adam. But then Adam was practically commuting between Bartonville and New York. Sara knew how hard he was working, Vicky told herself defensively.

While Bartonville was in the midst of its Fourth of July celebration—a town festivity inaugurated by Daniel twenty-six years ago—Sara lapsed into a coma. Vicky stayed at her bedside, hoping she might rally. The doctor left close to midnight and promised to be back early in the morning. By dawn Sara was gone. For Vicky it was as though she had lost her own mother.

Vicky sent Zachary to bring Adam to the house. Eleanor came with him.

"What can I do to help?" Eleanor asked, pale and shaken.

"Phone Clark and Jeffrey. Tell them. They'll contact Lily and Stephanie." Vicky was exhausted.

"Go and sleep for a while," Eleanor urged compassionately. "Adam and I will take care of everything."

* * *

Three days later Sara was buried beside Daniel in the Barton family plot. Lily and Stephanie—each wearing black crepe from Dior's new vertical line—clung to their respective husbands as though devastated by grief. The family servants were red-eyed and sorrowful. Vicky was pleased that so many people turned out. Sara would like that.

As when Daniel died, the family returned to Barton Manor for the reading of Sara's will. Why must it be now, Vicky thought in anguished reproach. This was too soon to dwell on material matters.

As the family gathered together in the library, Vicky was conscious of turbulent undercurrents. Lily had been complaining ever since Sara's first diagnosis of emphysema that Clark had not been called in to handle her mother's will. He served as company attorney in a limited number of matters, but he and Lily were affronted that Sara had turned to the old family firm for her will.

As at the reading of Daniel's will almost eleven years ago, Martin Woodstock seated himself at the library desk. Though in his early seventies, he was still an imposing figure. His eyes studied the faces of the family members gathered in the library for the reading. Vicky was conscious of an odd wariness in him.

"Let me say before the reading," he began, "that at her request Mrs. Barton was examined by a team of psychiatrists at the time her will was drawn up. She wanted it clear that she was of sound mind."

All at once the room reverberated with hostility. Vicky saw the exchanges of overwrought glances between Lily and Stephanie. Clark stared grimly into space. Adam moved restlessly in his chair.

Now the attorney began to read. Sara had left Barton Manor and all its furnishings to Vicky—"knowing that my beloved daughter-in-law will pass our family home down to her son Adam." There were cash bequests to the family servants and to the Daniel Barton Memorial Hospital. Next Sara's shares in Barton Tobacco Company—the major segment of her estate—were distributed.

Controlling interest was left to Vicky—"because without Vicky Barton the company would never have risen to its present heights." Vicky heard Lily's strangled shriek, Stephanie's outraged "I don't believe this!" The remainder of company stock was divided between her two daughters and her three grandchildren. According to the terms of the will, for the next fifty years stock could only be transferred among family members.

Pandemonium broke out. Lily and Stephanie—leaping to their feet—simultaneously screamed that they would sue to break the will. Clark and Jeffrey tried futilely to calm them. Adam said nothing, but Vicky could feel his inner rage. *He'd expected his grandmother to leave him controlling interest.* Only Kara seemed grateful to be remembered.

"Quiet!" Woodstock was furious at this reaction. "Let me say that the will has been drawn up so as to be uncontestable. Clark, I think you'll concur with this." But Clark maintained his grim silence. "Mrs. Barton felt this was the fair way to divide up her estate. Her daughters and their husbands, her grandsons and granddaughter will sit on the board of directors with her daughter-in-law. The younger Mrs. Barton will continue to operate the firm as she has in the past."

"We'll have no say!" Lily shrieked. "She—" Lily pointed a finger at Vicky. "She'll control everything! She's not even a Barton except by marriage!"

"Lily, shut up," Clark ordered, prodding her toward the door.

Lily and Stephanie, with their husbands, stalked from the library and down the hall to the front door. Vicky was sure that there would be long months—perhaps even years—of vicious efforts to invalidate the will. That would be for the lawyers to handle, she comforted herself. She had a company to run.

Chapter Thirty-nine

V ICKY WAS aware that her sisters-in-law were fighting with
Clark to launch a lawsuit to overturn the will. She suspected, also,
that they were outraged that Sara's estate would have to be shared
with the grandchildren—cutting back on their own bequests. At intervals Martin Woodstock gave her brief reports.

"Clark knows the case doesn't stand a chance in the courts,"
Woodstock told her late in the year, "but those two women won't
leave him alone."

Lily and Stephanie made it clear they would not set foot in Barton
Manor again. That which Sara would have hated most had happened; the
family was divided—except for their involvement in the company. Lily
and Stephanie had rejected the usual invitation to Thanksgiving dinner.
This year there had been only six for dinner: Vicky, Adam, Eleanor, tiny
Jill, and Kara and Derek—up from Atlanta for the long weekend. At the
rare social gatherings where they met, Lily and Stephanie avoided any
verbal contact with Vicky. But they'd made it clear through Martin
Woodstock that they would be present at annual board meetings—where
they could do no more than harass their despised sister-in-law.

Marc was Vicky's cherished confidant. He scolded her tenderly for
overworking, yet he understood. She welcomed the demands on her
time. They helped her to survive.

On a Thursday evening shortly after Anita's splashy New Year's
Eve party, Marc plotted another of their brief escapes.

"Marc, I'm dying to go," Vicky said, "but there's so much to be done here. I have to go to Roanoke again next week—"

"I'm going to Boston to deliver a paper," he pursued. "We can meet in New York—have at least a couple of days together. You can conjure up a business meeting in New York." His eyes held hers, pleading for agreement.

"All right," she said. "I'll call Frank and work out something."

"You're still worrying about Adam," he guessed. "Vicky, he's lacking for nothing."

"He's so bitter that Sara left me controlling interest in the company. He knows that eventually it'll all go to him." Her voice was sharp with frustration. "I can deal with Lily and Stephanie's anger. I've never known how to handle Adam. Even when he was little, I never knew what was the right way to deal with him."

"It's time to think about yourself." Marc inspected her somberly. "When are you going to understand that Vicky has rights, too?"

"He's never uttered a word of reproach," she admitted, her smile wry. "But I always feel that undercurrent of anger in him. I worry sometimes that it's spilling over on Eleanor. I've heard him be so nasty to her—without reason. Eleanor is one of the most gentle women I've ever known."

"*You* are the most phenomenal woman I've ever known. And that is not only the opinion of this love-besotted male—" He reached to pull her close. "I was so proud of that profile of you in the *Saturday Evening Post* last month."

"Frank insisted I go along with it. Great for business, he said."

"I'm concerned about what's great for Vicky," he murmured. "I worry about you."

Adam frowned as he listened to Frank's voice at the other end of the phone. With one hand he gestured to Carla, his latest secretary, to remain. She'd been with the company four months, and had been his personal secretary for five weeks. For a moment his thoughts were derailed from the phone conversation. God, that broad was built! And didn't she know it.

"Look, Frank, stop sweating," he said impatiently. "So a few people are making noises about the health hazards in smoking. The general public doesn't read those reports. We've got more doctors on our side to testify that there's no danger in smoking." The industry was out there fighting already—even though few people were paying any attention to those damn publicity-hungry doctors and scientists with their stupid claims. "Anyhow, people don't want to believe there's a problem—they would be miserable if they didn't have their cigarettes."

In moments, Adam was off the phone. Carla had sat down and crossed her legs. Her short skirt slid up her thigh. He cleared his throat. She knew she was making him hot as a pistol. And she didn't mind staying late—even though the office floor was deserted except for the two of them. She knew the next item on the program.

"Come here, baby," he ordered, swaggering toward her. She couldn't believe that at twenty-six he carried such clout in the company, he told himself smugly. There was something real sexy about being young and good-looking *and* powerful in business.

"No dictation?" she taunted good-humoredly.

"What do you think?" He reached out to pull her tightly against him. "Oh, wait a minute. I have to make a phone call." No point in going home to a cold dinner. "Let me tell my wife I'll be late." That was to remind Carla, too, that he was married. She could sleep with her boss. She'd never marry him.

At the cottage Eleanor went out to the kitchen to speak to Myra—her housekeeper/cook.

"There's no need to stay. I'll put dinner on the table when my husband comes home from the office. You run along, Myra."

"Yes'm," Myra said placidly. "The pot roast is all done—and the vegetables. I'll just put everything in the oven to stay warm."

"Thank you, Myra." Eleanor forced a smile. More nights than not these days Adam phoned to say he'd be late. She knew he worked long hours. But lately she asked herself if it was always work that kept him at the office. Twice she'd seen lipstick smears on his shirt. Not the shade she wore.

When Myra left the house to drive home in her ramshackle Ford, Eleanor walked into the nursery. This was the night that Jill's nursemaid went home to visit with her folks. Somehow, it felt good to be alone in the house with her precious baby.

She leaned over the bed to pull the comforter over Jill's sleeping form. She was such a restless little one, always throwing off the covers, Eleanor thought with a rush of love. She was so proud that she slept in a real bed now instead of a crib. For a moment Eleanor caressed the mass of dark curls that surrounded the beautiful little face. It was incredible, she thought, how much Jill resembled Vicky.

Mom thought it was disrespectful for her to call her mother-in-law by her given name, but Vicky herself had suggested it. It felt right, she thought guiltily. It was hard to believe that Vicky was forty-nine— she didn't look a day over thirty-five. She adored Jill, Eleanor thought with pleasure. Like Mom.

Sometimes Adam made a big fuss over Jill. Most of the time he seemed to be unaware of her existence—except when she annoyed him by being noisy when he was reading business reports. The only times she fought with Adam was when he yelled at Jill.

Their marriage wasn't like it used to be, she thought with recurrent alarm. Was she right in thinking he was seeing somebody else? *What was she doing wrong?*

Adam promised she could go up to New York late in the summer to spend a month with Mom. He'd be away on buying trips once the tobacco auctions began. She'd miss Adam, but it'd be so good to be with Mom. They'd have a little fourth birthday party for Jill, she plotted.

She wished Adam didn't carry on the way he did when she talked about going back to school. She could finish college right in Richmond. And it wasn't as though she'd be neglecting the house or Jill. She had so little to do—she'd enjoy going back to school. But Adam carried on every time she talked about it.

She left the nursery and settled herself in the living room with a magazine. Adam said he'd be home in an hour, but he had no sense of time. She reached for a cigarette, lit it. She remembered how she used to loathe cigarettes. Now she smoked two packs a day. It was something to do, she thought, and tried to focus on a short story in *Ladies Home Journal.*

Vicky was discovering that the food division of the company was demanding more and more of her time. She'd practically grown up in the tobacco business, she reminded herself—by the time she moved into the company she knew almost all there was to know from contact with Daniel. She was impatient that there was so much to learn in this division.

Ten days out of every month now she was traveling between their farm tracts and the cannery. She hadn't been up to the New York office in ages. Instead, Adam went up regularly for conferences with Frank and the executive staff. She was glad to be away from Barton Manor at regular intervals. The house seemed so empty without Sara.

Her working schedule these days had one distinct advantage, Vicky told herself as she drove toward Richmond after a four-day stay in Roanoke. She could manage more time to be with Marc since he was doing research on Virginia landmarks for a magazine article. Anita had no interest in going with him on these overnight jaunts.

Vicky watched for road signs now. She knew she must make a turn soon. She was meeting Marc at a cottage—midway between Roanoke and Richmond—which he had rented for the night. In the morning he would remain here to do his research while she headed on to Bartonville.

Her face lighted when she spied Marc's car parked in a driveway. She hadn't been sure that this was the cottage. The door swung open as she pulled into the driveway. Marc stood there with a welcoming smile. She always felt so young and carefree when they met this way.

Tonight Mark insisted on cooking dinner for her.

"I don't want to waste a moment in a restaurant. It won't be fancy," he warned, "but it'll be serviceable."

"I'll accept that," she laughed, following him into the strange kitchen. "And I'll do the dishes."

Over perfectly broiled steaks, baked potatoes, and a salad, Vicky shared her present anxieties with him.

"I worry about the way Adam treats Eleanor," she said somberly. "I know he's tense, always fighting to prove himself. I know how hard he drives himself at the office. But he shouldn't be so impatient with Eleanor. When they're at the house for dinner, he's always snapping at her. With no reason, Marc—except that he's tired. But it breaks my heart to see her hurt."

"Have you considered talking to him?" Marc asked.

"I've never really been able to talk with Adam about personal matters." She frowned, trying to express what she felt. "I could talk with Michael. But Michael would never have treated his wife that way."

Later she told him about the battle she'd had with Adam when she'd gone over a superintendent's head to appoint a black woman to the job of chief inspector in the plant. It wasn't being disloyal to Adam to discuss him with Marc, she thought, banishing an initial surge of guilt—under other circumstances Marc would have been Adam's stepfather.

"He said it was bad enough to break a precedent by giving the job to a woman, but I made it worse by choosing a colored woman. He yelled, and I yelled back," she confessed. "I warned him the time is coming when I mean to integrate the plant."

"Good for you," Marc murmured in approval.

Both she and Marc admired President Truman's stand on civil rights, as much as they decried the witch-hunting efforts of Joseph McCarthy and his ilk. And both worried about the continuation of the war in Korea. For Vicky it was the third war within her memory that American soldiers had fought on foreign soil.

In the morning Vicky reluctantly slid behind the wheel of her car and prepared for the drive to Richmond. There was a special poignancy about this parting. They wouldn't be alone together again until after the summer. Marc and Anita were heading for London in four days.

Perhaps Marc was right, she told herself as she approached Bartonville. Adam was her son—she ought to talk to him about how he was treating Eleanor. He couldn't ask for a lovelier, sweeter wife. Did he yell at Eleanor at home, she asked herself. Jill was almost four—old enough to notice such things.

At the office Vicky was instantly enveloped in a current business problem. She promised herself that before the day was over, she'd talk to Adam about how he was treating Eleanor. Perhaps he was even unaware of it. But endless phone calls—from the New York office, the cannery, the farm office—occupied every minute she wasn't in conference with one executive or another. Tomorrow for sure, she promised herself, she'd talk to Adam.

As usual she was the last to leave the office floor except for Adam, dictating to his secretary. She walked to her car, slid behind the wheel, then remembered she'd left a report from the cannery on her desk. She'd go over it tonight after dinner, she decided, and returned to the office floor.

She walked swiftly down the carpeted hall—night-silent now—then stopped dead at the sounds emerging from Adam's office.

"Oh, baby, you are terrific!" Adam's voice, thick with passion, filtered from behind the closed door. "The hottest little bitch in this town!"

Shaken, trembling, Vicky turned and hurried from the building, quickly forgetting the cannery report. Oh, yes, Adam was Daniel's grandchild, she thought bitterly.

All his life she'd been making excuses for Adam. There was no excuse for what was happening behind that door. And yet she knew she could never bring herself to accuse Adam to his face. She was afraid he might do something to destroy his marriage completely.

In August Eleanor went to New York with Jill. Vicky promised her tiny, much-loved granddaughter that there would be another fourth birthday party at Barton Manor when they returned. Waiting with them at the Richmond depot Vicky sensed that Eleanor knew her marriage was on shaky ground. *How much did she know?*

She remembered what Sara had forced herself to ignore in her own marriage. What was it Sara had told her? That she always knew Daniel would come back to her. But those were different times, she judged. How much would Eleanor forgive?

August seemed an endless month, with Eleanor and Jill away, Marc in London. She was delighted when Kara and Derek came up the last week in August to stay with her at Barton Manor. Stephanie and Jeffrey were in Newport. Stephanie was suddenly entranced by the yacht races.

"We wanted you to know first," Kara told Vicky their first night at the house. "Derek and I are adopting a baby. It's all arranged. I talked to Mother about it on the phone. She's furious. 'How do I know what kind of child it'll be? Why do we have to burden ourselves with somebody else's mistake?' What she's saying is that she can't bear the image of herself as a grandmother. She likes to pretend she's still thirty."

"Kara, I think it's wonderful." She pulled Kara into her arms and turned to Derek. "You two will be marvelous parents. That's a very lucky baby you're adopting." Just this year Kara had been told bluntly that she would never conceive because of some bungling of her abortion.

"Of course, we don't know if it's a boy or a girl. The mother expects to give birth any day. But whatever, we'll be happy with it."

"Eleanor will be so pleased," Vicky told her. She said nothing about Eleanor and Adam's shaky marriage. She didn't even discuss it with Marc. As though, she decided, the problem might go away. "She and Jill will be back in time for you to see them. It'll be so good for us all to be together here in the house. It's been so empty since Sara died.''

She'd thought of suggesting Adam move his small family into the house with her. But that would make it even more convenient for Adam to play on the side, she warned herself.

On the same day that Kara and Derek left for Atlanta, Marc and Anita returned to Richmond. Marc called Vicky from a pay telephone to tell her they were back.

"How was London?" she asked, so happy to hear his voice.

"We fought every day of the summer," he said tiredly. "It's the same old story. Anita's bored with Richmond. She wants me to look for a job in San Francisco. Suddenly she thinks she'd love to live out there."

"What did you tell her?" Vicky's heart was pounding. She couldn't bear the thought of not being able to see Marc.

"I told her flatly that I'm getting too old to keep shifting jobs. Hell, I'm forty-five. I can't keep starting up in a new job every two or three years. This is the longest I've stayed in any," he said. "I told her I'm not leaving this one."

"Marc, it would be awful if you weren't here," she whispered.

"I'll be here," he promised. "Vicky, you're what makes my life worth living."

She counted the hours now when they could be together. Sara had been so right. *"You and Marc have something precious. Don't squander it."* She'd die if Anita persuaded Marc to leave the university. Leave Richmond. Please, God, she prayed, don't let that happen.

Chapter Forty

ELEANOR WAS enthralled when Vicky offered to take her and Jill to the synagogue with her for the Hanukkah party.

"She's old enough to enjoy it," Vicky said lovingly.

"We won't mention it to Adam," Eleanor said, her smile evasive. Adam was on another of his trips to the New York office. He wouldn't bother to call Mom—he never did. It was as though her mother didn't exist.

The matter of his mother's faith had never been mentioned between them. Instinct told her it was wiser to be silent about this. Mom was upset that there was all this secrecy. She worried about how Jill would react when she was old enough to ask questions. "*A child should know who she is,*" her mother maintained stubbornly.

Eleanor enjoyed the Hanukkah party. It was nice, she thought, to be out with people. She lived such an isolated life since Kara moved to Atlanta. She wasn't one to make friends easily, she admitted to herself. Kara had brought her into her own social world. She was shy when left on her own. Adam turned down so many invitations to parties that people stopped asking them. He only cared about socializing with those he considered Important People.

Eleanor was so pleased that Doug would be coming home from Paris for Christmas. She'd never met him, but Vicky and Kara had talked about him with such affection. Adam said he was a jerk—

they'd never got along. *"Thank God, he'll run back to his queer friends in Paris after the holidays. He's only coming home because he knows about his inheritance and wants to find out how soon he can collect."*

It was wrong of Adam to be so furious because his mother inherited controlling interest in the company. Everybody knew she'd built it up into one of the top companies in the country. He kept bragging about how he and Frank Leslie had to fight to keep her from making major mistakes. *Not true.*

With the approach of Christmas, Eleanor drove into Richmond to shop for Christmas presents at Thalhimer's. Adam was leaving the shopping in her hands. When he bought himself that flashy new foreign car, she'd inherited his Cadillac convertible. He was still annoyed that his mother had backed her last year in her insistence on learning to drive.

She'd enjoyed her hours in Richmond, she thought in a surge of pleasure when she headed back to Bartonville. Three days later she decided on impulse to take Jill with her when she went into Richmond to shop again, this time at Miller & Rhoads. She reveled in Jill's wide-eyed delight at this new adventure.

"Would you like some ice cream?" she asked Jill tenderly when the shopping was done.

"Un–hunh!" Jill beamed.

"Then we'll go to the tearoom here." She juggled parcels to take one of Jill's tiny hands in hers. "You'll have ice cream, and I'll have chocolate cake and coffee."

"Can I have a piece of your cake, too?" Jill asked, intrigued at the prospect.

"A little piece," Eleanor agreed.

Driving back to Bartonville, Eleanor made up her mind that she would go into Richmond on a regular basis—even if only for some shopping and coffee at Miller & Rhoads tearoom. And Christmas at Barton Manor would be fun, she thought in anticipation—with Doug and Kara and Derek there. Jill would adore Kara and Derek's newly adopted infant.

Sometimes she wished wistfully that she and Adam would have another child. Adam refused to consider it—he always made sure that she didn't get pregnant again. He said there was plenty of time for that later.

Maybe it was just as well they didn't have a second child when he was so cranky much of the time. All at once she was somber. She had to sit Adam down and make him understand he mustn't yell at Jill the way he did sometimes.

She always picked her up to comfort her afterwards. Jill was too little and sweet to be treated that way. She didn't realize her daddy was just in a bad mood—that he wasn't really angry at her.

Vicky loved having family at Barton Manor. She rejoiced in the success that Doug and Paul were finding in Paris. Gary had always marveled at Doug's talent. And now Doug was arranging for Gary's symphony to be played in Paris in the spring. She was delighted that Kara and Derek were so happy with their adopted baby.

As always at holiday seasons, Vicky was painfully conscious of those now missing—Daniel and Sara, Gary and Michael. Thank God for her darling Jill—the first of yet another generation of Bartons. But she continued to worry about Adam and Eleanor's marriage. Since that day she'd discovered him with his secretary, she was fearful of what would happen if Eleanor discovered he was unfaithful.

Sometimes she fought against a sense of guilt that she was so angry with Adam when she herself was having an affair with a married man. But Marc had no marriage, she reminded herself repeatedly. What she and Marc shared was marriage.

Adam was doing well with the company. Even Frank admitted he was as shrewd as his grandfather. Because he was so young, he came up with some ideas that seemed revolutionary—yet there was always a visionary kernel in what he proposed. With Adam involved she felt less compelled to keep a tight rein on the cigarette division of the company. To Adam, of course—and to Frank—the food division was just a sideline. But she meant to build it up to equal importance. Daniel had established Barton cigarettes into an impressive business even before she arrived on the scene. But here was an exhilarating challenge to start from scratch and build a food empire.

Doug and Kara saw their respective parents briefly on their arrival. Lily and Stephanie and their husbands were flying to Palm Beach the day after Christmas for a two-week stay. It was like old times, Vicky thought, when Doug and Kara came home to Barton Manor on school holidays rather than to stay with their parents. Biological parents, she thought with distaste. No more. But already Kara and Derek were proving themselves devoted parents. She was proud of that.

Vicky salvaged only a couple of hours with Marc between Christmas and New Year's, but they talked regularly on the phone.

"God bless Alexander Graham Bell," she laughed on one late evening call. "At least, we can talk on the phone."

Like herself, Marc was concerned that the war in Korea, which most people seemed to be unaware of, continued despite truce negotiations. Again, American soldiers were dying in battle.

Marc was becoming involved in the local Democratic campaign. Both she and Marc had tremendous respect for Adlai Stevenson, but Marc declared there was little chance that he could defeat the very popular Eisenhower. Still, he felt he had to make the effort to fight on behalf of Stevenson.

"Maybe in '56," Marc said hopefully. "So we'll have to wait another four years."

Eleanor tried to tell herself she had too much idle time on her hands—that was why she was always suspecting Adam was fooling around with other women. Each time he returned from one of his trips to New York or to one of the new offices the company had set up in the Midwest, she looked for telltale signs. And was sick at heart when she thought she found them. Yet she couldn't bring herself to confront Adam.

Now she spent endless days in the Richmond department stores. Shopping helped fill the void in her life. She told herself it helped. Once again she considered returning to school. Next September Jill would enter kindergarten. She and her daughter could be in school together, she told herself in an attempt at levity.

On a balmy March day—with the first scent of spring in the air—she drove into Richmond to shop for a birthday present for Adam. She spent hours in the department stores until she finally settled on an expensive smoking jacket. Would he like it, she asked herself anxiously. Adam was so unpredictable.

Now she was in a rush to get home. Della—who no longer lived at the house—had asked if she might leave early today to help with a surprise party for her parents' wedding anniversary. She hurried to the car and slid behind the wheel. She remembered Adam talked about a shortcut to Bartonville. She'd save perhaps fifteen minutes that way.

She watched for signs that Adam mentioned were along the way—tense in her determination to save time. This wasn't right, she realized all at once. She must have missed a turn in the road. *Where was she?*

She drove slowly, watching for signs. The back road was thoroughly deserted. Maybe she ought to stop and ask for directions at a house, she thought. There were no houses in sight—just a stretch of woods on both sides of the road.

She slowed down to a crawl. There was a turnoff just ahead. She'd see where that led. No, it wasn't a road, she realized in disappointment. Some local lovers' lane. Then her heart began to pound.

The flashy foreign car parked just ahead had to be Adam's. There was none other like it in Bartonville or Richmond. Was he having trouble with the car and turned off in here to fix it? Yet while she tried to tell herself it was something like that, she felt ugly suspicions welling in her.

She stopped the car, pushed open the door, and approached the car that had to be Adam's. Then she heard Adam's voice drifting through an open window.

"Jesus, Melanie, don't you ever get enough?"

She spun around and hurried back to her car—dizzy with shock, her mind in chaos. Neither Adam nor that girl called Melanie was aware of her presence. Now she remembered the endless signs through the years that she had forced herself to ignore. And he came from all those women into her bed. *No more.*

She reversed her direction and found the missed turnoff to Bartonville. Always a cautious driver, today she sped, impatient to be home. She'd take Jill, and they'd wait at the Richmond depot for the next train to New York.

When she arrived at the house, Della greeted her with a relieved smile.

"I fed Jill her supper. She's listening to her records now," Della reported.

"You run along, Della. Have a wonderful time." She was too distraught to tell Della what was happening. Adam would have to tell her tomorrow.

She went into the nursery, reached to hug Jill with sudden urgency. She should have left Adam long ago, she reproached herself. He was a rotten father. It was better to have no father than a bad one.

"You listen to *Peter and the Wolf* now," she told Jill, struggling to sound calm. Let them be out of the house before Adam returned. But then, she reminded herself bitterly, Adam rarely appeared before seven or eight anyway. She'd send Myra home. There'd only be Adam for dinner tonight.

Fighting for composure she went to the kitchen.

"Myra, have you started dinner yet?"

"No ma'am. I'm making steaks tonight. I thought I'd best wait till Mr. Adam came or called to give us a time." *Did Myra know? Did everybody know?*

"We'll be going up to Barton Manor for dinner," she fabricated. "You run along home, Myra."

Eleanor went to their bedroom. She pulled down one valise from a closet. Pack just what she and Jill would need, she ordered herself. Do it quickly.

When the valise was half-filled, she went into the nursery, chose things that Jill particularly liked, carried them into the bedroom, and put them into the valise. Then she remembered Jill's stuffed giraffe and went to retrieve it. She trudged with the valise to the car, lifted it into the trunk.

From the house came the melodic strains of *Peter and the Wolf*. When Jill listened to her records, she was aware of nothing else. What was she to tell Jill? She would tell her that they were going to visit Grandma. She clutched at this explanation, since Jill adored Mom. She still clung to "Nana" for Vicky—her babyhood interpretation of "Grandma."

Eleanor returned to the house, went into the bedroom to take down a warm winter coat. March in New York could be bitter cold.

She stopped dead at the sound of a car pulling up before the house. She glanced out the window. Adam was emerging from his car. Did it still reek of whatever perfume "Melanie" wore, she tormented herself.

"Eleanor—" he called from the hallway. "Tell Myra to put dinner on the table." He sounded in rare high spirits. "I decided to leave the office early for a change." He paused. "Eleanor?" He paused at the entrance to their bedroom.

"I saw you with that girl." She spun around to face him, pale and defiant.

"What girl?" he hedged. "What the hell are you talking about?"

"I tried to take the shortcut home from Richmond. I got lost. I saw you there with that girl you called 'Melanie.' You were too busy to notice me," she said scornfully. She was trembling again. "I'm leaving you, Adam. I want a divorce."

"You leave me, and you won't get one red cent!" he yelled. "Not alimony! Not child support!"

"All I want is to be free of you!" she lashed back, heartsick and disillusioned. Let him keep his money—Mom would help her raise Jill. Somehow, they'd survive. "I want a divorce," she repeated.

"I get the divorce," he said after a moment. "Either I get it and you sign all the papers before you leave—or I'll fight for custody. And I'll get it," he said with a slow, triumphant smile. "No Bartonville judge will deny me my child."

She went ashen at the prospect of a custody battle. *She'd never let Adam have Jill.*

"What do I have to sign?" she asked shakily.

"Papers agreeing to a divorce, with no alimony or child support. I'll give you trainfare to New York—not another cent."

"Where are the papers?" She struggled not to fall apart. Not now. She had to get away from Adam.

"I'll phone Clark. He'll draw them up." He glanced at his watch. "There's a ten-twenty train out of Richmond. You'll be on it."

Adam charged from the room to phone Clark from the living room phone. Eleanor sat on the edge of the bed. Clark and Lily had never liked her, she remembered. She'd heard them call her a stupid New York liberal. Vicky was in Roanoke. She couldn't talk to her, anyway—not tonight, not feeling this way. Vicky would never believe how rotten Adam was.

Eleanor heard Adam arguing with Clark.

"I don't give a shit what you have to do, Clark! Just do it! Get the papers over here, and let me be rid of the little bitch. Remember, she agrees to never ask for a cent for either herself or the kid." There was a moment's pause. "All right, I'll come over there." Eleanor heard him stalk down the hall. The front door was opened, then slammed shut. She heard the car start up. Adam was meeting Clark at his office, she guessed.

She went into the nursery. Jill was beginning to yawn. She should have had her bath by now, be ready for bed.

"Lie down on your bed, and Mommie will read you a story," she said tenderly.

"Mommie, I'm not in my nightgown," Jill reproached. "You always read to me in my nightgown."

"Such a creature of habit," she crooned. "I've got a surprise for you, darling.'' She struggled to sound festive. ''We're going to take a train tonight. We're going to visit Grandma. But first, you have to take a nap.''

''After my story,'' Jill stipulated, but her eyes were wide with excitement. She wasn't likely to sleep now.

Despite her anticipation about the unexpected trip, Jill's eyes began to close by the time Eleanor was halfway through the story. She shut the book, switched off the lamp, and sat by Jill's bed. No doubt in her mind that Adam would be back with the papers in time for her to board the 10:20 PM for New York. He would be glad to have them out of his life.

When Adam had not returned in an hour—with every minute seeming endless, Eleanor went out to the kitchen to make herself a cup of coffee, reached into the drawer where she kept a supply of cigarettes. She kept telling herself she was going to stop smoking, but this wasn't the time.

At shortly past nine, the ashtray beside her littered with butts now, Eleanor snapped to attention. Two cars were pulling into the driveway. Exhausted from tension, she rose to her feet. Through a window she saw Adam approaching with Clark and a woman. She waited for them to come into the house.

''The papers are ready,'' Adam said tersely as he strode into the room, followed by Clark and the woman who'd arrived with them. Clark gave Eleanor a cold nod of greeting. The woman seemed annoyed at being here. ''Clark's secretary is a notary. She'll witness our signing.''

Clark thrust aside his topcoat, reached into an attaché case for a sheaf of papers, and spread them out on the coffee table.

''Sign each at the 'X,' '' he instructed Eleanor. ''There's a set for you.''

Without an effort to read the contents, Eleanor signed each line that Clark indicated. The secretary pulled out her notary seal and stood by.

''There'll be no need for you to appear in court,'' Clark told Eleanor, his eyes avoiding hers. ''I'll handle everything at this end.''

Eleanor watched the secretary notarize the copies. Her eyes strayed to the grandfather clock that sat across the room.

''You're all set.'' Clark took the papers from his secretary, folded over one set, and handed it to Eleanor. "Olivia will drive you to the depot."

"Thank you." Eleanor managed a smile for the secretary. Adam had dropped into a chair and was making a pretense of reading a copy of the papers. "I'll wake up Jill and get my things."

When she emerged from the nursery with Jill still half-asleep in her arms and struggling to manage her valise, Olivia came forward.

"Let me take your bag," she said gently, her eyes compassionate.

The two men were talking in low tones in the living room. It was obvious that there were to be no goodbyes. Silently she followed Olivia out to her car. Later Adam would drive Clark home, she interpreted. *He hadn't even bothered to kiss Jill goodbye.*

Eleanor laid Jill across the rear seat and climbed in beside Olivia.

"They're both bastards, you know," Olivia said as she started up the car. "You're well out of this town."

Chapter Forty-one

VICKY DROVE directly to the Bartonville offices rather than to Barton Manor when she arrived in town after a three-day tour of several of their farm tracts. She was exhilarated by the reports she'd received. The produce division was already showing a small profit.

She parked and hurried into the building, still fighting yawns because she'd arisen at five AM in order to be at the office at her usual time. It wasn't quite eight AM, she noticed with satisfaction. She relished that brief period at her desk before the others began to arrive. It gave her time to organize her thoughts, focus on the day's schedule.

While she skimmed the mail that had arrived in her absence, she heard someone striding down the hall. She looked up in surprise when Adam stalked into her office. In the last year he'd become the last of the executives to arrive, though she conceded he usually stayed later than the others. But ever present in a corner of her mind was the memory of that evening she'd returned to discover him in a passionate fling with his secretary.

"You won't believe what's happened," he said grimly. "I'm still dazed—"

"What is it, Adam?" she asked in soaring alarm. Her first thought, *"Something's happened to Jill!"*

"Eleanor—" He was seething now. "She's walked out on me. She took the kid and left. No warning—nothing. I got home last night—and they were gone. All that was left was that stupid note."

"What did she say?" Vicky felt sick with shock. She should have intervened. She shouldn't have let this happen.

"Just that she'd had enough of this town. She told me to divorce her—it was all over for us."

"Where's the note?" Eleanor had found out about those other women, she thought in pain. That had been inevitable.

"I went straight to Clark. I gave it to him. He'll need it in filing for the divorce."

"Adam, this is ridiculous." She was trembling now. "Call Eleanor's mother in New York. She must have gone there."

"Her mother moved to some place in California two months ago." He appeared surprised. "Didn't she tell you? Her mother said she was sick of New York winters."

"Find out where she is! Call, Adam!" Her voice was strident in her anxiety.

"Call where?" Adam just looked injured. "Don't you think I thought of calling her mother? But it's just as well." He made a show of being philosophical. "The marriage was dead even before Jill was born. You know how strange Eleanor can be sometimes."

"I know nothing of the sort," Vicky shot back. "And what about Jill?"

"I thought about fighting for custody," he said slowly. "I mean, if I ever catch up with Eleanor. But it wouldn't be fair to try to take Jill away from her mother. It would be bad for the kid."

"You and Eleanor could make a fresh start." Vicky bit back the recriminations that rose in her throat. *Let him stop chasing after other women. Stop belittling Eleanor.*

"It's over, Mother." His eyes went opaque. "I'd better get to work. I need some sales figures to take into the meeting this morning." He turned and strode from her office.

Vicky stared into space, her mind in chaos. She mustn't lose touch with Eleanor and Jill. They were both so dear to her. It was obvious Adam would do nothing to find them. *She* would.

Eleanor sat at the kitchen table with her mother. Jill was asleep in the bedroom. It had been an awful shock to Mom, she thought guiltily—to wake her up in the middle of the night that way. But nothing fazed Mom. Mom had taken one long look at her, knew she was overwrought and exhausted. *"Sleep, my darling, we'll talk in the morning."*

"Ellie, you shouldn't have signed those papers," her mother scolded, pouring a second cup of coffee for them. She'd called the shop, said she'd be in two hours late this morning. "You have a right to alimony and child support."

"I don't want anything from Adam." Eleanor reached for another cigarette. "Besides, if I didn't sign, he threatened to fight for custody of Jill. I couldn't let that happen."

"He doesn't give a damn about his child. I saw that," Rebecca said with contempt. "Ellie, when are you going to stop smoking?" she chided when Eleanor began to cough. "Young as you are, you're getting a real cigarette cough."

"I'm going to stop," she promised.

"You only learned to smoke to impress that bastard." Rebecca's face tightened with anger. "So he'd think you were so sophisticated."

"I'll find a job, Mom," Eleanor said determinedly. "Jill and I won't be a burden on you."

"You'll never be a burden to me. You and Jill are my life." Tears blurred Rebecca's eyes. "We'll raise her together. She'll never miss her father. We'll give her all the love she needs and more."

Six days after Adam told her that Eleanor had left him, Vicky received a brief letter from her.

"Dear Vicky, forgive me for taking Jill away from you. We couldn't stay with Adam any longer. We both love you. Eleanor."

There was no return address. But the postmark was Chicago. That was little to go on, she warned herself, but it was something. Saying nothing to Adam, she consulted a private investigator in Richmond. He made contact with a Chicago associate. But after long weeks of searching, the Chicago investigator came up with nothing.

Vicky was furious when she heard in June that Adam was seeing a Richmond girl. Lisa Feinberg reported this to her.

"She's Rowena Bristow, the congressman's daughter," Lisa told her. "Beautiful in an icy fashion. They're a stunning-looking couple," she admitted. "I suppose there's no chance of his reconciling with Eleanor?" Lisa knew how close she was with Eleanor, how much she adored Jill.

"No chance." Only three months since Eleanor left him and already he was publicly involved with somebody else. Was Eleanor all right? Did Jill miss her Nana, she wondered wistfully.

Not until November did Adam tell her he was seeing Rowena Bristow, and that they were serious.

"Is your divorce final?" Vicky asked tartly.

"No." Adam shrugged, unperturbed by this. "But it will be in March. Ronnie will be quite an addition to the family." She saw the glint of triumph in his eyes. "We'll have our own congressman in Washington to fight for us. Of course, what Virginia congressman would dare fight against the tobacco lobby?"

A month later Rowena's parents announced her engagement to Adam. There was to be a big church wedding in Richmond, preceded by an engagement party at the Commonwealth Club and a series of bridal showers. No doubt, the Commonwealth Club would be upset to discover that the bridegroom was half–Jewish. Jews were not welcome in their hallowed halls.

Shortly before Christmas the third board of directors meeting was scheduled at Barton Tobacco. Vicky insisted that the meeting—a charade—be held in the evening so as not to interrupt the day's business. Several days earlier she'd studied the reports that came from both Frank's office and Adam's division and was startled by the figures she saw. The afternoon before the meeting she discussed this with Marc at the cottage.

"I'm afraid I'm letting myself be carried away by the new division," she confessed worriedly. "I look at the annual reports, together with the projected sales figures for the industry as a whole, and I can't believe what I see. For the first time in nineteen years, Marc, cigarette sales are declining. Not just with us—the industry in general. I should have seen this happening."

"Vicky, relax," Marc urged. "You're enjoying the new division. You're making great strides with it. Sooner or later, the annual increases in cigarette sales had to level off. They've been jumping up every year since the war began. There are just so many people in the world who smoke."

"Daniel always used to say, you can't stand still—you have to keep moving. We need a fresh approach. I think it's time for us to move onto the TV bandwagon. I'll talk with the ad agency about our allotting some of our budget to TV."

"The company isn't losing money," Marc said.

"No," she conceded. "Profits are still good."

"Let Adam and the others worry about what's affecting sales," he said humorously. "You know you're getting a tremendous kick out of building the food division."

"I'd better get back to the office," she said with reluctance. "I have some calls to make before the meeting."

"Remember to go home for dinner," he teased.

"Zachary will bring me a tray," she promised. "Oh, God, I loathe these family board meetings. Lily and Stephanie are so venomous— and so stupid with their questions. It's all such a farce."

Adam dictated a last letter to his new secretary—the second since Carla—and then headed for the conference room. It galled him to see his mother sitting in the chair at the head of the table. *He* belonged there. She was paying little attention these days to what was happening to the industry. All she seemed to care about was that stupid food division.

But that was good, he told himself. His smile ironic. The less his mother knew about the craziness that was going on, the better. All those bastards claiming that cigarettes caused heart disease and lung cancer.

They were a bunch of publicity seekers—like that crazy surgery professor talking in Chicago last month to the American College of Surgeons, saying the cigarette companies ought to put up the money for research to find out how much at risk cigarette smokers were. His philanthropic mother just might want to lay out the money for it! *Fuck that.*

Before he opened the door to the conference room he could hear Lily complaining about what she'd read so far in the report—supplied to each director attending the meeting. Just Lily and Stephanie and their husbands, plus his mother and himself. Kara never bothered to come up. Doug was in Paris.

"Adam, what is this all about?" Stephanie demanded, her voice strident. "Are we losing money?"

"We're not losing money," he said calmly. "Sales just aren't going up the way they've done in the past years." He paused. "They've only dropped about one percent."

"What are we doing wrong?" Lily asked. "If my father were alive, this wouldn't be happening."

"Don't push it when my mother arrives," Adam warned. "Let her keep her nose buried in the food division. Some weird things are happening in the industry, but they'll all be smoothed out. The leaders of all the big companies are arranging to work together on this." He'd represent Barton. "Just don't ask questions about the sales figures in my mother's presence," he stressed.

Moments later Vicky arrived. She seated herself at the head of the table and called the meeting to order. Surprising Adam, she herself brought up the question of why cigarette sales were dropping.

"My father-in-law always said, 'When sales drop off, look to your advertising.' I'm suggesting we enlarge our advertising budget, allocate money for television. That'll be the thrust of our coming campaign. Let's face it," she said with a smile, and Adam silently mouthed her words, "there's little difference between one cigarette and another. It's the advertising that makes the difference."

Vicky was saddened when Simone wrote early in April that Henri had died. Simone wrote that she intended to remain on their small farm. Vicky worried about her. Simone was seventy-four and had worked hard all her life. Would she be all right alone on her farm? Perhaps she could persuade Simone to come to Bartonville. Whatever she needed would be provided.

With flights to Paris on a regular basis, why not fly over and see Simone, try to talk her into coming to Barton Manor? Those brief years in Paris had bound them together forever, she thought nostalgically. Simone had been so good to her.

Envisioning Simone's grief, Vicky prepared to leave immediately. The business could survive for a week without her, she told herself. Hearing her plans, Marc arranged to be in New York on business. She and Marc could salvage three days together before she would have to return to Bartonville. He'd meet her in New York at the airport.

"I'm terrified at the prospect of flying across the ocean," she admitted laughingly. "Twice! But the plane won't dare crash when you'll be waiting for me at the airport on the return trip."

Vicky reserved a suite at the Crillon for Simone and herself. She hoped that nostalgia would divert Simone for a while from her grief. It was a traumatic reunion for both women. They'd not seen each other, Vicky realized with a sense of disbelief, since Gary and she had come to Paris with the children in '29. Twenty-five years ago!

Outwardly Simone had aged beyond her years, but she insisted she was well and strong.

"But you, my love," Simone told her with pride. "You look a beautiful thirty-five."

Ever amused at the change in their status, Simone remained with Vicky at the Crillon for four days. Then she insisted she must return to the farm.

"My neighbors care for the animals, yes," she nodded, "but they miss me. They're like my children. And you'll be seeing Doug and his friend." Simone knew that she had spoken with Doug on the phone and was looking forward to seeing him. "You'll be fine. But don't stay away so long this time," she urged. "We live in such a wonderful world—when you can cross an ocean in a dozen hours."

Seeing Doug and Paul brought back poignant memories—Doug as a child, spending so much of his time at Barton Manor; Doug pleading with Gary to teach him to play the piano, too; Doug playing Gary's symphony for her at the cottage piano days after Gary's suicide.

But there was joy, too, in being with Doug and Paul. They were so happy about their success in musical theater. They brought her to the theater where the new musical they'd written was in production. She sat in the theater between them with tears of pleasure and pride welling in her eyes. Gary had been so right when he'd marveled at Doug's talent.

"I had a nutty hope that Mother and Dad would come over for the opening night," Doug said with a twisted smile. "They've got something else scheduled. Wouldn't you think I'd know that by now? But you and Grandma always came through for me," he said softly. "When I was a kid, I used to envy Michael for having you for a mother."

After the rehearsal Vicky took Doug and Paul to dinner at the Ritz. She had lunch with them the following day, and met Paul's parents that evening at dinner. She was touched by their gratitude at the Barton hospitality shown Paul during the war.

The following morning Doug and Paul took her to Orly and stayed with her until she boarded her plane. And in New York, she thought with joyous anticipation, Marc would be waiting for her at the airport. They would have three precious days together.

In New York Vicky and Marc played at being tourists. On their last day Marc decided they must go to the Metropolitan Museum. He was eager to see the two hundred paintings by James McNeill Whistler, John Singer Sargent, and Mary Cassatt that were on loan. They enjoyed strolling through the elegant halls of the museum, so rich in masterpieces. They felt lighthearted, in a special world of their own.

Then all at once Marc's hand clutched her elbow. She felt the sudden tension in him.

"Let's go back the other way," he whispered. "Quickly."

Not until they'd moved in silence down the long staircase, crossed the rotunda, and were out in the crisp April afternoon did Marc explain this sudden exodus.

"I'm sure Anne and Eric Walters were headed in our direction." His voice was troubled. "I had no idea they were coming to the city."

"Did they see us?" Vicky's throat tightened in alarm. Anne and Eric Walters were Anita's sycophants, always fawning over her.

"I hope to God they didn't. If they did," he said in rising apprehension, "they can't wait to tell Anita."

Chapter Forty-two

VICKY RETURNED to Bartonville five hours ahead of Marc. They'd never dared travel on the same train. Had Anne and Eric Walters seen them? She remembered with anguish that Lisa had referred to Anne Walters as "Mrs. Winchell." *Would they tell Anita?* The question ricocheted in her brain while she waited to hear from Marc.

Late in the evening Marc called her from a phone booth.

"No one's said anything to Anita," he comforted her. "If they had, she would have been screaming the minute I walked into the house. Eric and Anne didn't see us."

"Are they back from New York?" Vicky was still uneasy.

"I don't know." He was apologetic. "But don't panic, Vicky. For the moment everything looks fine." He was trying so hard to be reassuring.

"We've always been careful. Or so we thought," she amended ruefully. One little chance encounter could destroy something so precious. But didn't the whole world live only a moment from tragedy? Nobody knew what lay just around the corner.

"Don't think about it," Marc tried again. "A thousand to one we saw them and left in time. Everything's going to be all right."

Vicky avoided going to Marc's cottage. They talked on the phone. Then a week after they'd returned from New York, Marc reported that the Walters were in Richmond.

"They've been home for three days." Marc's voice telegraphed his relief. "Anita had lunch with Anne and a couple of other women yesterday. We're home free, my love."

Still, Vicky was apprehensive about meeting Marc at the cottage. Not until they'd been back home almost two weeks did he convince her they'd been worried for nothing. The reunion was poignantly sweet. Yet she tensed at any unexpected sound outdoors.

"Marc, what was that?" she asked in sudden alarm while he pulled up the zipper at the back of her dress.

"A car drove by. It happens, even on this road," he joshed. He'd chosen this cottage out of several shown to him because the road was so lightly traveled. He always left his car in the driveway so that Vicky's could be concealed in the garage.

"Honey, relax." He kissed the nape of her neck, his arms wrapped about her waist. "I can't tell you how much I've missed you these last days."

In the morning Marc phoned her at the office. Instantly she became worried. Marc never called her here.

"We need to talk," he said guardedly. "Not at the cottage. Can you meet me for coffee late in the afternoon?"

"I can get away from the office, yes." Why couldn't they meet at the cottage? *What had happened?* "Where shall I meet you?"

"There's a small restaurant about a mile out of Richmond, on the way to Bartonville. Between the gas station and that new supermarket."

"Bradley's," she said, recalling a rather shabby cafe frequented by drivers passing through the area. "What time?"

"Around four?" The constraint in his voice unnerved her.

"I'll be there," she promised.

Marc was sitting at a rear table in the sparsely occupied cafe when she walked inside. She hurried to join him.

"Sorry to drag you to a fleabag like this," he apologized. "But it seemed the best site."

"Marc, what's happened?" He looked exhausted, she thought.

"Anita knows," he said. "She had me followed last night. She knows we were together at the cottage. She knows about New York."

"Oh, Marc—" She felt dizzy with shock.

"She's given me an ultimatum," he continued in anguish. "I must give up my job at the university and move with her to London. Her 'civilized city,' " he added bitterly. "Either I go with her to London, or she'll divorce me and name you as the 'other woman.' I can't let that happen to you, Vicky.''

''Marc, this is unreal,'' she whispered.

A waitress sauntered over. They ordered, sat in silent frustration until she returned with their coffee and danish, and left them.

''I have to do whatever she asks,'' Marc said.

''When?'' Vicky's eyes clung to his face. Marc had helped her through so much. And now he would disappear from her life.

''School is over in two weeks. We'll leave immediately after that. I'm not likely to find a teaching job in London. I'll be Anita's devoted husband, catering to her whims.'' His anguish reached out to Vicky. ''I'll despise every moment of my life.''

''We won't see each other after today.'' The realization sent a chill through her.

''Vicky, if the time ever comes when I'm free—and if you're free—I'll come back to you. That hope will help me survive.''

Vicky sensed that Anita said nothing to the others about why she and Marc were moving to London. Hadn't she talked incessantly the last two years about wanting to live there? Intuitively, Vicky guessed that Anita had offered some excuse to Anne and Eric about Marc's being with her at the Metropolitan that day. Anita could not bear to have anyone believe her husband had been involved with another woman.

At a synagogue affair in early June, Vicky talked with Lisa Feinberg about Anita and Marc's leaving.

''I'm so sorry they've left,'' Vicky said, her smile wistful. ''Sometimes Anita was trying, but she and Marc lent something special to our little circle.'' Her life seemed empty, she thought in private anguish. In such a short span of time she'd lost Sara, Jill, and now Marc.

''People seem to move about more these days.'' Lisa sighed. ''I hate making friends and having them move away. Oh, have you heard anything of Eleanor and Jill?'' she asked sympathetically.

''Not a word since that short letter a year ago. I miss them.''

''In less than three weeks you'll have a new daughter-in-law.'' Lisa tried to sound encouraging. Adam's marriage to Ronnie Bristow would take place at the end of the month. ''But I know how attached you were to Eleanor and Jill.''

''I hardly know Ronnie.'' Vicky was somber. ''She's not the kind one gets to know easily,'' she admitted.

She gathered that Ronnie's mother had been giving every moment of her time for months now to wedding preparations. Thank God, nothing was required of her. She sensed that Ronnie's family accepted Adam. For an Old Family rich in tradition but hardly wealthy in cash, Adam was a good catch. She doubted, though, that they were enthralled with their daughter's Jewish mother-in-law.

Ten days before the wedding Adam approached Vicky about his future living arrangements.

"I can hardly bring Ronnie to live in the cottage on a permanent basis," he said, turning on his potent charm. "I mean, it's all right for a while—when we first come back from our honeymoon." They would be taking a three-week trip to London and Paris—the wedding present Adam had requested.

"If you'd like to build on Barton Manor property, that'll be fine." She thought she was anticipating him. With his trust fund, his inheritance from Sara, and his growing salary, he could certainly afford an impressive house. Appearances had always been important to Adam.

"I thought perhaps we could move into Barton Manor," he said ingratiatingly. "Ronnie could relieve you of the drudgery of running the household. And she'll be a wonderful hostess. It's time we started to entertain. I don't mean local people." His smile was disparaging. "After all, my father-in-law will be a congressman. It's important for the business—when industry bills come up—to know the Washington crowd."

"We'll talk about that in a year," Vicky stipulated after a moment, startled by the suggestion. She wasn't prepared to relinquish her role as head of Barton Manor. Nor was she ready to live under the same roof with Adam's second wife. Eleanor she would have welcomed. "There's something that I want to discuss with you, Adam. I was very disturbed about a news report I heard on the radio last night."

"What's that?" Adam was annoyed with her but trying to conceal it, she sensed.

"I know, of course, about the new tobacco industry institute." She saw Adam's glint of astonishment. Did he think she was turning the business over entirely to him and Frank and what they loved to call "the team"? "I'm aware that you're active on our behalf." She skimmed every report of substance that left the Bartonville office— no matter how wrapped up she was in Barton Foods. "But this commentator talked about an article in the *New York Times* last week.

Adam, that article said the American Cancer Society warned that some cancer researchers and surgeons believe cigarette smoking could lead to cancer!''

"I read the article. I read the *New York Times* and the *Washington Post* every day. Frank read it. Like everybody in the business, we were upset. We talked on the phone for over an hour. It was a totally biased and unscientifically prepared article. The truth came out. It was the usual crackpots, looking for publicity.''

"I remember your grandfather," Vicky said seriously. "He was a heavy smoker—and he died of lung cancer. Your grandmother—who spent most of her life trying to avoid his cigarette smoke—died of emphysema.''

"Mother, now you're trying to blame cigarettes for emphysema, too?" Adam chuckled. "Hundreds of top doctors blame lung cancer and emphysema on air pollution. They've made thorough, scientific studies. The same thing is happening in England," he pointed out in triumph. "Lung cancer has spiraled there in the past few years. But British authorities have come right out and laid the blame where it belongs. On pollution. We can't be carried away by hysteria that's based on ridiculous assumptions. If we do something about the pollution in this country—and in England—lung-related diseases will drop way down.''

"Frank believes this, too?" Vicky was ambivalent.

"He's furious at the way the press is spreading these malicious reports. He says the doctors and scientists that are making these accusations ought to be tarred and feathered. That's why the new tobacco institute is so important. It'll do thorough and unbiased research.''

"I want to know what's happening," Vicky instructed him. "It would be a terrible thing to discover we were dealing with death.'' She felt a sudden coldness close in about her. She remembered Daniel's painful last years. Oh, she wished Marc were here so she could talk with him about this. She missed him in so many ways.

"Frank and I will keep you posted," Adam promised. "Any major development arises, you'll hear it fast.''

Vicky was relieved when Adam and Ronnie's wedding was over. She was uncomfortable at seeing her son married in an Episcopalian church. This new marriage emphasized her feeling of loss that Eleanor and Jill were no longer a part of her life.

As always, Vicky sought solace in work. She spent little time at Barton Manor in the months ahead. She was constantly on the road. She was determined to expand the food division of the company, to make it show an impressive profit. She found a rich satisfaction in walking through segments of their vast acres of farmland as harvest times approached. There was something reassuring in the rebirth of the fields each year, she thought—a kind of Divine promise of the continuity of life, of lasting treasures.

On Adam and Ronnie's first wedding anniversary Vicky agreed to his renewed request that they move into Barton Manor. After all, she forced herself to acknowledge, Adam would one day own the house. Through Kara she'd learned that Lily and Stephanie looked upon Adam with favor now that he was the son-in-law of Congressman Bristow. She wished that she could look with favor on Adam's new wife. She found Ronnie cold, remote, and slightly supercilious.

Almost immediately, though, Vicky regretted having agreed to Adam and Ronnie's move into Barton Manor. Every week, it seemed to her, they were entertaining. She made it clear immediately that she had no time to share in this endless socializing. Food and liquor bills—which came to her—were staggering.

Sensing that Lula Mae and Effie were resentful of the added demands—plus Ronnie's arrogant attitude—Vicky informed Adam that if he and his wife insisted on entertaining, then they must arrange for additional help for such occasions. Lula Mae and Effie were not to take on these extra duties. Mattie Lou was now Vicky's personal maid and traveled with her—and was delighted with this arrangement.

Vicky was unhappy with the feeling of estrangement that was developing between Adam and herself. She was astonished when Adam and Ronnie decided to occupy separate bedrooms. But it seemed sufficient to Adam to have Ronnie serve as his hostess.

Without realizing it, Vicky began retreating into a separate world that revolved around the food division of the company. She was not concerned about the cigarette division. The drop in sales that had appeared in 1953 had disappeared by 1955. Sales were soaring to new heights.

But lying in bed in the strange hotel suites that were becoming more home to her than Barton Manor, Vicky wondered about the two most dear to her life—Jill and Marc—and prayed that they were all right.

Rebecca Kahn took the day off from work to prepare for Jill's ninth birthday. This August heat of 1956 was a scorcher, she thought, while she preheated the oven. The chocolate layers for the all-chocolate cake—as ordered by Jill—were ready to go in. While they were baking, she'd prepare the chocolate cream filling and the frosting. Her eyes lighted in affectionate humor as she envisioned Jill's momentary disappointment when she saw the white icing—but she'd break into her delicious, bubbly laughter when she discovered the icing was white chocolate.

She checked the beef stew, and nodded in approval. It would be ready by the time Eleanor picked up Jill at the day camp on her way home from work. Eleanor shouldn't have gone in to work today, she fretted. She'd been up half the night again with that awful cough. And she would never stop smoking.

She wouldn't say anything tonight because nothing must spoil Jill's birthday, but tomorrow she would insist that Eleanor go to see Dr. Evans. That cough just kept hanging on. It worried her.

Setting the table, bringing out Jill's birthday present, she felt a rush of love for her only grandchild. They'd managed all right between them, she thought with satisfaction. Right away Eleanor had found a job as a receptionist in a law office. She was bright and conscientious, and they appreciated her. And Jill was happy.

Those first months had been hard on her, poor baby, Rebecca recalled. To go from living in a lovely private house surrounded by woods—with her own bedroom and bath—to living in a one-bedroom apartment with her mother and grandmother was a drastic switch. Jill never once asked about her father, though for weeks she'd asked wistfully about "Nana."

Vicky was a fine woman, Rebecca thought. Eleanor had been afraid to get in touch with her, lest Adam change his mind and decide he wanted Jill. He'd worm her whereabouts out of his mother, Eleanor feared. Eleanor had given a letter to a neighbor who'd been going to Chicago and asked her to mail it from there. She said she had to let Vicky know she and Jill were all right—and that they loved her.

What a cross for Vicky to bear—to have a son like Adam. But like most mothers with sons like that, she probably made all kinds of excuses for his behavior. Vicky Barton deserved better. Eleanor said everybody had loved the son who died in the war.

Her face lighted when at last she heard Eleanor and Jill's voices in the hall. They might not have the Barton millions, she thought with pride, but they had such love in this apartment.

Their small birthday party was a real success, Rebecca told herself when at last Jill solemnly cut the white chocolate frosted cake.

"Grandma, I never knew chocolate could be white," she giggled. "You fooled me!"

"You like your new dress?" Eleanor asked, yearning for reassurance.

"It's beautiful, Mommie. Can I wear it tomorrow?"

Finally Rebecca insisted it was time for Jill to go to sleep. She and Jill slept in the twin beds in the bedroom, while Eleanor slept on the studio couch in the living room. Eleanor looked just exhausted. She couldn't go to bed until they were in the bedroom.

"Go wash your hands and face and brush your teeth," Rebecca ordered. "We all have to be up at seven AM."

"All right." Jill sighed exaggeratedly, kissed her mother, then her grandmother, and walked with her compulsively swift steps into the bedroom.

Together Rebecca and Eleanor cleared the table, and did the dishes. Not until Rebecca was sure that Jill was asleep did she venture to talk to Eleanor about her cough.

"I saw Dr. Evans," Eleanor confessed. "Today. I took off from work."

"What did he say?" Rebecca was sharp in her anxiety.

"He wants me to go into the hospital for tests," Eleanor said uneasily. "I think my health insurance will cover it—"

"When does he want you to go in?" Rebecca tried to appear calm.

"As soon as he can make arrangements," Eleanor told her. "Mom, I'm scared—"

"You're going to be fine," Rebecca insisted, holding out her arms. "The tests will tell Dr. Evans how to treat that rotten cough. You'll be well in no time."

Three days later Eleanor was admitted to the hospital. Rebecca fought to keep up a brave front. For both Eleanor and Jill this was necessary. But when the test results came through, the report was devastating.

"I'm sorry," Dr. Evans told Rebecca compassionately. "Eleanor has lung cancer. Immediate surgery is necessary."

"Those damn cigarettes!" Rebecca's voice soared in a mixture of anguish and rage. "How many people have to die before the government does something about them?"

Chapter Forty-three

A T THE 1956 annual board meeting—held as usual in December—Vicky realized with a shock that Adam had entered a new relationship with his aunts and their husbands. As long as she could remember, there had been only hostility between them. Now it was obvious that both sides had decided a friendly relationship was to their mutual advantage.

At thirty-one Adam was being recognized as the Boy Wonder of the cigarette industry. He had promoted their new king-sized cigarette into a top slot. The company's public relations firm was focusing on Adam rather than her, for which Vicky was grateful. She'd never been comfortable with being in the limelight.

When Adam went to Washington to confer with the tobacco lobby, he took Ronnie with him. They stayed at her father's D.C. townhouse, and entertained lavishly there. Adam used his father-in-law's influence at every possible turn, Vicky sensed.

She could understand that Lily and Stephanie relished Adam's new connections. However, she was curious that Adam was cultivating his relationship with his aunts and their husbands. True, Clark continued as mayor of Bartonville—but that was a minor position. There was no doubt in her mind that Adam saw some advantage to the new warmth between himself and his aunts.

At this year's board meeting Vicky relinquished her chair at the head of the table so that Adam could report on the status of their cigarette division. The others—including Adam—were bored with her own report on their growing food division, she comprehended. They couldn't see its potential. Kara never bothered to come up for the board meetings, though she and Derek and tiny Sara—named for Kara's grandmother—regularly came up from Atlanta to visit Vicky. Now they stayed in Richmond at a hotel rather than at Barton Manor or at Kara's parents' home. Lily abhorred the image of herself as a grandmother.

Vicky's mind wandered as Adam talked enthusiastically about the state of the industry and current profits. She remembered Kara's reply when she'd called about their coming up for the traditional Thanksgiving dinner.

"Come down to have dinner with us," Kara had urged. "Barton Manor doesn't feel like home anymore with Adam and Ronnie taking over. I feel like an outsider."

Not until Adam startled her with the announcement that he and Ronnie were going to her parents' plantation for Thanksgiving dinner did she decide to go down to Atlanta. She would have been alone at Barton Manor. On the train to Atlanta she'd thought nostalgically about the last real Thanksgiving at Barton Manor—the Thanksgiving before Eleanor and Jill had disappeared from her life.

Where were Jill and Eleanor now, she asked herself wistfully. Where was Marc? Their absences created such a void in her life. Through the years, she had intermittently consulted with private investigators, but they had had no luck finding Jill and Eleanor.

"Adam, when are we going to go public?" Lily demanded loudly, as she did at every board meeting.

"We can't," Adam reminded, clearly displeased at this restraint. "We're the only major tobacco company that hasn't gone public, but the will prevents this."

"What about the international field?" Clark asked. "The British market is out there waiting for us."

"We don't have the votes to carry through that development." Vicky heard the reproach in his voice. He was constantly on her back to approve the company's move into the international field.

"This is not the time," Vicky said casually. "I feel it's wiser to diversify right now." She frowned at the sounds of exasperation that echoed around the room. She felt herself alone against the rest of the family.

But she still held the majority vote, Vicky reminded herself defiantly. Adam had much leeway—and, in truth, he handled his responsibilities well—but *she* plotted the direction of Barton Tobacco Company. That was how Sara had wanted it.

Early in 1958 Doug wrote jubilantly that his latest musical was scheduled for production in Paris in April.

"It's the best Paul and I have ever done. We're terribly excited about it. Why don't you and Kara come over for the opening? You should share this with us. If it hadn't been for all your checks while I was at Columbia, I couldn't have kept up with my music."

Joyous at the news Vicky immediately phoned Kara. It would be an opportunity, too, to see Simone, who wrote regularly, always insisting she was well and managing nicely alone on the farm.

At first Vicky and Kara plotted to take Sara—now a bewitching seven-year-old—with them. But conscientious little Sara objected to missing school.

"I'm in second grade," she said solemnly. "I can't miss school. I'll stay home with Daddy."

"We'll bring you something very special from Paris," Vicky promised. "But you must be a good girl and do exactly what Daddy tells you."

"I will!" Her eyes were bright with anticipation. "Oh, I love you, Aunt Vicky!"

Hugging this precious little grandniece, Vicky asked herself if Jill remembered "Nana." Was she all right? Was she happy? But she knew, of course, that Eleanor and Rebecca would lavish love on Jill.

When she and Kara planned their trip, she at first held back when Kara suggested extending it to include two days in London. But that would be unfair to Kara, she promised herself. Of course, they would fly to London for two days, then fly home. And all the while—in a corner of her mind—she remembered that Marc was in London.

She wouldn't see Marc. That was impossible. But she could look up his address in the phone book and just walk past the house where he lived, she thought with simmering excitement. It would be something special to go back home and to visualize his home, the streets where he walked. Nothing would happen. There was no way they'd run into each other. One chance in a million that would occur. But she had this childish yearning to envision where Marc lived.

*   *   *

On a blustery April morning Rebecca waited on the surgical floor of the hospital with Jill. For the second time Eleanor was having lung surgery. Rebecca was resigned to the knowledge that Eleanor's cancer was terminal, but the doctor hoped they could buy a few more years with this latest operation.

Her eyes revealing her terror, Jill sat beside her grandmother. At intervals Rebecca reached out to take one small hand in hers. Without words Jill knew her mother's time in life would be brief. Together Rebecca and Jill prayed for as many years as could be saved.

Rebecca tried to convince Eleanor to write to Adam or Vicky about her illness. Despite Eleanor's health insurance, their savings were all but exhausted. But Eleanor was terrified of any contact with the family. *"Adam might take Jill from us."*

That would never happen, Rebecca vowed. Nor did she suspect Adam of having any interest in his child. *She* would raise Jill, see her through college. Eleanor had dropped out to marry that bastard Adam, but Jill would earn a college degree. She prayed she would live to see Jill married and with a family of her own.

"Grandma?" Jill lifted her violet eyes to Rebecca. "When can we see Mom?"

"Soon, darling," Rebecca comforted. Ellie'd been in surgery so long, she thought in anguish.

Even before the doctor spoke to her, Rebecca knew that Eleanor's hold on life was extremely fragile. His somber demeanor as he emerged from surgery told her this. Subconsciously she tightened her grip on Jill's hand. Together they would stand by Ellie, but soon they must go on alone.

Three days after surgery Eleanor died. Rebecca and Jill were with her to the end. During the next forty-eight hours, Jill refused to leave her grandmother's side for a moment, though friends strived to be helpful. She even went with Rebecca to choose her mother's coffin. And after the funeral they came back to the apartment where a small group of friends waited to comfort them. She would raise Jill by herself, Rebecca vowed. But what would happen to Jill if *she* became ill?

Rebecca waited until Jill's private school—necessary because it provided afterschool care—closed in mid-May and she herself was able to take a week's vacation from work before going down to Bartonville.

"You're going with me, my darling," she told Jill. "I want to talk
to your father. If something should happen to me—God forbid—I
have to know that he'll be there for you."

"Nothing's going to happen to you, Grandma," Jill said fiercely.

"Not for a long time," Rebecca soothed, "but for my peace of
mind I have to tell him that your mother's gone."

"Couldn't you write him a letter?" Jill asked.

"I could," Rebecca acknowledged, "but I think it would be good
for you two to meet again. He's your father."

"I don't want to meet him!" Jill's eyes were dark with rejection.
"He's a mean man. He hurt Mom."

"Well, you may not have to," Rebecca soothed. He might refuse
to see Jill—but she had to give him that opportunity. She hesitated.
"Do you remember him?" It was six years since Jill saw her father.
She was only four and a half then.

Jill squinted in thought, as though reluctant to recall that earlier part
of her life.

"Sort of," she said after a moment. "But I remember Nana. She
was sweet."

"Maybe you'll see Nana," Rebecca said, striving to sound cheerful.

"I don't want to see *him*." Jill's small face was taut with rebellion.
"Promise me, Grandma."

"Only if you decide when we're down there that you do not want
to see him," she said after a moment. They'd have to wait to see how
this visit played out.

Arriving at the beautiful Richmond depot, Rebecca recalled her earlier trip. Right from the beginning she had been apprehensive about
Ellie's marriage. But then Jill arrived, and she prayed everything
would work out well. Much as she continued to dislike Adam, she'd
been impressed by Ellie's comfortable new lifestyle. Right away she'd
been drawn to Vicky Barton. Ellie had loved her mother-in-law, she
remembered, all at once fighting tears.

Rebecca registered at a modest Richmond hotel, where she and Jill
expected to stay only one night—unless Jill showed signs of wanting
to see the area where she'd spent the first years of her young life.
They left the hotel to find a place to have lunch, and Rebecca struggled
to make this seem a festive occasion.

After lunch Rebecca went back with Jill to the hotel, dug out the
latest *Nancy Drew*, and gave it to Jill.

"You sit down and read till I get back," she said cheerfully, though she was dreading the encounter that lay ahead. "You don't leave the hotel room. You don't even open the door for anybody."

"Okay." Jill reached for the book. "But don't stay too long."

"I won't," Rebecca soothed. Of course, Jill was still shaken by her mother's death. It was heartbreaking, Rebecca thought with pain, the way Jill followed her about the apartment every minute they were there together, as though terrified that she might disappear. "Just remember, darling, you stay right here in our room."

Rebecca left the hotel in a taxi, en route for Bartonville. Questions ricocheted in her mind. Was Adam in town? Eleanor used to say he often went on trips. But she had to take that chance—she didn't want to write or phone. She wanted to talk to him face to face. He wouldn't refuse to see her? Now she battled fresh apprehensions. She had to know that if something happened to her, he would be there for Jill. *She was his daughter.*

The day was hot and sticky. The faint breeze she'd felt in the drive from Richmond seemed to disappear as they drove into Bartonville. It was such an ugly town, she thought in distaste. She paid the driver, alighted from the taxi, and approached the office division of the Barton Tobacco Company. Opening the entrance door, she was immediately aware of the lush interior—in such contrast to the plain, strictly utilitarian exterior.

At the reception desk she asked to see Adam.

"Do you have an appointment?" The receptionist at the burnished mahogany desk seemed puzzled by Rebecca's appearance here.

"No, but he'll see me." Rebecca contrived an air of confidence. "Tell him it's Rebecca Kahn, from New York." He wouldn't dare refuse to see her, would he?

Moments later she was being escorted from the reception area down a long, carpeted hallway to a private suite. Here she was instructed to wait while the girl who had brought her this far disappeared into an inner office. Rebecca sat on the edge of a chair, conscious that her heart was pounding.

The girl—probably Adam's secretary—emerged from his office. "You may go in now, ma'am." The woman seemed oddly wary, despite her polite smile. Had Adam made some distasteful remark about his ex–mother-in-law?

Adam sat behind a huge, highly polished desk. He was heavier than she remembered and expensively dressed.

"Please come in." His face was impassive, his eyes guarded. She heard the door close behind her.

"I felt that I must tell you in person rather than by letter." Rebecca's voice was strained. He hadn't asked her to sit down, nor had he risen. Most Southern men would rise in the presence of an older woman, she thought. "Eleanor died in April. Of lung cancer." Because *he* had goaded her into becoming a heavy smoker.

"I'm sorry to hear that. But we've been long divorced," he reminded. "I've since remarried." He was shuffling papers on his desk now, as though to indicate she was interrupting important work.

"I'm here only to remind you that except for myself Jill is alone in this world. If—"

"Eleanor deserted me," Adam said coldly. "She disappeared so completely we could find no trace of her." *Had he tried? His mother might have tried. She'd dearly loved Jill.*

"I'll raise Jill. We want nothing from you," Rebecca said proudly. "But if something should happen to me, I—"

"I don't know that Jill is my child," Adam interrupted. All at once his face became flushed, his eyes hostile. "Eleanor was rather profligate with her favors—"

"How dare you!" Rebecca was trembling, her face ashen. "Ellie never looked at another man! And Jill is the image of your mother! You are despicable!" She turned and strode from the room. *She* would raise Jill. They would survive. They must forget Jill's father was alive.

Out on the street Rebecca walked without seeing, her mind in chaos. She hadn't expected to be welcomed—but she hadn't expected Adam to vilify Eleanor.

Now she looked around for a phone booth. She had to call for a taxi to take her back to the hotel. She found a booth at a nearby coffee shop. Inside she hesitated, then on impulse decided to try to reach Vicky. She clutched at this. Vicky would look after Jill if *she* was the first to go. She dialed the company, asked to speak to Mrs. Barton.

"I'm sorry," the switchboard operator told her. "Mrs. Barton is in Europe. She's not expected back for another ten days."

"Thank you." So much for that, she thought in disappointment.

Now Rebecca phoned for a taxi. She'd have a cup of coffee until it arrived. She'd make Jill understand that they'd be all right without her father, she told herself in grim determination. The words formed in her mind. *"It's all right, darling. I promise to live to be an old, old lady. I'll always be here for you."*

Jill kept saying she didn't want to see her father—she had only unpleasant memories. Still, it would be yet another painful memory to understand that her father had rejected her.

Chapter Forty-four

THOUGH THE YEARS seemed to be racing past, Vicky was conscious of a sense of waiting for her life to begin again. To keep her mind off the loneliness, she focused on expanding the food division of the company—though she relinquished her plan to change its name when Frank and Adam together marshaled a campaign against this.

Now—as the world moved into another decade—she embraced the prospect of adding a frozen food division to the company. Even ten years ago she had been fascinated with the possibilities this offered. But everything went on hold when Frank died suddenly of a heart attack. His death was a devastating shock.

She attended the funeral in New York along with Adam and a contingent of company executives. It was the end of an era, she thought. Frank was irreplaceable.

She was conscious even at the funeral that Adam was involved in a whispered business discussion with Cliff Stanton, a man new to the company. That afternoon at the New York office Adam told her this was the man he had chosen to fill Frank's role in the company.

"Adam, he's only been with the company a few months," she protested. His promotion was sure to create ill feelings among others who were being bypassed for someone still an outsider.

"Cliff Stanton is as sharp as they come," Adam insisted. "He's got great contacts inside the other companies. We can't afford not to hire him."

"Make sure he understands this promotion is subject to a review at the end of six months," Vicky ordered. "I don't want us locked in with a contract."

Only now did Vicky realize that Adam had set up a spacious apartment for himself on Sutton Place in Manhattan.

"It's cheaper than constantly renting hotel rooms," he pointed out. The apartment was a company expense, she interpreted. "And it's a place for Ronnie to stay when she's in town."

She had come to accept Adam's marriage as a kind of business arrangement. It was unlikely that Adam and Ronnie would ever present her with grandchildren. Always, Jill was present in her mind. How was Eleanor? Was she managing all right?

Vicky was out of town so much of the time these days that she had drifted away from the synagogue friends, though at intervals Lisa called to report on a birth or a marriage or a death. She was unnerved when Lisa called just before Passover of '61 to tell her that an article by Marc appeared in a Southern periodical.

"You remember how Marc was so interested in civil rights," Lisa said, clearly entranced by the article. "He's written about race relations in Richmond during the forties and fifties. Can you imagine, he wrote it without being here for—how long is it?"

"Seven years," Vicky said softly. It seemed a lifetime.

"It's awfully good. I gather he and Anita are still living in London. You know how they sometimes give a little background about writers. It mentions that he lives in an eighteenth-century townhouse and that he'd lived in Richmond for several years. I'm tempted to write him a fan letter care of the magazine," Lisa said, an anticipatory lilt in her voice. "Shall I give him your regards?"

"Please do." She *knew* where Marc lived. She'd walked by that house.

"If you're not already booked, we'd love to have you come to our Seder the first night of Passover," Lisa invited. "It seems we just never get to see you anymore."

"Thanks for asking me, Lisa, but I've meetings scheduled in San Diego. I do miss seeing you," she apologized. "Maybe after this round of business trips, I'll be able to settle in for a while." The trips were compulsive, she reproached herself. She was forever running away.

In the following months she did exhaustive research on the frozen food field. Her imagination had long ago been captivated by the possibilities of dealing with world hunger through canned and frozen foods. Perhaps the time had come to launch a foundation—the Sara Barton Foundation to help reduce world hunger.

By 1962 company profits had soared to heights that would have amazed even Daniel. Wasn't it time to give some of that back? Lily and Stephanie would be indignant, she mused. As though she was robbing them of the food on their table. No matter that she'd point out the tax benefits, that a charitable foundation would do much for the company's public image. But she'd have the final word, she reminded herself. Sara had made certain of that.

Privately she began lengthy consultations with Martin Woodstock's son and his associates in the law firm. Martin had finally retired last year. They understood that not a word of this must leak out before she was prepared to set the foundation in motion. She recoiled from the anticipated rage of Lily and Stephanie and their husbands. Clark still hadn't forgiven Sara for not allowing him to draw up her will. Instinct warned her that Adam, too, would fight this.

Then in late May of '62, word came from Simone's neighbor that Simone had suffered a stroke and was in a Paris hospital in critical condition. Vicky immediately booked a flight to Paris aboard one of the new jets that made the trip in a miraculous seven hours. Aboard the Pan Am jet—cruising at five hundred and ten miles an hour—she relived in her mind her chaotic escape from Petrograd—now Leningrad—with Simone. The years in Paris—where Simone had been her lifeline to survival—were still so vivid in recall. She prayed that Simone would survive this stroke. She had long ago convinced herself that Simone was indestructible—but she was close to eighty and had worked hard all her life.

Landing at Orly at nine AM Paris time, Vicky went directly to the Ritz, registered at the hotel, and then headed for the hospital. Vicky learned that Simone was tenaciously clinging to life.

"She was determined to see you," a nurse compassionately reported as she led Vicky to Simone's room.

Vicky sat beside Simone's bed and reached to take one hand in hers.

"She drifts in and out of consciousness," the nurse explained.

Moments later Simone opened her eyes. Her drawn face seemed to shed years.

"I knew you'd come," she whispered.

Five hours after Vicky arrived at the hospital, Simone died. Inundated with grief, Vicky took care of all the arrangements. The small farm, she learned, had been left to her. Simone had long been out of touch with her sisters—she had not even known if they were alive. Vicky gave the farm to a local orphanage, with the stipulation that they provide perpetual care for Simone's grave.

She couldn't bear to go back home yet—but being in Paris now was torture. For her the city was full of ghosts. Doug and Paul, she knew, were in Rome. She wouldn't see them on this trip. Spend a few days in London, she told herself—until she felt able to cope with life again. Marc was in London. She couldn't see him, but just being where he lived would provide comfort.

On impulse—remembering Doug had mentioned that he and Paul would be staying at the Grand Hotel in Rome—Vicky phoned him from her hotel suite. When he eagerly suggested she fly to Rome for a few days, she fabricated a business conference in London. In her present mood she was not fit company for anyone.

"Then you must stay at Claridge's," he told her. "It's beautifully private and the service is impeccable." He understood how upset she was by Simone's death. "Let me call and make arrangements for you. It's very difficult to acquire reservations unless they know you."

"Doug, how sweet. I'd appreciate that." In a corner of her mind she recalled that Claridge's was considered by many the most exclusive hotel in the world. That Doug could call and get reservations for her was an indication of his success. "And do come home soon for a visit. Kara and I miss you."

Twenty minutes later Doug phoned back to say that he had reserved a small suite for her at Claridge's.

"You're probably flying," he said, a hint of amusement infiltrating his voice now, "but if you were arriving by ship you'd be met at the wharf by liveried footmen, who'd take care of your baggage and conduct you to reserved seats on the boat train. The train would be met in London by more footmen and—"

"No, Doug," she interrupted with laughter. "I'll take a flight."

Arriving at the hotel from the airport, Vicky viewed the building with interest. No one would think this faded red brick building—its door flush against the sidewalk, with only a tiny canopy identifying it as Claridge's—was the host to titled royalty and the world's wealthiest individuals.

The atmosphere in Claridge's was that of a fine private club, Vicky thought as the uniformed doorman—brass buttons glittering and top hat elegant—ushered her through the marble foyer and to the lobby. She was welcomed by an assistant manager with the same respect he might have welcomed a member of a reigning royal family.

She was charmed to find red roses in the sitting room of her suite, but soon understood that a hotel employee had asked Doug for her preference. Because the evening was unusually cool for spring, a fire had been started in the bedroom fireplace, providing a cheery atmosphere. Oh, in her present mood it was good to be pampered this way, she thought gratefully.

She slept little this first night in London. Out of habit she awoke early. Too restless to linger in bed, she arose, showered, and dressed. A brisk walk would clear her head, she told herself. She left her suite, hurried downstairs, through the columned lobby into the already busy street.

She walked a few blocks, and then realized she was hungry. She spotted a pleasant restaurant just ahead and decided to stop for breakfast. At this hour the restaurant was all but deserted. She was seated, ordered breakfast, and leaned back in her chair with an almost overwhelming weariness. Had she made a mistake in coming to London? Yet she felt a need to be here—close to Marc.

An attractive, smartly dressed woman in her middle forties came into the restaurant and was seated at the next table. An American, Vicky surmised, as the other woman chatted with the waiter.

"May I start off with coffee please, and then I'll decide what else I'd like," she told the waiter.

Vicky's neighbor opened her purse, searched among its contents, and then muttered in annoyance. She reached for the menu, squinted, sighed. Now—with a smile—she turned to Vicky.

"I've reached the age where suddenly all print looks smaller than it should be. And I've left my glasses up in our hotel room. I told my ophthalmologist that the telephone books were using smaller print—" She chuckled in recall. "And he told me I'd arrived at the age where glasses were a necessity of life."

"Are you having trouble with the menu?" Vicky asked sympathetically.

"It's so frustrating." The other woman hesitated. "Would you mind serving as my eyes?" Her smile was ingratiating.

"I'll get out my glasses." Vicky reached into her purse.

"Oh, you've reached that age, too."

"I reached it quite a while ago—" Vicky hesitated. "Would you like to join me?"

"That would be nice. I'm Hilda Ashley," she introduced herself as she moved to Vicky's table.

"Vicky Barton," she said with a smile. "You're American, aren't you?" But her speech seemed a blend of American and English, Vicky thought.

"I was born in Philadelphia," Hilda explained. "Then during World War II—I was an army nurse—I met my husband, who's British. We live about an hour out of London. He's a physician, here in the city to talk with his publisher." Now Vicky and Hilda Ashley conferred over the menu. When Mrs. Ashley had made her choice, she put aside the menu with a grateful smile. "My husband's planning a series of articles based on that report just issued by the Royal College of Physicians."

"That sounds exciting," Vicky said politely.

"Lord, it was about time the government was told to stop the 'murder by cigarettes' that's been swept under the rug for so many years!" she said.

"What's the report about?" Vicky stammered, her heart suddenly pounding.

"The link between cigarette smoking and lung cancer and heart disease—and heaven only knows what else. I haven't smoked since that article in *Reader's Digest* back in 1950. I have my sister in New York send me a bunch of American magazines three or four times every year—to keep in touch with home. Did you read that *Reader's Digest* article?" She chuckled. "If you had, you wouldn't have forgotten it."

"I didn't see it." In 1950 her mind had been torn between Sara's illness and the new food division of the company. "I didn't even hear any discussion about it." Vicky struggled against a battering ram of alarm.

"It shook up the cigarette industry, I'll wager." Hilda was grim. *Why hadn't she known what was going on?* "It shook the hell out of me. And then Hal came home that September with an article from the *British Medical Journal*. These two doctors suspected lung cancer was the direct result of smoking." Vicky was lightheaded with shock. Then she hadn't been off the mark when she suspected Daniel's lung cancer came from his heavy smoking. "From then on," Hilda pursued, "Hal was drawn into the research being done on the subject. It's become an obsession with him. The British government is just as guilty as the American government for not attacking the cigarette manufacturers. They ought to be tarred and feathered. They're selling death, and they know it!"

"But most of the public are not aware of this," Vicky said defensively, stunned by what Hilda had said. "I've read nothing in the magazines or newspapers—"

"Oh, you haven't been reading about it—except for several articles in *Reader's Digest* through the years—because advertising departments of magazines and newspapers are terrified of losing all those cigarette ad dollars," Hilda said scornfully. "And politicians play along with the tobacco companies because they're greedy for campaign funds." Barton Tobacco contributed regularly to campaigns, Vicky remembered. It was a precedent set by Daniel. "But *Reader's Digest* doesn't run ads—they can afford to run those articles."

"I've read nothing," Vicky confessed, ashamed of her ignorance. She was part of the industry—she should have known. "I've heard nothing on radio, seen nothing on television." Just that once, she recalled now. Around eight years ago a radio commentator had talked about an article in the *New York Times* that said the American Cancer Society warned that some researchers maintained cigarette smoking could lead to cancer. But Adam—and later Frank—had convinced her that many other researchers complained that report was biased and unscientifically prepared. *Why hadn't she checked further?*

"You won't see anything on television or hear it on radio," Hilda clucked, then paused as her waiter approached, smilingly approved of her move to Vicky's table, and took her order. "You won't see or hear anything on TV or radio," Hilda resumed, "because the stations don't want to lose that enormous revenue. Except for two telecasts by Ed Murrow on his 'See It Now' series, back in 1954. I still wonder how those two got through."

"I'm afraid I've been in a vacuum for the last dozen years." Vicky was reeling from Hilda's attack on the cigarette industry. "I remember in World War I—and then again in World War II—how the government was always saying how important cigarettes were to the war efforts. President Roosevelt made tobacco a protected crop for that reason.'' She was fighting to retain her poise, not to give away her mental chaos.

"Times are changing," Hilda said with satisfaction. "The report from the Royal College of Physicians warns that it's urgent to take 'decisive steps' to curb the growing use of cigarettes—and what more respected medical body is there than the Royal College of Physicians?''

After breakfast Vicky wandered about the London streets and saw nothing. The facts that Hilda Ashley had poured out to her ricocheted in her brain. *Cigarette manufacturers were selling death.*

The people who said this were not crackpots—as Frank and Adam had pointed out with such contempt. They were eminent scientists and doctors who had conducted exhaustive research. Impatient to read for herself what had been written through the years, Vicky canceled her London stay and managed to book a flight for New York the following day.

From Idlewild she phoned the hotel where she had stayed with Marc. Yes, they had a vacancy for the evening. Again, it was as though Marc were with her when she checked into the hotel for the night. In the morning she would head for the public library at Fifth Avenue and Forty-second Street and search through the files of magazines and newspapers of earlier years.

For much of the night sleep eluded her. How had she allowed herself to be so blind in the years when the dangers of smoking were being brought out in ugly clarity? The old skeptics of an earlier century who had labeled cigarettes ''coffin nails'' had not been wrong.

She arrived before the imposing flights of steps that led up to the Fifth Avenue entrance to the New York Public Library, and hurried up as though on a desperate mission. She made inquiries, found her way to the proper section, and discovered her quarry. Her heart pounding, she sat and read for an endless time the collection of articles— admittedly few—that had made their way into print.

When she left the library, Vicky knew that what she meant to do would evoke loud recriminations from some members of the family, namely Adam, Lily and Clark, Stephanie and Jeffrey. They would drag her into court, perhaps label her insane. But the publicity would be great, she thought. Newspapers and magazines would carry dramatic reports of her battle to destroy the cigarette division of her own company.

The message would be loud and clear, she told herself in triumph. Every living being must understand that to light up a cigarette was to court death. She remembered Daniel's final pain-wracked years—a terrible punishment for what too long had seemed a harmless addiction.

The cigarette division of Barton Tobacco Company would be eliminated. The company would become Barton Enterprises. She would enlarge the food division to include a frozen food subsidiary. The food division was already showing a substantial profit. That would increase with the addition of Barton Frozen Foods.

She would refuse to sell their equipment—it would be melted down as scrap metal. All the employees in the cigarette division would be retrained to work in the food division in its varied aspects. *The company would still make comfortable profits.* But it would be selling health—not death.

She was not afraid of taking on the family. Not even Adam. She held the voting stock in her hands. If she were alive, Sara would back her up all the way.

Was Sara, too, a victim of cigarette smoking? She hadn't smoked—but she'd grown up with a father and brother who were heavy smokers. Despite her rules about no cigarettes in her bedroom or the dining room, Barton Manor—before Daniel's death—had reeked of cigarette smoke. Had Sara, too, died because of cigarette smoke?

Chapter Forty-five

WALKING INTO the library to-night, Vicky was glad that Adam had long ago persuaded his grandmother to have Barton Manor air-conditioned. Outdoors the air was heavy, sultry, cloyingly sweet from the flowers rushed into bloom by the heavy rains of the past two days. And shortly, Vicky warned herself, the atmosphere inside the house would be overheated.

She had ordered this special board of directors meeting to be held at the house and in the evening because she expected a savagely bitter uproar when she made her announcement. At the house what was discussed at the meeting could be kept secret for now from company employees. Later—at the proper time—they would be told. She had given the domestic staff the night off so that they wouldn't witness the anticipated uproar.

She glanced at her watch as she sat in the chair behind the desk. It was exactly 8:25. She had called the meeting for 8:30 PM. Adam had not been home for dinner. He'd been in conference at the office—or so he claimed. Ronnie—who was not on the board of directors—was at The Homestead for a few days with her mother. Lily and Clark would be late, as usual. They'd drive over with Stephanie and Jeffrey.

Clark had become such a pompous ass, she thought, since he'd been elected a local judge. Kara never came to board meetings, and Doug could not be expected to fly in from Paris.

Adam arrived at exactly 8:30. He appeared annoyed rather than curious about this unorthodox meeting. Was it interfering with some personal rendezvous? She doubted that he was faithful to Ronnie, doubted that Ronnie cared. But he ought to do something about the weight he was putting on. At thirty-seven he shouldn't have that paunch.

"I hope this isn't going to take long, Mother. I've got a batch of reports to go over tonight."

"Not long," she promised. He wasn't curious, she realized all at once, because he expected her to talk about the food division—what he called "my mother's obsession." She'd mentioned that she was pleased by the last quarter's earnings.

Adam sat down near the TV, and fiddled with the dials until he found a news program. He was ever hostile toward the urgent call for integration in the South. He took no pride—though to Vicky this was a cause for joy—that Richmond had recently been lauded by the *Washington Post* for leading the way in race relations. He had unmasked distaste for what he called "coloreds who've gotten too big for their britches."

At ten minutes to nine Lily and Stephanie and their husbands arrived.

"Adam, why do we have to have a board meeting now?" Clark complained. "What's up?"

"My mother called the meeting." Vicky saw the loaded exchange between Adam and Clark. They were beginning to behave as though she were senile, she thought in simmering anger.

"I have an announcement to make," she said, making an effort to sound calm. She might be sixty, but she felt a long way from retirement.

It was pointless to play games, she'd told herself earlier. Now—in succinct language—she told them how horrified and sickened she'd become when she realized what research had brought out about the link between lung cancer and smoking.

"That's a crock!" Adam exploded. "Those phony reports have been exposed a thousand times. They're—"

"They're proven facts," Vicky interrupted him with determined calm. "As far back as 1938, a professor at Johns Hopkins reported to the Academy of Medicine that a major study he had directed indicated that smoking was life-threatening. In May 1950, an article in the *Journal of the American Medical Association* linked smoking with lung cancer. In 1953 four studies did the same, and in addition linked it with heart disease. In—"

"What the hell are you digging up this shit for?" Adam demanded, his face florid with rage.

"We have to face what we're doing—and stop it," Vicky shot back. "We can't go on selling death." The stunned silence of the others was suddenly ominous. "I harbor a terrible guilt for not realizing what was happening these past few years. I'm not selling my stock in the company. That can't be done for another thirty-eight years," she said, reminding them of the terms of the will. She also had no plans to sell—that would be only passing on the plague. "But I'm closing down the cigarette operation."

"What are you talking about?" Adam's voice soared in disbelief. "You can't do that!"

"I'm closing down the cigarette operation," she repeated. "We'll focus on the food division, add a frozen subsidiary—"

"That's insane!" Lily shrieked. "We'll lose hundreds of millions of dollars!"

Vicky flinched as the other five leapt to their feet and verbally assaulted her—their words a jumble of nasty invectives, a cacophony of outrage.

"You're out to ruin us all!" Stephanie was hysterical. "Jeffrey, tell her she can't do this to us!"

"This meeting is over." Fighting for poise, Vicky rose to her feet, also. Head high, pale and trembling, she strode from the room while the voices rose to a screaming crescendo.

"Quiet!" Adam shouted, his face flushed with fury. "Jeffrey, close the door."

Stephanie dropped into a chair, sobbing wildly while Jeffrey went to the door.

"Stephanie, shut up," Lily said impatiently and turned to Adam. "How do we stop her?"

"We can't let her get away with it," Adam said grimly. "She's off her rocker. Clark, how do we handle this legally?"

"Look, let's face it." Clark was somber. "She holds all the cards. The only way to stop her would be to prove she's mentally unstable."

"Nobody in their right mind would do what she talks about doing." Adam was triumphant. "She's mentally unstable," he declared. "What's our next step?"

Clark was startled. He glanced about at the others. All eyes were focused on him.

"To put her into conservatorship will be tough," he warned.

"What do you need?" Adam challenged. "A doctor to testify that she's mentally incompetent. That's you, Jeffrey. Family to state that she's behaving erratically. Lily, Stephanie, and me. A judge to hear the case. That's you, Clark. We can work it out in a thoroughly legal manner." *He'd waited a long time to take over the company.*

"It's for her own good," Lily pounced. "Like Adam said, no woman in her right mind would take such steps."

"I'll have someone in my own firm represent her," Clark plotted. "Jeffrey will officially declare her mentally unstable."

"Hey, this is going to be rough—" Jeffrey was nervous.

"Nothing is going to happen to my mother. This is for her own good," Adam said. "And we have to protect the family. Each of us stands to lose millions."

"Jeffrey, don't be an ass. You'll do it," Stephanie told him.

"We have to move fast," Clark pointed out. "Before she goes into the office and starts throwing her weight around. Don't forget—she owns controlling stock. Even if we all voted against her, it wouldn't mean a damn."

"We'll start tonight." Adam's mind charged ahead. "Everybody knows how devoted she was to my father and brother. She turned the cottage into a secret shrine to their memory. And tonight vandals broke in. She couldn't hack it—she fell apart. A nervous breakdown."

"Adam, what do we do with her?" Lily demanded.

"We'll tell the public she's had a severe breakdown and is in a sanitarium—in another state. She'll be in the cottage behind a chain-link fence—"

"How do we explain the fence?" Stephanie broke in. "The servants will get suspicious."

"We're outraged about the vandalism, so we put up the fence." Adam's mind was in high gear. "Anyhow, the servants have no reason to go to the cottage. To them it's spooky."

"Suppose people want to visit or send flowers?" Jeffrey demanded. "Hell, she's an important person!"

"We'll tell everybody the doctors say, no visitors. Only her son," Adam drawled smugly. "Nothing will go wrong," he promised. "We'll set up an arrangement with some sanitarium hungry for funds to cover for us. You have contacts, Jeffrey."

"That's asking for blackmail," Jeffrey warned.

"No." Adam paused. "Not if we motivate it properly," he said. "You'll explain that you have a psychotic patient whose family is embarrassed by her state. They want to keep her home in familiar surroundings, but to keep away possible visitors they'll circulate that she's in a distant sanitarium."

"We're flirting with disaster," Jeffrey said gloomily.

"We're saving our hides!" Lily shrieked at him. "Stop being an ass!"

"You and I will go up to the sanitarium." Adam refused to be derailed. "We'll work out the details. If somebody shows up at the sanitarium—like Kara, who can be damned persistent—we'll have a routine all worked out. When my mother's better, they'll be notified."

"I still say it's dangerous," Jeffrey said.

"We can handle it. The fence goes up first thing tomorrow morning. I'll bring out a rush crew from that new firm in Richmond. They'll do the job quick and get out. Now let's—"

"Adam, suppose somebody wanders onto the estate, sees the fenced-in cottage, and starts asking questions?" Stephanie challenged, and Lily grunted in disgust.

"For God's sake, Stephanie, this is estate country. Nobody has less than a hundred acres. Nobody wanders onto somebody else's property any more than they'd fly to the moon. Folks around here cherish their privacy. They don't trespass unless they're invited. And we won't be issuing invitations to roam about our land."

"How long can we keep it up?" Jeffrey exchanged an anxious glance with Stephanie.

"As long as we play it smart," Adam shot back. "We have no other choice. She'll be safe. Nobody's going to hurt her. But she won't be able to rob us of millions of dollars that belong to us! That money is our birthright!"

"You'll have to put her under sedation," Clark warned. "And fast."

"I'll go up to her room in a little while—pretending to be in a conciliatory mood after our little explosion. I'll bring up coffee for the two of us. Jeffrey, get me a strong sedative. My coffee is always heavily laced with cream and sugar. Mother takes hers black." Unexpectedly he grinned. "No chance I'll get the wrong cup."

His eyes questioning, Jeffrey turned to Stephanie.

Stephanie hesitated, then lifted her head in a gesture of defiance.

"Give her a double dose of my sleeping pills." She was too greedy to mess this up, Adam told himself in satisfaction. "That'll put out a horse." She fished in her purse, brought out an enameled pill box.

"She'll be conscious in the morning," Jeffrey said, "but her head will be too fuzzy for her to cause any problems for a few hours. Then we—"

"Don't worry about tomorrow morning," Adam interrupted briskly. "This is what we do." He was exhilarated by the prospect of being in total command of the Barton empire. "In a few minutes I'll go up to her room with the coffee tray. I've done this before. I'll pretend to try to persuade her to change her mind—which will never happen," he conceded. "I'll leave her. She'll fall into a drugged sleep. At two in the morning I'll call you. All upset. My mother came to my room—I helped her back there, but she's terribly distraught. You'll come over with an ambulance—that's a cover in case one of the servants wakes up and asks questions."

"How am I supposed to get an ambulance?" Jeffrey asked.

"You're the chief administrator of the hospital," Adam said impatiently. "Bring over an ambulance. We'll take her to the cottage. When the servants wake up in the morning, we'll say she's been taken to a private sanitarium. We'll give them reports every day until the deal is closed. She'll never come back to Barton Manor."

"You can't just dump her in the cottage," Clark pointed out. "There has to be a hearing."

"That nurse in your office, Jeffrey." Adam was searching for an answer. "She's been with you forever. You said she'd do anything for you."

"Yeah, she's trustworthy." Jeffrey avoided Stephanie's eyes. "I took care of her daughter twice when the kid got pregnant. I can have her stay for a few days with Vicky—but what about after that?"

"We keep her sedated until Clark stages a hearing and the papers are filed. Then I hire somebody to live in the cottage and do the cleaning and cooking—and make sure she stays put."

"Who?" Lily was anxious now. "Suppose that person talks?"

"We'll work that out later. We can't waste time thinking about that part now," Adam said briskly. "Don't worry—we'll handle it. The rest of you get out of here. I'll take coffee up to her. Jeffrey, stand by for a call around two AM. You know what to do."

* * *

Vicky stood at a window and stared into the night. She was still trembling from the raucous encounter in the library. But hadn't she expected that, she reproached herself. She had to be strong, carry this out as planned. They didn't have to be among the one hundred richest families in the country. The food division would still provide heavy profits. None of them would have to change their lifestyle because the company was no longer peddling death.

She started at the light knock on her door. That had to be Adam. The servants wouldn't be home until at least ten o'clock.

"Yes?" She struggled to sound matter-of-fact.

The door opened. Adam walked in. He carried a tray with two cups of coffee, playing the charming, irresistible son.

"I thought the two of us ought to have a private talk." He flashed the ingratiating smile that often served him well. But not tonight, Vicky told herself.

"Adam, I don't want to talk any more about my decision to close the cigarette division."

"Mother, cigarettes *are* the company," he protested. "I know you enjoy the foods division. It's like a cherished hobby." His smile was indulgent.

"The food division represents twenty-five percent of the company income," she pointed out. "And it's growing. When we add a frozen subsidiary—"

"You're throwing away hundreds of millions of dollars in the next twenty years," he pointed out. "Here, drink your coffee."

"Adam, you won't change my mind." She reached to take the coffee from him. "I was devastated when I was told the details of that report from the Royal College of Physicians."

"A bunch of old fogies," Adam protested, sipping at his coffee.

"They are one of the most respected medical bodies in the world. And there's plenty of support for their research here in our country. Adam, I've read everything that's been written in the last twelve years—and it's frightening!"

"Mother, drink your coffee," he urged again and she lifted the cup to her mouth.

"Where did you learn to make such good coffee?" She knew the servants were not in the house.

"One of my secret talents," he drawled. "My college roommate taught me.'' He drained his cup, put it on the tray. ''I have some reports to read. I'd better get to them. Finish your coffee, and I'll take the cups down to the kitchen.''

Vicky drained her cup. She was relieved that this had not become a nasty encounter. She was exhausted from these last days. And sleepy. She'd go straight to bed.

Adam went to his room, and sat down to study the report he'd brought home from the office. He'd tell Cliff to start right away exploring the international situation. No need now to delay moving into the international market. He would talk to Roger at the ad agency about doing a sales promotion film to go to foreign nations who might welcome cigarette imports.

Too stimulated to nap until his two AM rendezvous, Adam decided to go down to the library and fix himself a drink. He was whistling softly as he strolled down the hall of the lower floor and back to the library. He'd take the company up to Number One in the industry. He knew just how to do that.

At a few minutes before two AM Adam cautiously opened the door to his mother's bedroom. Wow, those pills must have been potent, he thought. Still fully clothed except for her shoes, she lay sprawled across the turned-down bed. Okay, get this show on the road.

From the phone in Vicky's bedroom he called Jeffrey, played the scene the way he'd plotted.

''And Jeffrey, for God's sake, don't use the ambulance siren. No need to wake up the servants.''

In less than ten minutes Jeffrey drove up in a Barton Hospital ambulance. Adam met him at the door. Together they went up to Vicky's bedroom, carried her—in a drugged sleep—down the stairs and out to the ambulance.

Only now did Adam realize a woman had come with Jeffrey—his office nurse. Doris something or other. He was sure Jeffrey had been sleeping with her for years. She'd play on their team.

They drove to the cottage. The two men carried Vicky inside. Doris followed. Jeffrey gave her instructions, and a small package.

''Doris will give the necessary injections,'' Jeffrey told Adam. ''The men working on the fence won't suspect anybody's in the cottage.''

''I'll insist the fence company send out a large crew. I want the fence set up in a few hours. When they've gone,'' Adam plotted, ''we'll take my mother downtown to your office, Clark. You arrange for the hearing. If anybody in town recognizes her—with a nurse and solicitous family hovering about, they'll be convinced she's in a terrible mental state.''

When the servants appeared in the morning, Adam played the distraught son. He explained how his mother had gone to the cottage, discovered the vandalism—and later went berserk.

''We all know what a terrible strain she's been under these past few years. This was the final blow. Dr. Jeffrey has had her admitted to a private sanitarium with a fine reputation for handling cases like my mother's. And I'm having an electrified chain-link fence installed around the cottage. No vandal will ever do his dirty mischief there again.'' They were all upset, he decided. He'd played the scene well. And they needn't worry that any of the servants would go to the cottage—they had superstitious fears about it since Gary killed himself there.

At dusk—accompanied by Jeffrey—Adam returned from the office and drove over to the dirt road that led from the public road to the cottage. Together with Doris they guided Vicky from the cottage into the car. Adam made a mental note to close off the entrance to the dirt road with plantings. He and Jeffrey would handle this personally tonight.

Most of Clark's office staff and his associates had left for the day by the time they appeared. If anyone there was curious about the arriving procession, they would see this as a situation that saddened the whole family, Adam reassured himself.

Dazed and incoherent, Vicky was led into Clark's elegant private office in the care of a nurse and her two sisters-in-law. Jeffrey was there to offer testimony that Vicky Barton was mentally unstable. Her sisters-in-law and son reluctantly admitted that she had been behaving oddly for weeks. An office secretary dutifully recorded all the testimony.

''There's no question in my mind but that she should be placed in conservatorship,'' Clark concluded in his role of judge. ''All necessary papers will be duly filed.''

Adam fought not to show his elation. It was done. He was his mother's conservator. He was in control of the business and master of Barton Manor.

* * *

Jeffrey's nurse remained in the cottage with Vicky while Adam and Clark argued in the privacy of Clark's home office late that evening about how to manage in the years ahead.

"We can't afford any slipup, Adam." Now that all the technicalities had been handled, Clark was apprehensive.

"We'll have no slipups," Adam insisted.

"We can't keep her under sedation on a permanent basis," Clark pointed out.

"Look, my mother is in conservatorship. For her own best interest we have her secluded—that's better than putting her into a mental institution. She'll lack for nothing."

"Jeffrey can't keep his office nurse there indefinitely," Clark warned.

"Don't you think I know that? I made all the right arrangements this afternoon. Tomorrow morning Jeffrey's nurse will be relieved. One of the workers at the plant has a retarded thirteen-year-old sister-in-law. He does some gardening for me on the side, and he asked if there was some job for her in the house. I told Lula Mae to see if she could use her in the kitchen, but the kid's scared to death of people. She'll live in the cottage, be my mother's personal maid and cook. She'll be all right as long as she can stay in the house and not have to face anybody else. Her name is Amy, and she'll live with my mother forever." His smile shouted victory. "Once a week I'll personally see that everything that's needed will be taken to the cottage. When I'm out of town, you or Jeffrey will handle this. I'll take you both on a dry run," he joshed. "It's a small price to pay for saving ourselves millions of dollars."

Two mornings later—when the ten-foot, electrified chain-link fence was already installed—Adam personally conducted the terrified thirteen-year-old to the cottage. He'd told her brother-in-law that she was to live with his invalid cousin in a town in North Carolina. They shouldn't expect to be seeing her—and, of course, she couldn't write to them. The brother-in-law, Adam congratulated himself, was happy to have the retarded kid out of his hair.

"There's nothing to be afraid of, Amy," he soothed. "You're going to live in the cottage with my mother. You'll cook and clean for her. If there's anything special she wants—like magazines or something special to eat or clothes—you tell her to write it down and it'll be

taken care of.'' He understood the girl couldn't read or write—but
that was no problem. "She won't hurt you," he soothed, "but you
have to remember that she's not quite right in the head. She'll probably say all kinds of crazy things. You just listen and pretend you
believe her.''

His mother was still in a dazed state when he arrived at the cottage
with Amy. Doris was clearly relieved to be off the case.

"The injection I gave her will wear off sometime this afternoon,"
she reported, gazing doubtfully at Amy. "You're sure she can handle
her?''

"She's young and strong and willing," Adam said confidently,
touching his head in a silent communication. "You'll be fine, won't
you, Amy?''

"Yes sir.'' The small teenager nodded in agreement. Her brother-
in-law would knock the shit out of her if she messed up on this, he
guessed. The jerk wanted her off his hands—one less mouth to feed.
Dumb as she was, she knew that much.

"Okay, Doris," Adam said briskly. "I'll drive you home.''

Vicky felt herself emerging from a murky haze. Slowly she opened
her eyes. Oh, her head ached! She frowned, closed her eyes again,
and cradled her head between her hands. Now she became aware of
an unfamiliar, childlike voice singing close by. With a shattering suddenness she was aware that she was not in her bedroom. She was not
at Barton Manor.

She opened her eyes again, glanced about the room. *She was in the
cottage.* When had she come here? What was this nightmare closing
in around her?

"Who's there?'' she called out sharply.

Instantly the singing stopped. A small, reed-thin colored girl of
about twelve or thirteen with enormous dark eyes walked fearfully
into the room.

"I'm Amy," she said, hanging in the doorway as though afraid to
advance further. "Mist' Adam say I'm your maid. I'm to cook and
clean and everything.''

"Amy, don't be afraid of me.'' Vicky was touched by her obvious
fear. "But I don't understand. How did I get here?'' She drew herself
up into a sitting position. "I don't remember coming here.''

"Mist' Adam say you been sick.''

"I want to go to my house, Amy." She realized now that she was in a nightgown. "Where are my clothes?"

"Oh, I hung everything away, just like Mist' Adam told me," Amy told her with a momentary pride. "But we can't leave here. They put up a big fence—and Mist' Adam say not to touch 'cause if we does, we get a bad shock."

"What kind of fence?" Vicky gazed in astonishment at Amy, then swung her legs from the bed and darted to the window. She gazed out at the chain-link fence constructed within the hedges—now a dozen feet tall—that years ago Sara had ordered the gardener to plant to provide Gary with privacy. "Oh, my God!"

Dizzy with disbelief she dropped into the Boston rocker that Sara had sent to the cottage when Eleanor was nursing Jill. Adam—and probably Lily and Stephanie and their husbands—had conspired to stop her from closing the cigarette division of the company. *In their greed they had resorted to this.*

"Miz Vicky, you want me to make you some coffee and breakfast?" Amy asked solicitously. "My sister say I cook real good."

"Just coffee, Amy—" She forced a smile. Why was this poor child made to share her imprisonment? "Please bring me coffee."

In mid-afternoon Adam drove up to the cottage, lifted out of the car a carton of food staples and reading matter along with the valise he'd instructed Mattie Lou to pack—"to be sent to the sanitarium for when Miss Vicky is well enough to wear her own clothes."

"Damn!" He saw the door of the cottage swing wide. He'd hoped to make this first delivery before his mother emerged from her stupor.

"Adam, what the devil is going on?" Vicky stood in the doorway, pale and accusing. He sensed she was still partly dazed.

"You're going to be all right," he soothed, unlocking the gate and carrying the carton and valise inside. She wasn't going to be physically violent, was she? She knew he could overpower her in a minute. "The family decided you need to be protected from yourself." Amy cowered behind her. "We're doing this for your own good. Anything you want, you just tell Amy, and it'll be brought to you. We—"

"You've imprisoned me!" Vicky lashed at him. "I can't believe this is happening!"

"It's all legal. You've had a court hearing. I was appointed your conservator."

"On what grounds?" she demanded.

"You're off your rocker, Mother. We had to take action." He put down the carton and the valise and began to edge back toward the gate. "You'll have everything you need to be comfortable. Once a week one of the family will come here to bring supplies. Make a list and—"

"How could I have given birth to a monster like you?" Vicky felt sick with contempt. "But you won't have the final word. Kara and Derek will find out what's happened. They'll get me out of this insanity! You'll not run my company for long, Adam. I swear to that!"

Chapter Forty-six

PULLING INTO the driveway of her charming house in the Buckhead section of Atlanta—paid for by awesomely large dividends from her Barton Tobacco Company stock—Kara heard the phone ringing. She hurried from the station wagon and into the house. Sara and her nursemaid were at a children's party this afternoon, and this was the housekeeper's midweek day off.

"Hello," she said breathlessly.

"Hi, Kara." She was surprised and alarmed to hear Adam's voice. He never called her.

"Hi, Adam," she said, a hint of tension in her own voice.

"Something terrible has happened to my mother." He sounded unfamiliarly subdued. "You know how hard she works. Well, vandals broke into the cottage. I don't know if you're aware of it, but she's been kind of keeping it like a shrine to my father and Michael. She just went berserk. She's in a sanitarium now, under treatment."

"Where?" Kara sought a memo pad and pen. Derek always made sure every phone had these. "I'll come right up—"

"The doctors won't allow anybody to see her. It just sets her off again. They don't want to keep her under heavy sedation all the time because there seems to be some minor heart problem. They won't even let me see her."

"Oh, my God," Kara whispered, cold with shock. "How long do they think this will go on?"

"The prognosis is not good. The doctors say that she's been work-ing up to this for a long time. You know, Michael's death, my father's, our grandmother's. All we can do is sit back and hope."

"Give me the address of the sanitarium. At least, let me send her flowers. Let her know we're thinking about her."

"You can send them, Kara," Adam said, "but she won't under-stand. She doesn't recognize anybody. She doesn't know where she is, the doctors tell me. She didn't know me."

"The address of the sanitarium, Adam?" she asked, churning with anxiety. How could this have happened to Vicky? She was always so strong and in control.

"Got a pencil?" he asked.

"Yes."

She scribbled down the address of the sanitarium. She recognized the name. It was a posh, private sanitarium seventy miles south of Richmond. She'd drive up there in the morning.

"Look, will you write Doug and tell him?" Adam asked. "I'm tied up like crazy with business now."

"I'll write Doug," she promised.

Off the phone with Adam, Kara called Derek at his office, reported on the situation.

"Shall I drive up with you in the morning?" he asked.

"Honey, I know how involved you are in the Taylor Building. Besides, you should be home for Sara if I'm away overnight. I'll drive up first thing in the morning. I'll call you from there—" It was too long a drive for one day. She'd stay overnight in a motel, drive back the next morning. "I just can't believe this—" Her voice broke. "Vicky of all people!"

"She'll pull out of it," Derek comforted. "Like Adam said, she's been through a hell of a lot. It finally caught up with her."

At the sanitarium the next day Kara was shaken to discover she would not—as Adam had warned—be permitted to see Vicky.

"Mrs. Barton is in a special wing," the head nurse told her when summoned by the sanitarium receptionist. Delicately the nurse indi-cated that this was a wing reserved for violent patients. "Mrs. Barton is being attended by round-the-clock private nurses. We have to make sure she has no opportunity to harm herself."

The head nurse appeared professionally detached yet compassionate.

"I'll see that she gets your flowers." She reached to take the florist box containing Vicky's favorite red roses. ''Her son is in constant touch. If there's any change in her condition, he'll be advised immediately.''

Vicky struggled to cope with her situation—never doubting for a moment that this would be of short duration. She had quickly realized that there was no way she could physically escape on her own. Adam had made sure of that. But weeks became months and nothing changed. *How had Adam managed to head off Kara and Derek from trying to find her? What about Doug? Wasn't he upset that he received no letters from her, as in the past?*

Each Saturday morning she made a list of items she wished, and twisted it through a segment of the gate for pickup. She guessed that it was collected somewhere in the middle of the night. On Sunday mornings she and Amy would find a carton just inside the gate. She'd given up trying to encounter Adam. What would be the use? Now she had reconstructed what happened—but she remembered nothing from those moments when she had drunk drugged coffee until she awoke in the cottage.

After the first frustrating ten days, she'd forced herself to plot a survival course. She must keep her sanity in an insane situation. The area around the house was too small to allow for walking. She asked for an exercise bike. She requested a television set—which was an instant delight to Amy. She ordered extensive reading material. And all the while she fumed that no one seemed to recognize her true situation. Adam had been diabolically clever.

She'd made an effort from the first day to brush away Amy's poignant fear of her. By the end of their first month together Amy had learned to relax with her. She viewed living in the cottage as an impressive luxury. For Amy's sake she masked her own rage at this incarceration.

Vicky soon suspected that Amy was extremely shy rather than retarded. Because she'd been considered retarded, she'd never been sent to school. She couldn't read or write. Use this time, Vicky ordered herself, to help this sweet little girl.

Determined to improve Amy's life—and fill the infuriatingly empty hours—Vicky asked for pencils and paper. She would teach Amy to read and write. They would hold ''school'' for several hours each day. They would take turns on the exercise bike—because it was important to preserve their health. If either fell ill, she guessed with caustic humor, they would be treated by Jeffrey—obviously a part of this whole plot. Fleetingly she conjured up a vision of herself summoning medical help, and then with Amy's help overpowering Jeffrey and fleeing from the cottage. Logic told her this would be a physical impossibility. Knowing Adam, she was certain Jeffrey would arrive with backup to thwart an escape.

In time, she promised herself, Kara and Derek would understand something was desperately wrong. They would fight for her release.

Jill finished summer school in August of 1962 and enjoyed the brief respite before the regular school year began right after Labor Day. She knew her grandmother was against her rushing through school this way, but she had set a schedule for herself.

"You're working yourself to death," Rebecca scolded as they sat on a bench along Riverside Drive on this Sunday evening of the sultry Labor Day weekend. "I don't understand your mad rush to get through school."

"I want to be able to graduate in three years," Jill tried to appear casual.

"But why?" her grandmother demanded querulously. "What are you trying to prove?"

"I want to start college when I'm seventeen—and graduate in three years Then I'll work for a while to save up money and go to Columbia for a master's in journalism."

Her grandmother was silent for a moment, but Jill felt her tender approval.

"You've been planning this for a while," she guessed. "You may be a few weeks short of your fifteenth birthday, but you have a twenty-five-year-old mind." She chuckled with pride. "If you want to go to a journalism school, you'll go. You won't have to work to save up money. I'll manage to see you through. But why, my darling, must you always be in such a rush to do things?"

"Because there's so much I want to do, Grandma," she said earnestly.

Didn't Grandma understand why she chose journalism? Because that was the way to help in the fight against the cigarette companies. Smoking had killed Mom. She and Grandma had to stand by and see Mom suffering—and there had been nothing they could do to ease her pain. Nothing the doctors could do. Even now she could feel her own pain in watching Mom those awful last months.

Grandma hated the cigarette companies. She said there was proof that smoking killed more people than wars. She said Mom never would have smoked except for Adam Barton. She refused to allow herself to think of him as her father. Grandma hated Adam Barton more than anything else in the world.

Someday, she fantasized, she'd go back to Bartonville—which was only a vague shadow in her memory. She'd expose her father for the disgusting human being he was. She'd help to expose those big cigarette companies that were killing people.

The only good memory she had of Bartonville was of her other grandmother. She'd called her Nana, she remembered. The stuffed giraffe that Mom had brought along when they came to live with Grandma had been a birthday present from Nana. She had vague recall of the pretty house in the woods and of the big house close by where Nana lived.

Grandma said she'd read in a magazine that Nana was locked away in a sanitarium somewhere. She'd lost her mind. Mom had kept snapshots of Nana and of her cousins Kara and Doug. It was so weird to have cousins she hadn't seen since she was tiny. She couldn't even remember what they looked like.

She didn't know why she never told Grandma about meaning to go back to Bartonville one day. Maybe because she thought Grandma might be afraid she wouldn't come back. But she didn't want to live down there. She just wanted to see Adam Barton suffer the way Mom suffered.

As the months rolled by, Vicky was touched by the love she saw in Amy's eyes. Amy was not retarded—she was a bright and eager pupil. When she and Amy emerged from this exile, she would keep Amy with her. She would campaign to see that children such as Amy were given an opportunity to learn.

She began to clip from the myriad magazines and newspapers she read every item that dealt with the cigarette industry. She relived in memory that chance encounter with Hilda Ashley in the London restaurant, when she'd come face to face with her abysmal ignorance of cigarette research. She asked for a subscription to the Congressional Record and received it in time.

She vowed to follow every bill that came into Congress that might

deal with the effects of smoking on health—and was astonished when
several were introduced in the House and Senate. But soon she realized that none of these bills were being seriously considered. The
congressmen and senators from the tobacco states fought against any
bill that was a threat to the sale of cigarettes. She came to realize that
there was little real public support for these bills. Still, she clung to
the news that the Surgeon General had announced appointments to
the Advisory Committee on Smoking and Health. *Something must
come of this.*

For Vicky each day blended into the next. Weeks into months, and
then it was a year. How could this happen? Why didn't Kara and
Derek come looking for her? Couldn't Doug—over in Paris—understand something was wrong?

She'd asked for a subscription to *The Atlanta Constitution.* At intervals she saw Kara and Derek's names on the society pages. She
was delighted to read about a new building in Atlanta, where Derek
was the architect. After so much pain Kara had found herself, Vicky
thought thankfully.

She read about Doug's success in French musical theater and was
happy for him. *What had Adam told Doug that he never tried to find
her?*

With mounting excitement she followed the increasing number of
stories about the cigarette industry that were showing up in the newspapers and magazines. People had to take notice now, she told herself.
Facts were coming out into the open. She should find her "house
arrest" a little less repugnant, she told herself—knowing some progress was being made in alerting the public to the death being sold by
the cigarette companies. Yet, she strained at what would be solitary
confinement except for Amy's presence. It was Amy's determination
to learn to read and write—and now there was simple arithmetic—
that kept *her* from sinking into despair.

From her reading she knew that Adam had catapulted the company
into the multinational scene. And always she tried to deal with the
realization that Adam—her own son—could have so brazenly and
mercilessly thrown her into conservatorship. This would not go on
forever, she promised herself.

On January 11, 1964, the Advisory Committee on Smoking and
Health released its report to the public after over a year of study. The

committee concluded that cigarette smoking was related to lung cancer and increased the risk of dying from chronic bronchitis and emphysema. The committee further said that it was wise to assume that cigarette smoking also caused coronary disease.

Early in April Vicky read in the Richmond *Times-Dispatch* that Adam had bought a townhouse in Washington, D.C.—so he could personally supervise their lobbyists, she interpreted with distaste. Adam was reveling in his power.

"Miz Vicky, what are we going to see on television tonight?" Amy asked avidly as she cleared away the dinner dishes. Television brought the outside world to Amy, and she was intrigued.

"Do you really want to watch TV tonight?" Vicky teased.

"Yes ma'am." Amy was emphatic.

"All right. I'll let you choose," she promised. It was amazing, she thought affectionately, the bright young mind that had been buried beneath Amy's shyness.

They watched in quiet enjoyment the program of Amy's choosing. Then Amy turned to Vicky.

"Now it's your turn," she said with a bright smile. "We share, like you always say."

Vicky found a news program and leaned back to watch. She and Amy might be sequestered from the world, but TV brought the world to them. They had followed the tragic assassination of President Kennedy, had seen photos sent back to earth from space by astronauts. They had seen two hundred thousand people gathered together in Washington, D.C., to demonstrate for civil rights—and heard Martin Luther King's now famous "I have a dream" speech. But when would she be freed from her prison?

Kara stopped off at the florist shop in Buckhead to order the usual dozen red roses she sent to Vicky each month. She exchanged wistful complaints with the florist about the July heat wave that lay heavily over the area.

"I can't wait for the last two weeks in July when my wife and I will be up at my son's cottage in Pine Mountain. That's living." His face lighted in anticipation.

"Derek keeps urging me to go off to the seashore or to the mountains, but I told him I'll wait until he takes off three weeks next month and we can go together.'' Sara was in Europe for the summer with a group from school and having a ball. "Thank God for air-conditioning," she laughed. "How did we ever survive without it?"

Driving to the house Kara realized with a shock that Vicky had been in the sanitarium for just over two years. *Where did the time go?* At regular intervals she prodded Derek to check with the sanitarium about Vicky's condition. A man always received more respect. The response was always the same: *"There has been no change in Mrs. Barton's condition."*

Dad said the doctors taking care of her were top drawer and the sanitarium was luxurious—though he scoffed at their astronomical schedule of fees. And she understood, too, that Adam was his mother's conservator—it was his right to make all decisions. Still, she was frustrated that Adam had twice rejected their suggestion that other specialists be brought in to examine Vicky, and perhaps, offer alternative treatment.

On Thursday evenings the household staff was off, but Elvira always left a cold dinner in the refrigerator. After she and Derek ate and she'd stacked the dishes in the dishwasher, Kara plotted, she'd talk to him again about prodding Adam into some action. She and Adam just got into screaming battles when she tried to talk to him.

Exhausted from a long day on the job, Derek accepted Kara's offer of clearing away the dinner dishes, without his usual help, and bringing their coffee into the den.

"I know everything's air-conditioned at the office, but you've been spending so much time on the construction site—and in this weather that's ghastly."

Ten minutes later she came into the den with the coffee tray and discovered Derek asleep in his chair. Poor darling, he was so tired, she thought with a surge of tenderness. Moments later he came awake with a guilty start.

"I didn't mean to conk out on you," he said ruefully.

"I sent roses to Vicky today," she began and sighed. "I can't believe she's been in that sanitarium for over two years."

"Cases like hers are tricky, I understand." Derek's eyes were compassionate. "Suddenly one day she could come right out of it."

"I still think Adam should consult other specialists," Kara said. "He's always been so damn stubborn."

"I've asked around from time to time about the sanitarium she's in," Derek said. "It appears to be quite prestigious—"

"Derek, couldn't you try to talk to him once more? We just get into a screaming battle when I try."

"I'll phone him," he promised. "But you know what'll happen. Adam will yell and tell me to butt out. I gather he's spending a fortune on that fancy sanitarium and its specialists, so he's sure it has to be the best. He's never had any respect for me. He knows," Derek said humorously, "that we wouldn't be living in such style except for your inheritance. And Adam only respects money."

Adam sat across from Ronnie in the recently redecorated living room at Barton Manor and glared at her in silent rage. He waited for the servants to leave the room before he spoke his mind.

"What the hell do you mean? You want to plan a fox hunt at Barton Manor in the fall? Are you out of your mind?" First, the nonsense—again—with Kara and Derek, and now this.

"My father would bring down some important people from Washington," she pointed out. "Why not have the fox hunt?" she challenged.

"Why do you think Clark and I personally posted all those No Hunting and No Trespassing signs all through our acreage? We don't want strangers charging all over the place."

"Why don't you move her somewhere else? Wouldn't that be the smart thing to do?" Her smile was mocking.

"It would not be the smart thing to do," he said grimly. "That's a situation that has to be monitored at regular intervals—and by close family members."

"Adam, you're absurd. You have conservatorship—you can do anything you want."

"I like a contained, safe situation, Ronnie. She stays here."

It annoyed him that he had to pay off that damn sanitarium on a regular basis—all because Kara and Derek had to have a place to send flowers a dozen times a year, he thought in contempt. Even Doug wired flowers on every holiday that came up.

"I gather you don't want me to call on your cousin Doug when I'm in Paris next week," Ronnie sulked. She was going to Paris for the couturier shows. "He's so famous—and so good-looking."

"He won't be interested in *you*," Adam reminded. "Maybe in that couturier you're so crazy about." As usual, Ronnie would spend an obscene amount of money on new clothes.

"Yves Saint Laurent," she said complacently. "He's a marvelous designer. And so attractive." She gazed at him in speculation. "I can't imagine why you want to go to New York tomorrow in this heat."

"Business, Ronnie." He enjoyed these jaunts in the company jet. "That's what pays for all those goodies you like." When the bills came in, he was always mad as hell. Still, he liked having his wife's picture in all those slick magazines. "*Beautiful jet-setter Rowena Barton.*" It added to his own image.

"Dad asked me when I was up in Washington last week if that report from the Surgeon General—you know, that links smoking with lung cancer—is causing the industry any trouble."

"Tell him not to worry." Adam's smile was smug. "Smokers don't want to think about those crazy reports. Sales may drop for a while, but they'll pop right up again. People are not ready to give up their cigarettes!"

Chapter Forty-seven

IN THESE EARLY DAYS of her freshman year at NYU, Jill was awash with sentiment. This was where her mother had briefly studied. And in three years—by attending summer sessions—she would graduate and go on for a master's in journalism up at Columbia. Life had become beautiful, she told herself with relish.

At the end of the third week of classes she met Howard Levine, an NYU medical student, when both went to the rescue of a terrified Beagle pup being attacked by a nasty Doberman in Washington Square Park. The pup's owner—whose rescue efforts were being hampered by a rambunctious toddler—rushed forward in gratitude when the Doberman was sent into retreat. Afterwards, Jill and Howard decided to go to an Eighth Street coffee shop to discuss their mutual love for all four-legged animals.

From the first meeting Jill knew Howie was to be important in her life. It didn't matter that she was only a freshman and he was in his last year of medical school. They thought alike on almost everything. And Grandma always said, she reminded herself, that she was very mature for her age.

She hesitated to introduce Howie to her grandmother. Her mother had met her father during her freshman year at NYU—and that had been a disaster. But this was different. Howie was wonderful.

Except for cousins in Atlanta, Howie was alone in the world. He was an only child, and his parents had both died of cancer in his junior year of college. They'd left him funds to see him through medical school. When he talked with such dedication about becoming a doctor, she was convinced they were meant to share their lives.

Not until the first night of Hanukkah did she bring Howie home for dinner. She'd said very casually—fearful of upsetting her grandmother—that she'd invited somebody for dinner that night. It had been a habit ever since she was a little girl to bring somebody home the first night of Hanukkah. It made a party of the occasion of lighting the first Hanukkah candle.

"Oh, fine. Tell her to be here early," Rebecca reminded. "Before sunset."

"Him," Jill said, trying not to make it sound important.

"All right, him," Rebecca accepted. But Jill saw her grandmother's fleeting unease. It was the first time she'd invited a man to dinner.

Before they were half-through dinner, Jill began to relax. She watched her grandmother's face as Howie talked. *It was going to be all right.*

"I want to be an old-fashioned G. P.," Howie said earnestly. "I want to set up a practice—when I'm finally through training—in some small town where I don't have to charge my patients a lot of money. Low overhead, low fees," he said humorously. "I don't worry about driving a Jaguar and buying a big house in Westchester County and a second home on Fire Island or in the Hamptons."

Already Howie was plotting where to serve his internship and residency.

"Not in some huge city hospital," he stipulated. Jill suddenly felt lonely at the prospect of his living somewhere else, though they knew they'd be married eventually—once all their schooling was behind them. "I'll work the same insanely long hours, but let it be in a smaller city where people aren't on the crazy big city treadmill."

After Howie left, Jill turned to her grandmother with a conciliatory smile.

"Do you like him?"

"I like him," Rebecca nodded in approval. "He's a *mensch*."

Jill talked to Howie in total candor about her rage at her father, her avowal to be part of bringing him down. She spoke unflinchingly about her feelings toward the cigarette industry. *"They're guilty of more deaths than all the wars this country has ever fought!"* He listened with compassion and in agreement.

But she knew Howie was concerned about her hatred of her father. "Jill, don't let him poison your mind," he exhorted regularly. "You're hurting yourself in this obsession for revenge against him."

Early in the new year Rebecca Kahn suffered a massive stroke. Jill was devastated. Howie was constantly at her side as she waited for her grandmother to emerge from the coma. Late in the evening of the sixth day Rebecca rallied briefly.

She looked up at her granddaughter, then Howie.

"He's a fine boy, my darling," she whispered and closed her eyes. An hour later she was dead.

Jill moved through the next forty-eight hours in a daze. Howie took care of all the necessary arrangements, never leaving her side. After the funeral he told her firmly that they would be married immediately.

"Your grandmother would want that," he said, holding her in his arms.

He listened while she poured out her heart—about her love for her mother and her grandmother, about her anguish that her father had treated her mother so brutally.

"I hate him," she said, her voice muffled by tears. "But what about my grandmother on his side? Mom loved her. Why did she never try to reach us, Howie?"

"Maybe she did try," Howie reasoned. "She didn't stop loving you because your mother left your father. You said your mother didn't let anybody know where you were," he reminded.

Ten days later Jill and Howie were married by a rabbi in her grandmother's apartment. They would finish out the school year, Howie had decreed, then Jill would go with him to wherever he was to intern. She was bright and conscientious—she'd find a job there. And later she'd go back to school to earn her B.A. degree and then a master's in journalism.

"So I won't make much money as an intern," he conceded with wry humor. "With both of us working, we'll manage."

On a gray morning in early April Anita Roberts was laid to rest in a cemetery outside of London. Marc guiltily tried to repress his sense of being freed from a long prison term. Anita's moods had not improved by living in England. She'd antagonized almost everyone they knew in her last years. He'd remained at her side because he considered it his obligation.

He left the cemetery with Anita's attorney. They were the only mourners except for Anita's last nurse, who had been accompanied by three friends. *"Nobody should go to their grave without a few people there," she'd told Marc.*

Over a drink in the attorney's office Marc learned that most of Anita's fortune was gone.

"I know she didn't tell you," the attorney said compassionately. "She was a strange, hard woman—if you'll forgive me for saying so. When she knew she had only months to live, she disposed of most of her estate. It went to a British orphanage."

"I didn't know," Marc stammered. "I hadn't thought about it."

"You'll have whatever there is in your joint checking account," he told Marc. "You can go home now," he said with a faint smile.

"Yes." Marc was startled by his financial situation yet not alarmed. He would survive.

But where was home? They'd lived in so many towns in the course of their marriage. But only Richmond had seemed like home. Because Vicky was only a few miles away.

Was there a chance that he and Vicky could pick up their lives again? *Could* that happen, after all these years?

Late in April, Jill came home from a late class to find Howie had made dinner for them, set the table, and placed a bottle of champagne in a makeshift cooler on the table.

"What's the celebration?" A celebration, she thought in a fresh surge of grief, was an affront to her grandmother.

"Two replies in today's mail on my application for internship. Both acceptances." He reached to pull her close. His eyes pleaded with her to share his satisfaction.

"From where?" Out of New York, she was sure. Howie was firm about going to a smaller city—or even a small town. "Where are we going to live?" She tried for a festive note. Howie hadn't told her where he'd applied. *"I don't want you to be disappointed if your favorite place turns me down."*

"Honey, I don't have to accept it—but I think one of them would be good for both of us." His dark eyes were anxious now.

"Howie, where? Why are you being so mysterious?"

"Barton Memorial," he said softly. "In Bartonville, Virginia."

Jill stiffened in his arms. Shaken. Recoiling from the prospect of living in Bartonville. *How could she go back there?*

"Howie, it would be a nightmare," she whispered.

"You need to face up to the past," he told her. "You need to know about your family on your father's side."

"I hate him!" she said passionately. "I know more than I want to know about him. Howie, how can you ask me to live in the same town with him?"

"He won't know you're there. You'll be Jill Levine, a New Yorker whose husband happens to be interning at Barton Memorial. I want you to know about your grandmother on your father's side, your aunts, and your cousins—"

"My grandmother is in a mental institution," she reminded him.

An inchoate alarm welled in her. Mom said she looked just like Nana. Was she like her in other ways? Did that mean *she* might end up in a mental institution, too? "And why should I care about her? She never tried to find Mom and me—"

"Jill, nobody knew where you were," Howie reminded. "Your grandmother told you your mother was terrified that the family might track you down and take you away. She threw them off the track."

"She should have tried," Jill said stubbornly, even while she knew this was a childish reproach.

"It's right near Richmond," Howie cajoled. "You can pick up a journalism degree at the university."

"Where is the other hospital?" Jill asked.

"Out in Kansas." He told her the name. It was a prestigious institute, Jill recognized—one most interns would welcome. "It's up to you."

He'd hate interning at a huge hospital, she remembered. He was so anxious to try living in a small town.

"Okay, we go to Bartonville." The prospect was terrifying, but for Howie she would face it. "Now get dinner on the table before I die of hunger."

Two weeks later Howie left for Bartonville for his interview. Jill clutched at the excuse of preparations for finals to avoid accompanying him. She insisted that whatever house or apartment he rented for them would meet with her approval.

"But as close to Richmond as possible," she'd instructed. Please, God, not in Bartonville. She'd find a job in Richmond. Later—when they'd built up a bank account—she'd look into classes at the University of Richmond.

Howie came back jubilant. He'd found the hospital well-equipped and staffed. He'd liked the people he met.

"Oh, the chief administrator is married to a Barton. Stephanie Barton," Howie told her. "I gather he's chief administrator in name only. And he'll never win a popularity contest at the hospital."

"That's Nana's sister-in-law," Jill pulled from her memory. "Her son is named Doug. Mom said she'd read that he'd become a very well-known composer in Paris." She might meet the Bartons—but they wouldn't know who she was. She clung to the comfort this provided. Mom used to say she'd liked Kara and Doug, though she'd had nothing good to say about their parents.

"What about an apartment?" Jill asked Howie. "Did you find a place for us to live?"

"I found a house. A little one, midway between Bartonville and Richmond—five miles in either direction," he told her. "We'll have to pick up a cheap secondhand car. You can't survive down there without a car."

"When do we have to be there?" They could afford a secondhand car, she thought in a corner of her mind—relieved that they wouldn't be living in Bartonville. Howie had saved some money, and she had some money from her joint savings account with Grandma. They weren't one of the "Hundred Neediest Cases."

"I had to take the house right away," he explained. "We'll head there immediately after graduation. That'll give me a little time to help you settle in before I start at the hospital. Oh, I bought a box spring and mattress," he added grinning. "That with my card table and your folding chairs will be our furniture until we shop."

"I'm scared," she confessed.

"About being married?" he joshed.

"About going to Bartonville, silly." Her laughter was shaky. Thank God for Howie, she thought.

Marc was assaulted by memories as he walked through the Richmond depot. He should have written Vicky, he chastised himself. But in a corner of his mind he'd harbored a fear that she might have remarried—that she wouldn't welcome a letter from him.

Every moment of the train ride from New York to Richmond he had thought about her. He remembered every detail of her face, the sound of her voice, her gestures. He visualized the way her face lighted up when she was pleased. He relived the precious hours they'd spent together in what they thought was their secret hideaway.

The early June day was humid. No breeze from the river alleviated the discomfort. He'd register at a hotel, go out to an air-conditioned restaurant for dinner. In the morning he'd call Vicky. He was almost lightheaded at the prospect. He would call her at the office rather than at Barton Manor. If she had remarried, he had cautioned himself, it would be better not to intrude on her at home.

Later—sitting in a comfortably air-conditioned restaurant—he tried to analyze his reactions. At moments it seemed as though he'd been away a century, at other moments as though he'd hardly been away at all. Before coming into the restaurant he'd taken a long, exhausting walk about town. He was amazed at the number of new buildings that had gone up and how the skyline had changed. Seeing a black couple seated at the next table, he recognized that integration had made great strides in Richmond. That must please Vicky. Reading about the problems of integration in the *International Herald-Tribune* had been enlightening. Seeing it in effect in Richmond was much more dramatic and satisfying.

He knew he would sleep little tonight. He was impatient to hear Vicky's voice on the phone, to learn if they could bridge the years between them. He had never stopped loving her. The memory of those years they'd shared had enriched his exile.

He returned to the hotel, tried to read. Images of Vicky kept invading his mind. It was unlikely that he'd find an opening at the university—or at any of the other colleges in Richmond, he warned himself. He was fifty-nine years old and away from teaching for thirteen years. Instead he'd decided to invest his modest funds in a bookshop. Richmond was a "bookstore town."

The first gray streaks of dawn were seeping through the blinds of his hotel room when he finally succumbed to sleep. He awoke with a sudden start, realizing almost immediately that he was in a strange hotel room—in Richmond.

He turned to the clock on his night table. It was eight AM. Was Vicky still the first one in the Barton offices, he asked himself with a surge of anticipation. Wait a while, he cautioned himself. Shower, dress, have coffee sent up from room service—then call Vicky. Oh, God, he couldn't wait to hear the sound of her voice.

Just before nine AM—his heart pounding—Marc called the business offices of Barton Tobacco Company. Had her feelings toward him changed in the intervening years, he asked himself. His instincts told him they had not. They'd shared something so precious. Could even the years of separation kill their feelings for each other?

"Good morning, Barton Tobacco Company," a young Southern voice greeted him.

"May I speak to Mrs. Barton, please?"

"Mrs. Barton hasn't been with the company for three years," the switchboard operator said with an undercurrent of surprise in her voice. "Can somebody else help you, sir?"

"Thank you, no." His throat tightened in disappointment as he put down the phone. He couldn't conceive of Vicky leaving the company. Was she all right? Alarm triggered him into action. He reached for the telephone book again. He'd call Lisa Feinberg.

He located Lisa's phone number—relieved to find that she still lived in Richmond and at the same address. Why had he expected nothing to have changed in the years he'd been away?

He waited expectantly for Lisa to answer the phone. It was ringing steadily. Was she still asleep? Had he called too early?

"Hello—" Lisa's voice was faintly breathless as though she had hurried from some distant point in the house to reply. For Marc, it was as though he had heard her voice yesterday.

"Lisa—"

"Yes—"

"I don't know if you remember me—" All at once he was self-conscious. In many ways time had stood still for him through the years. "Marc Roberts."

"Marc, how lovely to hear from you!" Her warmth was reassuring. "Are you in Richmond?"

"Yes, I arrived last night," he explained.

"Do you know, I almost wrote you a fan letter a few years ago. I read that marvelous article of yours about Richmond. But then I thought, all these years later, you might not even remember me."

"Lisa, how would I not remember you?" he chided. "You all made me feel so welcome here in Richmond. After years of being nomads

I felt that Anita and I had come home." He hesitated. "Anita died three weeks ago in London."

"Marc, I'm so sorry," Lisa said compassionately. "We often talked about you and Anita and wondered how you were."

"Tell me about everybody," he encouraged, striving to sound casual. "How is Vicky? Still the hard-working business executive?"

"Oh, you haven't heard about Vicky." Lisa's voice activated alarm signals in him. "She's been in a sanitarium for the past three years. She had a nervous breakdown, and still hasn't seemed to come out of it. We were all shocked and upset to hear about it."

"What brought that on?" he asked, his dream world collapsing about him. "I know she worked terribly hard."

"I suppose it was an accumulation of things. We hadn't been seeing much of her in the years after Adam's remarriage. She was terribly upset when Eleanor left him and took off with Jill. Do you remember how she adored her granddaughter?"

"Jill was the center of her life," Marc said gently.

"I don't think she's fond of Adam's second wife. Adam and Ronnie moved to Barton Manor about a year after their marriage—and Vicky just seemed to spend all her waking hours at the company. We'd talk on the phone, but sometimes I didn't see her for months on end."

"Where's this sanitarium?" Marc asked compulsively. "I'd like to send her flowers."

"I don't know just where it is. But from what we've been told, she's completely irrational. She doesn't even recognize Adam. Nobody's allowed to visit her. The doctors say this just makes her condition worse. Vicky, of all people," Lisa said with frustration. "It's hard to believe, isn't it?"

"Vicky's always been so strong—" Disconcerting questions flooded his mind.

"Marc, why don't you come to dinner tomorrow night?" Lisa urged. "Just a dinner party for a few of the old crowd. Everybody will be so pleased to see you."

"I'd like that very much. But I warn you, I'm not just passing through town. I've come to Richmond to settle down. If I can find the right spot, I plan on opening a bookshop here."

"Oh, that's great news! And you couldn't have chosen a better place for a bookshop," she said with pride. "I heard that the American

Booksellers Association declared Richmond one of the nation's prime retail book markets. People in Richmond buy more books per head than those anywhere in the Southeast between Washington and Atlanta—and we may even buy more than people in Atlanta."

"If you hear of a nice one-bedroom apartment, let me know," Marc encouraged. "I hate living in a hotel."

"We'll have to fill you in about how Richmond has changed at dinner, Marc. Welcome home!"

Off the phone Marc sat immobile, trying to digest everything that Lisa had told him. He didn't want to believe that Vicky had had a nervous breakdown. He must make an effort to see her, he promised himself. He'd never rest if he had any doubts about her really being ill.

Now he forced himself to deal with the practical matter of looking for an apartment, and locating a vacant store that would be suitable for a bookshop. He realized he couldn't accomplish all this in one day, but making preliminary inquiries would keep him busy until this evening. Tonight he would call Adam at Barton Manor and ask about seeing Vicky.

He waited until past the usual dinner time to phone Adam. Even so, the maid who answered the phone wasn't sure he was through with dinner.

"I'll just go see if Mr. Adam can come to the phone," she said politely.

"Tell him it's an old friend of his mother's who's just arrived in town after a long absence," Marc told her. "I can call back later if this is an inconvenient time."

In a few moments Adam was on the phone. His tone indicated that he was annoyed at this intrusion.

"I've been living in England for the past thirteen years," he explained to Adam. "A mutual friend told me of your mother's illness, and I thought—"

"My mother sees no one," Adam interrupted. "Doctor's orders."

"I'd like to send her a card or flowers," Marc told him. "Just for old times' sake. Where is the sanitarium?"

Marc wrote down the name and address given him with obvious reluctance. Tomorrow he'd rent a car and drive down to the sanitarium. With luck he'd get in to see Vicky. *Was she receiving the best medical care? Was there a need to bring in other doctors?*

Immediately after breakfast he rented a car, stopped at a florist shop to buy a dozen red roses. Vicky had always loved red roses, he'd remembered. Now he headed south for the sanitarium. Who had committed her? he asked himself. Was he being melodramatic in his suspicions that this was an effort on Adam's part to gain control of the business?

The sanitarium was a lush complex set in acres of exquisitely landscaped grounds—a haven for the very rich. He parked, and walked into the spacious lobby.

The receptionist was polite but firm.

"I'm sorry. Mrs. Barton is allowed to see no one. But we'll make sure she receives your flowers," she promised.

"I'm an old friend who's been living in London for the past thirteen years," he tried again.

"We have our orders, sir." She opened the box of flowers, smiled down at the cluster of long-stemmed red roses. "She must have loved red roses. A box arrives every month from a niece down in Atlanta."

That would be Kara, he realized. Then it was true. Vicky was here in the sanitarium and allowed no visitors. *Knowing this, did he want to stay in Richmond?*

Chapter Forty-eight

Vicky watched the national news on TV while Amy prepared dinner in the kitchen. She was upset by the nation's intensifying activities in Vietnam. With the four thousand Marines who'd landed in Vietnam last May, the total U.S. forces there was now over forty-two thousand.

"Come to the table, Miz Vicky," Amy said. "You have to eat your dinner while it's hot. You can watch more television later."

"All right, Amy." Vicky switched off the television set and followed Amy into the dining room.

"I just don't understand all this fighting," Amy confided.

"There seems to be no end of wars, Amy." She never watched the news without thinking of Michael. "All those young boys killed or maimed. So many missing in action. Pray," she said compassionately, "that the war will soon be over and they'll be free to go home again. I guess you could say you and I are missing in action," she added, her smile whimsical. Sometimes it was hard to believe she and Amy had been here in the cottage for three years. Amy talked about asking for paint and brushes so she could paint the walls. "Of course, we're not sitting in prisons with God only knows what kind of food—and no television," she teased because Amy adored television.

"Can we see 'Father Knows Best'?" Amy asked, serenely sure that they would.

"We'll watch it," Vicky promised.

While Amy did the dishes, Vicky sat down to read the last copy of the *New York Times*—brought to her from Richmond each week. Tonight she was searching for more word on the Federal Trade Commission's ruling on cigarette advertising. If the health warning about cigarettes was not used in advertising, the ruling would have lost its teeth, she thought in frustration.

Then Amy hurried into the living room, though their program would not begin for another few minutes. Their TV time and Amy's "school time" were the important periods of their waking hours. Amy dropped to the floor before the set and began to fiddle with the dials.

A commercial came on and captured Vicky's attention. The little girl in the commercial reminded her of Jill. But Jill would be grown now, she thought wistfully. Someday Jill would be a major beneficiary in her will—but would the lawyer who was her executor ever be able to find this cherished grandchild? Would some miracle ever bring Jill into her life again?

On a gray, dismal morning shortly after graduation, Jill and Howie loaded their newly purchased secondhand Valiant with all their personal belongings and headed south. Jill made an effort to laugh at Howie's comments as they emerged from the Lincoln Tunnel into New Jersey. She knew he was determined to build this trip into a small adventure, to make her forget that they were cutting themselves off from what had been home for most of their lives.

"I feel like we have a backseat driver," Howie joshed, as they waited at a traffic light. Jill's stuffed giraffe sat atop a pile of blankets and linens on the rear seat.

"Hoppy's good at that," Jill laughed. "Remember, we haven't been separated since my fourth birthday." When Nana had given her the giraffe, Mom had promptly named it "Hoppy" for Hopalong Cassidy— whom she'd adored on television. She hadn't thought of her Barton grandmother in such a long time—but suddenly she was "Nana" again and one of her few good memories of Bartonville. Nana and their pretty little house, surrounded by flowers and trees. She harbored images of a huge white house with tall columns out front. Nana's house.

"I hope you like our house," Howie said. At intervals now Howie expressed concern. "It's tiny but nice. And we look out on open fields on every side. It's a long haul from West Eighty-fourth Street in Manhattan.''

"It's close to Richmond, you said." Jill clung to the knowledge that they wouldn't be living in Bartonville.

"If you think you'll be scared at being alone there," Howie said anxiously, "we can get a dog." He was remembering the grim stories of the hours interns worked at every hospital.

"I won't be afraid," she promised. "Later we'll get a puppy. Once we're all settled in." A dog-lover like herself, Howie knew she'd always regretted never having a dog in her growing-up years. Grandma said it'd be unkind to keep a dog cooped up in the apartment when they would be away so much of each day.

The drizzle that began when they were only minutes out of the Lincoln Tunnel became a downpour for the next hundred miles. Then all at once they left the rain behind for brilliant sunshine.

"It's an omen," Howie told her with mock solemnity. "We're moving into great times."

They stopped to picnic at a particularly lovely park. Howie dug out his camera and insisted on taking endless snapshots of her. He was a long-time photography buff. "I'm making the spare bedroom my darkroom," he warned in gleeful anticipation.

As the miles sped past, Jill grew tense. She didn't want to go to Bartonville, yet she was conscious of an obsession to know about what Mom had called her "other family." At intervals Mom had talked almost compulsively about them. Names jogged into her memory now. Nana and Doug and Kara, whom Mom had liked so much—and her great-grandmother, who was dead. Lily and Stephanie and what Mom had called "the husbands"—all of whom she'd disliked. Mom never talked about Adam Barton—as she herself preferred to think of her father. Grandma had been blunt in her hatred of him—but Mom just said he'd been a bad husband and father. *"We couldn't live with him anymore, so we came to live with Grandma."*

She remembered that strange trip to Richmond when she was eleven. Grandma wanted her to meet with her father—*"It'll make me feel better to know he's there for you if something happens to me."* Grandma hadn't said it in so many words, but she'd understood he hadn't wanted to see her.

When they approached Richmond, Howie took a cutoff that was a shortcut to the house.

"Shall we take a drive to Bartonville first?" Howie asked gently. "I'll show you the hospital where I'll be interning."

"Not yet." She was involuntarily sharp. She wasn't ready to deal with Bartonville. "Let's go home." Her voice was softer now.

She was glad that Howie didn't have to report for duty right away. She needed his presence in the house. She liked the large, sunlit country kitchen. There was a fireplace in the cozy living room, a corner of which must serve as their dining area. On cold nights, she told herself, they'd be able to have dinner and watch logs burning in the fireplace.

Together they painted the four rooms of the cottage, and shopped for the absolute essentials. Later—when she was working—they'd fix up the house so that it was really attractive. Everything was so expensive.

They became familiar with Richmond. They drove to the campus of the university—where in time Jill planned to attend classes. Twice they went to the movies. They were impressed by the presence of a symphony and an Opera group—though they couldn't afford such luxuries at this point.

Now Howie insisted that Jill do most of the driving. She'd just learned to drive a few weeks ago. He was eager for her to feel comfortable at the wheel.

"I don't want to leave you stranded at the house," he said solicitously. "You'll have the car. You'll drive me to and from the hospital."

Her first drive into Bartonville was traumatic, though she had no recall of the town itself. She felt a tightening in her throat, a dryness in her mouth. She fought against an urge to turn around and head for home.

"It's an ugly town," she said with distaste, driving slowly along Main Street, en route to the hospital.

"Like most company towns," Howie dismissed this cheerfully. "But look ahead. That's a beautiful park area coming up."

They paused to admire the small park, then drove past rows of dreary small houses. Soon, a more affluent area came into view. Here beautiful houses sat surrounded by extensive, landscaped grounds.

"Probably the homes of company executives," Howie surmised. "Oh, the hospital is just ahead, on the right."

Jill turned off the road onto the driveway leading to the hospital parking area. This was the Daniel Barton Memorial Hospital, erected in memory of her great-grandfather. She didn't feel like a Barton, she thought defiantly. That was just an accident of birth.

* * *

Now Jill and Howie settled into a routine. He insisted she wait until the fall to look for a job.

"Honey, you've worked your beautiful little butt off these last three years—you need some time off."

Each morning she drove Howie to the hospital and picked him up when he called to say he was off-duty. On her fourth morning she drove to Richmond after leaving Howie at the hospital. Her destination was the Richmond Public Library.

Forgetful of time, Jill sat at a table in the library and scanned the pages of back issues of the local papers. Her heart pounded each time a Barton was mentioned. Now she plotted a course for herself. She'd learn about the Barton family by reading through the years. Start far back, she ordered herself, then come up to the present.

Hesitantly she told Howie about what she meant to do.

"That's good," he approved. "Because they're your roots, too. But don't sit there in the library all day and forget to go out to have lunch," he warned, drawing her into his arms. "I don't want to see you melt down to a shadow."

Jill felt as though she were living in two worlds—the world of yesterday, inhabited by family she knew only by name, and the warm, precious world that centered around Howie. She was always grateful that Howie had come into her life.

She read about her great-grandfather, tobacco tycoon Daniel Barton, her grandfather Gary, who committed suicide, her uncle Michael who died in World War II, her great-grandmother Sara—whom Mom had loved. She learned about her cousins Kara and Doug, and her great-aunts, who were the family jet-setters, and their husbands. One husband, who was once the mayor of Bartonville, was now a judge. The other—as Howie had told her—was the chief administrator at Barton Memorial. She read birth, wedding, death announcements. With a sense of unreality she read the announcement of her own birth. She was the youngest Barton.

She was struggling to become accustomed to Howie's extended working hours. He said the schedule for interns was meant to train them to cope with emergency situations even when they were exhausted. Still, she loathed seeing him so dragged out, she thought while she waited this morning for a call to pick him up at the hospital. He'd been on duty for twenty-four hours.

Her introspection was shattered by a shrill sound of the phone. She hurried from the kitchen to answer. She told herself it would *not* be Howie, calling to tell her he was stuck with another back-to-back shift. She was supposed to leave in ten minutes to pick him up with the car. They'd have breakfast, then he'd sack out for a few hours. In the three weeks that he had been an intern at Barton Memorial he'd been caught twice on back-to-back shifts.

"Hello," she said breathlessly. Actually, nobody but Howie or Kathy—the wife of another intern—ever phoned the house. They didn't know anybody yet.

"Baby, I'm sorry. I'm stuck for another twelve hours."

"Oh Howie, you must be so tired. You never get enough sleep."

"You know I'm not fooling around with other women," he joshed. "I wouldn't have the strength. If I get off earlier, I'll call you to come and get me."

"Okay."

"Drive into Richmond and go to a movie," he urged her. "This is a day for air-conditioning."

"I'll go floating around the book stores," she told him. She felt guilty that she hadn't started looking for a job yet. Howie kept insisting she wait until the fall. Right now she was engrossed in furnishing the house as cheaply as possible, buying only what was essential. "Kathy says there's a new store in town that has a great suspense section." Jill was addicted to paperback suspense novels.

"Live dangerously," Howie laughed. "Buy yourself an armful of paperbacks."

In his small but attractive new bookshop—open only four weeks but already showing signs of making the grade—Marc was rearranging the window to include five newly arrived titles. It was rare that anyone came in this early, but he preferred being in the bookshop to his apartment. He felt less lonely here.

He glanced up with a smile when a slim young girl left her car at the curb to walk purposefully toward the shop.

"Good morning," he began—and stared at the lovely face of the new arrival with a disconcerting feeling of déjà vu. It was unbelievable, he thought—her resemblance to Vicky. The same mass of dark hair, the same features, the same violet eyes. But then, everybody has a double somewhere on this earth, he told himself. "Forgive me for staring," he apologized, "but you remind me so much of someone I used to know."

"I have that kind of face." Even the lilt in her voice reminded him of Vicky. "A friend told me you have a great suspense section."

"Yes, right over there—" He pointed to a far corner of the shop. "If there's anything special you'd like that I don't have, I can order it for you."

"Thank you." She smiled—Vicky's smile, he thought in torment.

He waited behind the counter while she browsed, glad she was the sole customer in the shop. If she and Vicky were in the same room, he mused, strangers would take them for mother and daughter. Vicky always looked so much younger than she was, he remembered nostalgically. All at once, he couldn't bear to have this young replica of Vicky walk out of the shop without further exchange. For a little while he would feel he was with Vicky.

When she came to the counter with her three paperback books, he began a compulsive conversation. Feeling awkward yet obsessed with a need to talk to her.

"Are you a student at the university?" he began. "I taught there years ago."

"No. I just finished my freshman year at NYU in New York," she told him. "I'm hoping to earn a degree later on at the university. My husband just started interning at Barton Memorial, so I figure on waiting a while before going back to school. I mean, his hours are so crazy."

"I hear interns have a rough road," he sympathized, just now noting her wedding band.

"Howie always says, 'Jill, anything worthwhile comes hard.' "

All at once Marc's heart was pounding.

"Jill?"

"Yes—" She smiled uncertainly.

Suddenly the atmosphere was electric.

"Before your marriage, were you Jill Barton?"

"Yes," she whispered. "How did you know?"

"You're the image of your grandmother. She was very dear to me." His voice was uneven. "She loved you so much, Jill. For months— after you and your mother left—she had detectives searching for you."

"I thought she had forgotten me—" Her eyes searched his.

"She never stopped hoping she'd find you," Marc said. But now Vicky would never know that Jill had come home.

"I'd like so much to talk with you about her," Jill said urgently. "Could you—would you come to dinner with Howie and me? Tomorrow night," she said. "Tonight he'll come home and just fall into bed."

"I'd like that very much." Marc felt himself encased in unreality. Vicky had prayed to find Jill for so long. Now Jill was here—but she wasn't.

Jill awoke early after a restless night. Despite the morning heat, Howie slept soundly beside her. He'd sleep well into the afternoon, she guessed with a rush of tenderness. He was so beat. But at least he was off-duty until tomorrow morning.

Howie would be here for dinner with Marc Roberts. She lay back against her pillow and went over in her mind—as she had a dozen times already—the startling encounter in the bookshop. She suspected that Marc Roberts and Nana had once been in love, and that he still loved her grandmother. And he'd known Mom.

Impatient to talk with Marc again, Jill tried to fill her day with activities, pushing away the hours until dinner. She wished their little house was more completely furnished. They had not yet bought real dining room furniture, but the table bought at a rummage sale would be hidden at dinner by one of Grandma's fine linen tablecloths. Thank goodness, they'd brought along the four folding chairs from New York.

By four o'clock the pot roast filled the kitchen with savory aromas. Not until the last moment would she steam the vegetables she'd bought at a nearby roadside stand. The salad was ready. Dessert—a colorful fruit salad to which she'd add raspberry sherbet later—was chilling in the refrigerator.

She walked to the bedroom, quietly opened the door, and peered inside. Howie was still asleep. She'd let him sleep until the last moment.

The three hours before Marc Roberts was due to arrive seemed awesomely long. Her mind raced backward through the years. She remembered the pretty cottage that sat on a knoll with a view of the river. Mom had loved the river. On hot days like this one Mom used to walk with her at the water's edge and tell her fanciful stories.

All at once she felt an obsessive need to walk along that river again. Nobody would know, she soothed herself. She'd park on the road and find her way down to the river. *No one would see her.* For Mom she had to walk beside the river again.

She hurried out into the kitchen, turned off the heat under the pot roast. When she returned, she'd let it simmer again. In a burst of impatience she left the house and went out to the Valiant. No breeze from the river here, she thought subconsciously. The house was too far from the water.

She knew that the Barton estate sat not far off the main road between here and Bartonville. There was a sign pointing to Barton Manor. How many times had she been drawn just to drive past—but at the last moment rejected the prospect?

Now she watched for the sign, all the while trying to remember the path along the river. Did she truly remember, she asked herself—or was she imagining it? *No, she remembered walking there with Mom.*

She drove the equivalent of at least three city blocks past the entrance to the estate before she parked. Her heart beating wildly, she left the car and walked toward the woods. She searched for a path. There was none. Blindly she pushed her way through the overgrown bushes, past trees that were a century old toward what she sensed was the river, ignoring the endless display of No Trespassing and No Hunting signs posted on the towering, summer-lush trees.

A faint breeze told her she was approaching the river. An odd exhilaration charged through her when the river came into view. *Here was where she had walked with Mom.*

The water level was low. In spots she could see the river bed. Wild flowers grew in profusion along the bank. Mom had been happy when they walked here together. Why did she have to die so young?

I hate my father! Grandma said he made Mom a smoker. She'd be alive today if she hadn't smoked. Damn the cigarette companies!

The view blurred by her tears, Jill walked until the first clap of thunder made her realize the sun had disappeared and a summer shower was imminent. She gazed about the woods for a path that would take her back to the car. Panic gripped her for a few moments when no path seemed in sight. She'd just plowed through the woods when she came in—

Try this way, she ordered herself. Perhaps it would lead to the road.

Rain began to fall in huge, cooling drops. She walked quickly, anxious now to be back in the car. She'd die if anyone found her here.

She paused, startled by the sound of music. Her eyes followed the sound. How strange! In the midst of the woods a gigantic circle of evergreens towered perhaps a dozen feet or more. Her heart began to pound again. Instinctively she knew that behind those evergreens—taller than she remembered—was the cottage where she and Mom had lived. Who lived there now?

Trembling, she walked to the circle of evergreens, searching for the entrance. She halted before a tall, wooden door, read the message scrawled in large red letters: Private Property. Trespassers Will Be Prosecuted. She hesitated only an instant, pulled the door open. She stared at the chain-link fence that surrounded the cottage. Here a sign read: Beware. Fence Electrified. *Someone was imprisoned behind this fence.*

"Amy, let's bring in the clothes before they get soaked." A slender woman was at the clothesline, her back to Jill.

"Yes ma'am," a youthful voice called out.

The woman turned around. A coldness closed in about Jill. *That was Nana.* The face she remembered, only older now. The face so like her own.

"Nana!" she cried out involuntarily.

"Who's there?" The woman inside the fence was moving toward the gate, trying to see through the pelting rain. *Yes, it was Nana.* All at once her face was luminescent. "Jill? Jill, is that you?"

"Yes," she managed to gasp. She saw a young black girl emerge from the cottage, and walk toward them as though mesmerized. "People told Marc Roberts that you were in a sanitarium. We thought—"

"*Marc?*" Vicky's voice was hushed in astonishment. "Marc's in Richmond?" Astonishment gave way to joy.

"Yes. When I said my name was Jill, he asked if I had been Jill Barton. He said I had to be your granddaughter—we look so much alike."

"Jill, my darling—" She extended fingers towards an opening, then suddenly remembered not to touch the fence. "This is a dream come true. You and Marc, both here in Bartonville."

"I don't understand." Jill's eyes clung to her grandmother's. "What have they done to you?"

"Jill, go to Marc," Vicky said urgently. "Bring him here. Tell him Adam had me put into conservatorship. No doubt Jeffrey declared me mentally incompetent. Clark must have been the judge who signed the papers. Marc will get me out of this insanity. What is today?" she asked in sudden caution. "Wednesday?"

"Yes—"

"Good, on Saturdays somewhere before dawn someone comes to bring me supplies. No one comes at any other time. Bring Marc to me, my darling. He'll know how to get me out of this prison. But go quickly. Nobody must see you here."

Chapter Forty-nine

SOAKED TO THE SKIN but refusing to stop at the house to change into dry clothes, Jill drove into Richmond. The summer thunderstorm was at its height now. Lightning lit up the sky. Thunder roared like some demoniacal god out for revenge on a thoughtless earth.

Grateful for an available spot, Jill parked near the bookshop, darted across the sidewalk and inside. Marc was in conversation with a customer at the counter. Another pair of customers browsed in the rear. She stood near the counter and waited with strained patience for him to finish with the customer.

She saw the concern in his eyes when he turned to her. She was clearly distraught.

"Jill, what's happened?" he asked.

"I have to talk to you," she began, took a deep breath, then poured out in hoarse whispers what she had just encountered. Marc listened with a mixture of incredulity, elation, and grim determination.

"Everything's going to be all right now," Marc soothed her. "I'll close the shop in a few moments." He nodded toward the browsers. "I'll explain that a family emergency has arisen and get them out. Go home, change into dry clothes, and I'll pick you up in fifteen minutes. We'll go out to Vicky. But don't expect us to gain her release immediately," he warned. "Everything has to be handled through attorneys and the court. But I promise you, we'll get her out of that prison."

Jill smiled through tears of relief. "I'll be waiting at the house for you."

"Do you have a camera?" Marc asked.

"Oh, yes. Photography is Howie's hobby," Jill told him. "He's even set up a darkroom in the house."

"Bring the camera with you," Marc instructed. "We'll need it."

"Yes." Jill hurried from the shop and back to the Valiant. She clung to what Nana had said: "Marc will get me out of this insanity."

Walking into the house, Jill sniffed the pungent aroma of percolating coffee. Howie was awake and in the kitchen.

"Howie!" She darted into the kitchen and in a burst of rage told him what had happened.

"Marc Roberts is driving by to pick me up," she finished. "We're going back to the cottage. Come with us, Howie."

"You bet I'm coming." His face mirrored his shock and anger. "Go change into dry clothes," he said gently. "Your grandmother needs strong supporters—not a sick little granddaughter."

A few minutes later Marc arrived.

"I'm already in contact with a lawyer," he reported. "One with top credentials and out of this area. Someone who won't be intimidated by Adam and his cronies. This isn't going to be easy," he warned her again. "We're taking on a so-called eminent local doctor, a law firm that obviously takes its orders from Adam Barton—and a court judge who does the same."

"The truth has to come out!" Jill was frustrated that delays lay ahead. *Why couldn't they get her out immediately?*

Jill looked up with a smile as Howie walked into the living room. She introduced him to Marc, and he held up his camera.

"I assume you want snapshots."

"Absolutely," Marc confirmed. "We must have photos of that fence, photos of Vicky, and a statement from her—witnessed by you and me, Howie, that she's being held against her wishes. We'll have to prove that the whole trial to put her into conservatorship was a fraud."

"When will the lawyer take action?" Jill prodded.

"He's driving into Richmond early tomorrow morning. We're to meet him at a highway diner a couple of miles out of town—where we can talk in private. I'll pick you up at around eight AM—we'll go to meet him together. Is that all right?" He gazed from Jill to Howie.

"I'll be on duty in the emergency room," Howie explained, "but Jill will be waiting for you."

"You'll be swearing out the complaint, Jill," Marc explained. "You're a blood relative. Now please, take me to Vicky."

"I hope I can find the cottage again." Jill frowned in recall as they walked to Marc's car. "There's no path from the road. I just pushed toward the river."

"We'll find the cottage." Marc was unperturbed. "We'll find Vicky."

All at once they were aware that the summer storm was over.

"Look at that magnificent rainbow." Marc paused beside the car. "It's a symbol," he said, smiling whimsically.

"They won't try to move her?" Jill asked in sudden panic while she slid onto the front seat beside Marc and Howie climbed into the rear.

"They don't realize we know," Marc pointed out. "By the time they find out, it'll be too late."

When they arrived on the road that flanked the vast Barton Manor acreage, Jill directed Marc to where she believed she'd entered the woods earlier. The three hurried from the car—Jill in the lead.

"This way, I think—" Her throat was tight with anxiety. *She had to find the cottage again.*

They pushed their way through the woods, ignoring the droplets of rain that fell from the branches above.

"I feel a breeze from the river. We're going in the right direction." Marc's voice was electric with anticipation.

A few minutes later they heard music.

"She's kept the record player going so we'd have a beacon," Marc guessed. "Beethoven's Fifth," he recognized. "One of her favorites."

Now they charged forward with fresh intensity. As the sound of the music grew louder, Marc paused.

"Please," he asked apologetically. "May I have a few moments alone with her? Just a few moments—"

"Of course." She'd been right, Jill thought sentimentally. Marc and her grandmother had been in love. Were still in love.

She and Howie fell behind Marc, deliberately slow in their approach. Howie's hand reached for hers. He, too, understood.

Marc opened the door and gazed into the fenced-in circle. The front door of the cottage was open. How awful, he thought in rage, to bring Vicky here where Gary killed himself.

"Vicky?" His voice didn't carry above the music, he realized. "Vicky!" he called out in joyous abandon.

"Amy, turn off the record player—" he heard Vicky say. After all these years he recognized her voice instantly. Now she hurried from the cottage. "Marc?" She gazed at him, immobile for a moment. Now her face was alight with joyous comprehension. "Oh, Marc—" She ran toward him, her arms outstretched. Then she frowned. Her hands dropped by her side as she approached the fence. "Don't touch it," she said anxiously.

"I know," he said, his eyes seeming to embrace her. "I told you I'd come back to you when I was free," he said tenderly. "I didn't expect you to be the prisoner now. Oh Vicky, you haven't changed a bit—"

"Marc," she laughed, "it's been thirteen years."

"I told you long ago—you discovered the Fountain of Youth and bathed in it every day."

"I can't believe you've found me." Her voice was a caress. "Here I am—sixty-three years old—and I feel like twenty again."

"We'll make up for the lost years," he vowed. "But first we have to clear up this madness." He turned and gestured to Jill and Howie to join him.

All at once there was a burst of activity. Howie took snapshots of Vicky, of Vicky and Amy, and of the chain-link gate that separated them. At Marc's instructions Vicky wrote a statement about her fraudulent conservatorship, and signed it with Marc and Howie as witnesses, and rolled it up to slide between the links of the fence.

"We'd better get out before we're discovered," Marc said reluctantly. "I know—no one comes except on Saturdays—but let's not take chances. Not when we're this close to happiness."

Jill sat on the small veranda of the house and waited for Marc. Howie had already left for the hospital. She'd stacked the breakfast dishes in the sink, too tense to do them now. Marc kept warning that the three involved in her grandmother's conservatorship—Adam, Clark, Jeffrey—were powerful in Bartonville.

"It's dangerous for Bartonville residents to cross them. We could have a tough fight ahead."

But they would win Nana's release, Jill vowed. Tears filled her eyes as she remembered what had precipitated the conservatorship. Nana meant to close the cigarette plant, to lobby against the tobacco industry. In doing that, she thought with exultation, Nana was honoring Mom's memory.

She rose to her feet. Was that Marc's car? It was. She hurried to the car, slid onto the front seat beside him. While they drove to their destination, Marc explained that the attorney they were meeting was the son-in-law of a friend of his and of her grandmother's.

"Lisa's son-in-law has a reputation as a brilliant lawyer and a man with high principles. He'll make no deals in Bartonville," Marc said with satisfaction. "He'll do whatever needs to be done to overthrow the conservatorship."

The attorney was already in a booth at the diner. Marc and Jill hurried to join him. Marc brought out the witnessed statement. Jill produced the snapshots that Howie had developed in his darkroom last night.

"Okay. We're in business," the attorney said briskly. "Let's go over to the courthouse."

Adam glanced at his watch as he signed the letters his secretary had brought in and left for his signature. It was almost noon. He had a lunch date with that sexy little redhead who had just opened up a new dress shop in town.

They'd eat at that Italian place a mile down the road. If anybody saw them, they were discussing business. He was considering investing in the shop. And after lunch they'd make a quick stop at the motel next door.

He scowled when his secretary buzzed him.

"What is it?" His voice was sharp.

"Judge Thompson is here to see you," she reported.

"Tell him I have to leave for a business appointment." What the hell did Clark want? "Tell him to call me tonight at the house."

"He says it's urgent—" She sounded nervous. Clark did that to people.

"Tell him to call me—" He stopped dead as Clark threw the door wide and charged into the room, his face flushed, his eyes apprehensive.

"Don't give me that bullshit, Adam!" he said tersely and slammed the door shut behind him when the secretary made a hasty retreat. "We've got ourselves a peck of trouble!"

"What are you talking about?"

"One of my people down at the courthouse just called me. Some smart-ass out-of-town lawyer is there along with some woman who says she's your daughter. They're filing a complaint about Vicky's conservatorship. Adam, they know she's there in the cottage!"

"You're out of your mind!" Adam pushed back his chair and leapt to his feet. "Now calm down, Clark. Who's this little bitch who says she's my daughter? And what does she know about the conservatorship?"

"She says she's Jill Barton. Your kid—" Clark's voice soared. "Somehow, she got to your mother. I don't know where we go from here—"

"Somebody's out to blackmail me!" Adam yelled. "That's all it is—" He paused, grimaced. What was this awful pain in his head? All at once his speech was unintelligible. He saw the strange look on Clark's face. *What the hell was happening*? He staggered, fell to the floor.

"Oh, Christ, this is just what we need!" Clark groaned and dropped to his haunches beside Adam. "Adam, don't conk out on me now—"

Adam was unconscious. A stroke or a heart attack, Clark guessed, fighting panic. He grabbed for the phone, dialed Jeffrey's office.

"Dr. Nelson's office," his longtime nurse said crisply.

"Doris, this is Clark Thompson. I have to talk to him right away."

"He's with a patient. He left word he was not to be disturbed."

"Tell him to stop screwing the broad and get on the phone," Clark ordered. "Keep ringing until he answers."

While he waited for Jeffrey to come to the phone, Clark reached for another and dialed Barton Memorial.

"Send an ambulance and a doctor fast to Barton Tobacco," he barked into the phone. "Something's happened to Adam Barton." For a Barton they'd come fast.

"What the hell's going on?" Jeffrey's voice filtered through the phone as Clark reached to retrieve it.

"Get your ass over to Barton Memorial," Clark ordered hoarsely. "Adam's on his way there—he's had a stroke or a heart attack. And some little bitch who claims she's his daughter is downtown filing a complaint about Vicky's conservatorship. We've got a lot of work to do. Move it, Jeff!''

In the emergency room at Barton Memorial, Howie was part of the team that was working over Adam Barton. What a way to meet his father-in-law, he thought, in the midst of his having a massive stroke.

"Come on, we can't afford to waste a minute here!'' The cardiovascular surgeon who'd been summoned from making rounds scowled at a nurse, who didn't move fast enough to please him.

It was clear that Adam Barton was no ordinary patient. The atmosphere in the emergency room was electric with this knowledge. But the patient wasn't responding, Howie recognized. It looked bad for him.

For almost two hours the team worked over Adam Barton. Then—slowly—he seemed to be regaining consciousness.

"Okay, take him to the VIP suite,'' the doctor in charge ordered at last. "Nurses around the clock. Did anybody notify his wife?''

"She's somewhere in Europe,'' one of the nurses said. "I read an item on the society page of the *Dispatch*.''

"Is he going to make it?'' Howie asked softly.

"Probably,'' the doctor in charge said. "But he may wish he hadn't. He's paralyzed from the neck down. I doubt that even with therapy he'll ever beat that rap. And he can't speak.'' Unexpectedly—involuntarily, Howie suspected—the doctor in charge smiled. "For Adam Barton that'll be the worse curse of all.''

Downtown in the courthouse, Clark and Jeffrey were fighting to defend themselves.

"All right, so we cut a few corners,'' Clark conceded defiantly. "But she was off her rocker. She wanted to close down the whole cigarette division of the company. It would have cost us all millions of dollars.''

"She's filed a complaint through a lawyer. She says she was drugged, put through a mock hearing, and held under incarceration for three years.'' The district attorney glanced apprehensively from Clark to Jeffrey. "This is going to get ugly. Why don't I arrange for a new hearing and—''

"No.'' Clark was reaching for a lifeline. "Let's just say that her condition has changed, and we'll approve the dismissal of conservatorship. The old girl won't press charges," he said with shaky bravado. "She won't want to disgrace the Barton name."

"If you're wrong, we're in bad shape." Jeffrey was grim. "Damn it, I told Adam this would backfire."

With Marc's arm protectively about her waist Vicky walked into Adam's suite at Barton Memorial. So much had happened in the past seventy-two hours, she thought. She was free at last. She had pressed no charges against those responsible for her incarceration. How could she do that to what had been family? For Sara's sake she couldn't disgrace the Barton name. But Clark would lose his judgeship and would be disbarred. Jeffrey was to be shorn of his license to practice medicine. For two greedy, ambitious men and their wives that would be sufficient punishment.

"Are you sure you feel up to this?" Marc asked solicitously.

"I have to see him, Marc." Vicky tensed, steeling herself to face her son. "Wait for me here."

Leaving Marc, Vicky walked into the room where Adam lay in his stark hospital bed. A ribbon of late afternoon sunlight seeped through the drawn draperies and lent a spurious cheerfulness to the room.

"May I be alone with my son for a few minutes?" she asked the private nurse who sat at his bedside.

"Of course, Mrs. Barton," the nurse said sympathetically. They knew—didn't they—what Adam and the others had done to her.

Vicky looked down at Adam. The doctor had warned her that he was paralyzed from the neck down. That he couldn't speak. He stared into space, seemingly without seeing. Ronnie had been notified at some resort on the Riviera. She hadn't bothered to come to his side. It was the end of his marriage.

"Adam," she said softly, her mind all at once free of the anger that had haunted her for so long. Now she felt only sadness. "I don't know if you can hear me—or understand me. I want you to know that I'll make sure you have lifetime care. When the doctors say you can be moved, you'll be taken to the cottage at Barton Manor. You'll have round-the-clock nurses to care for you. Whatever can be done to make you comfortable will be done. No matter what has happened, Adam, you're my child. A mother looks after her child."

Blinded by tears Vicky walked slowly into the sitting room. Marc reached to pull her into his arms.

"I'll take you home now," he said.

For the first time in three years Vicky walked into Barton Manor. The servants came forward to welcome her, their eyes bright with affection and compassion. Vicky knew that Marc had come to the house, called them together and explained what had been happening. The mistress of Barton Manor was coming home.

Only Mattie Lou remained of the early staff. She—who had nursed Adam through babyhood and made excuses for his temper tantrums— came forward to embrace Vicky.

"We're all so glad to see you, Miz Vicky." Mattie Lou's eyes were tear-drenched, but her smile was serene.

"Remember Jill?" Vicky asked tenderly.

"Yes ma'am. She was the prettiest little thing I ever saw."

"She'll be here for dinner tonight with her husband."

"Oh, Miz Vicky, we're going to be a family again." Mattie Lou beamed.

"Next month Mr. Marc and I will be married here at Barton Manor." The rabbi from the synagogue would perform the ceremony. "Miss Kara and Mr. Derek have promised to be here—and I'm writing Mr. Doug and insisting that he come, too. It'll be almost like old times." Almost.

Vicky ordered dinner to be served in the library—on the small table she'd bought at Thalhimer's when Adam and Ronnie moved into the house. This was where she had preferred to dine on the frequent nights when she had been alone. There was a charming intimacy here that she sensed Jill and Howie would welcome.

Like herself, Vicky discovered, Jill was always punctual. On their arrival, Vicky showed Jill and Howie through Barton Manor—the house, she thought with sentimental pleasure, that would one day be theirs. But not for quite a while, she promised herself with a surge of joyful anticipation.

Over dinner Vicky talked with candor about her impatience to dismantle her tobacco empire and focus on a new frozen foods division.

"And I'm setting up the Sara and Eleanor Barton Foundation," she said softly. "It'll be dedicated to work in the fight to make every human being understand that to smoke is to court death."

"How wonderful!" Jill was radiant.

"I've always needed a crusade," Vicky mused. "Now at last I have it. I want to join all those others who're fighting so hard to spread the word. It'll be a long battle—'' Her eyes reflected determination. ''I hope to see it won in my time.''

''We want to share that fight with you.'' Howie's eyes swept from her to Jill. ''It'll be our crusade, too.'' Oh, yes, Vicky thought exultantly. They were a family again.

Jill and Howie made a point of leaving early. Vicky intercepted their visual exchange. They were romantics, she told herself tenderly.

''Howie has to be at the hospital at seven AM,'' Jill said, striving to sound casual. ''I don't want him falling asleep on his feet in the emergency room.''

Hand in hand, Vicky and Marc walked with Jill and Howie to the veranda, and stood there while the younger couple walked down the steps and to their car. They exchanged jubilant good nights yet again, and then Howie slid behind the wheel and Jill joined him on the front seat.

''They're so sweet. They were plotting to give us some time alone together,'' Vicky told Marc, clinging to his arm as they watched the other two drive away. Now she lifted her laughter-lit eyes to his. ''Before we kiss a chaste good night.''

Marc lifted an eyebrow in reproach.

''Vicky, are you sending me home tonight?''

''Not a chance,'' she told him with a joyous lilt in her voice. ''The young think love and passion were invented just for them. We know better.''

Arm in arm Vicky and Marc walked into the house and up the long, curving mahogany staircase. Together they walked down the exquisitely carpeted hallway to the bedroom where Vicky had slept alone for so long. They were opening the door to a whole new beautiful life, Vicky told herself.

''I plan to live to be an old, old man,'' Marc joshed as he pulled her into his arms. ''To make up for all the years we've missed.''

''I'll go along with that,'' she began, but his mouth aborted further conversation.

It was the way she had dreamt through those awful years in the cottage. Marc and she together, forever.